ISBN: 978-0-9936345-2-9
Second Edition, First Printing

Many thanks go out to Jon Sprung, Stephen Orser, Linda Demissy, and Jocelyn Baxter for your hours spent beta reading and giving me honest and helpful feedback. Without you, this would not have been possible. I would like to thank the Bonavista Writers' Circle and its predecessor, the St. Norbert's Writers' Circle, for inspiring and challenging me to become better and reach higher.

Thank you also, to Sarah Cloutier, my cover artist for providing such beautiful art to be the face of my dream come true. You are attentive, dedicated, and generally a joy to work with.

My thanks to Kristy Laporte for the cover's graphic design. Your patience and skill continue to impress me.

Thank you Alexander Nachaj for your excellent editing and formatting. You caught screw-ups I never would have seen and polished my manuscript into something I could truly be proud of.

To my friends, thank you for helping me stay mostly sane and being the family that life's lottery saw fit not to give me.

To all the artists, authors, musicians, and poets who have inspired me over the years, thank you for igniting in me the passion to create and keeping that flame alive when the light at the end of the tunnel was too far away to see.

To my wife, Kaitlyn Kincaid: for being the hero who continues laugh at destiny and forge her own path.

Blood of Midnight

The Broken Prophecy

Chapter 1: The Message

Damon spread the fresh hay over the corner of the stall and plumped it. His paper-white fingers plucked apart a bunch of dried sweetgrass before spreading it throughout the horse's bed. He usually did not do such things for the others, but Silhouette was his horse and he felt entitled to show a little favouritism. The large stable doors were open to the field. None of the grazing horses out there felt cheeky enough to pester him today. The deepening of autumn occupied them with fattening up while there was still grass.

He set down the hay fork and stretched. At last, the morning chores were finished and he could return to the house for some leisure time before lunch. Perhaps he could work at finishing that flute he'd been carving, though a flaw in the wood was threatening to make it crack. *No*, he decided as he re-bound the messy locks of black hair out of his face, today he was feeling lazy. It was more a day for writing songs and reading.

Outside the barn, horses wandered the fields making of themselves blotches of gray, black and the occasional spot of white against the green. Beyond them, the forest had donned its fall colours; the birches, tamarack, and poplar in gold, and the steelwoods in their ghostly white. Glasshammer was too far north for the reds of maple to be found. Evergreens shrouded the shoulders of the mountains that made a wolf's-jaw border around their lands, open only to the south. The snow-caps were already beginning to swallow the upper portions of that covering. Far in the distance, the White Blade, the tallest peak in the kingdom, pointed its jagged finger north.

Damon turned and tromped up the cart track alongside the barn, a distinct clinking of metal accompanying each step. He wore iron plates bolted over the toes of his boots. It made them expensive and weighty but heavy hooves and farm equipment made the investment worthwhile. A crushed foot could take a good worker down for quite some time.

The track cut through their apple orchard and he scanned the trees to either side of him, looking for his sisters. He'd thought that Sunev and Rebecca were taking in some of the apples today but he didn't see them. They'd been talking about the orchard or the herb garden and he couldn't remember which they'd chosen. Ah well, he would find out soon enough when he got to the house. If they were not in the little fenced-in patch along the south side, then they would be wanting help carrying the apple bushels.

The practicalities of the day flitted out of Damon's head as he spotted his father, Erik Stonehart, striding off down the track that led to the main road. He glanced in the direction his father was headed and spotted a bright blue splotch in the tall grass. He could make out the livery of King Harlon after a few more paces and realized he was looking at a herald.

Now that was a rare sight! No one came to Glasshammer unless absolutely necessary for they feared the Stonehart curse; no one but bandits or slavers, those desperate or foolhardy enough to laugh off the threat of dying young, and dying badly. Damon picked up his pace to a trot, eager to see what could be so important that it could not be entrusted to a messenger bird.

They were only a few yards away from the man in blue when the lad caught up with his father. Erik turned at the sound of his footfalls and frowned.

"No, Damon. I need you to go to the house," he said and held up his palm to halt him.

"What? But—" Damon stuttered.

"Now, please."

At nineteen hands high, Erik was a man to be looked up to by many, and a man whose tunic Damon could not even fill out yet. He would, in time. Nature had favoured the boy with his father's build though not his chestnut hair, nor his sun-kissed complexion. No matter how many hours Damon spent in the fields, his skin took on neither colour nor warmth and the oddity often drew the stares of strangers. He had not gotten his father's pale blue eyes either. Those eyes were fixed on him now, as hard as ice and his crossed arms told him that Erik was not going to budge until his request was fulfilled.

"Can't I just—"

"No. I want to know exactly where you are. No sneaking around and no silly ideas until I've heard what this man has to say."

The herald held onto his sweating horse by the riding reins - something Stoneharts never used. Was it true that other horses were so stupid that they needed to be steered by the mouth? Why was the pommel of his saddle so small? He was bursting with questions but his father gave him a light shove.

"Damon, go inside." The stern tone of his voice brooked no disagreement.

With a mutinous glare, Damon turned down the path and headed for the house. He did, however, take his time, glancing often over his shoulder.

"Is he alright, Lord?" the messenger asked. "His colour's a bit off."

"He's fine. Wait until he's indoors, if you would. He hears like a hound." Erik looked toward his son and shooed him emphatically.

Damon quickened his pace, but only slightly. To his disappointment, his dawdling did not glean him any more news as the messenger remained silent. He lifted the latch and ducked inside.

The central fireplace still smoldered from breakfast. It was the only motion in the kitchen. Damon tapped clods of damp earth from his boots and bent to unbuckle them. Neither of his sisters' boots were by the door which told him they were still out working. He wondered if they had any idea what was going on.

The shutters and windows had been thrown open wide to let in the fresh air; though, the emptiness of the house deprived it of some of its cheer. He sat down quietly by the window and rested his elbows on the kitchen table as he watched the two men outside talk. The sun was still strong enough to be warm on his hair and bring out the scent of the herbs in the garden. He rested his chin on his hands and frowned. *What were they talking about?* Hardly anyone called Erik "Lord" as the messenger had done. Leaning forward, he tried to read their lips.

The messenger gesticulated wildly. He begged for something, ducking his head and shoulders and clasping his hands together, shaking them in fervour. Damon sighed and resisted the urge to sneak out. Their summer-house had only one outer door and it faced the road. The doors on either side of the main room all stood ajar to let the air circulate, even the storage room, and the dust motes drifting through the bars of light as they fell across the floor only stirred his restlessness further.

Why does he always keep things from me? I'm not going to break in half if I hear something distressing. Still, a shiver crawled down his spine.

Erik stood quite still except for the occasional nod of his head. Damon kicked the table leg, his foot making a steady bump, bump, bump in the empty kitchen. The wind chime over his head tinkled as though to mock his sour mood. He had made it when he was ten. It was almost as big as the kitchen table and had three tiers to it. He had searched for feathers all the same shape and shade of grey to hang on the ends with the weighted beads. It had taken months to put together and another month to get the hollow brass chimes from Tuador, but he loved things like that. Anything he could poke and tinker at over several days held appeal for him as a craft as he found that he learned things best when doing them slowly.

Over the window there hung a wooden plaque decorated with thistle designs. An invocation to the Vies, spirits of the air, land, and water to protect the house and all within it.

Aervie, guard the air I breathe,
Lanvie, all the steps I leave.
Vanvie, give me sturdy health,
Blotvie, wisdom, cunning, wealth.

The decoration had been made by Erik's great grandfather and was old enough to refer to the ancestors as Blotvie, a word few people still used anymore. In the past, it had been a custom to pray to one's forefathers for assistance, just as one would petition and make offerings to the other Vies. Damon could see why the practice had fallen into disuse and the word with it. He was fairly sure that there was nothing some old bones could do for him that the combined might of the earth, wind, and water could not. Nevertheless, the blessing was well-cherished and engraved in nearly every Stonehart house.

Damon tried to imagine what the messenger wanted. Perhaps a large order of horses that would take a long time to pay off? A loan for a desperate farmer? He'd heard that there had been vandals setting crop fires in the lowlands south and east of Tuador Village. Perhaps someone needed wolves chased off? Sometimes Damon tired of the requests, but his father always said that the strong must protect the weak.

"As long as I live, men may call upon me for aid," his father would say, quoting from the Code of Valour. He always seemed to refer to that passage whenever someone asked something of him, no matter the job.

Damon shook his head. No, it didn't look like something that simple. Had someone died? Veins stood out on the backs of Damon's hands as he clenched them. *Not another one of us? Surely not? We can't take many more losses.* An image of his mother, Anna, buried a year now, swam unbidden into his thoughts. He shook his head again, with more force. *No. A Stonehart messenger would carry news of a death in the family.*

The kitchen was quiet and still with no one else in it. He began counting the jars of preserves, herbs and spices on the shelves that covered the walls. He left off after forty-three and swung around to look at the fireplace with the water pump in front of it, then beyond it to the raised

10

benches that served as steps up to the rooms surrounding the main hall. Only the doors on the left side of the main room were open more than a thumb's width and those rooms had been empty since Uncle Jacenth had passed on and his boys had gone up to live in Autumn's stedding.

Erik reached over and patted the messenger's shoulder, nodding. Damon sat up as he started back to the house. The way his shoulders were braced, as if against a heavy load, informed him that something was wrong. Was there trouble in Tuador? Large bands of thieves and even the odd audacious slaver were always a threat to the people of the Northern Kingdoms. As if the weather conditions weren't bad enough, he thought. This was the first day of sun after two weeks of driving rain and high winds.

Kingdom Stonehart—if it could even be called that anymore—just didn't have the manpower to defend itself as it once did.

They hadn't even had a proper king for a long time. Over the years, their numbers had dwindled down so far that it seemed ridiculous to use such a title. The last Stonehart to call himself "King" had died four generations ago. His daughter, Ursula the Black, in her grief, had wanted neither crown nor coronation and had simply taken up leadership as "Chieftain." It had been that way ever since.

In any case, it was the heads of the households that decided everything so there was not much point for kingship anymore. Erik was considered the chieftain now, though Damon didn't know if there had been any ceremony proclaiming him so.

The door swung open and startled him; he had been daydreaming Erik stomped the mud off his boots. The rain had made a spongy mess of the fields. Damon rose to his feet, hardly able to wait for his father to come inside. That was a rule of the house: "Don't bug a body 'til their boots are off."

Erik took off his leather work coat and hung it on a hook. Only then did he turn and look at his son. His eyes were full of sorrow.

Damon straightened up, squaring his shoulders. At times like these, when Erik had that heavy look on his face, he always felt so small.

"What's the trouble, Father?" he asked, hoping he sounded like a competent man. He was not a big lad and if not for the physical labour on the farm to pad his frame, he would be downright willowy.

Please Da, tell me. I'm not a child. His father looked at the long shadow Damon threw across the floor. Damon stared at the rolled-up parchment in his father's hand as if somehow he could read what was on the inside if only he tried hard enough.

"Sit down," said his father, seating himself at the table. He let the parchment fall next to a glass vase, containing three purple thistle flowers and some stalks of late wheat. Sunlight danced through the water and threw rainbows across the cup and swan seal of King Harlon.

What does a king want with us? It was his deep respect for his father that kept him from reaching out and snatching up the letter to read for himself. Instead, he stayed silent, clasping his hands between his knees.

"Damon," he began. His voice sounded strained, as though it didn't want to come out at all. "You know these are rough times and we all find ourselves having to make decisions. Sacrifices."

He stopped for a moment, staring at the table.

"I'm sure you've heard the rumours of war in the south circulating among the village lads." Erik closed his eyes. The hand he rested on the table curled into a fist.

Damon waited, hardly realizing he'd moved towards the edge of his seat.

"They're not rumours." His father looked at him again. "What's more, there are forces pushing north. King Mido Solara has been slain and all his family with him."

Damon felt his jaw drop. "But Mother's vision—"

"I know." His father looked tired. "Your Reflection is supposed to be of the Solara family. There are rumours flying about the youngest daughter escaping but ... ah, I don't know. I'm sorry, Damon. It could be possible but what that means... I just don't know."

Erik went silent.

It was said that, when a Stonehart was born, their power was too great to be held in the body of a small child; that it had to be split in half. One half stayed in the child, while the other half, the Reflection, went into the body of second person. In time, the two would be drawn together. The Reflection would inevitably be taken by a wanderlust so strong that they would find themselves heading for the Northern Kingdoms without knowing why. Only when they embraced the Stonehart to whom they were called would they understand. An Embraced Stonehart was complete, their power stable and strong. All the best healers and fighters of the clan were always one of the Embraced.

Since his mother's gift of farsight had told him where his Reflection was, Damon had expected a long and difficult journey. He would probably have to ride down and meet them halfway instead of waiting for them to come up and find him. If there were no more Solaras, though, he would have to accept the possibility of living the rest of his life incomplete. With his mother gone and Rebecca's gift still too weak, there was no one to ask for guidance.

Erik's voice broke through his thoughts.

"King Harlon has just told us that scouts have been sighted at the edge of his borders. They're not slowing down and no army has yet been able to halt their progress. They just ploughed right through Howweld and swatted the armies of King Regaid and King Dulmir like flies. Duke Freston actually had to flee Boarsback after his initial defences were crushed. I have no idea how they got all those men across the Silver Ribbon in the middle of the rain season..." He trailed off. "Do you know what I'm trying to say?"

"They're coming here." The statement fell out of his mouth before he could stop it. The thought of the Southern Kingdoms falling to any force was mind-boggling. The idea of such a force ripping through their peaceful backwater settlement chilled him. An image of armoured soldiers riding chargers through their fields and churning up the still waters of Lake Glasshammer flashed through his mind and a curious anger swelled up inside him. It was like a memory, but of something he had never seen before.

This is my land. The thought struck him as strange but seemed right to him.

"Do we know who it is?" he asked.

Erik raised his eyebrows. "I didn't think that'd be your first question. There are reports of sightings of flag bearers carrying the standard of the White Asp."

Damon thought he was hearing things. Why would anyone carry the flag of a storybook villain? He'd heard tales of the legendary sorcerer, Lyre, since he was a child but none of them were to be believed. He was a myth used to frighten children and explain inexplicable misfortunes. Damon remembered being terrified that the White Asp would come in the night and steal his voice if he ever told a lie.

If anyone wanted to identify himself with such a despicable, murderous character, he couldn't understand why. One nagging thought tugged at him. *What if they're not just stories?* Ridiculous. No. Clearly, someone was just trying to terrorize the people into submission.

Something still didn't fit. Why the letter?

"So, he sent us a warning?"

Erik shook his head and sighed. "It's a call to arms. 'All able-bodied men and women are asked to take up weapons and fight for their lands and the future of the Middle Kingdoms.' In short, he's asking us to stop the threat before he takes over all of Silan."

"The whole world …" Damon murmured. He couldn't begin to imagine someone that powerful. He realized he was chewing his lip and stopped.

"If this is any indication." His father gestured at the parchment on the table. "There have been battles all through the duchies, many of them all happening on the same day if reports are to be believed. I don't know how he manages to command a force that vast with such precision but his general must be the most brilliant man who ever lived, and the most fearsome. Harlon is as practical a man as I've ever known. He doesn't scare easy; that's why he's a good king. He wouldn't panic over hearsay, and this is as nervous as I've ever known him to be. He must be pretty desperate to extend the call all the way up to the high Northlanders."

He shook his head.

"It'll be hard travelling this late in the fall."

Damon wrinkled his nose. "You're not seriously thinking of going, are you?"

"We must go. The Treaty of Emmesford binds us to protect our allies from invaders. Regaid and Dulmir would answer the call as well if they weren't too busy making war on each other. We must 'protect the weak,' remember?"

"King Harlon is hardly weak."

"Neither were Kings Paros, Delan, or Shrana, or the Southern Kingdoms, and they all fell to the White Asp," he said. "Empress Tlube was only able to manage a single call for aid and no one has heard any more from her. The Deep South Empire: gone."

He thumped his hand on the table. "Like blowing out a candle. I've told you stories of the southern fighters. Their armies are not trifles."

Damon rubbed his hands. He did remember the stories but this was no simple request. He didn't think it fair that the Stoneharts should have to respond to the call while others ignored it, especially those who, by all rights, should know better. During the War of the Bloodplains, when Kyax, one of the chieftains of Howweld, got it into his head that he should be Emperor the whole of the Middle Kingdoms had banded together to put an end to the carnage and ruin. Rell and The Silver Ring had been hit the hardest but their gratitude had swiftly devolved into endless land disputes that continued to this day. Granted, the war had been three hundred years ago but nearly twenty years of violence and terror should be a hard thing to forget.

If King Harlon had wanted wolves chased away, he wouldn't have hesitated. But he didn't. He wanted the Stonehart magic to protect him. He wanted them to be like the warriors of the old legends and save the world, but there weren't many of them left. *We could still do it, couldn't we?* His pulse raced. The prospect of war both frightened and thrilled him. He had always wanted to be one of those warriors. Even if his Reflection was dead and he could never reach his full potential, he still wanted to do something. A feeling of intense pride swelled up in his chest. *I could still defend my homeland.*

He drew himself up in his seat.

"Then we've got to fight," he said solemnly. "I know I'm not old enough to ask by tradition, but it seems we don't have two years to wait, and I'll be damned if I'm going to stand by while others die for Glasshammer."

He stood up and cleared his throat, preparing to ask the time-honoured question from son to father on the day of his coming-of-age.

"Father, may I have a sword?"

Erik regarded his son in silence. Damon knew denial was coming. Many boys tried asking their fathers for the hallowed weapon that would mark their passing into manhood. But an Eve of the Sword could not be rushed. Tradition stated that it must be the eighteenth year, when a man could properly support a family and a business. But Damon wasn't trying to be what he was not or to show off to his friends. There was evil afoot and he wanted to fight it.

Still, very few ever requested formally before their time and the ones who did earned a tongue-lashing for it. He sighed, realizing how foolish his request must seem. He was just a boy. Harlon had a standing army in Shirfeild and the rest of the Middle Kingdoms had plenty of soldiers. They didn't need children getting underfoot.

"Da, I'm sorry I—"

"Yes, my son," Erik cut off the apology. "You may."

Damon was stunned. The traditional response had been given. His father looked both sad and proud at once. His eyes shone with moisture and he wore a pained smile.

Why did I ask? And why did you say yes? There was no going back on it now.

"Thank you," he whispered, too astounded to say anything else.
"Thank you."

Damon saddled Silhouette, his black stallion. The long-legged charger tossed his mane and thumped a silver hoof on the ground in excitement. The still-lush grasses couldn't tempt him. He was ready to run. "Easy, boy," Damon said, patting his neck. "We'll be off soon." Truth be told, he was just as anxious.

Sunev stood with her back to him, saddling her grey mare, Torrent. She was twenty with her Eve of the Sword two years ago. He didn't know if she knew of his upcoming ceremony. He was sure when she found out he was going to get the chastisement of his life. Sunev wasn't exactly known for her gentle spirit. She had the unfortunate combination of their late mother's sharp wit and their father's temper, but whatever she said to him, he could understand. She had patiently waited her full eighteen years.

The sunlight made her hair as bright a gold as the birch trees, turned to their autumn colours in the forest beyond. She turned to him suddenly, making him jump. "Right. Damon, I'm heading for the west path to talk to Lorne. You'll go east to Jae. Tell her about the meeting in Stonehart Hall and head back home. Hearing me?"

He smiled. That was Sunev. She didn't believe in small talk. "Yes."

"Good. You'll be back later than the rest of us. When Da and Rebecca get back from Autumn's you'll be in, say, an hour afterwards. Don't dally. Keep your head up. There's still thieves about from the raid in Tuador. Listening?"

"Yes."

"Wipe that grin off now. You look like a fox into the chickens." Her grey eyes were tight at the corners. "It's no adventure, Damon. Hard business today."

He sobered his face and nodded. Sunev straightened the scarlet wool wrap over her shoulders. Damon was sure she could make any garment look dignified. She grasped the high pommel of the saddle and swung up onto Torrent, sitting as straight-backed as though she were to ride in a parade.

"Be careful," he said.

She nodded and clicked to her horse and took off at a brisk canter. He watched her receding over the meadow. Briefly, he cast a glance over the sloping, sod peak of their summer house, standing in the tall grass and autumn wildflowers.

There was a heavy shove on his shoulder. He turned and rubbed Silhouette's nose. "Alright, let's go." He grinned as he launched himself into the saddle. "We've got to hurry. The news we've got is more important than you can imagine." The horse turned and leapt into a gallop for the east path. He let out a whoop, not loud enough for Sunev to hear, but enough to show his appreciation. He leaned forward over his horse's neck as they plunged into the forest. "I bet we can beat Everlasting," he whispered fiercely.

Silhouette and his father's horse, the smoky-coated Everlasting, were always racing each other in the fields. They hurled themselves over rocks, streams, fences, always daring each other to accomplish greater feats of wildness. Maybe on other days Everlasting would beat him home, but Erik was taking Rebecca with him to see Autumn; he would be slowed. The road to Jae's stedding was a little more narrow, but Damon hoped the thinning leaves would give him an equal chance.

He shook his head. Whether or not he won his little bet, he was determined to do the best he could in all his father asked of him. He didn't know if the assent to the traditional question could be withdrawn but he wasn't taking any chances. He would prove himself worthy no matter what it took. He stayed low as green and gold foliage and the dark fingers of wet branches blurred past his vision. Silhouette's wild spirit was infectious. He was sure the horse believed he could outrun the wind. He felt the hoof beats deep in his chest like the throb of a heart.

Bird calls were the first thing that warned, or rather, a lack of them. Silhouette's ears flipped up and he slowed so quickly that Damon lurched forward in the saddle. Stonehearts were a part of this land as much as anything else. The birds would not cease their chatter for only him. He shivered. Sunev's warning came back to him. Could it be the bandits from the attack on the village? Silhouette had come to a full stop. Leaves and vines pressed in close on all sides. The underbrush was so dense it gave nothing away. He swallowed and tried to stay as quiet as possible. For once he wished for the hastening of autumn for the simple fact that the leaves would not obstruct his view. The path needed to be cleared and cut back on either side. *Such wonderful ideas I have when it's too late.*

A twig snapped somewhere to his right. He turned but it must have been several yards away. He could see nothing but greenery. He held his breath, listening. *Do they know I'm here?* He strained his eyes, looking slowly around him. He searched for anything that might give them away. There was no money on him but before he left the house he had slipped the dirk with the bejewelled pommel his father had given him into his boot. Now that he thought about it, that golden hilt would probably be more likely to get him in trouble than protect him.

"Where are they?" he whispered to his horse. Silhouette nickered. He took two steps forward and a few back, swinging his head about. He would not go on. "Surrounded?" Silhouette nodded his head up and down. He cursed himself for being so foolish. His throat was dry. He felt like he had a mouth full of ash. *Idiot. Couldn't think to bring a flask of water but I could bring a fancy knife into a pack of thieves.*

He cleared his throat. "Hello?" he called out. His voice quavered. *Some brave soldier I am.* He forced himself to sit up straight and grip the pommel firmly.

There was a swish of leaves ahead and to his left, nothing else. Nothing but the cries of ravens. He squared his shoulders and put on his father's card-playing face. "I carry an important message. Please let me pass." The birds were starting to quiet. He could hear his heart in his ears.

Suddenly, a man burst out of the bushes aiming a crossbow at Damon. Silhouette reared and shrieked, pawing the air with his silver hooves. The upper part of the thief's face was covered with strips of cloth, his dark eyes peering out of holes burned through the fabric. The eyes were wide and flicked all around like startled fish. His clothing was worn but of good quality. "Yeh be gettin' down that beast now, prinny." His exposed arms were heavily muscled. On his right shoulder there were a series of straight scars counting off a tally. Two groups of five and two lines. "Doncha be thinkin' 'bout tryin' on me fer a tussle. I sees yeh lookin' here." He shrugged his shoulder at him. "These is all the weasel-squeezers I knocked down and they was big ol' brawlers. Skinny lil' goat fucker like you'll be havin' naught but sod. Get down now, boy."

More men were coming out of the woods. Damon's hopes of defending himself flew away before his eyes. *Oh Aervie, please just let me get out of here alive.* A man with the bottom half of his face masked by a scarf made a grab for Silhouette. There were no reins to snatch and he foundered in confusion for a moment. The horse shoved against him and he fell. His comrades howled with laughter.

"That'll be a Stonehart horse, ya shite muncher!" a man with a stringy grey beard called. "He'll not be lettin' yeh touch his master." He spied at least two more men with crossbows in the cover of the leaves. He knew he

18

didn't have a chance of escaping while they had those trained on him.

"Please, good sirs," he tried again. A little flattery couldn't hurt. "I carry word of war."

"And like as not some gold too and that's the sort of what I'll be interested in," the apparent leader of the bandits said.

"I've got no money on me." He knew full well that they would not believe him; not with a golden dirk winking at them from his boot. Two men tried to seize his arm and tug him off his mount. Silhouette snorted angrily and rounded on them kicking out with his hooves. He saw the aim of one of the bowmen shift. What if they shot his horse out from under him?

"Easy, boy!" he cried. "It's alright." He pulled his arm from the grip of the thieves. "I'm getting off," he told the bearded man, and pushed himself out of the saddle. "Don't harm him, please!" He landed awkwardly on his feet on the soft layer of leaves covering the path.

"I'd say not!" The leader chuckled as if he'd made a joke. "Fine piece of horseflesh, that!" Damon could have wept when it hit him at last. They were going to take Silhouette. The dirk he could bear but not his beloved horse. The stallion had quieted and turned around to look at him. He swallowed and tried not to gag on the lump in his throat.

Please, someone help me. Somehow. Looking into the calm, dark eyes of his four-legged friend, he was certain the horse knew what was happening.

"Now, 'bout that gold…" The leader swaggered towards him, crossbow down but ready to fire at a moment's notice. He grinned savagely, giving a hoarse bark of a laugh. "Lad's scared outta his mind! White as gull shit, lookit that!"

"No color t'all!" cried the bearded man in response. He and the other man who had tried to pull him from the saddle came forward and seized him by the arms. He gasped and let go.

"Cold as the grave he is, boss!"

"Aye?" The leader reached out and brushed Damon's face with two dirty fingers. He frowned, clearly perturbed by the frigid flesh. "Well, more a-scared than I thought!" he proclaimed, some of his earlier bravado creeping back into his voice, though it was strained now. "I think you'll be handin' us the goods now, eh? There's a peachy boy."

"I already told you—"

"Nice piece, this." He felt the dagger slide from his boot and heard the thieves behind him exclaiming over it.

19

"Aye, I'd say it, too," the leader said. "Where'd a chicken shit like you come by such a pretty sticker?"

"My father gave it to me," he sighed. "I don't suppose you'd care."

"Not like yeh mean, but I'll be wonderin' who this da of yers is. Wealthy, eh?" He was close enough to smell his rancid breath. Damon swallowed. If they thought he was someone of importance, they would surely hold him for ransom. He clamped his mouth shut. It had been a mistake to ever speak in the first place. This was his mess now. It was time to be a man. "Come out, don't play shy whore with us. Who's yer da, boy?" He glared at Damon's silence. "Don't get stubborn, it'll do ya a harm and nothin' else. The Stonehearts live up here. You a prince, eh?"

Damon stared at him. He hoped his face didn't show how frightened he was. Even if he wanted to speak, he doubted his voice would get past the lump in his throat.

"Best start talkin', boy." The bearded man pressed a knife to his neck. He trembled but held his tongue. It didn't matter if he looked brave now. He just had to keep silent.

Silhouette shrilled angrily, drawing all attention. He was fighting off the three thieves who were trying to catch hold of his saddle to restrain him. The leader laughed raucously as the horse put his back hooves into the chest of one hapless man. Damon thought frantically. If only his power would kick up for a moment. Just a second would do it. Maybe while they were distracted, he could do something. Any other time he would have vanished into the shadows of the forest by now.

Why haven't I faded to shadow yet? Now that he had a moment to think about it, he should have already escaped. It was dark enough here, wasn't it? *Maybe if I concentrate hard enough.* He fought to clear his mind but the knife at his throat bit into his skin as the thief laughed at his comrades.

Salvation came suddenly, but not the way he expected. A shriek erupted from the man with the beard and was echoed shortly by many more. The thief stared at the blue liquid on his blade, then dropped it as though it were on fire.

"Great fuckin' she-god!" he cried. "He bleeds blue!"

"Demon!" shouted another. Several broke and ran.

The leader stared at him through the burned holes in his mask. His eyes were big. "So yer da's the Evil One, then..." he whispered, licking his lips and backing away. Damon touched his neck and looked at the blue blood on his fingers. He blessed whatever force had given him such a unique aspect and whatever superstitious nation these thieves hailed from.

Silhouette, no longer harried by the villains trying to capture him, took this opportunity to butt his head into the small of the leader's back. The man howled in fear and took off running with the rest of his crew.

He watched them go until he couldn't see or hear them anymore. Among Stonehearts, it was not strange to have darker blood, usually red but rarely drifting closer to purple. After birth, the colour of an infant's blood was measured against the spectrum of the altar stones in the Hall. Darker blood meant more magic. Damon was the first to have outright sapphire blue since antiquity but it didn't really seem to bother anyone but outsiders.

Another accidental rescue. He wasn't sure what to make of it this time. It was funny, he supposed, but he was shaking too hard to laugh. His stomach was doing cartwheels. It was a few minutes before he trusted it enough to bend down, pick up his dirk and return it to his boot.

"Let's get out of here," he whispered to Silhouette and mounted. The horse did not need to be told twice. He bolted down the path as soon as Damon had his seat. They raced for Jae's stedding, not slowing until they could see the smoke from the chimneys ahead. He just wanted to deliver the message and get back home.

They burst from the tree line and pounded up the path toward the four houses clustered around the little garden courtyard. Samuel was just coming out of the one nearest to him on the left and he turned to the sound of hoof beats. He raised a big hand to shade his eyes against the sun. In the dark of the woods, Damon had completely forgotten the sun was shining. He could see his name forming on Samuel's lips and the look of confusion.

"Damon, what..." He didn't finish but gasped seeing the blood on his neck. "You're hurt! Marel!" he called back to the house. "Bring bandages. Erik's lad's been injured!"

"I'm alright," he said as the big man helped him dismount. The sun made his red hair orange. It occurred to him that he didn't know if he was alright but it was the first thing that came to mind. Marel, Samuel's wife, came running out with a roll of linen strips. She wore slacks and a tunic like her husband. Not many Stonehart women wore dresses anymore. Except for Sunev, of course.

"Damon, Damon, what *has* happened to you?" she scolded, half out of breath as she reached them. Her light curls bounced with her movements. She yanked the collar away from his neck and touched her fingers to the wound. He hissed at the sting.

"I was caught by bandits on my way here," he explained. Samuel

21

grunted, a sour look on his face. He punched his fist into his palm and glared into the underbrush but there was nothing there to direct his anger at. "They harassed me a bit but when they saw the blood they thought I was a demon and ran off."

"Lucky lad, lucky," he murmured, still staring murderously at the trees. Damon lowered his head only to have it raised forcibly by a clucking Marel. She wound the cloth tightly around his neck. He would have warned her not to choke him but he knew her temper.

"Aye. I've got a message, though. There's a meeting in the old Stonehart Hall five days from now. King Harlon's calling us in for war."

Marel dropped the end of the bandage and it uncoiled to the ground. "War?" She stared at him for a minute before starting to gather up the linen.

"With whom?" Samuel pressed.

Damon took a deep breath, hoping no one would laugh at him. Then he realized that this was far too absurd to be considered a joke.

"The White Asp," he sighed. "If you can believe it."

Neither of them said anything for a long time.

"The ... demon?" Samuel stuttered finally.

Damon nodded.

"The demon that eats souls?" Marel furrowed her brow.

They had all read the legends, the darkest tales of Stonehart lore. He had no explanation to offer. He just nodded again.

"I don't like it," Samuel declared firmly at last.

"Neither do I." He tried to loosen the bandage at his throat but Marel slapped his hand away.

"None of that, you," she scolded. "You want to bleed to death?"

He thought it best not to answer that question. "Can you please tell Jae about the meeting? It was her I was supposed to get the message to, but I think I should probably make for home before those thieves find their nerve."

"You will not." Marel pushed him toward the house. "Not all by yourself and not until that cut stops bleeding. I'm not letting you ride off until I hear all about these bloody bandits and the call-to-arms. In you get. You're having a drink and something to eat and I'll not hear another word about it."

Damon wisely kept his mouth shut and obeyed. He looked down and was surprised to find a large blue stain on his over-large grey work shirt. The thief must have been so startled that he'd cut him more deeply than intended. He strode up to the stone and timber house and ducked under the doorframe into Marel's kitchen.

It was smaller than his own but the construction was mostly the same. Central fireplace with raised benches built into each wall. There were only two rooms off the back of the main area so the sunlight could come directly in through the windows along the sides. Marel had already brought out the seating cushions that usually lined the benches in the autumn as her family huddled in closer to the fire for the cold season. Soon, Sunev would do the same. It was always one of those tasks done with reluctance, not because it was difficult but because it was an acknowledgment that, yes, the summer was well and truly ended and they had a long stretch of snow and darkness ahead of them.

The smell of chicken stewing in a rosemary broth coming from the pot over the fire made Damon's stomach rumble. While he was sorry to see the sun diminish, the sharing of savoury harvest-time dishes was something he looked forward to. *Ah, well, he thought. At least I'll get some food out of the deal.*

After Marel had finished fussing over him, Samuel went to inform Jae of the situation and gather a contingent to send with him for protection on the way home. She left him alone to tend her garden and he was glad to finally relax. He hadn't had the opportunity to do that since the messenger had arrived this morning. He watched the sunlight play across the stone floor through the lily patterned curtains and rested his head, cradled in his arms on the table. The copper pots and pans hanging on the wall over the hearth glowed warmly in the waning sunlight. The cut on his neck still stung when he moved but not as badly as before. He knew it would heal soon. By late tonight, it would be gone as if it had never been there.

It wasn't certain why the Stonehart magic had concentrated so densely in his body. It was so strong in him that its natural blue hue was ingrained into his very blood. There were other Stoneharts with darker blood but none truly blue. Strange things had continuously happened to him since he was very young, that forced him to unknowingly unleash odd talents he never knew he had. He didn't usually think about it until something like this happened. He didn't really know how to use these powers that appeared seemingly at random. Every Stonehart had a Showing, when their fully matured power manifested itself in some way. Usually, it happened in late adolescence. Earlier and later Showings were not unheard of but Damon's case was different. He had had his Showing shortly after his birth.

They had thought he was dead when he entered the world because he was so pale and his flesh was cold despite having been in his mother's womb. After a few moments of breathless silence, however, he began to cry. As his mother held him, the earth gave an ominous rumble. Everything in the house rattled and she held him close, trying to soothe away his fear. Instead of calming, he released a blinding burst of blue light that danced wildly around the room until the shaking stopped. They all knew then that he was special.

His father had told him not to try to push himself to hone these talents fearing he would harm himself. It was dangerous for a child to try to wield a magic so obviously potent. Yet, even without training, his power often came to his aid, saving him from the notorious foul luck of the Stonehearts. It occurred to him now that if it had been anyone else at the end of that knife in the woods, they would have died or been taken hostage. His kinsmen rarely made it past the age of forty before something terrible happened to cut their lives short. It was why no one ever sought to take land in Glasshammer. Not even the lush green hills could tempt a farmer with the threat of an early death hanging over them.

Is that why you said 'yes' father? He thought. He couldn't afford to let his power rest and wait until he was older. Not anymore. There was no more time to grow up. He resolved to deliberately hone his talents as soon as his Eve of the Sword was held. All his strength would be needed to fight this battle. He shivered, trying to imagine himself charging the banner of the White Asp. He tried to imagine the sound of steel on steel and the cries of wounded soldiers the way it was described in the stories. He tried to envision cutting down his enemies and driving them back. He couldn't do it. The image wouldn't come to him. Lake Glasshammer was strong in his mind however, its perfect mirror surface sullied by mud as he had seen it before. It made him just as inexplicably furious as it had the first time. He thumped the table with his fist.

"Are you alright Damon?" He sat up. Marel stood in the doorway with a basket of herbs on her hip.

He sighed and ran a hand through his hair. "Yes. Just frustrated."

"Ah now," she said soothingly. "It could have happened to anyone." She set the basket down on the table and sat across from him. "What were you supposed to do? Fight them all off?"

"I don't think I could have." He stared at the grains in the wood of the tabletop, tracing them with his finger. "But I can't help thinking that I could have gotten away. It's happened before, when I was scared."

Marel tapped her fingers on the table and made a thoughtful sound. "You're talking about that shadow thing?"

He nodded. "I was really scared today. I could hardly keep my knees from buckling under me." He blushed. Marel lifted her eyebrows in concern. It always shocked people when he blushed. Because of the colour of his blood, his face turned blue instead of red. But Samuel and Marel were his clansfolk so, although it was still surprising it didn't warrant any questions. "I can't understand why I didn't turn into a shadow. It's happened three times so far. Once when the tree almost fell on me, once when I saw that party of slavers when we were out hunting and once when that bear scared me in the woods, *that* time when I tried to turn back I changed into a wolf by accident." He looked up at her. "Today of all days when I really was in trouble I didn't do anything useful. It just so happened that they were superstitious about my blood."

"That's your fantastic luck at work again Damon," she said smiling. "It might be that your magic knew it wasn't going to be needed to save you. But..." She became serious. "The greater possibility is that you are maturing. Your magic will become less wild and unpredictable and more easily channelled. It's a little early, but then, we all expected that from *you*." She reached out and patted his hand. "Don't worry about it Damon. If I'm right it will be a lot safer for you now. Your magic will be less likely to get out of control and accidentally hurt you."

He sighed and returned his gaze to the swirls in the wood.

"Damon." The tone in her voice made him look at her again. "Do you remember when you were very young, four years old I think, and those older boys in the village tried to pick on you?"

He furrowed his brow. He remembered his father had just turned his back for a few minutes to barter with the shopkeeper. He didn't remember which shop in Tuador it was or even what the boys looked like only that they had been much taller than him. "They thought I looked funny because I was pale," he said at last. "I wandered away from my father and they followed me. I think one of them pushed me into the shelves and knocked me out or knocked the wind out of me. Something like that."

Marel smiled but it was a sad smile. He frowned at her. This was an expression he'd seen too much lately and he couldn't understand why. "Damon, I know Erik didn't want to frighten you and that's probably why he didn't tell you. But I think it's alright now that you're older." She cleared her throat. "There were three boys in the village that picked on you in the cobbler's shop that day. The oldest was about seven and he's the one who pushed you into the shelves of boots. But you weren't knocked out. You were angry and you got up and took a swing at him. Since you hadn't matured yet, your magic was still very wild. It didn't help at all that it was so powerful either. The fact is, you laid him out flat."

"What!" Damon half rose from his chair but she took his hand and gently pulled him back down. "But you said I was only four," he protested. "A four year old can't knock down someone almost twice his age."

"Let me finish, please," she said gently. "You have to understand what happened. You see, you didn't actually hit him. At least not with your fist. Your father never would have known you were being bullied if not for the tremor that rocked the room. The other two boys said the space between you two rippled like a heat mirage, only it was freezing cold like a winter wind. Then the magic slammed into the older boy and threw him into the racks behind him. The impact was so strong it knocked the racks over too."

"That's crazy," he whispered rubbing his temples.

"Your father came running to see what had happened," she continued as if she hadn't heard him. "You were just recovering from the swing and preparing to defend yourself against the other two boys. He told you to stop, knowing that the magic could overwhelm you. For one so young, it could even mean death to try and wield such power. He took hold of you and you stopped trying to defend and instead tried to pull the magic back. He doesn't know what happened. I don't think any of us could explain it except that you received a backlash from the power you unleashed unknowingly. All he knows is that you started getting really cold."

"I've always been cold," he interrupted.

"Not like this. Not your normal temperature, like the lake in the autumn." She shook her head. "No Damon. It was different. Your temperature dropped suddenly even as he held you tightly. You passed out and it just kept plummeting. He had to lay you down on the floor and run for some blankets because no one could touch you with their bare hands. You were so cold that your clothes and the floor around you became layered with frost. They had to dump a bucket of hot water on you just to pick you up because your clothes were frozen to the floorboards.

"They took you to the healer's immediately and sent for all the Stonehart healers to come help. We tried everything to rouse you but you just fell deeper and deeper into sleep. There were long periods of time when you would stop breathing and we thought we'd lost you. Finally as a last resort, we built a pyre and set you on it. We wrapped you in wet blankets and lit a fire underneath you."

Damon gasped.

"It was dangerous, yes, but we didn't know what else to do. You were frozen like an icicle. We kept the fire away from you as much as possible but the blankets still caught eventually. Yet you never moved an inch. We thought we had failed, but just as Erik was lifting you off the pyre you opened your eyes and asked him what was going on."

"I thought…" He trailed off, unsure of himself. "I thought I just hit my head. Was I… What happened then?"

Marel shrugged. "You had a bit of a fever afterwards but it was very mild. How you didn't die from dehydration we don't know."

He rubbed his forehead with the heel of his hand. "I remember being sick but not… Not any of the other things."

She shook her head. "No I didn't expect you would. You were unconscious for nearly a week in that strange icy state." She reached across the table and took both of his hands in hers. "Damon, what I'm trying to say to you is if you are maturing and your magic is coming under control it is a good thing. It's much more frightening to have your power act on its own at random. You never know what might happen. That's why all of us say you're so lucky. It's not just because you seem to escape the Stonehart curse when it falls on you. It's because your magic, in its wild state, has emerged out of nowhere so many times and yet you've only been seriously harmed by these outbursts only once. Other Darkbloods have killed themselves. You remember Lorne's sister."

He shuddered. They'd collected all the pieces they could.

"Just be happy Damon. You're starting to grow up. The sooner you can control your magic, the sooner you'll be out of danger."

He nodded, unable to think of anything to say. He could understand why his father hadn't told him this. It disturbed him deeply that his own power could do him such lethal harm. Suddenly, his Eve of the Sword held much more meaning to him. *But even after I'm safe from myself,* he thought, *will I be safe from the enemy?*

It was waxing late afternoon when Samuel returned. Damon looked up and was startled to see Jae Stonehart herself step through the door. The sun behind her made her light golden hair almost white. As soon as her pale green eyes fell on him, her sharp face tightened into a scowl. He felt a tremor pass through him.

"Inexcusable!" she snapped, suddenly stamping her boot on the stone floor. He lowered his eyes, unable to continue staring at the fury he saw in hers. He found himself staring instead at the golden hilt of her long sword, wondering how he could ever be worthy of such an object. He heard her draw in a breath and braced himself for the tirade he knew was coming. "That the son of Erik Stonehart himself should be attacked in this manner! Those highwaymen have gone too far, and on *my* territory!"

He looked up then, relieved as he realized he was not the object of her anger. He was relieved. Jae's violent temper and prowess with a blade was legendary. Most bandits knew better than to trespass near her stedding. She rode far and wide throughout the vast expanse of Stonehart land to the east, driving out any criminals skulking there. She was married into the clan rather than being born into it, but that didn't make her any less Stonehart. Where the defence of her clan was concerned, she was a wildcat.

She put a hand on his shoulder. "Rest assured, Damon, they will not escape unpunished. I will hunt them down myself if I have to!"

He blushed under her attention.

Jae withdrew her hand, startled, then grasped the pommel of her sword to cover the motion.

"Thank you," he said, unsure of what else to say.

"On the contrary, thank *you*." She sat down in the chair beside him. She had a small build, but the presence she exuded made her seem larger. "Carrying word of war is a matter of great importance and a dangerous task in these evil times." She glowered at the trees outside as if they were somehow responsible for the attack. "You displayed great courage today. You certainly are growing up fast." She smiled.

But is it fast enough, he wondered. What would she say if she knew his father had already promised him a sword two years before his time? Even if Erik *was* the leader of the Stonehart clan and even if he *was* special in terms of his magic, he was sure there would be disagreements about it when the council was asked to give their blessing on the ceremony. It occurred to him that quite soon he would know who truly believed in him and who did not. *I guess now I'll know exactly how many friends I have.* It was this thought that disturbed him perhaps more than anything else. He was beginning to earnestly regret ever having asked his father for this thing that would change his life. If there was one thing he was sure of, it was that he was not ready for this. Not by a long shot.

Jae sent twelve armed Stoneharts with him to see him safely home. It was getting dark by the time Damon and his escort rode into the clearing around his house. He was still feeling a little light-headed from losing blood, but he declined his cousin Derek's offer to help him off his horse. Samuel was Derek's Embraced. They had met while he was on a trip to Sunsfield to sell horses. After they had returned to Glasshammer, he married into the Stonehart clan as was usually the case.

Damon couldn't help but wonder what would have happened to him if he could have met his Reflection. The embrace of one's match was different for each person. The powers uncovered were as unique as the person themselves. He couldn't stop thinking about what his father said. If his Reflection was dead, did that mean he'd never reach his full potential?

He looked up at a shout from the direction of the house. His father had already seen them riding in and came running to meet him.

"Damon, what happened?" he said, breathless from running to meet them. "It's almost sundown! I was just about to saddle Everlasting and come looking for you." His eyes grew large at the sight of the bandage wrapped around his neck.

Damon was glad he had been given another shirt to wear. The other one had a huge bloodstain down the front and he was sure that would cause his father even more worry. "It's ok, Da," he said. "I'm fine. Marel took good care of me."

Derek stepped forward. "It was thieves, Sir. An ambush." Erik Stonehart's face grew dark.

"I'm sorry," Damon said quietly, lowering his head. "I shouldn't have taken the dagger with me. I wasn't thinking ..."

"Nonsense!" He reached out and pulled him into a hug. "What were you supposed to do? Go out unarmed? Your older sister and I both have swords with jewelled hilts. It could have happened to either of us."

Damon looked down at the weapon sheathed in his boot and couldn't help but wonder if the thieves might have let him be if it were a sword instead.

He was amazed. For all the stupid things he'd done today, no one seemed to be angry with him. In fact, they all seemed to think he'd had his own reasons for doing them. He resolved to make better judgement calls in the future. *Do I really look like I know what I'm doing?* In a way, he was proud of the trust they showed him, but worried about the responsibility that trust implied.

His father released him and patted him on the head affectionately. "Are you alright?" When Damon nodded, he continued. "Why don't you go inside and get some dinner? Your sisters have already started deciding what's to be packed for the trip. I'm sure Derek and the others can explain what happened."

With a look of gratitude, he started walking toward the house while Erik talked with his cousins, stroking Silhouette's neck while he listened. Damon knew that he had caused a delay that would mean they wouldn't reach Stonehart Hall on schedule, but it couldn't be helped. The long wet grass shushed around his legs as he plodded toward the long wooden house. The hayfork still leaned, forgotten, beside the door. He was too tired to put it away just now.

As soon as he opened the door, a distraught little sister flung her arms around him. "Damon! We were so worried about you! What happened? Are you alright?"

"Easy Rebecca," he said, prying her off and pushing her long brown hair out of her face. "I'm alright. Everything's fine."

"Maybe, but you look awful." He looked up from the big, brown, tearful eyes to see his older sister standing with her arms crossed in the doorway leading off to the sitting room. He always marvelled at her ability to detect changes in his skin colour when even he had trouble doing so. "Your other shirt?" She snapped her fingers at the brown sweater he was wearing. "Not the one you had this morning."

"You don't miss anything, do you?" He adjusted the woollen affair around his shoulders, giving a half-hearted smile. "The other one got blood on it." Rebecca made a sound and clutched his wrist.

"It's *alright*," he said again. "It's a scratch, nothing else." And by now it really was no graver than that, healing just as fast as any other wound he'd ever received. "Da said my things are all ready?"

"Yes. Packed while you were gone. Your dress clothes are on the bed."

"Thanks, Sunev." He moved to go past her but she stopped him with a hand on his arm. The expression on her face was unusual as if she'd just bit her tongue.

"Don't hurry or anything," she told him. "Take a rest, even. Da said we're not leaving right away. Got some things to sort out before we go."

Damon was puzzled. Being treated like a hero one minute and an invalid the next was confusing. "It's alright," he said for the third time. "Honestly."

"Of course it is," she stated flatly. "But you're walking like a drunk. Just go lay down until the dizziness passes, Damon. You knock your head into a wall, I'm not taking the heat for it."

He grinned. That was the Sunev he knew, observant and sharp-witted.

30

"Alright, alright," he sighed and walked through the main room his bedroom. He realized that she was correct, as usual. He was teetering ever so slightly as he moved. Only Sunev would have noticed, but then that was her talent. When she pointed things out to him, he just couldn't understand how he hadn't seen them before. That was why he really enjoyed hunting with her. He was better at the actual task of hitting the target, but she could find tracks and dens where he saw nothing.

On his bed there was his black formal tunic with the high, stiff collar and his good breeches. His dress boots were polished to a glossy shine. His knee-length riding cloak hung from a post on the headboard accompanied by a few things he didn't recognize as his.

He picked up the amulet first. It was a small vial of blue liquid attached to a silver chain. A white feather was bound to the stopper along with three small glass beads, two green and one blue. The next thing was a thick leather strap with large round studs through it that, after some playing around, he found was a baldric and it hung over his left shoulder where the family crest was displayed on a medallion about the size of his fist. Below the traditional winged horse galloping from a thundercloud there hung a fringe of metal pieces that reminded him somewhat of a wind chime. The third and last thing he picked up was a strap of fine leather with a buckle on it and a reinforced loop in the middle which he recognized as a thigh strap to hold his dagger.

He smiled at the gifts and flopped down on the bed beside his clothes. He supposed he had to take his sister's advice and have a rest; already his eyes were growing heavy. *Just a little nap*, he promised himself as he fell into a deep sleep.

A bright light greeted him when he opened his eyes and he slit them against it. *The sun?* "Ah!" He twisted around and promptly fell out of bed. He was still in his room and still not dressed in his formal clothes. It was morning.

"Uh, are you alright?" Rebecca popped her head in the door in time to see him haul himself up off the floor.

"What's going on? Why didn't someone wake me? We're late!" He went to the window and observed that the sun was closing on its zenith. Not morning anymore. "We're *very* late!"

"Hey, don't yell." She stepped in and he could see she was already wearing her bright blue tunic and breeches without its accompanying belt and cape. "Sunev said not to wake you up because you got hurt and you'd be tired. Everybody knows what happened. Nobody thinks it's your faul—"

"*Everybody* knows?" He sighed and sat down on the bed. "Wonderful."

Rebecca crossed her arms. "Well not *everybody*, but yeah everybody will once we get to the Hall." She twisted the end of her braid around her finger. He kneaded his temples.

"Is there any way to *not* spread this around? It's embarrassing enough."

"Why's it embarrassing?"

He stared at her, wondering how he could make her understand. "I wanted to beat them up," he said, hoping the simple statement would suffice.

"But you said there were a lot of them!" She uncoiled the hair from her finger and began wrapping it around the other way. "You couldn't beat them all up. You can't even beat Sunev when you spar."

"I know I couldn't but I just…" He clenched his fist. "*Wanted* to. You know? I just wanted to *do* something."

Rebecca smiled and shrugged. "Yeah, I know. Next time just run away!"

He didn't bother arguing. It was hard enough not to maintain a conversation with her that didn't devolve into a hundred questions.

"It'll be better when you get your sword. You'll be scarier." He looked up sharply. "Sunev said to get dressed. We're leaving after lunch." Before he could say anything she turned and whisked out of the room. So she knew about it. How many others did as well? She didn't seem jealous about it, but what of Sunev? She must surely know by now. Nothing would escape his shrewd elder sister.

He shut his door and got dressed. It couldn't be helped. He was just going to have to apologize for his impetuousness and hope she would understand. He buckled the baldric over his shoulder and secured the other strap under his left arm. Then he took a deep breath and made his way to the kitchen.

Rebecca grinned at him. "Well that's better. Can't be a hero if you smell like shit in the fields."

He flushed. "Rebecca…"

She tugged his cloak. "Come on. I'm going to eat your soup if you don't." He sat beside her at the small table and tried to keep his eyes away from Sunev. She stood stirring the soup over the fire in the hearth. The heat from the flame and her red velvet dress combined to give her a rosy complexion. Any moment he knew she was going to turn and lecture him or stride angrily out of the room. There was never any reasoning with her when she was angry. She had a righteous temper.

He sipped at the soup. Chicken, tomatoes, beans, white corn... It was very good. He listened to the breeze stir the wind chimes above his head in the window and tried to ignore the sound of his sister's footsteps coming near. He felt a hand descend on his head and looked up. She had an odd sort of half-smile on her face and her eyes looked like glass.

"I think you've gotten taller," she said, ruffling his hair. He wondered if her gold choker was restricting her breathing a little. She walked out of the kitchen and he heard faint rustling which he assumed was her packing a travel bag.

"I guess she approves," he said quietly. He only realized he'd said it out loud when Rebecca nodded. He looked at her but she didn't meet his gaze. "And you?"

"Huh." She tried to smile but it didn't work. It just came out as a sour face. "I'm way too young for a sword. Even the wooden ones are heavy for me. What would I do with it anyway? Probably cut my own stupid foot off or something like that." She pushed a carrot around with her spoon. "We knew it would be something like this. I mean, at least I did. I've been listening. Lorne read that book of prophecy to us last winter during the Vigil Nights. 'A shining youth shall come with hands raw to the sword. A shining youth shall come and be the salvation of his people.' And I've been seeing things. Like Ma did. Not really good but I see a lot of fights.

"All the old stories of Stonehart heroes had someone like you, A Darkblood who's nice to other people. And then when there's war he picks up a sword and we get someone like Serrus."

As flattering as it was being compared to a folk hero like that, Damon doubted he could hold Stonehart Hall during an invasion by himself. A thousand years ago, people did things he would never be able to. Not even with practise. He said nothing, waiting for Rebecca to talk herself out.

"If there's a war going on, I shouldn't be surprised ..." She trailed off. She looked at him finally. "Just don't get killed. Alright? If somebody writes a song about you, it's not going to mean much to me if you're not there to hear it."

"Oh don't be silly," he said perhaps a little too harshly. "No one's going to write a song about me. I'm not a hero. I'm just doing what I have to. What makes you think this 'Shining youth' business has anything to do with me? Every Stonehart has power. If I'm a hero then every Stonehart is a hero."

Now, she did smile. "But you're excited aren't you?" Rebecca's smile was infectious. She socked him in the arm. He smirked and shoved her shoulder playfully.

"Well, I can't say I'm not. I mean it's pretty scary but ... I'll probably never have a chance to fight in a war ever again." He looked out the window at the trees. The golden leaves of the birches and the white of the steelwoods swayed and waved in the wind. "I'll be defending my home. That feels pretty good." He ate his soup in silence as Rebecca busied herself about washing the dishes in the water basin. He wondered about this weird feeling welling up in him lately. This righteous anger that bristled unexpectedly. It was so powerful and pure he was certain that it couldn't be his own. Yet it felt more real than anything else before it. When it came, he felt as if all his previous emotions had been a dusty parody. Then he would calm down and feel like himself again. Perhaps he would understand it better when the battle came? Perhaps the fiery rage would save him from the fear of charging the enemy?

I can't be a hero, he scoffed to himself. *Heroes don't get angry. They're always calm. They always know what's going on and how to deal with it.* He could see how he must seem to other people. He contained powerful magic. He was a descendant of kings. He was patient and kind and did good things as was expected of him. They just didn't understand that he was as mysterious to himself as he was to them. The thought had never disagreed with him before. Now, things were changing.

"Just don't say anything to the others about the 'shining youth' thing alright? It's just ... strange. I don't like i—"

"Ah! You're awake!" His father knocked the mud off his boots on the rug and smiled at him. He'd been so lost in thought he'd not even heard him approach. "That's good. How are you feeling?"

He smiled back but not very well. His face felt tight. "Much better. Someone should have woken me though. We're very late."

"Nonsense. I'll not have you falling off your horse in your dress clothes because of a dizzy spell." Erik turned his head toward the first door on the right. It was still closed. "Sunev, are the bags packed?"

There was silence for a moment. "Yes, Da. Be out in a minute." Her voice sounded a bit muffled. Erik frowned but it didn't last long. Now *his* smile looked fake. Perhaps everyone was just as nervous as he was about the war? That comforted him in a strange way. At least no one would think him a coward if his knees shook a little.

"Ready for your big night?"

Damon sat bolt upright. "So soon? I thought you would have to go buy a sword."

"I had one forged for you already. It's locked up in Stonehart Hall."

Damon tried not to let his anxiety show. He thought he'd have more time to prepare himself for this. "When did you have it forged?"

This time Erik's smile was real and he didn't like what he saw there. "On the night of your birth." Damon felt his skin crawl. All these strange happenings coming one after another were beginning to pile on top of each other in his mind. Would things ever be normal again? "I knew you were special. I knew you'd need it someday."

He knew it now. There was no one who didn't believe he was some kind of miracle. Believe it so strongly that even if he told them it wasn't so, they wouldn't believe him. Believe it so blindly that they would give him whatever they thought he needed to complete some fantastic destiny that he couldn't see and probably wouldn't want to even if he could. He was certain of it. They would thrust him into the fray believing that he could somehow call his fickle magic to do something wonderful. They would all be very surprised when he fell to the enemy after his arms became too tired to lift a weapon he should never have asked for. He couldn't believe he had wanted this. He must have been dreaming. And yet …

Muddy water. Thundering hooves. Desperate cries. Pillars of smoke rising where the homes of his family should be …

He clenched his fists. "I am ready," he said in a low voice. "I would go mad had I to wait any longer." His tongue didn't feel like his own and he pinched the tip of it between his teeth lest he say any other strange things. He could feel his pulse beating in his temples. He forced himself to uncurl his fingers. They were tingling. It was that foreign anger again. Somehow he couldn't make it leave him. Couldn't cut it off and discard it any more than he could his own hand. He wondered when it had become a part of him and what it could mean.

His father was staring at him. He forced himself to breathe deeply and slowly. "Well," Erik said, the strained smile coming back to his face. "I'm glad for your confidence. We'll surely need it in the days to come."

Sunev came into the kitchen carrying two leather packs. Her eyes looked a little puffy and Damon wondered if she'd had trouble sleeping. "All packed up," she said, handing him a sack. "I knew you'd forget everything if you packed your own bag so I just did it."

"Ah, thanks," he said wondering if he should take offence.

"Let's be off then," Erik said and held the door while they stepped outside. Their horses were already saddled and standing at attention in the field before their house. Damon sighed. They had all obviously been up much longer than he had. Sunev came out and started towards Torrent. Silhouette saw his master and trotted over. He nosed Damon's chest and whickered.

Were you worried too? He wondered. He smiled and patted him on the neck before tying his pack to the hooks on the back of the saddle and mounting. This time the bejewelled dagger looked right at home glittering against his good black trousers. *And this time, no one will try to take it from me*, he thought. Soon, he would know the weight of a sword against his back and petty thieves would be a little more reluctant to harass him.

Everlasting moved toward the tree line carrying his father and Silhouette followed. Sunev rode to Erik's right and Rebecca to Damon's left. The cool breeze in the woods helped wash away the tense feeling the unnatural anger had left in him. The birds sang blissfully in the trees. Soon, many would migrate south for the coming snow. Already he could hear more sparrows and ravens than robins. *It seems like everything is changing.*

Chapter 2: Princess

Wind whipped her hair and dust blew in her eyes. The thin cotton nightgown she wore did little against the stinging sand storm.

She didn't know how long it had been storming nor when she had eaten last nor even what day it was, or night for that matter. What she did know was she must be somewhere north east of Dunkhar and had to keep moving away from the city.

She had had no time to grab anything, not even the sword she had carried with her since childhood. As was the way with her people, every new born Solara had a blade forged specifically for them. As far back as the cradle, that sword had been by her side; she had even learned to walk with it strapped to her back. Now, its absence ached like lost a limb.

Her bare foot struck a hidden stone and she yelped but not before placing a hand against her mouth and listening. Though the winds shrieked wildly, she was still afraid *he* would hear: that man with the piercing green eyes that peered out at the world like venomous twin stars; that being with the face of an angel that had killed her family.

She choked down a sob. *Why me?* She thought desperately. *Why this?* He hadn't even tried to negotiate. Her father was a reasonable man. Why this sudden savagery? She was sure there could have been an agreement. Some sort of compromise. Anything but this. *He must be mad, this man. He must have no soul inside him. Or perhaps he is possessed by a demon? Perhaps he is a demon?*

She coughed violently, trying to dislodge the sand that collected in her mouth and nose. This couldn't continue for much longer. Her legs were getting tired and she was afraid that any moment she would step into a pocket of loose sand and go down. Suffocating in some Gods-forsaken dune was not a way she had imagined herself dying. Maybe in battle, or by the hand of an assassin, or even honourably by old age, giving herself to the next generation in the Feast of Life, but never suffocating because of a blind blunder. *There is no glory in this,* she thought. *Let it never be said that Princess Phoenix perished by stupidity.*

Such a storm was out of season in Kingdom Solara, especially so close to Dunkhar. If it had happened a couple of months ago, she wouldn't have been surprised. *What if it had something to do with the sorcerer?* She stopped, legs seizing as she tried to force down the tremors of panic. Could he have called up this sandstorm in the hopes that it would kill her out here in the desert? *What if he knows where I am?* She thought. *What if this is some kind of demented execution?* She could imagine it now; just on the other side of this unnatural gale was a clear calm morning. And here she was wandering in circles while he toyed with her. *But if that is so...* Her knees were shaking. *If that is so, I should just give up. I should-*

"Stop it!" she cried aloud, gripping fistfuls of her short black hair and pressing her knuckles into her cheeks. "Stop it! Stop it! Stop it!" It was this wind, howling unceasingly, that was grating on her nerves. She had to get a hold of herself. *Think Phoenix, think. If he already knows where you are then you don't have to think about being found. If he doesn't, maybe he can't find you in this storm. Maybe he thinks you're dead or unimportant. In any case, all you can do is look for shelter and wait for the storm to stop.*

She raised her head in spite of the sand beating against her. *This is not how it ends. I will not die this way. I will not.*

She clenched her fists and glared into the shroud of dust, deep green eyes squinting. It was all the same formless wall on all sides. She coughed and when she lifted her foot she found it covered to the ankle. The sand was making her throat dry and her eyes watery. She bent down and tore off the bottom of her nightgown and tied the strip of fabric over her mouth and nose. It wasn't much but it would keep her from suffocating at the very least.

Unable to find any indication of which way to go, she simply started walking. Her older sister Darsa had told her that one day she would teach her to find north with her senses alone. She remembered how excited she had been to hear that. She could almost remember the child she had been, jumping up and down with glee. "Really? You can do that?"

"Oh yes. All Solaras can do it. Just like we can all talk to each other from far away with this." She had tapped the red stone on Phoenix's forehead. The gem shaped like a tear pointed on both ends that was fused to the skulls of all Solara children when they had survived their first year in this world. "I'll teach you how someday. When you've had your first Feast of Life. Then you can lead the way when we go hunting."

Phoenix sobbed. Beautiful, proud Darsa with her flowing black hair. Her perfect white smile flashing against her deep copper skin. *Now, I'll never learn,* she thought. She fought the urge to weep with all her strength. She was having a hard enough time breathing as it was. She chastised herself for being so foolish. *Of course you will learn. There has to be someone left. There has to be.* She bit her lip. *Kingdom Solara is too strong to be crushed just like that.* She tasted blood but kept her teeth clenched anyway. Even to her unpractised mind, she couldn't feel anyone else out there. She balled her hands into fists and squeezed until her nails bit into her palms. She would not weep, not here, not now. She would not stretch out her mind to seek the others; but not just yet, because if she did, and there was nothing, then it was all over, and she knew she would never be able to take another step.

Phoenix braced her hands against the hard structure she had bumped into. Her fingers groped over the stone, trying to discern what it was. It was rounded like a pillar. *What is this? Have I come back to the city?* She walked forward, arms outstretched, and soon collided with a second pillar. As she walked, a low wall on her right grew taller and taller, until it reached high over her head. It blocked some of the wind, enough to see something looming in the distance, something huge and dark with jagged peaks like a broken mountain range. At least three large triangular forms crowded at the base like the points of a crown. She could not make out what it was.

She quickened her step. Something flashed in the middle of the central triangle. She slowed, then stopped. It was not the habitation offering shelter that she was hoping for; it was one of the temples built outside the city in ancient times. Unlike the palace, they had not been cared for nor preserved; they were cursed places and it was forbidden to enter one without expressed permission from the deity that resided therein.

Phoenix felt her eyes tear up and the lump in her throat tighten. It was so unfair to finally find a building and not be allowed to enter. Though, being so near to a temple also meant she was a lot further from the city than she'd thought. Hundreds of years ago, when her ancestors had fled southward out of Howweld from the slaughter that had been the War of the Bloodplains, they had found these strange edifices scattered in the desert. At the centre of them all, there had been a great ruin of a palace home only to passing traders, explorers, and the highwaymen who preyed on them. From those humble stones, Dunkhar was born.

Though the temples offered little in the way of shelter they could be used as landmarks for navigation. She clenched her fists and ground her teeth. *Might as well get closer*, she thought. *Even if I can't go in, perhaps it will offer some respite from the wind. Maybe I can determine which temple it is and use it to find my way somewhere safe.*

She approached the structure cautiously, keeping the stone wall near her shoulder so as not to get lost again. Details began to emerge from the swirl of sand in the air. The three triangles were irregularly shaped buildings all connected at the bottom. The other smaller pieces were monoliths of varying sizes stretching out in a rough circular shape behind the main buildings. They might have been pristine and triangular once upon a time, but now they were pitted by wind and storm, rising jagged from the earth like the teeth of some ancient monster. She had seen the temples before on fairer days and knew what they looked like. The central triangle had a huge oval stone mounted on its front, still strangely smooth after all these years. It was framed in gold with etchings all around it, long obscured by weathering.

Through the blowing sand, she could only see snatches of the features she knew were there. She peered up at the crystal, trying to discern its colour. If it was blue, then it must be the temple south of the city. If it was green, she was south east of it. She strained her eyes as hard as she could, trying to overcome the veil dance the wind played with her vision.

Suddenly, a brief lull in the wind revealed a bit of the bottom. It was a red stone. *Red?* She searched her memory. *Where was a temple with a red stone?* Surely, she couldn't have come so far. She looked around hastily. If she were killed on cursed ground, the Gods would automatically cast her into the second hell with the blasphemers and the heretics. The blowing sand betrayed nothing.

She recalled something else from her gazelle hunts with Darsa. There was the temple to the North West to be sure, but there was also one directly east of the city. If she remembered correctly, the door was broken on that one. She crept closer, hoping none of the vengeful spirits would take offence.

Yes! The top left hand corner of the door was broken. She was at the temple of Thenun Ekht, a temple that was difficult to find even in good weather. On clearer days, the mirages played deadly games with travellers, sending them off in the wrong direction. It was a miracle that she had found it through all this.

"Thank you Elstoe," she whispered. It was said that He was particularly fond of the blind, and so He must surely have guided her here. But why?

She looked at the one-winged sphinx glaring out at her from where it was carved into the door. The sand covered the creature to just below her breasts and brought Phoenix uncomfortably close to her face. Through the storm she could make out a snarl, angry over the loss of its right wing which had broken off and fallen inside no doubt.

Perhaps… she thought, then shook her head. *No. I can't go in. A one-winged sphinx is still a sphinx. I dare not even try. Still…* She coughed and cleared her throat.

"Honourable guardian," she said bowing to it. "I do not mean to trespass. I am lost and I only wish for your guidance. Please tell me what I can do to save myself from this storm."

The sphinx stared at her and remained motionless. Phoenix furrowed her brow. Had she not asked right? Even if the guardian didn't want to tell her, she should at least ask a riddle. Or say something. But there was not even the slightest hint of change in her expression. There was nothing to indicate if she was irritated or amused by her petitioner.

"Honourable guardian, can you hear me?" she tried again. Nothing. The slanted eyes gazed at her intently but otherwise there was no indication that she was even paying attention. *What a lazy guardian you are!* She thought but kept it to herself. She approached the lion creature and pressed a hand boldly on her paw. The stone did not yield in the slightest. "Honourable guardian!" she shouted. "Speak to me!"

Suddenly an idea struck her and she gasped, stepping backward. What if the guardian was dead? Was it possible? *It cannot be. If the guardian was dead, anyone could just walk right…* Phoenix licked her lips behind the makeshift mask.

She screwed up her courage and grabbed a rock from the base of the door. She hurled it at the black space where the stone was broken. It passed through and made a muffled clattering noise on the floor inside, nothing more. At the very least, Thenun Ekht was not really a vicious God, he governed travellers, messengers, and the migrations of animals and the like. Phoenix could think of worse deities to anger, certainly.

She set her hands into the grooves of the sphinx's foreleg muscles, hauling herself up. She tried to ignore the fierce eyes as she clambered up over her shoulder and began inching up what was left of her right wing. The grains of sand clinging to the stone made climbing difficult. Her hands and feet slipped and slid over the pock-marked surface.

When she reached the end of the broken wing and peered into the blackness beyond, she nearly lost heart. She had no torch and there was no way of knowing what was inside. She tried to think rationally. If the spirits were opposed to her being here they would have attacked already wouldn't they? "Hello!" she called. Her voice echoed back to her. She shivered. It must be bigger in there than she thought. "I am sorry about this, but I must come inside. If I don't I will die in the storm. Please forgive me!"

There was no reply. Phoenix breathed deeply, or as much as she could behind the sand-encrusted cloth over her mouth and nose, and pushed her hands through the hole. She pulled her head and shoulders in, expecting at any moment to be grabbed by some unseen horror and gobbled up but nothing touched her as she struggled; nothing save the rough stone which tore her nightgown and scraped her skin.

She leaned down into the temple on the other side of the door and pushed against it with her arms. She fell forward into a somersault and landed awkwardly on her behind on the floor inside.

Phoenix sat utterly still, trying to calm her laboured breathing to hear if anything was moving. Her heart hammered against her ribs. She could hear nothing but her own breath, echoing weirdly off the walls. She coughed. It seemed unbearably loud in the dead quiet. Still, nothing jumped on her. It was strange. She had expected rats at the very least.

Very slowly, she began to unwrap the cloth from around her face. The crust of sand crumbled and scattered on the floor. She dropped it beside her and sat still again. Maybe there were no ghosts in here? Had they all escaped through the broken door? She wasn't taking any chances.

The air in here smelled stale and dusty but at least it was mostly free of blowing sand. She took a deep breath and savoured the feeling of filling her lungs. The thought of going further into the temple made her tremble. She would stay here. It was better than risking the wrath she might incur if she disturbed some sleeping spirit. She stretched out her legs, touching nothing but the cool stone floor. The walls inside were much smoother than outside as they had not been battered by the wind and the elements. It wouldn't be so bad to sleep here, as long as nothing happened.

But first, she had to know. Now that she was safe, it was time to reach out for the other Solaras and in the relative quiet it would be easy to focus. Phoenix close her eyes and breathed deeply, relaxing herself. Her breath rasped a little in her raw throat and behind her eyelids there was darkness. The empty black field stretched on forever in her mind. She concentrated harder, they had to be here. She searched for the little red spot, that tiny ruby beacon in the dark which signalled, a stone on another living person.

Nothing.

She tried again, raking through the darkness with all her might, screaming into the emptiness with her mind, but there was no sign of life. *No, it can't be.* The lump rose in her throat. She searched again. *Please no. There must be someone. Someone!* There was no answer. "Please, please," she whispered aloud. She could not understand it: how could an entire bloodline be gone?

Hot tears spilt from her eyes. "No." It was all she could force out. She felt herself shaking though she wasn't cold. She couldn't stop herself. Her body seemed to detach from her and she collapsed on her side. With what strength she had left, she pulled her knees to her chest and hugged them there. All the world was darkness now, before her eyes and within her mind. She closed her eyes and gave in to grief.

She hadn't realized that she'd fallen asleep until a deep growling noise jolted her awake. She sat upright and grazed her forehead against the wall. Her hand went immediately to her hip and grasped air where the hilt of her sword normally rested. She sat still, listening. It didn't take her long to remember where she was. Though she was sore and cramped from lying curled on the hard floor she didn't dare stretch out for fear that whatever was lurking in the temple might attack.

She heard a second rumbling, but this time was only her stomach. She sighed; there was nothing to eat and less to drink.

She kept listening. Apart from the roiling of her empty belly, there was no sound whatsoever. She stood up and looked toward the opening in the door, or at least where the opening should have been. As it was, she couldn't see anything at all; the temple was dark all around. She shuffled over to where she could stand under the break, scuffing her feet so she wouldn't trip. Her feet slid over smooth stone for the first two steps before she trod on something softer: sand, and not just a little of it; there was veritable a pile of it that grew deeper as she went forward. With outstretched fingers she brushed the ceiling. Sand shushed around her knees, before she realized what had happened. She put her hands down and after a moment of gentle patting she recognized the conical shape of the sand pile. This sand had not blown into the temple; it had poured in because the door was buried, something she had seen many times before when she been part of rescue efforts during especially savage sandstorms which sometimes buried homes on the unprotected outskirts of the city. There was no way of knowing how much sand had piled up against the door or how long it would take to blow away; it could take days or years.

Phoenix felt a cold sweat trickling down the back of her neck. She was trapped. *I knew I shouldn't have come in here.* She punched the door with her fist. She didn't care that it hurt. She was alive when everyone else was dead. Maybe this was right? *I just walked right into this. I even buried myself in my own tomb.* There was nothing to be done. She'd seen her kin blast away layers of sand and rock with their crystals alone but she did not yet know how to do such a thing.

The enormity of it all swept over her. She let herself fall hard on the sand pile. Tears fell from her eyes faster than she could wipe them away. "I'm trapped," she said quietly. Her voice was hoarse and felt like it didn't belong to her. "I'm trapped and it's all your fault," she said a little louder. If anything heard her it didn't jump out. She was beginning to doubt there were any spirits here at all. Even Thenun Ekht Himself seemed to be absent. Had He abandoned His own temple? "Shorah damn you!"

It was probably unwise to call on the God of strife and violent death in a temple but the silence alone was worse. She was shouting, and shouting felt good. She wished she knew the name of the demon man in white so she could curse him by name. "Thero take His divine retribution on your miserable head! Alsteh drive you mad with Her screaming! Wasune fill your bed with scorpions and curse all your offspring! You bastard!" She punched the wall again and again. She kicked the sand and screamed at any God who might be listening to bring ruin to the man who destroyed her world. She wanted to see that beautiful face break. Her curses deteriorated into an incoherent wail.

Her shouting didn't last long. The sobbing had caused her breath to spasm and the hiccoughs that resulted made her more frustrated than angry. Exhausted, she stared into the darkness and pressed her knuckles against the grains below, grinding them slowly in little circles while she waited for the spasms to stop.

What if there's another way out? It couldn't hurt to look. *If I will die anyway, there is no use in cowering here waiting for the end.* She wished she had her sword, though what good that would be against an angry spirit she couldn't guess. Nevertheless, just the feel of the blade by her side would still make her feel better.

She stood up, shaking a little and leaning on the wall for support.

Once she had her balance, she started forward. She shuffled her feet out of the sand and felt her way along the floor with her toes. It seemed like forever before she finally hit something and when she did she was so startled she almost fell. She felt it with her hands; it was a block of stone. *Another wall?* It was impossible to tell. It stretched high above her reach. She turned right, running her hand along the wall until it disappeared from under her fingers. She swiped at the empty air then stepped forward.

Phoenix gasped. *Stairs!* However, her enthusiasm didn't last long; the stairs led downward and the last thing she wanted was to go any deeper underground. Who knew what could be down there? Still, if there was anything in this place, it surely would have woken up at her screams. She sat down on the top step, trying to decide what to do. Her stomach growled again. At least the hiccoughs were gone now.

She closed her eyes. Strangely, this didn't make her any more afraid. There was nothing to see in the dark anyway. She tried not to feel the weight of stone over her head. She wondered if she would ever feel safe in a stone building again. Maybe she *wasn't* safe here? The temple of Thenun Ekht had stood for hundreds of years; thousands even, if the legends were true. Surely it wouldn't fall down today? Then again, she had thought the same thing of the Palace. Those towers were meant to stand forever. *Maybe it would be safer deeper underground ...*

Before her doubts could stop her, she began to descend the steps. After the first set, it began to get noticeably cooler. She tried counting the steps. *Twenty, thirty, sixty, one hundred. How far down does this go?* Her legs were starting to get tired. She lost count after three hundred and decided to sit down again. *Why would anyone build something so deep into the ground?* The bottom could be a couple steps down or a thousand, there was no way of knowing. Then, a chill ran up her spine: what if there was no bottom? What if the ancients had devised some arcane portal to the gates of the four Hells?

That is just ridiculous. She shook her head; these were foolish thoughts conjured in the darkness, nothing more. She couldn't believe that only a little while ago she was considering giving up. How would it be to die by the door of the temple only to find out in the afterlife that there had been another door somewhere? *I am going to search every inch of this temple and only then will I concede defeat.* Even then, she could still try and dig herself out if she could find anything to use as tools. She had to give every effort.

She rose with a groan and continued downward. After a long time, she reached a flat surface. It startled her so that she fell forward onto her knees. *No more stairs. Now what?*

She walked forward, still shuffling her feet so as not to fall over anything, or *into* anything for that matter. Her feet found nothing but more smooth stone. She found herself wondering just how far this temple went. It hadn't seemed nearly so big from the outside. She deviated from her path to find a wall. It would be easier to get her bearings if she could feel her way along the borders of the room, or tunnel, or whatever this space in the earth was.

She hadn't gone far when her foot hit something. It wasn't stone like the rest of the temple, it was metal. She reached out with her hand and grasped it. It was a metal pole. As she moved to retract her hand, she hit something else beside it. She felt along that too. It was another metal pole. She took a few steps, keeping her hand out so her fingers bumped against pole after pole.

Oh no. Panic crept up into her throat. *Oh no, no. I don't like this. These are bars. There are cells down here!* She took her hand away quickly and backed away from the bars. *Cages!* She did not want to think about what could be beyond those bars. The desiccated bodies of some unfortunate prisoners left here to rot no doubt. She began trembling and could not stop. *No, I don't want to die down here. Not like this!* She fell to her knees and clasped her head between her hands. She would die here. She would starve. She would go mad. She was sure of it. It was said that the Old Man laughed with a wheezy voice when he came to take the dead beyond the veil. She listened for the thin, reedy chuckles, the popping and cracking of bony fingers reaching for her.

"Shut up!" she growled. Her voice rasped, throat raw from screaming. For a moment she held her breath, almost believing that it was someone else who had spoken the words. *Don't be stupid. You are alone here.* "I am alone," she said out loud, more to hear some sort of noise than anything else. She was rewarded with an eerie echo. Then, an idea struck: what if she could use that? Perhaps with a little testing she could get an idea of how big this place was or what it was shaped like? *Bats can do it. Let's see if I can try.*

"Hello!" she called as loudly as she could manage. The word came back to her as surely as if someone had shouted back. Three times. She shivered. Perhaps that was not such a good idea. *The troubling thing about echoes is that they never really sound like your own voice.* Though, perhaps it would be nice to have someone to talk to. Even if it was only an imaginary someone. She'd heard of prisoners who had salvaged their sanity in solitary confinement by talking to the wall or themselves. "Greetings ghosts!" she called. The call came back to her. She started to walk forward in the same direction she had been moving before. She found that the centre of the room, or at least she assumed it was the centre, was a little more worn than the rest of the floor.

"I am Princess Phoenix Solara!" Again, the message returned to her.

"No, you're not!" she teased the echo. "I am! Oh you're a contrary lot aren't you?" As strange as it was, it made her feel a little better to talk to the air. "I am not here to disrespect you," she clarified in case there really was anyone listening. "I am trying to find a way out of here. I came here by mistake. I was chased here by a storm. If you are ancestors of the Solara family or indeed any of the city-dwellers, it may pain you to know that the Palace is destroyed and the city sacked. I need to leave this place so I can take revenge for the destruction of my people. Please help me if you can!" After the echo faded, there was no answer.

"Hello!" The echo came back much louder this time though she hadn't raised her voice. She stopped for a moment, then called again. The room must be large indeed. The echoes cascaded together and went on and on. She caught her breath. This was what it sounded like to shout into the gorge in Sorgana. It was said its depths went on forever. Was there some sort of chasm here? She went forward with even more caution, dragging the balls of her feet and leaning back in case she came to the edge of an abrupt drop.

Her right foot hit open air. She gasped and slowly eased herself into a seated position. She dropped her legs down over the edge, but they didn't go far; her feet set down on a shelf of stone just a foot below where she sat. She stretched her legs out and her heels found a lower shelf of smooth stone. *More stairs.* She sighed.

Her legs were aching from walking down all those stairs. The prospect continuing such torture did not appeal to her in the least. She lay back on the floor, stretching her tense muscles. This oppressive silence was not helping her nerves nor was the unadulterated darkness. She could not stay still for long despite her weariness. The sound of her footsteps was better than nothing. She stood up and began to make her way carefully down the stairs.

To her surprise, they ended after only about two hundred steps. She walked forward for about twenty paces and then barked her shins sharply on a stone jutting up from the floor. She yelped and the echoes turned the sound into a weird series of cries cascading into each other. Phoenix stood for a moment with one hand cradling her leg and the other clamped over her mouth. She reached out and felt the stone and found it to be some sort of smooth shelf. Then her fingers reached the end of it and descended into something cold and wet.

She jerked them back. *Water?* There was a strange shimmering before her eyes. She blinked several times, thinking that the darkness was playing tricks, but the shimmering grew brighter. What began as a mere clump of little white stars soon spread out into a sheet of radiant blue, letting her make out the pool in sharp detail. Before her was a large, round fountain about thirty feet across. The glowing water threw ribbons of light over a statue in the centre. The statue was of a man, bundled up in a ragged travelling cloak shading his eyes with one hand and gripping a long walking stick with the other.

"Thenun Ekht?" There was no reply. It didn't really look like any depictions of him that she had seen before.

She looked down at the frayed edges of the robe and the worn boots and blinked her eyes. The statue was not standing on a raised dais, platform, or pedestal of any kind. It was simply floating about a foot over the water, completely motionless. *It must be a trick.* Phoenix looked up to the figure's head expecting to see some thin cables suspending it from the ceiling. There were none that she could see. It was supported by nothing but thin air. *What have I come across?* She wondered. A feeling of dread began to well up in her stomach. Perhaps she had disturbed some slumbering spirit after all?

"Excuse my intrusion, Silent One," she said bowing to the statue. She did not know his name and called him by the only thing she could identify about him. "I hope I have not disturbed your rest. I am Princess Phoenix Solara and I am trapped in here. If you will only tell me how I may get out, I will leave you in peace."

The traveller did not answer. She was not sure if she should have expected him to but there was no need to be careless in a strange place. She would address any stone on the floor if she thought it would help her escape. The gleam of the water continued to get brighter, revealing a second set of steps on the other side of the fountain. She stared at them.

The steps were not attached to the platform on which she stood nor were they anchored to the floor up to which they led. Each stone slab simply hung in mid-air much like the statue. Phoenix turned around and let out a little cry to see that the steps she had just descended were the same. Staircases leading to the left and right were of the same construction, suggesting that the platform on which she stood was floating in midair over what indeed looked to be a deep pit. She inched over to the edge and peered down. She could not make out the bottom and had nothing to throw to see if it even had one.

She went back to the fountain and looked up. She could not see the ceiling either. She was suddenly grateful for the lack of light she had until now. Had she seen these strange stairs, she never would have tried them; though, what other options would have been left to her were a mystery. At least there was light here and she hoped it would last. The water, she knew, would certainly be stagnant after sitting still for so long and would be undrinkable. As well, she was not sure that she wanted to drink glowing water either.

Phoenix shrugged and stooped to wash her face free of sand and clean the scrape she'd gotten from bumping against the temple door. When she was done, she decided to explore her surroundings. If she found nothing else of use, she would come back here and at least have some light. She walked over to the stairs on her right.

As soon as she put her foot on the step, it dipped under her weight. She gasped and stepped back. The stair bobbed back up again and was still. She pushed harder on it. It would not support her weight. *Perhaps the magic that holds it up has broken down on this side?* She went to the stairs behind the fountain and found them the same way. The ones to the left would also not endure her stepping on them. Well that was no good! It was not as if she could make a run for it without plummeting to her death! She went back to the stairs she had come down. Perhaps there would be another way to go if she searched around the room she had come in first, or perhaps there would be a bowl or something to hold the gleaming water so she could use its glow to search.

The step sank under her and she almost fell. "What?" she said aloud. It echoed back at her. She tried again. It still would not hold her. "But I came down this way!" she protested. The echoes mocked her. "What good is a stair that only goes down?" She looked back to the fountain. The traveller, for all his human appearances, still did not seem inclined or indeed able to respond.

She slunk back to the fountain and sat down heavily on the edge of it. It wasn't fair. She had come so far to be denied even the small consolation of exploring the temple ruins. *Now I really will go mad*, she thought. There was nothing to do. Nowhere to go. She wondered if she would starve before she decided to drown herself or leap into the oblivion below.

"Well, if you will be keeping me here, Silent One, the least you can do is afford me the privilege of a bath." She stood up on the rim and looked defiantly at the traveler, almost hoping it would tell her she couldn't. It remained still. The water looked to be about up to her chest or perhaps a little shallower. "Fine then." She hopped down into the water.

Phoenix's feet hit the bottom but much farther down than she'd expected. She stood up and gasped. She was not in the water. She was not even in the cavern. The traveler was nowhere to be seen. Her torn nightgown dripped on a floor of ribbed red stone, or at least it felt like stone; it was warm and felt oddly soft. The tunnel was roughly cylindrical and all composed of the same strange red rock. There were torches on the wall at intervals along the otherwise uninterrupted passage. The tunnel twisted up ahead and when she turned around it was the same in the other direction.

"How did I get here?" she said aloud.

"Phoenix Solara, what are you looking for?"

Though the voice was silky and calm, it made her jump. She suddenly found a woman standing there where there had been nothing before. Her skin was pale as a corpse's and her lips, painted red, stood out starkly against it. She had long black hair to the waist but it was straight and fine unlike the usually coarse hair of Phoenix's people. A streak of red stood out from the otherwise undisturbed ink-coloured tresses. Her clothing was also like nothing she had ever seen.. She wore a long black robe which fitted her form perfectly except where the sleeves dropped down to the floor like a pair of wings, exposing their red insides. The robe was cut at the neck like a "v" revealing another shirt underneath which clung against her body up to her chin.

The woman took a step forward and Phoenix saw that the robe was split up almost to the hips on either side exposing snug-fitting red breeches covered up to the knee in black leather boots with laces up the front. The red gloves she wore lacked fingers and exposed her elegant hands from the knuckles down. Her nails were painted red like her lips.

"You entered a gate," the woman said.

"Excuse me?" Phoenix realized she had been staring and searched for some appropriate words of apology.

"You came through a gate. You are now in the Planar Gateway." She smiled but the expression did not soften her demeanour. "But I would not expect you to understand this. What is important is that I am the Gatekeeper and I would like to know why you are here."

"It was an accident, Gatekeeper!" She bowed quickly, hoping there was no honorific she was supposed to be attaching to that.

Now the Gatekeeper looked amused. "It often is. You see, everyone who comes here is looking for something. I help them find it if it pleases me. What is it you are looking for?"

She looked around. "I *was* looking for a way out of the temple but it seems I have already found that."

The Gatekeeper nodded in reply.

"Where can I go from here?" Phoenix asked.

"Anywhere." The Gatekeeper folded her porcelain hands, as if waiting patiently for Phoenix to make a decision.

Phoenix wet her lips. "There is a man, a demon man ..."

"The White Asp," the Gatekeeper interrupted.

"The ... what?"

"He who destroyed Dunkhar and many others to the south. What of him?" The Gatekeeper waited for her answer.

She peered at the strange woman for a moment. *Can she read minds?*

"Of course I can."

Phoenix jumped.

"May I ask then, why do you ask me what I want when you must surely know already? Why should I speak at all?"

"The thoughts of mortals are chaotic and convoluted. Speech is much tidier." She waved a hand dismissively. "Words said aloud are a contract."

They are? Phoenix thought hard. *What have I agreed to already without knowing it? I must speak carefully.* "Is there danger still, in Duhkhar?"

The Gatekeeper canted her head to the side. "Yes."

"The demon man, is he there? What did you call him?"

"The White Asp. Though, you call him something else." She sighed. "Take care. Know that I do not like to answer questions in my realm, it is my right alone to ask."

Phoenix pressed her lips together tightly. *Call him something else? He is known to my people?* She rifled through her thoughts. There was a snake God that many of the common people worshipped but He was harmless. It didn't make any sense. She took a deep breath. *Words said aloud are a contract. I must say only what I really, truly want.* "I want to go somewhere safe. Somewhere I can grow strong. I must aid my people. I ... I may be the last ..." She could not make herself say it.

The Gatekeeper cast her eyes to the ceiling and considered for a moment, pursing her red lips. She stood very close to one of the torches and Phoenix wondered if she was uncomfortable in its heat. "Somewhere safe. Somewhere to grow strong." She nodded slowly. "You will want retribution, yes?"

Phoenix wrinkled her brow. "The ... White Asp? He is too powerful. I could never hope for revenge."

"You speak with such certainty." The bright red lips curved in a smile. "Yet, you are mistaken."

"Can I truly avenge my people?"

"Again, a question." The Gatekeeper set her hands on her hips and frowned.

"I apologize." Phoenix hastily dipped her head and shoulders. "I meant ... yes, I desire retribution, as you said."

The smile was back. "Good. Vengeance pleases me. As does your request."

"My... " She stopped just short of finishing the question. Before she could say or even think of anything else, a sound like an approaching sandstorm filled the tunnel.

"Farewell Phoenix Solara. Grow strong."

An invisible force latched onto Phoenix and she founder herself being yanked through the air down the dim passageway.

Chapter 3: The White Asp

Lyre closed his eyelids, showing only the barest hint of vibrant green glow beneath his lashes. Raach, his concubine and captain of the berserker regiment, crouched to his left with her hands on her knees, cackling. Despite the wealth he afforded her, she was still in the blood-stained hides she'd worn to battle and her long black hair hung in disarray. Aside from the bits of grey that touched her temples, she was no different - no less hard and rangy - than she had been when she'd first been sent to assassinate him.

It had been nearly ten years since that initial encounter. She had been the first to know of his power and the first to show no fear. In turn, he had been the first man to defeat her in single combat. As he was 'pretty enough' for a woman of her tastes to enjoy, he let her have her fill. She swore her arms to his service and in exchange he led her and her cadre of madwomen to blood and glory. He had expected her to one day betray him but her loyalty continually surprised him.

Her careless appearance made a stark contrast with his pristine white battle robes. The many layers, complete with heavy silver pauldrons and an ornate coronet were far too oppressive for the heat of the desert. They were, however, needed at the moment for inspiring the appropriate level of awe in his newly-gathered troops.

He compromised by removing the veil that covered the lower half of his face and kicked his boots aside. Reclining on his lectica couch with a slave fanning him, he felt comfortable enough to conduct the day's affairs. The wind rippled the sides of his command tent like waves but the blowing sand from a nearby storm made it too unpleasant to open up the flaps.

Raach thumped the couch's single arm as she tried to catch her breath. "They opened the gates!" She stamped her feet and hooted. "I can't believe ... they opened their gates for you! Shit-heads! I can't believe it! I thought you said the Solaras were dangerous?"

"They were," he said. He rolled a piece of sweetbread between his fingers and dipped it into a bowl of cream and apricot sauce.

"But why?" She sat down on the foot of the couch, unasked. He moved his legs out of the way and resisted the grumble of annoyance that wanted to slip out. "You said we could not break the will of the Solaras. You had to rip down the walls of Dunkhar before we could start the assault. That's what you said! I remember. But they opened the gates as soon as they saw your standard!"

The sorcerer sighed and waited until he had finished his mouthful of food before answering. "Those were not of the Solara; Solara is the name of the royal house."

Raach shrugged and stole a piece of bread off of his plate. "Kingdom Solara. They're all Solarans to me."

"In that, you err. Apart from the sojourners come for knowledge or trade, the people of this place are forged from steel and cunning. They are Az Taeorans. 'Blade of the Sands,' and rightly called. They enfolded this place in their palms when it was but a wayward trading post in all this sea of nothing. Their hold upon it has been steely from that time on." Lyre watched her brow furrow in thought and despaired, not for the first time, of her grasping the subtleties of the peoples she hacked through. "This word, Solaran, is but a fancy of yours."

"I thought the Az Taeorans were just their soldiers?"

Lyre nodded. A delicate strand of pearls hanging from the side of his coronet slid down over his shoulder. He pushed it back. "They are armsmen, yes." He waved away the question she opened her mouth to ask. "All of them. It is their way."

"Ahh ... A warrior nation. Good!" Raach nodded her head. A smile softened her features. She might not be considered pretty by most. Her savagery, her body sculpted by muscle and etched with scars distracted from the comeliness that she did possess. On occasion, some facsimile of gentleness did peek through and Lyre treasured those moments though they never lasted.

"Why did they open the gates then?" she asked.

"Traitors."

The berserker made a noise that was somewhere between surprise and disgust. "Did you know about them?"

"I suspected." He looked away from her glare. "I hoped. I have lived almost four thousand years, Raach. Think you that I have done nothing in all of that while? I have planned a long time and far is my reach. Generations of my servants have gone forth at my bidding to seed the minds of the peoples over all Silan in accordance with my wishes. Now ..." He swept a hand out in front of himself in a lazy arc. "All that remains for me is to collect the fruit."

Raach remained silent while he finished his food and it was just as well; it was tedious having to explain everything to her. Most of the time, she was content to watch over him and follow his orders. As long as she and her Blood Seekers, as they called themselves, could engage in battle, they were happy.

"I wondered why you attacked a superior force," she said finally. "I thought you had decided to die in glorious combat and, truth be told, I was excited. I can see that you mean to augment our army with these ... Az Tae ... Az Taeorans?" Lyre nodded. Her pronunciation was appalling but she was close enough. "Still, I hate that you hobbled our opponents for us."

"The Solara fought you," he protested. The anger smouldering in her dark eyes told him that he was going to have an unpleasant evening. "Like demons they fought you. Many of your sisters fell to their blades."

"They fought us and they fought their own people besides!" She jumped up from her seat strode to the head of the couch. "I wondered what madness had gotten into them! You don't tell me anything! I would not have been nearly so hot-blooded for this fight if I had known you'd sabotaged our foes beforehand."

"The victory is yours." He looked away.

"It's a lot less satisfying knowing that you cheated!" she stormed. "You don't understand what this means for my sisters who died. The honour of their deaths is much less because of this."

"They will not know."

"*I* will know!" Her hands clenched and unclenched spasmodically. She turned on the slave who was still fanning Lyre and delivered a savage blow to the side of his head. The young man fell on his side and did not move.

Lyre ignored her and gazed at the profusion of potted plants and flowers that sat along the wall of the tent. Gifts from the peoples he had brought under heel from the Deep South all the way to Dunkhar. There was more, of course; lords and princes could be quite generous when trying to buy their lives out of the mouth of the Asp. He kept most of it tucked away in the supply waggons but for a few token chests and statuettes he thought particularly fine. Plants, however, could hardly be stored; not that he would had he the option. The greenery lent him a sense of calm. A sanctuary away from the ugliness of war where he could think.

"This campaign is my quest. It is-"

"All my focus," Raach interrupted. "I know that very well! You don't care about anything else. You don't even look at me anymore!" She ripped open the lacing of her short leather jerkin and threw it at him. The slap of the coarse hide against his cheek snatched him from his contemplation. "Look at me!" Lyre deposited the jerkin on the floor in front of the lectica.

55

"Calm yourself, Raach. You behave like a child and I have not the time for hysterics."

She lunged forward and grabbed the front of his robes. "Bastard!" She lifted her fist. He stared back at her, unflinching.

"Will you kill me?"

Raach stopped. Her knuckles were as white as her snarling teeth but she did not bring them down. Slowly, her fingers uncurled from the silk. "No. I will keep my vow." The fire was leeching from her eyes. "You know that."

"My hold on your leash is a loose one. You have greater freedom than others who serve me. Keep in mind that my affection for you is borne up by your usefulness and that you are my *servant*." His voice was soft but his brow was still furrowed in annoyance.

"Yes, I am," she conceded. "You should treat me better though. I'm the only one who loves you, King of Death."

For a moment, it was too bright to see anything. When the dancing spots cleared from his vision he saw Raach picking herself up off the ground. Steam rose from a blossom of sear-marks across her chest. She gritted her teeth in pain and uttered a growl. Lyre lowered his hand, the glow fading from his fingertips. Raach straightened and grasped the tent flap before he could speak. She turned and shoved past the guard who was peering in to see if assistance was needed. Glancing over her shoulder, she glared at him but kept her mouth shut.

He sat in silence for a time. The slave Raach had struck did not stir so he leaned down and felt his neck for a pulse. There was nothing. Lyre grimaced and sat back. He gestured at a slave standing in the corner a few paces behind him. "Take this refuse from my sight."

The girl hesitated and he turned a glare on her. She was one of his newer acquisitions, picked up from a village on the northern shore of the Rift of Storms. Whatever life she'd led before, it had not included much heavy labour and it showed when she clasped the corpse under the arms, trying to drag it out of the tent. Her bare feet dug into the rugs and furs as she struggled. She succeeded in displacing the floor coverings down to the sand underneath, but not moving the body.

He watched her, silently cursing his concubine for bringing death into his sanctuary. Now was not the time to be dealing with disobedient servants. Anything that could not perform its function was a waste of resources. Slowly, he let out a breath. The girl glanced up at him as he rose from his couch.

"I apologize. This thing I have tasked you with is too heavy for you."

A look of relief washed over her face but vanished when he drew his sword. The slave was too shocked to flee. She just stared at the curved blade and kept tugging ineffectually at the corpse in her arms. He brought it down in one quick slice and she tumbled backward, holding onto the upper part of the torso that had come free of the rest of the body. She muffled a scream behind her hands, realized there was blood on them, and proceeded to gag. Lyre brought the edge up level with her eyes. There was only the sound of the chimes on his sleeves and the soft grunts of the girl as she tried not to vomit.

"Sully my tent any further and there will be two corpses to carry."

She swallowed repeatedly. Her eyes, wide and dark like a doe, remained fixed on the steel, hypnotized by it. Lyre placed the flat of the blade against her shoulder and wiped it clean on her linen dress. It was only when he sheathed it that she moved again. She gathered the severed torso in her arms, her gagging muffled behind tightly closed lips. He tucked his hands in his sleeves and watched while she removed the body. Tears threatened to spill down her face. She kept blinking and swallowing, glancing at his left hand that he kept resting on the pommel of his sword. When she had dragged the legs out of the tent flaps, he pointed at the rugs marked by the sprawling red puddle. She knelt and piled the sullied furs, scooping handfuls of wet sand onto them to carry away. She picked up a glistening bit of flesh but her hands shook so violently that she dropped it. She whimpered, picked it back up and tucked it under the topmost rug.

The girl made the trip out and back, breathing heavily through her nose; she never once opened her mouth. He watched her in silence as she dumped bowls of fresh sand, raked it flat, and brought in clean rugs. When she had finished, she knelt before him. She was trembling all over and held her hands spread out in front of her as though she could not bear to let her fingers touch each other.

Lyre resumed his seat on the lectica. He flicked his fingers in dismissal and she ran from the tent. In the quiet, he relaxed and looked over his potted garden. At least one servant had proved herself useful today and it went a long way toward improving his mood. She would be alright, he decided, if she managed to overcome her fear of blood. There was a practical reason for the campaign trail being drawn on his maps in red.

The moaning of the wind had lessened, or at least moved further away from the city. Tent walls had been tied back, allowing him a view of Dunkhar and the orderly peaks of his army's tents surrounding it. The forces of the White Asp spent little energy arranging defensive positions; they knew there would be no attacks. Dunkhar was beaten, its iconic towers lay in ruins. Lyre studiously kept his eyes away from the void where they should be.

He had known the Solara would not submit and their defiance was of little surprise. Centuries of planning could only do so much against the stubbornness of royalty. The other inhabitants of the city, however, had been more pliable to his indoctrination. *One need not push the boulder. Merely move the sand beneath it.*

Before him now stood the fruits of his labour. The Az Taeorans who had sworn themselves to his service were ranged in tidy rows for his inspection. Despite the subtle suggestions by his bodyguards, he kept the new additions armed. He wanted it known to all and sundry that the White asp feared no man and was indeed as invincible as the legends claimed. All the same, the long curved sword that hung at his hip was not just for show and neither was the barrier he placed between himself and his audience. Though invisible to those gathered there, the shield shimmered in his eyes like a curtain of crystal beads and the voices of the Arcana he had used to summon it whispered and sighed in his ears.

He watched from behind the veil as his general, Emeka, walked along the ranks. Lyre was in the habit of covering his face before he went among his troops. Emeka's old and grizzled visage was the one they interacted with; the one they associated with his commands.

Ingvor Emeka had been a former army general in the Deep South. His flesh was darker even than the bronzed Az Taeorans he inspected now, and crossed with many scars. He had been forced into retirement and replaced by a younger man years before Lyre had ever launched his attack. His people had thought him worn-out and ready for pasture. They had heaped honours on him but it had only made him bitter. He wanted the field and his spear in his hands.

When Tlube's forces had broken and scattered after his initial assault, Emeka had gathered them up and played the greatest game of cat and mouse Lyre had ever experienced. The wily old general had outfoxed and killed the Asp's then-commander, Charlot. For the first time in a long time, Lyre had been forced to enter the battle and fight alongside his troops, allowing him to finally trap and capture the old man.

Lyre had lived long enough to know the kind of hunger he saw in the man's eyes. He knew even before he offered him the dead commander's sash what his answer would be. Emeka did not possess the same madness as Raach but the cry of his heart was identical: give me blood and glory and I will fight for you until I die. The sorcerer, of course, offered plenty of both. As long as they were victorious, Emeka was content.

The general approached his sitting cushions, drawing Lyre back from the past. He bowed and the White Asp titled his head in response; the folding dais on which the cushions had been placed allowed him to look down on his general and nearly everyone who came before him.

"My Lord, they're as fine a body of men as you could want," Emeka told him without preamble. He was one of the few who could get away with speaking without being asked. His accent made him pull his tongue back in his mouth a little more than Lyre was used to hearing but it did not impair his ability to make himself understood. "Strong, body and mind. Intelligent and not easily cowed. I fear you may find some of them wilful." Emeka waited for a moment for a response. Receiving none, he continued with his report. "But they revere you, to be sure. A few more men like this and some mercenaries and your armies will be more than enough to crush the Ice Kingdoms."

Emeka stalked toward the large hide upon which a map of Silan had been painted. Small wooden symbols dotted it where Lyre's forces sat, where the enemy's might had been mustered, and reported locations of kings, princes, lords, and other landholders and lawgivers of any notable strength. At first glance, it looked like a fool's gamble. The groups were all small, often no more than fifty men to a raiding party, and they were scattered all over the place from the Great Barrier Desert all the way up to the southern tip of Highseat, a few days' ride from Emmesford.

On closer inspection, the large red X's drawn through cities and villages alike, forests and fields, told a very different story. Emeka took up a block representing a squad of twenty men and moved it from Boarsback, hundreds of leagues away to the west coast of Clowry. Lyre watched him play his war game, taking note of where his General determined he should strike next, where further scouting was needed, and which green areas of the map they needed to march for.

The attacks were so widespread and so sudden that his foes had no choice but to presume his army to be at least a hundred times larger than it actually was. He cultivated this assumption with great diligence, for enemy commanders were far more likely to surrender if they believed resistance to be hopeless. They could not conceive of the power to travel leagues of distance in an instant and so believed that the legions of the White Asp were so vast as to cover the entire length and breadth of the kingdoms.

Emeka knew precisely where to strike and how hard. He had a deep understanding of human nature, and of war. Like the sorcerer, the general was rarely surprised by anything. He could predict the reactions of his opponents almost perfectly. If he said they would surrender, they would lay down arms. If he said they would fight to a man, they charged to their deaths. Lyre had ceased to doubt him long ago. He had been wrong only twice and both times, the unexpectedly resistant villagers had been crushed to a pulp with the application of a little more force.

It was a joy to watch him work, walking round and round the map with all the grace and hunger of a hunting cat. Though he could not see inside the man's mind, Lyre could almost feel the satisfaction as the general thrust his spear toward the surface of the leather to move a piece, as though he were imagining impaling the foe himself. There was a kind of magic in it, he supposed. A desire to kill, to dominate, that was so pure and fervent that it bordered on the religious.

Lyre sat back and allowed himself a small smile behind his veil. This was what he had come for: the next green patch on his map. So many of his plans had rested on the keystone of the Az Taeorans and now they were his. He had waited out centuries for the old northern magics to weaken and the population to dwindle under his careful manoeuvring. Generations of piracy, slaving, and raiding had been financed and planned by delegates of his. It had taken no more than a hundred years for nearly every kingdom to forget that life had ever been any different and it had taken even less time for his "prophets" to change from raving lunatics to respected spiritual leaders. Now, all that remained for him was to stretch his scythe from north to south and reap his harvest as he gathered the faithful and burned the resistance. When they finally reach Glasshammer, their combined momentum would be too great to stop.

Somewhere in those frozen reaches, there was a fount of power that flowed in the veins of a single person. The Arcana had whispered that the one he sought would be born close to this time. though they were vague towards the exact when, as they always were. He consoled himself that all he had to do was take Glasshammer and hold it until he could find the source of that magic. Once he did, all of this miserable warfare would be a thing of the past and he would never have to work with the Arcana again. He hated dealing with those spirits along with their perverse pacts and bargains; freedom could not come soon enough.

"Their leader wishes to speak with you."

The White Asp nodded. He stood and walked out of his tent, slaves following a few feet behind carrying his chair. His steps were unhurried and the assembled soldiers were so quiet that the only real sound was the wind passing through the chimes that hung from his sleeves. He stopped a few feet from them and resumed his seat, folding his hands neatly in his lap. The ranks of new Az Taeoran recruits parted and an old woman leaning on a long staff slowly made her way forward. The light robe she wore was too long for her and had been gathered at the waist with a plaited chain belt. Under her scarf, her head was clean-shaven and though age had diminished her, yet Lyre remembered the report of her taking on the mantle of priestess as a maiden. He fought the urge to look away from her wrinkled face.

She stopped a few paces away from his seat and bowed low. "I greet you, Lord. On behalf of my people, I am high priestess of Ostarok the serpent God ..."

"I know you, Ndiro," he said, nodding his head. "I beheld you as a child. You have carried my voice to your people all the years of your life. I am well pleased."

Ndiro hesitated before she managed to speak again. "I th-thank you, O blessed Ostarok for Your guidance, for Your assistance in troubled times." Her face had reddened quite a bit. "We have suffered under the rule of the heretics who did not understand Your superiority over the other Gods but we held fast. This is a joyful day for us, when we welcome You at last. Many have turned their hearts to You today O Lord. Now, they understand Your power."

Lyre smiled.

"If it would please You, we have held a gift for You for a long time and we would like to present it to You now." She carefully removed a sheaf of grain from her bag. It had been dried, preserved and bound neatly with twisted oasis grass. He recognized it from the reports. It was the holy object kept sequestered behind the altar of the temple where they worshipped their snake-God Ostarok.

Ndiro strained to lift it up to him but he sat too high for her to reach. One of his bodyguards moved forward but Lyre waved a hand to stop him and rose from his seat. A heavy silence descended as he dismounted the dais and stood before the old priestess. She quickly knelt and held up the offering to him. He brushed her scarf away from her face and smiled.

As soon as he took the sheaf of grain from her hand, he could feel the power that emanated from it. He wanted to peer at the structure of the magic but it hummed so strongly in his fingers that he decided not to risk blinding himself in public. The Az Taeorans had surprised him and he was suitably impressed. His smile widened as he lifted the scarf from her head and let it fall back over her shoulders so he could place his hand upon her bare scalp.

"I accept your offering, and my blessings do I give to you. *Alleo camunda invitmasua,*" he murmured the words of power over her, speaking to the Arcana in the language they understood. The whispers of the Arcana teased his ears shadowy voices reminding him of pacts, conveying obedience to his order. The cords of magic woven through his body twisted and pulled, shifted position in accordance with his will. The bright beads of light as the Arcana raced along the threads to complete the spell remained invisible to the eyes around him.

The priestess knew nothing of the spell until the barren scalp under his hand sprouted thick, lustrous white hair streaked with locks of silver. It fell down her back in spirals and came to rest just above her knees. She gaped with amazement and he had to hold back his laughter.

"You will instruct your acolytes to grow their hair long and wear it unbound. This is a sign of my returning and a mark of the covenant between you and I. Your faith has remained a wall both hard and unassailable. Your reward is nigh."

The priestess did not rise from her knees; she wavered as though she might fall but the staff leaning over her shoulder gave her enough stability to remain upright. "It will be as You say, Lord," she answered reflexively. Her voice rasped in her throat, thick with emotion. "Will ... will You return to Your temple in the city that we might serve You there?"

Lyre shook his head slowly and closed his eyes for a moment. "I cannot stay. The oases from which you draw life are renewed, as I have promised. But there is a great evil in the north. It is an evil I must silence with my fangs for eternity." The imagery of the snake God served him well, as it did in so many cultures. "They have stolen a portion of my powers and hoard it unto themselves. They care not for others. No plague, no famine, no drought suffered by your people has moved their hard hearts. That is why they are called Stonehearts. I will go and take back what is mine. Then, I will return and you will know glory and forget the taste of hunger."

Ndiro's gnarled fingers tightened on her staff. "O Lord, You are wise and courageous! Ask anything You wish of us. We will help to smite Your enemies if we can."

The fluttering in the White Asp's chest made him want to laugh. Those eyes peering up at him sparkled with trust, like a puppy that had never known the feel of a boot. "Your armsmen have pledged their service unto me. Their blades shall savour the blood of evil men. They shall be instruments of justice. But for me, you can do more. Gather together all your witches, your sorcerers, your wielders of magic. They too shall come with me. To me, they shall lend their strength and be transformed. You shall all become more than what you are. I reward my faithful servants richly."

"It will be as You say, O Lord!" She struggled to her feet eagerly.

"Go now, and do my bidding, Ndiro." He put out his hand, signing his benediction as he watched her hurry away as fast as her old bones would let her. Then, he looked down at the bound sheaf in his hand. He had reaped more than he had thought he would today, and all for the love of some natural springs he had never touched. *Surrounded by fools. Praise Ostarok.*

In the quiet of the evening, Lyre lifted the coronet from his head and set it on the bed beside him. Long years of practice had made him accustomed to sitting at attention all day, but there never was anything to be done for the mind. He looked over the maps spread out over the sheets. They had done nothing to quiet the chatter in his head. He picked up the one nearest to him and began slowly rolling it up. At this time of night, there were few sounds aside from his fingers on the worn parchment.

It had shocked him, seeing the mighty towers come down; it really shouldn't have, but it did. They were older than he was and their destruction irrevocably changed his mental map of the world. The threads of magic had soared around them, the ghostly Arcana roaring, laughing as their bright eyes circled the ancient structure. Everything had gone as expected, better than he had hoped in fact. His plans had been fulfilled, yet something unsettled his thoughts.

His troops had dutifully bathed themselves before coming in sight of him, as ordered. Fragrant flowering plants in bloom and in bud were arranged around his room, tended by his servants as though they were minor princes in their own right. Offerings of fresh fruits and choice cuts of lamb had been presented to him earlier. Perhaps it was the body of the young princess - the one they had been unable to find - that troubled him?

Solaras were not to be underestimated. Their wills had remained unbendable in all the years he had tried to sway them. It had been a constant struggle to keep the commoners loyal to Ostarok and stop the royals from swaying them back to the old Gods. Their rule had been both firm and fair and bred a nation of hardy people, tenacious and gifted in survival. In spite of all his preparation, if the king had managed to rally the people, the battle could have differently. There was no doubt in his mind that he still could have taken the city but the cost would have been so much higher. It was bad enough as it was even with everything going according to plan. Though Az Taeorans might think him a God but, people did not easily forgive and forget such slaughter. Even now, they were still burning the bodies and cleaning up the rubble. All of his soldiers were instructed to watch not only the newcomers but their own behaviour.

Lyre looked down at the half-rolled map sitting in his hand. He finished the task and slid a tie of cream-coloured ribbon over the rolled parchment, setting it aside and moving on to the next map and as he continued to tidy his bed. He resisted the urge to pour over the routes and battle plans, knowing that he needed to sleep.

There was a quiet murmur outside the divider. He sighed and considered chastising the guards for disrupting his work. The words died in his throat as his berserker queen threw the curtain aside. Her chest was bandaged and she smelled of ointment. She had abandoned her shirt completely, no doubt finding the pressure intolerable. One breast was uncovered while the other was bound under the bandages, giving her a somewhat unbalanced look. He had quite forgotten this morning, while she had clearly had not. Her fingers were squeezing and kneading the pommel of her whip as she did when she was plotting something particularly unpleasant.

He lifted his palms, as though picking a cord up from the floor. "*Shitosa ven durinshta.*" The air prickled around them, swirling with feather softness before expanding out to the walls of his sleeping area. Silence descended as the muting spell took hold. He would not tolerate having his personal life intruded upon by an incompetent guard.

"You're still in your battle robes." Raach tossed the sack she had been holding against the side of the bed.

"I-"

"Don't answer. Just take them off."

His hands complied, stripping off the layers of white silk one at a time. His eyes remained focused on the pommel of her whip. Her fingers drummed idly on it, making soft tinkling noises.

"My fury is too great for a simple flogging."

The words vibrated up his spine and he closed his eyes for a moment. His hesitation seemed to snap her patience as she strode forward and pulled the loincloth off of him in a few quick jerks.

Her fingers were warm against his belly and Lyre knelt on the bed for a moment longer, resting his skin against the back of her hand. She pulled the hand away and thrust her fingers into his hair. Her grip forced his head back uncomfortably. She covered his mouth with hers, emitting a growl deep in her throat.

He did not attempt to move. Years ago, he ceded control in the bedroom and though the fear that tightened his gut might sometimes make him regret it, he never went back on the decision. *That which one needs and that which one wants is not always the same.* Raach tilted her head to the side and dragged her teeth lightly down his throat. She pressed a hand to his chest and shoved him backward onto the bed.

Lyre turned his head, hearing the crinkle of paper as the bedding shifted under his weight. There were still several maps laid out from his studies. Raach sent them scattering over the floor with a sweep of her arm. He winced.

"Raa-"

She brought her arm back swiftly, and backhanded him across the face. He saw nothing but tiny pinpricks of light for a few moments. Then, he felt the pain from where the impact had caused his teeth to cut the inside of his cheek. He sucked the blood back from his lips and swallowed quickly, not wanting her to see; but it was futile, her ilk had nostrils like hounds. Raach pressed her mouth over his and wormed her tongue in between his lips, digging it into the wound.

His whine of pain was muffled by the kiss. A trickle of blood ran down his throat as he drew breath and it made him cough. His consort sat back and laughed at him. Then, she snarled and hit him again in the same spot.

"Don't you dare glower at me like that! You've earned this ten times over."

He hadn't even realized that he'd been glaring until she said it. He looked away but she seized his jaw and forced him to face her. The steely grip made his cheek ache and he had to keep swallowing to keep the blood from choking him. Her eyes bored into him as she slowly dragged her nails down his thigh, causing him to shudder. He closed his eyes for a moment but opened them as soon as he felt her weight lift from him. He knew that it wasn't over as he had yet to discover what was in the sack she'd brought. It would certainly be unpleasant; Raach was the sort who didn't care if he enjoyed himself, only that she got what she wanted from him.

This is why I keep you, is it not? He watched her back muscles stretch as she leaned over the side of the bed, searching for whatever implement of torture she wanted to use first. He sighed. There was beauty in this strength.

His thoughts came to a halt when she returned with a spear head. It was a savage piece of art, made of flint and flaked on the edges to a razor-like sharpness. Raach held it by its central groove and moved the jagged edge back and forth across his vision as though trying to hypnotize him. She pressed the flat of it against his face and he held his breath. She'd never put out an eye before but he always wondered if she would someday. How angry would she have to be? All he could hear was his pulse, his consciousness balanced on the point of sharpened stone.

She dragged it lightly down his face and brushed it ever so gently over his jaw. He couldn't tell if she'd drawn blood or if that was only the trickling of perspiration. The warm roll of liquid intensified as she pulled it further down his neck where it culminated into a blossom of pain as she began to cut him. His fingers curled tightly in the sheets. He could - and always did - heal himself, after each night when she performed her duties for him, but if she made a mistake or slipped...

Raach leaned down and ran her tongue up the wound. He fought to slow his breathing, fought the reactions of his body as his eyes closed. He groaned softly.

"You missed me. I know you do." She whispered it against his ear, her breath making long strands of hair tickle his face. He did not move to brush them away. "Every day. You think you can keep your mind on your quest, your army, but I know better. I'm the only one who loves you, you white demonspawn." He turned his head away, hating the word and hating the blade biting into his collarbone even more. She snarled and pushed harder. He gasped in pain, feeling it grind against the bone.

"Please ..."

She withdrew the blade and pressed the heel of her hand against the wound.

"You're begging already? Over *that*?" She pushed harder and turned her wrist forcing the cut to rip a little deeper, a little wider. He panted and squeezed his eyes shut. His tongue unconsciously brushed against the wound in his mouth, pain distracting from pain. "You pathetic little bitch."

She seized his shoulder and thigh and rolled him onto his belly. Lyre breathed a sigh, glad that at least lying like this the sheets would staunch the bleeding. He watched over his shoulder as she pulled rope from the sack. He wondered idly if she was going to bind him, before he noticed she was fashioning a harness, slinging it around her waist and between her legs with expert hands. He hated her "toys", as she called them. One of these days he was going to find out the blacksmith who made them for her and have him executed. The corner of his mouth curved up.

No, he would not do that; Raach was merely painfully creative with her anger. Even if he took all her tools away, she would just fashion new ones, probably with far less skill than her current set. Whichever of the smiths travelling with them made these things, at least he had the propriety to keep the rough edges to a minimum.

"Are you laughing at me?" Raach crawled back across the bed and peered at his face. He shook his head. "You were smiling just now. Why?"

"Thinking," he said.

"Thinking of what? Conquest? Plans? Hmm?"

Lyre stared at the steel reptilian head held fast in Raach's tidy knot-work. An artistic rendering of a serpent's head. The scales of its belly stood out in exaggerated ridges while its back was smooth and polished enough to see his own green eyes looking back at him. He did not answer.

"I'm going to pull those damned thoughts out of your damned pretty head." She leaned down and whispered in his ear. The metal was cold on his thigh. "You think too much. You know what I told you about that. If you think too much you'll go screaming mad. You should be glad I'm here to save you. Are you glad?"

He nodded again.

"I see it in your eyes sometimes. I can see it sinking its roots into you. Madness. If you must think of something then think of me. I keep telling you that." She pushed her fingers through his hair, scratching along his scalp. He shivered. "I am the monster that will eat your fear and every crazy thought. I tell you this and you don't listen to me because you're a stubborn little *bitch*." She wrenched his head back, causing him to gasp for air. The awkward angle of his neck coupled with her sitting on his back made breathing difficult. She held him there for a moment, watching him struggle, then she let his head down again.

"What do you have to say for yourself?"

What indeed? *I thank you?* There was more to it than that, he thought. *And, forgive me ... perhaps, though I think it improper to--*

67

A blinding pain ripped through his right hand. He wasn't quite sure if he screamed or if the ringing in his ears was simply his mind trying to tune out what was happening. He stared at the spear tip that she had rammed through his hand, pinning it to the mattress. He wanted to stop shaking for the movement pulled on the wound but his muscles refused to obey him. He wondered how much energy it would take to heal this later but the thought didn't stay with him; his mind was emptying itself of everything in the world beyond the livid red streams seeping out around the stone.

Raach's fingertips came into his vision again. She grasped his wrist and pulled the blade free. He jerked and groaned at the rough motion but she paid no attention. There were lines of pain being drawn on his back. He did not know what the picture could be. The best thing to do at the present moment would be wadding the sheet around the bleeding puncture. He just stared at it. The idea was very far away. Warm drops rolled down his sides, following his ribcage to the mattress, pooling in the small of his back. She laughed at her drawing. Something obscene and uncomplimentary, no doubt.

Her hair dragged over his face as she rubbed herself against him. The bandages around her chest chafed the shallow slices on his back. Lyre stretched his arms up over his head and gripped the rumpled sheets. Swathes and splashes of red marred the clean whiteness like the scene of a winter hunt, yet no beast had been slain and the berserker on his back lusted for more than blood. She growled against his ear and pushed at him, giving in to her desire to rut at last. He submitted with a whimper.

"You think you're in control," she hissed. Her voice was becoming animal, her mouth producing more grunts and pants than actual words, but before she let loose completely, she spoke one last time. "You're not. Don't forget that."

He understood. It was her way of forgiving him. He looked at his bloodied hand, remembering the towers falling. He couldn't feel it. He watched it claw at the silk, smear the scarlet pool. Someone else's hand. It was always someone else's hand choosing the way. He might have been angry, or elated, but he was too far away, and blessed by the sweet welcoming bosom of numbness. No thoughts. Only the perfect black of the void.

Lyre sat in silence, legs folded under himself. The candles had burned low enough that he could only see half of his face in the mirror. No matter, he didn't need to see to write out the sigils on the smooth glass. It had taken enough time that the blood near the top was dry before he finished drawing the ones on the bottom. He leaned his head against the wooden frame of the mirror, lest his hair drag through the writing and foul up his summoning.

A tired and bloody hand pressed to the glass. He spoke the words of the spell slowly, taking care not to mumble in his exhaustion. Threads of light stood out in violent green in the darkness, weaving their patterns around the curve of the sigils and around his fingers. When he saw a face there that was not his own, he withdrew his hand. A shadowy reflection followed, palm-to-palm but the skin was black and scaly rather than a delicate cream.

A head crowned with a profusion of curving horns emerged from the mirror and turned to look at him. The slits in the plain white mask revealed nothing. He could not see the lips that moved behind the mask's laughing mouth; they never let him see their faces. He'd once asked why.

"We are to you what we show you of us. That is all we wish you to see. The face that you imagine is how you shall know us. That is all we wish you to know." It had taken a few centuries for the reply to make sense but it had taught him the value of wearing a veil in public.

"Meirgloth of the Arcana, I beseech you for your aid this night."

"This and many nights, you seek us." The voice was a whisper, like rushing wind against his ears. The mask moved until it was nearly touching his face. He did not pull away. "Your sacrifices we recall, your gifts we yet hold in memory of our pact."

"I wish for healing. What payment would you take from me for this work?"

Its breath stirred his hair. It was warm though strange-smelling. They never would tell him what they ate.

"Heal another human with your own power. Do this in honour of me."

Lyre sighed. He would have to petition another Arcana later to help him restore his reserves of magic. Healing took so much more energy than destruction. So the cycle of pacts and promises went.

"It will be done."

"Swear it."

He did pull back from it this time, his eyes narrowed in anger. Meirgloth simply waited in silence. There was nothing for it. The spirit would be appeased or it would not help him.

"On my oath, it will be done." He pressed his teeth together until his jaw hurt, wanting to spit curses at it. The hand that was still resting against his palm abruptly sank into him. Lyre held himself still while the Arcana seeped into his body. Once it was settled, he wove the threads of power around himself and the net of light fell down over his skin shrinking wounds and clearing bruises. Chanting the same healing spell over and over lulled him such that he nearly failed to mark when he had finished. The pain had vanished, leaving a vague sense of wellbeing.

The brilliant green light from his eyes obscured the rest of his features in the mirror as the Arcana looked out from behind his face. He scowled at the crown of black horns overlaid on his hair.

"Your body is healed. Sad that I can do nothing for your soul. Unless you care to--"

"Get out," he snapped.

The Arcana drained from him, the same way it had come, leaving him feeling oddly empty. The sensation would pass., it always did. The Arcana merged itself with the mirror with a sigh of wind that perhaps contained a trace of laughter.

The White Asp placed the coronet upon his head, checking the mirror to be sure that it was straight. The morning light permeated the tent roof, suffusing his room in pale gold. The face that looked back at him was blank and distant, like a statue. One of the guards called from the other side of the divider. "General is here to see you, my Lord."

"Send him in." He turned on his cushion to observe the slave gathering up his sheets to be cleaned and brought back white and innocent as the day they were sewn. The girl was the same one that had cleared the corpse and the mess from his tent earlier.

Emeka gave a curt bow and stood by the door. "You desired to go through our travelling plans when we break fast, Lord," the general reminded him. He looked around the room, before adding "how was your night?"

"Peaceful," Lyre said, folding his hands in his lap.

The slave paused in her folding, staring at a blotch of red. He had missed a spot with his cleansing spell, under the pillow. She glanced at him hastily, looking for all the world like a trapped animal. He held her gaze for a long moment, then he dragged the tip of his tongue along the underside of his upper lip. She stuffed the stain under a fold in the fabric and gathered the rest of the bedding in a flurry. She bowed to him and trotted out through the flap. He smiled, perhaps she would last long enough for him to learn her name? It was possible, if she kept out of Raach's notice and leaned the right attitude.

Think the worst and be silent.

Lyre smiled at Emeka and put out his hand for the morning reports.

Chapter 4: The Sword

A trip to Stonehart Hall usually brought Damon a sense of excitement and an eagerness to reconnect with his kin who lived too far away to see on a regular basis. This time, however, tension pervaded his muscles as the reality of his upcoming Eve of the Sword sank in.

Sunev rode to his right, close enough to touch, but she kept silent as though she sensed the gravity of his contemplations. She watched their father chattering quietly with Rebecca as they rode a few paces ahead. The hilt of her blade gleamed on her hip and kept drawing Damon's gaze, reminding him that he would soon bear more than the weight of his doubts.

Damon flexed his fingers. He'd been gripping the saddle hilt too hard and he wished that whatever courage that had inspired him to ask for a sword would return to help him accept it. He hoped that the talk of war would distract everyone just enough to ease the stress weighing heavy on his shoulders. That morning in the kitchen had been so simple: there was a threat to his homeland and he needed to defend it; but now that the mysterious fire in his heart had died down, it seemed he couldn't think of anything but the eyes of his clan on him. It made him cringe to think of what their reaction would be.

The trees began to thin and the three Great Towers of the Hall came into sight; three huge towers that reached for the sky, their windows glowing with a golden light like giant eyes staring into the darkness. Though normally of a blue-gray hue, in the moonlight the stones of the castle appeared shamefully black and he could only barely make out the magnificent winged horse statues that adorned the turrets.

The central tower always drew his attention. At its peak, a strange stone construction spiralled around and around like four giant serpents with a large blue stone trapped in their midst. It was so large a couple horses could have squeezed inside. Once, his cousin Vivian had climbed up there to see what it was made of. She said it was glass but Salen wasn't convinced so he climbed up himself. Unfortunately, he never managed to prove her wrong; a strong wind had come up and made him lose his footing. Stonehart healers could do amazing things, but they could not raise the dead.

Damon looked away from the mysterious crystal shining in the moonlight. Dwelling on death would not help him drum up his fortitude.

There were two smaller towers in the front that guarded the main entrance. From the way they approached it, they could see a bit of the main building behind the towers. There were a few smaller turrets in the back which seemed hardly necessary as Stonehart Hall was built on the top of a cliff. If anyone wanted to attack it from behind, they would have to trek through dangerous moor land, rife with sinking bogs, and then scale a sheer rock face rising hundreds of feet straight up. Not that anyone ever attacked it, mind you; the Hall was empty most of the time. Even in the event that someone did attack, the Hall itself was picky with its guests. Someone had once told him a story about a band of thieves who spent a whole week trying to ram the doors in. They had had to give up, the enchanted wood would not yield to their demands.

However, as Damon approached, the doors opened.

Silhouette's hooves clattered as the horse ascended the broad steps. Ahead, Autumn Stonehart stood between the open doors. He had a smile on his face but the corners of his eyes were tight. A bit of silver had snuck into his dark hair at the temples. He'd been thirty six when he'd married Remin Stonehart and taken on the proud family name and legacy. Now, at thirty nine, he was one of the oldest Stoneharts Damon knew. He wondered what his surname had been before marriage, though it didn't matter now; married or born, a Stonehart was a Stonehart.

"Erik," he said warmly, helping him down from Everlasting's back. "Thank Aervie. We were worried." He looked up to Damon. "Okay there, son?" Damon couldn't help smiling. He always thought it was funny that Autumn called everyone 'son'.

He nodded. "Yes." He couldn't think of anything else to say. The wound was gone. There might still be a scar there but it would be gone by the morning.

"I told you he was the luckiest Stonehart of all," Derek said. He helped Damon down, then Rebecca. Silhouette trotted off to the indoor stables to the right. "Rebecca?" Derek held her at arm's length. "Oh no! How can you do this to me?" They all looked around. "You're going to be taller than I am! Oh now that's just not fair…"

She giggled and stood up on her toes. Everlasting, Torrent and Rainfall walked down the hall after Silhouette. Damon looked down to where Sunev's foot was tapping her impatience.

"War's on," she said flatly. She snapped her fingers at the hallway in front of them. "Everyone here?"

Autumn stopped smiling and nodded. "Almost like having your Anna here with us eh Erik?" Erik nodded, looking wistfully at the floor. "Let's go then." He led the way through the base of the main tower into the huge throne room. The large ornate throne at the far end of the room sat empty as did the countless seats that rested in orderly rows along the risers ascending toward the walls of the room. Everyone stood clustered around the huge fire pit in the middle of the floor; apparently, no one bothered to light the chandeliers overhead.

In total, there were about a hundred and twenty of them gathered there. It had been too short notice to call in the many thousands of capable fighters from the far-flung reaches of Glasshammer and only the heads of the various hamlets and steddings could be reached in time. Damon felt a sinking sensation. It should have seemed like a lot of people, but it was painfully obvious this ancestral dwelling was built for so many more. Something inside him squirmed at the sight of dust on the throne.

"So to echo Sunev's question, is everyone here?" Erik asked.

Autumn nodded. "Derek's just closing the doors. Then we can start going over the register we've been working on. You know, who's going, who's staying, provisions and the like. We'll have to send all the Darkbloods we can to Harlon's aid, if we're facing a sorcerer..." They walked over to where Jae and Lorne were sitting. The two heads of household contrasted starkly. Lorne's inky black hair, half-flopped over his face looked dull when compared to Jae's neat and shining locks.

Sunev left them to join her friends near the back. Rebecca tugged at Damon's hand. "C'mon, let's go sit over here." He looked over to where she was pointing. His friends were sitting to the far right almost out of reach of the fire's glow; dark haired all of them, except for Adi's brilliant red standing out like a battle flag.

Indigo had grown taller since he'd last seen her and now sat a half head taller than the twins, Piadrom and Roddoc. They all sat shoulder to shoulder in a circle with heavy furs wrapped around themselves for warmth. At first, Damon could not spot Solen, but when Piadrom moved to tug a lock of Indigo's hair, he saw the small boy nestled in the bear fur under his other arm.

Rebecca liked his friends and took every opportunity to follow them around. Like most of the other Stonehart children, he only saw them once every couple of months, and Adi every four or so. At any other meeting of the families, they would all be running around playing Hunter, or Wardens and Bandits, but tonight there were no games and the young were quiet and keeping out of the way.

Damon was glad that his friends were nice to his little sister even if he suspected it was only because they were a little afraid of him. He wished they wouldn't be. He would never hurt any of them. He frowned. The things Marel had told him came back to him. What if he *did* hurt one of them by accident?

"Come *onnnnnn!*" Rebecca, pulled hard, jarring him out of his thoughts. He hesitated but she was insistent.

"Alright, alright, take a breath." He followed her. Indigo was the first to see them and waved. Like most Stonehearts, her hair was dark. She'd gotten her name from her vividly colored eyes. Adi looked up at the motion and pushed his bright orange-red curls out of his eye. He was *forever* playing with his hair. The girls all loved it and he was well aware.

"About time!" Piadrom and Roddoc said at the same time. They were twins. Solen ducked as Piadrom whacked his brother on the head with his palm.

"Now you owe me a sweet!"

"Oh, I owe you *something* alright!" Roddoc cracked his knuckles.

"If you two are going to fight can you wait until I'm not sitting between you?" Solen quavered. He had the same black hair as they did but a darker complexion and a much slighter build.

"Oh no Sully-pants!" Roddoc wrapped his arm around Solen's neck and rubbed his knuckles against his scalp. "We wouldn't want to break you!"

Piadrom wrapped his arms around the boy's waist and began tickling mercilessly. "Roddoc stop being so rough with my dolly! You know he's fragile!"

Solen squealed helplessly under the onslaught. Damon couldn't help but smile. At least in these dark times he could count on his friends to stay constant. He sighed and sat down, waiting for the twins to stop torturing their prey.

Indigo reached over from braiding Rebecca's hair to poke him. "What's wrong? You look tense."

He looked down at his boots. He really didn't want to tell them. They were all the same age or, in Solen's case, a couple years younger. His Eve of the Sword would change things between them. He would be a man. They would still be children.

"You guys aren't worried about the war?"

"Why?" Adi asked, lying back on the floor. "*We're* not going to fight."

Damon fidgeted with the dagger on his leg. "But still..." he muttered.

"Well if you're not going to tell me what's wrong you can at least stop sighing like an old man." Indigo shrugged.

"I'm getting my sword," he confessed. He studied the polished surfaces on his boots. "Early." No one said anything. It was so quiet that he wondered if they'd heard him at all. He could hear murmuring voices where his father and the others were discussing matters. "So, I am going to fight."

"But what if you die?" Solen asked.

Damon looked up. Solen was staring at him with dark eyes wide like a deer's. "Then..." He stopped. He had no idea what it would mean to lose his life on the battlefield.

"Then the Stonehearts lose, dummy," Rebecca said. "Everyone knows if the hero dies the story's a tragedy. I hate tragedies."

"Hero?" Adi snorted. "Don't be stupid. Damon's not a hero. Maybe you think he's so great because he's your big brother but the army's not going to fall because of one man." He passed a hand through his rusty curls again. "Well let's hope that luck of your holds out Damon." He looked agitated. Damon could well understand. He'd wanted to go fight the bandits every time they struck. And why not? They had taken his parents from him.

"You're going to wish you believed it when he comes back," Rebecca stated confidently. She crossed her skinny arms. "I was paying attention last High Winter when Lorne read from the books of oracle. 'A shining youth shall come--' "

"Oh, *enough* of that!" Damon interrupted her. She opened her mouth and he levelled a finger at her. "I'm serious. I don't want to hear it again." Every year on the solstice, it was tradition to throw the rune stones and read from the ancient books of prophecy in accordance with what the divination determined to be relevant to their clan for the next year. Eerily, for the past four years, the runes had given then exactly the same passage.

"You think that referred to him?" Indigo asked from behind his sister. "To Damon?" Rebecca looked over her shoulder and nodded.

Damon threw up his hands and let out a sound of frustration. He turned away from them and watched the adults move around the fire, dark shapes flickering in the dim light.

"Makes sense ... Might not be but, these are some pretty dark times." Indigo's voice was contemplative. "They're not telling us much but I've not seen them so scared before."

"I'll try to bring something back for you," he offered, wanting to change the subject. "All of you." He glanced back over his shoulder. None of the others would look at him. Solen looked like he was trying to pick something out of his eye without much success.

"Unless it's a pretty wench, don't waste your time," Adi retorted.

Indigo's hand came up out of nowhere and cuffed him on the ear. Roddoc stifled his own laughter, not wanting to be next. "Don't you be like that around him, or around me." She looked about ready to strangle him. "Your mother and father are both in the spirit world but the rest of us have family to worry about."

Adi rubbed his ear but said nothing more. Apparently, his fear of Indigo's temper outweighed his jealousy of Damon. He hated it when people mentioned his parents. For some, talking about death was almost a taboo, especially the young. Personally, Damon thought that talking about death would neither prevent its coming nor attract its attention; that was what his father said anyway.

"Alright everyone," Erik called from his place near the other heads of household. Everyone shifted so they could see him. "There are some things we need to take care of tonight. As you all know, there is a war on. King Harlon has asked us to come help him fight the White Asp."

A murmur rose up from the assembled Stonehearts. Erik nodded in agreement. "Yes, I can see you are all just as disturbed as I am. However, in the way of the Stonehearts who have gone before us, we must heed that call. There is a roster drawn up of who will go to fight and who will stay home to defend." His light blue eyes gazed steadily at his kinsmen.

"There is a matter that must be taken care of before any of us can go to war."

Damon swallowed. *Well, this is it.* His heart thudded in his chest. What if too many people disagreed with his decision? Perhaps he would not have to go to war and leave his friends after all? But he wanted this; he burned to defend his homeland.

"Many of you know of the blood bond that exists between all Stonehearts. There was a time not long ago when that strong bond was used to communicate over long distances between the hearts of our people and to defend our homeland from evil magic." Erik closed his eyes for a moment, then opened them again. "This bond has fallen into disrepair and tonight we must mend it. One Stoneheart must climb to the top of the towers and rest a hand upon the blue stone while we perform the ceremony to restore it."

There were more murmurs, a little more panicked now. Everyone remembered what had happened the last time someone had climbed up there. Damon was confused; he had thought for sure his father would announce his ceremony. Had he misunderstood? Were they going to do it when they returned from war? Or on the way to the battlefield? Erik held up his palms.

"We have already chosen who will do this."

Damon felt like he'd swallowed a brick. *Oh no, not that.* His father extended a hand in his direction and he bowed his head. *This is madness.*

"My son Damon will have his Eve of the Sword tonight. As his trial before receiving his sword he will be the one to make the climb."

He'd known he'd have to perform some kind of feat before he could be given a sword but he hadn't thought it would be so dangerous. Not only was he being asked to climb to the stone but to do it at night. The gathered Stoneharts murmured amongst themselves but he could only make out the comments made nearby.

"That's murder!" Roddoc whispered. His twin just sat there with his mouth open. Adi had his eyes closed, but he was definitely not asleep. The corner of his eye twitched. Indigo stared at the chestnut coloured braid in her hands as if Rebecca's hair had just become a snake's nest. Damon couldn't see Solen's face, he had it covered with is hands and was slowly shaking his head back and forth.

Damon sat in silence for a moment. He felt the eyes of his clan on him but he only stared at his father. He could always decline the challenge, if he had to say he accepted he could just as well say he did not accept it, but he'd never heard of anyone saying no to their task regardless of how risky it was. His father stared back at him with no expression. Had he chosen the task or was it one of the others? What if he expected Damon to decline? No, that was preposterous. Erik Stonehart did not set anyone up for failure.

The honour to defend my people is within my grasp. I must not back down now! He wondered where that errant thought had come from. Nevertheless, the stirring in his heart had returned. *No one will sully the waters of Glasshammer. Not while I stand guard.*

Damon smiled at his father and gave a small nod. "I accept this task for the honour of the Stonehart clan," he spoke the ceremonial words clearly into the large chamber and heard them echo ever so slightly off the rafters. There were a few quiet murmurs from the others but he did not take his eyes off his father's face.

Erik smiled and nodded to him. That same look of sadness and pride made him look older than his years. He would try his best. Perhaps his people believed in him too much for their own good, but even if failure was certain, he could not give up without trying.

The Stonehearts gathered outside the front door. Damon had doffed his cloak, his dagger, even his boots. Anything that might hinder him in his climb he couldn't afford to bring with him. The shadows cast from the torches inside painted weird shapes on his kinsmen below him. He stood in the window of the tallest tower and gathered his nerve.

As was the tradition, no one came with him. His hair tickled his face in the night wind. He put one foot up on the windowsill, then the other. His skin was stark white against the black fabric of his clothes and the dark stone.

He couldn't afford to look down at the faces of his family and turned his back. His friends hadn't said much to him, as if somehow by talking to him they would be tainting themselves with ill luck. Aervie must have turned a blind eye on him tonight, for the moon kept hiding its face behind the clouds. He reached up and gripped the window frame, slowly pulling himself up. *Just like climbing a tree,* he told himself, but he knew it wasn't; there were fewer handholds and the stone was much less yielding than wood.

His fingers found the ornate drain spout overhead and he held onto it. He slowly straightened up, moving one hand after the other up the spout while rising onto his tiptoes on the top of the window frame. *Don't look down,* he told himself. His feet left the frame and his legs dangled below him. The muscles of his arms and back complained at the abuse. Thankfully, the builders had included ridges on the drain spout which aided his ascent. He just kept reaching for the next one and hoping the trembling arm holding his whole body weight would stand up to the pressure. His palms were starting to perspire and his fingers slipped once. A groan escaped him at the pulled muscles in his left arm. He promised his body a nice long rest if only it would get him up to the stone.

Finally, he was up high enough to use his feet. He gripped the ridges in the stone with his bare toes and he rested for a moment squatting there like a frightened squirrel. There was no good in looking down, it would only tell him how far he had to fall if his friends' fears proved right. Instead, he just stared at the smooth stone under his hands; it was amazing, lifetimes of rain had failed to beat the details out of the masonry.

The muscles in his legs cramped and he knew he had to go on. He straightened his legs slowly, crawling forward with his hands. In this fashion, he slithered up the spout and onto the slate tiles on the roof. The gradient was steeper than it looked from the ground. *I don't think the Aervie love me anymore,* he thought in despair. The blue stone shone enigmatically in the moonlight. Indeed the moon had appeared just when he didn't need it very badly. He decided not to complain. Better some light than none at all. He crawled on his hands and knees up to the stone and grasped one of the twisting serpent-like formations holding it. He inched to his feet and put a hand on the cool surface of the blue stone. It was indeed made of glass.

Only then did he allow himself to look down. He saw most of his relatives had their hands clasped together in prayer. The wind pushed against him. He gripped the stone clasp more firmly and swallowed. He could hear his heart in his ears and something else too. Chanting from far below.

There was a long stream of white among the Stoneharts gathered below. Someone was reading from the sacred scroll that held the words to strengthen the blood bond and make communication possible. With so few Stoneharts left, it would be difficult to forge a reliable bond. In reality, only some with the inherent gift would be able to transmit actual messages because of their small numbers. The rest would only be able to convey feelings or images.

Damon nearly fell off the roof when the crystal under his hand hummed to life. It glowed with an ethereal blue light and the deep resonating sound was like a giant hive of bees all droning at once. The moon itself seemed to get a little brighter. A wisp of blue wound up his arm from out of the glass and stroked over his chest. He stared at it wide-eyed. He heard whispers in his ears though the voices from down below could hardly reach him. No, it was the crystal itself.

He leaned closer, trying to understand. At first he didn't comprehend the language, but bit by bit it became more familiar. It was as if the person speaking was slowly transferring into the common tongue from some ancient language. His forehead touched the surface of the glass and the world melted away around him.

"I remember… I remember the past… those days…" The crystal was whispering. Was it talking to him or to itself? He could see a woman in black and red. There was a flurry of black wings and feathers before his eyes and she was gone. Then there was a battle. "They have forgotten… yes, even *he* has forgotten… but the blood remembers…" A white horse reared, pawing the air. Its rider, wreathed in black robes, glared from under a savage helm. Green eyes flared with an unholy light. A red flag with a black crescent moon rose up from a sea of soldiers and on the other side a blue bearing a flying horse. "Stonehart... I recall... They may forget but some things... some things the land itself remembers... the wind speaks of... the water dwells on..."

Damon's breath caught in his throat. A line of cavalry charged a phalanx of spears, leaping high over the barbs as though hurled by the roaring wind itself. The ranks behind the spearmen scrambled to retreat but it only gave the horses more room to manoeuvre. Flesh was ripped, skulls cleaved. All around him, death and terror ruled the field and he watched it, unable to look away. "For Glasshammer... for Kingdom Stonehart... the earth will never forget the taste of their blood..." Tears streamed down his cheeks. Farmers with crude weapons were hewn down by a warrior clad in iron, wielding a giant axe. "Here is the force that cannot be vanquished by fear... It will not yield to pain... It will not be sullied by hatred... This is holy ground... made so by the blood of a valiant people... There is courage in such blood... as there is life... as there is resurrection... Glasshammer will testify when all else is dust... her people will watch over this land... For the grave cannot hold such hearts as these."

An anguished wail resonated in his skull and he jerked back, clapping his hands over his ears. He felt weightless for a moment. The wind whistled through his hair, his eyes snapped open and he saw the tower above him, receding into the starry darkness of the heavens.

I'm falling! That one panic-stricken thought was all he had before the world spun strangely and he came in contact with the ground, but the touch was soft. Now, he really was weightless. *Oh Aervie, am I dead?* He looked around. He had fallen from the tower and now he lay on the ground. No, not quite lay. In fact he had no limbs or body to speak of. *I turned shadow,* he realized. *Must have changed at the last second.* He was just too relieved to be alive to be worried about his powers acting without his consent once again.

His family stood huddled around the scroll. No one had moved to roll it back up again. They all looked where he landed. Solen's face was buried against Indigo's shoulder and Damon understood then: they were waiting for him to come back, to come back to the true world, to show them he was alright.

He always felt slightly cooler in this bodiless form; that and he felt a strange calm when he was suffused in darkness like this. Everything was infinitely clearer. The blades of grass stood out individually even in the deepest shadows and he could see every detail; nothing was hidden to him, nothing could escape his sight when he was one with the shadows.

Indeed, he could see the reflection of the night time world in the tears that fell from Rebecca's dark eyes. Something stirred in him, something that reminded him of his humanity and his life among the living. He suddenly felt his back resting against the stone wall. Blades of dew-wet grass tickled his bare feet and hands. He was sitting with his eyes closed but he could tell from the sighs of relief that he was back among them. His muscles ached but he didn't think he was hurt seriously.

Suddenly, he was being embraced by a small sobbing flurry of braided hair and skinny arms. "Damon! Are you alright?"

He opened his eyes and looked down on the half-finished braids of Rebecca's hair. A smile curved his lips. "You'd think you'd ask me *before* you tackled me." He heard her giggle against his chest. The sound was slightly hysterical.

She looked up at him, scrubbing the tears out of her eyes with the heels of her hands. "What happened? What was it like?"

Damon frowned. "Well…" He remembered the battle, the screaming, and the wings… then there was that horrible wail. He shook his head. "It was… strange. I didn't like it much. What did you see from down here?"

"It was amazing!" She plunked herself down in his lap and looked up at him with her brown eyes as big as coins. "We saw the crystal glow and then it wrapped around you and went in you and all through you until it came down and crawled down the walls and touched the scroll and it touched all of us and I got a sort of buzz in my head and it was like this huge chain of light!" Rebecca took a big breath and he tried to keep in a chuckle. Despite his trepidation, she lifted his spirits. He wondered what would keep his hopes up without her near him when they rode to war. "And then you sort of jerked like somebody punched you and you fell and I was so scared! Are you sure you're ok?"

"I'm as sure as I can be."

"Nevertheless." Damon looked up to see his father standing over him. He had an intense look of relief on his face. "You should have a healer look you over before we proceed with the ceremony. I'll not have you collapsing on your own Eve of the Sword." He reached down and rested a hand on Damon's head. "I am so proud of you my son. I hope you will know one day just how much you mean to me. To the rest of us as well, but as your father, I thank Aervie and the ancestors every day for making you one of my children."

Damon smiled. He didn't trust himself to speak right now so he remained silent. Erik helped him to his feet. He felt a little dizzy but otherwise he was fine. Had he really channelled so much power from the crystal to his clan? He felt he should be burned somehow like one struck by lightning, but he reminded himself that not all power was the same. He tried to think of how he felt. Something was different but he couldn't place it. It was like he was wearing more clothes or he had gotten wet somehow. It was like he was carrying something extra though he had not yet received his sword yet.

Heavier, he thought. *I feel heavier.* It didn't make sense but it was the only way he could describe it. He looked down. His feet made no more of an imprint as he set them down and his shoulders did not slump any more than they had before. Even though he leaned on his father, he felt he could still walk as straight as before. Perhaps it was not a weight *on* him as much as a weight *in* him. He could feel it somewhere in his chest whenever he thought of those things the crystal had whispered in his mind.

He looked around at the others. His friends followed closely, watching him. They wanted to come closer but he got the feeling they had been told to stay away. He sighed, feeling somehow contaminated.

"Da, why don't you go get ready for the ceremony?" It was Sunev. Her voice had that same strange choked quality that he hadn't understood that morning. At the moment he just wanted somewhere nice and dark and quiet to release the tightness in his chest. He turned to his sister and noticed that the torchlight made glass of her grey eyes.

Erik nodded and she replace him at Damon's side. He leaned against the soft velvet of her dress. She tossed part of her cape over his shoulder and Rebecca, at his other side, pulled it around him before slipping her little hand into his. The majority of the Stonehearts went back to the throne room. Marel and a couple other skilled healers came with him and his sisters. Matthew and Arra Stoneheart never went without their bags of herbs and remedies. Most of the Stonehearts who could reliably do something useful with their magic were healers. The rest could only command simple cantrips like keeping a blade from rusting, finding game in the forest, or protecting crops from pests. He wondered if they would be coming to war or staying at home.

It was probably a good thing that it wasn't up to him to make these decisions. He didn't think he could. King Harlon probably had many in his army. They were probably as good as the Stoneheart healers. Yet, he wondered if they employed magic with their antidotes. He'd heard that magic wasn't used as much in other places. Indeed, he hadn't seen any sorcerers or witches anywhere else when they'd journeyed to trade horses.

Matthew led the way into one of the guest bedrooms. He was tall and willowy, his hair a chestnut brown like Rebecca's. His long brown braid swung behind him as he opened up the heavy drapes on the windows while Arra, the shorter one with curly black hair that hung to his shoulders, lit the lamps. While the two healers looked nothing alike, it was their movements that truly set them apart: where Matthew was slow and peaceable, Arra was quick and flighty. Sunev refused to leave until she'd properly beaten the dust out of the blankets on the bed. Marel helped her and Rebecca just stood by Damon's side, holding his hand. He wasn't sure if she was trying to comfort him or herself. Perhaps a little of both.

"Miss Sunev, are you quite satisfied?" Arra asked, lifting an eyebrow.

Sunev straightened with a sniff. "Hardly, but it'll do." She came and took Rebecca by the hand. She put her other hand on Marel's shoulder. "Take care of him," she said quietly. Marel smiled and nodded. Damon thought for a moment that Sunev said something to him as she left but her lips didn't move except to smile. He could not recall any words only a comforting feeling of warmth in his stomach. Perhaps this was the new bond? He was curious to see if he could use it. After all, he *had* climbed the tower and channelled the stone's magic.

"Alright Damon let's see if that *thing...*" she waved her hand over her head to indicate the crystal "...did anything nasty to you."

She sat him down on the edge of the bed and examined his left hand, the one he'd touched the crystal with first. There were no blemishes on it. She pressed on his palm with her thumbs. "Does that hurt?"

Damon shook his head. "Tingles a little." He could still feel traces of where the magic had coursed through his body.

Matthew lightly took hold of his chin and examined his eyes. He moved a candle in front of him. "Can you see this alright?"

"Yes," he responded.

Matthew moved the light back and forth. "Now follow this with your eyes." Damon did as he was told and he didn't have any trouble following the light.

"Matthew stop mucking around," Arra scolded him. "You're going to burn his nose with wax if you keep at it."

"I'm not mucking around," he said, offended that his colleague would accuse him of such a thing. "I'm checking his eyes for damage. We have no idea what channelling pure magic does to a person, especially not that kind, and if he's had any sort of knock on the head you'll be sorry we didn't check."

"It's alright," Damon said quietly holding up a hand. "Do whatever you need to. We all know I can't burn anyways."

They were all quiet for a moment. The healers looked at each other, remembering the pyre his father had built for him, the fire, and the desperation to save a young life at the mercy of his own icy power. He saw the unease in their eyes, and the guilt in Marel's.

"You told him, Marel?" Arra asked. "You know Erik told us not to. He didn't want to panic him."

"Well, he had to know," she retorted defensively.

Damon closed his eyes and waited for them to stop arguing. He could actually feel the healers standing around him, even with his eyes closed. His muscles hurt and he wondered if this was what it was like to be old. He felt ancient; it was as if he was sitting here, living on after the whole world had stopped. Had time ended while he wasn't looking? Did it matter? He didn't want to be left alone with the memory of the battlefield and those terrible screams. He shuddered. It was a sensation that defied description. If he could put words to it, he supposed he would say it was like seeing what they felt. Prickles of anxiety. Flames of agitation. Swirls of affection. It was a sense that was somewhere between seeing, hearing, and tactile sensation. Strange and unfamiliar, but no less compelling. If he let his focus drift out farther, he found he could actually hear a humming sound. Were those the voices of his kin? This Blood Link was a bizarre thing.

"Hey now." He felt hands bracing his shoulders. "Wake up Damon. Don't go away on us." He opened his eyes and saw Matthew's concerned face. "Can you hear me alright?'

"I can hear everything just fine," he said dully. Frown lines creased Matthew's face. His brown eyes went squinty at the corners.

"Poor thing," Marel cooed. "You must be tired and here we are all nattering around you. Let's be about our business boys and leave the discussion for later." The other two nodded. "Well off with this then." She tugged at his shirt. He removed it without question. Arra probed his shoulders.

"Ack, these are all pulled and tight," he clucked behind him and he felt some kind of cool salve being applied to his back. Damon gave a little sigh, feeling the muscles loosen. Marel examined the front of his torso and his arms. The tingling sensation went all the way up from his hands, through his shoulders and back and chest. It seemed to follow his blood vessels and he guessed that must be how the crystal channelled power through a person. He wondered if only a Stonehart would be capable of it. Probably.

His thoughts were cut short by a sudden pain in his chest. He gasped and doubled over. Matthew hissed between his teeth. "Marel what did you do?" the healer asked.

"I just touched him with my fingers," she replied. "Damon what is it? What's wrong?"

He stayed bent over for a moment. No one touched him and he was glad for that. He took some deep breaths. His chest felt like he'd been stabbed. "I'm alright," he murmured quietly after some time. He straightened up and rubbed the place that had hurt. It was right over his heart. It looked like a large ugly bruise.

"Aervie!" Arra hissed. "He must be bleeding down within the flesh. Damon can you breathe alright?"

He took a breath; no problems there. He nodded. "I'm fine, it's just a bruise." He looked at Marel but she shook her head.

"A bruise that big and with that colour?" She ran a hand over the skin lightly. It stung and he jerked. "Strange. Help me lay him down," she told the other two. "Don't you move, Damon."

He sighed and let them move him up further onto the bed so he could lie down. *Well if Marel says it's serious then it must be serious.* He laid still while they checked out the rest of him and then swaddled him in the blankets. They talked among themselves while he rested and he could tell they had forgotten how good his hearing was.

"We should go and tell Erik to postpone the ceremony. We don't know exactly what kind of condition this is," Marel advised in a hushed tone.

"No," Damon said without even opening his eyes. He heard a rustle as they all turned to him. "I'm fine as long as no one touches the bruise. The mark of the sword goes on the back not my chest."

Marel sighed and came over to sit on the side of the bed. "Damon you must not strain yourself. We just don't know what's happened to you. You've channelled a huge amount of raw magic through your body and I think it's done some damage. We have to be careful." He opened his eyes a crack.

"I'm not going to do any straining. The trial is over." It was his turn to sigh now. "It's important that the ceremony is done as soon as possible."

The healer frowned, her eyebrows coming together. "Damon we don't

even know when the war party is heading out. A few nights rest won't..."
She trailed off, seeing him shake his head. "Why is it so important? I don't
understand."

Damon opened his eyes and stared at the canopy of the bed. The
patterns of gold in the purple velvet glinted dully in the lamplight. "The
stone..." He thought of how best to describe it. "It talked to me... he
frowned "...or at least I think it did. It may have been someone speaking
through the stone. Whoever it was, it said it was important to defend
Glasshammer. That the Stonehearts must fight. That was what I got from
what they said. There were images too, it was like seeing someone's
memory; maybe that's what it was. The stone said it remembered and I
saw a woman and there was a big fight..." Marel was looking at him like
he'd started speaking another language. "You think I'm crazy."

She hesitated. "No..." It seemed like she was going to say something
else but instead she just repeated it. "No, of course not." She reached out
hesitantly and placed a hand on his forehead. Perhaps feeling for a fever.
Damon rarely got fevers and by the look on her face he could guess that he
didn't feel any different to her. "Maybe you're stressed from the
channelling. Maybe you're tired and anxious. Who knows maybe there are
things stored in that crystal that we don't know about. Our ancestors were
as mysterious as they were powerful. Who can say?"

Matthew cleared his throat. "I will go give Erik our report if that's
alright with you?" The other two healers nodded. He gave a quick smile
and a nod to Damon before ducking out of the room.

"You really should rest," Arra said after a moment. Damon looked up
at the healer's dark eyes and smiled wanly.

"After the ceremony I promise to sleep for a whole day," he said
solemnly. Marel smiled and stroked his hair. Damon's eyes slowly closed.

Quiet murmuring roused him. He must have only been asleep for a few
minutes.

"Yes, he was concerned but he said that whatever Damon says we
should go along with it." Matthew sighed. "He knows something big is
happening, as we all do. Even if there's no way of knowing how to react to
this kind of situation it seems... I don't know... harsh. He's so young
Marel. I hate to see so much resting on his shoulders."

"He's insistent," she said finally. "He wants the ceremony done
tonight. I'm just going to let him sleep though. He'll wake up when he's

ready."

Damon reflected on the success of his trial. The constant hum emanating from the newly-established Link was still there and this made him frown. Was he just going to have to get used to that? Did any of his other kin hear it too? He decided he'd rather not ask in case they didn't. He was quite finished with having worried looks thrown his way. He made a point to make some noise when he yawned.

Matthew and Marel turned to him. They looked almost guilty. "I think I'll get up now. Is everything ready?"

Matthew sighed as if he'd expected that. "Yes, they're waiting for you whenever you're ready."

Damon sat up and slowly swung his legs over the edge of the bed. His head wasn't spinning nearly so badly now. His toes were slightly colder than the stone floor, nothing unusual. He put on his trousers but there was no point in dressing himself entirely for the ceremony; if he put on a shirt, he would just have to take it off again. He walked over to where the healers were standing and Matthew straightened up at his approach, holding the door for him. He eyed the ugly hand-sized bruise on Damon's chest but didn't say anything. Arra was nowhere to be seen.

Marel walked at Damon's side. He could tell by the way her arm kept crooking that she wanted to link arms with him to support him. "I'm feeling much better now Marel. Don't worry." Marel smiled but her lips were tight. He knew she wouldn't feel better until he was back in bed. He looked away from her face and kept his eyes on the walls, following the rune-covered border which ran just above eye-level. He eyed the runes suspiciously; they felt familiar. It was as if the meaning of the lost words was ghosting around the limits of his vision. He felt certain that if he could stand there and stare at them for a time their meaning would become clear.

He shook his head. *That's ridiculous. I don't know the ancient language.* He stared at the floor in front of him as they walked through the eerily silent halls.

But what if he could make out the runes? Could it be one of the things the crystal had passed to him along with the sounds and sights? Had he gotten memories from the crystal? He shivered a little and this time Marel did touch his arm. He smiled at her reassuringly. What would it mean to walk about with ancient memories in his head? No, he was jumping to conclusions, surely.

They arrived in the throne room. He felt less nervous than he expected and even with everyone looking at him, he didn't tremble. Perhaps he was better prepared than he'd thought? Well it was only natural, he supposed; he'd seen plenty of Eves of the Sword and he knew what was to happen. He held his back straight and didn't look to either side as he approached the front. His father stood there waiting for him in front of the throne, his face tight and serious. Damon could see the pride in his eyes, even as they wandered to the bruise on his chest and a hint of worry was added to them.

Damon half-wished that he'd sit on the throne as it used to be in the old days but Erik Stonehart would not accept the title of king. He would be a leader to his people, not a ruler. *Maybe someday, when we are stronger.* What a strange thought; he let it go, but it was only natural, after all, to want his people to grow and prosper, both in strength and number.

He stopped in front of his father and ducked his head. His father let himself smile before turning to retrieve the sword lying over the arms of the throne. The sheath was covered in black leather but about a hand's breadth of the sheath was uncovered at the top. He could see dark cherry wood where with straps fastened securely around it, allowing him to attach to his baldric so that he could carry it on his back, rather than at his hip. Not as if he had a choice of how to carry it, not at his current height in any case.

Erik drew the sword. Brightly polished steel glittered in the firelight. The crosspieces and pommel were adorned with blue crystals much like the one that had spoken to him earlier tonight. The grip was bound in a layer of leather dyed blue and wrapped in a coil of silver wire to ensure his hands would not slip. His lips turned up at the corners almost against his will. It was sturdy and beautiful, everything a sword was meant to be. He would carry it with him for the rest of his life even if it broke, as was the way of things, and when he accepted this weapon, he would be a man.

The pommel of the sword was placed against his forehead. "Damon Stonehart, tonight is the night when your childhood comes to an end," his father began. "It is time for you to take on the responsibilities of a grown man. This is not something to be taken lightly but something of grave importance. Now, as you receive your sword you must recite the Code of Valour and swear to live by it as have your forefathers."

Damon swallowed and cleared his throat. He'd heard this many times but he was still a little nervous that he might say a wrong word in the wrong place. Yet even through his nervousness the still calm stole over him. "I solemnly swear to love, guard and uphold the innocent. To bring justice firmly and swiftly upon the heads of the wicked. To enforce the laws of justice rightly and fairly in all corners of the world and to lay down my life for the people when they have need of salvation. This is the Code of Valour. I hereby swear to live by it."

Erik nodded proudly at his correct recital. "Then kneel young Stonehart and receive the mark of the sword."

Damon got down on his knees and placed the hilt of the sword on his left shoulder, resting it there as he'd seen so many other boys and girls do. He rested the tip against the base of the throne so it wouldn't slip. Arra came forward and set up his tools behind him, giving him a quick smile before setting to work. He slid the glass cartridge of black ink into the back of the tattooing needle and measured the ancient steel pendant against the skin of Damon's back. He felt a sharp pain just below the small of his back and his fingers tightened on the crosspieces. He clenched his teeth as the healer skillfully tattooed the image of the sword on his back. He was determined not to make a sound.

He closed his eyes and let his thoughts drift away from the pain. Everyone was very quiet. Arra shifted the waist of Damon's breeches down a little more so he could start work on the blade. All in all the mark was only a little longer than his thumb and he was glad it was no larger. He kept himself still and pondered over the words of the crystal but stopped when his chest started hurting again.

Arra stood up behind him and he wondered what had happened for a moment before he realized the tattoo was finished. He must have been concentrating very hard for so much time to have passed without him realizing it.

"Arise Damon Stonehart," Erik said. Damon looked up at his father and saw a smile of pride. His father's eyes sparkled like light blue jewels. "And be a good man, steadfast in your promises and courageous of heart."

He stood up slowly and gave a quick bow as was customary. He was handed his sheath and he put his sword into it. He felt somehow completed by it and though he had never known the weight of it before, he felt as if he had somehow been missing it up until that point. His father pulled him into a hug.

"I'm so proud of you my son," he said quietly. The next thing Damon knew, Rebecca was there and had her arms around his waist. He was glad she took care not to touch the new tattoo. Someone cleared her throat behind him and Rebecca reluctantly let go. His father straightened up and made an effort not to chuckle. Sunev tried to hug him while looking as dignified as possible. Damon smiled.

"Congratulations little man," she said, pulling back and brushing imaginary dust off his shoulder. "I'll be watching out for you in battle so don't you think you get out from under my wing so easy."

Arra cleared his throat and Damon turned to him. "Yes Arra I know. I will be steadfast in my promises and go to bed now." He smiled again. "If I can?" He turned to his father. Erik nodded.

"Get a good sleep Damon," he said. "Take however long you need. We won't be leaving without you."

The three healers who had attended him before came forward to escort him back to the chamber he'd stayed in. He gave his worried friends a wave on the way out. He was relieved when they all waved back, even Adi; though he looked like he was still a bit miffed about the whole affair.

He was glad to lie down. He lay on his side to avoid resting any weight on the tattoo or the mark on his chest. After extracting promises from the healers not to let him roll over in his sleep, he let his eyes drift closed. Marel leaned over and kissed him lightly on the forehead.

"Goodnight Damon. May Aervie watch over you."

But as he surrendered to sleep, his dreams were troubled. Wandering in darkness, buried and trying to find a way out. Alone in the silence but for the sound of his own breath. He reached into the blackness, seeking the comforting presence of his kin; but all he found was a roaring wind, snatching him up and pulling him away.

Chapter 5: Queen of the Skyless

It was still dark when Phoenix finally lurched to a halt, landing on her side and skidding across a cold, hard surface. At first, she wondered if it was night, but when she stood and banged her head on rough stone, she realized that she still indoors.

Did she send me back to the temple? She wondered. *Did I misunderstand what the Gatekeeper said?*

Her fingers groped along the low ceiling and she shuffled forward. Unlike the temple, the rock around her seemed uncut and unshaped, a natural cave. Grit and broken bits of stone scratched at her feet as she moved.

As her eyes adjusted to her surroundings, she was began to make out a faint light somewhere up ahead.

There was a certain blue cast to it, much like moonlight, but it flickered. She paused for a moment, controlling her breath. In the mouth of the cave, she could see movement, but no distinct figure. She kept one hand on the rock above her, scanning the ground for any loose pieces she might use as a weapon but none were larger than her hand.

The ceiling grew higher as she drew closer to the light but it wasn't long before she no longer needed it for guidance; in front of her, just a few metres away, was a large stone bowl with a bright blue flame inside. It gave no heat, no smoke, and made no sound as it burned. She crouched down beside it, trying to see what manner of fuel could make such a fire. There were two sticks inside; one crossed over the other. They glinted like metal.

"What do you want?"

Phoenix jumped back. A man with skin so dark he looked to be carved from an ebony block stepped from an alcove in the rock. His head was bald except for a topknot of meticulously kept dreadlocks and held tightly in a golden clasp. He stared at her with dark eyes that glinted like the edge of a blade and seemed to pierce through her with them as if he was searching her very soul.

"I am called Phoenix Solara." She boldly announced herself; now was not the time to allow her apprehension to creep into her voice. She could sense magic on this man, radiating from inside him; how she knew this, she couldn't quite say.

The man made no movement and no sign that he understood what she had said.

Suddenly: "You answer a question I did not ask." He spat. It sounded almost like the croak of a raven. "What claim have you to such a name? Are you human?"

She held out a palm apologetically. "I'm sorry sir, very sorry. I didn't mean to agitate you." Anything to stop him from trying to harm her. She could not see any weapons on him but that meant nothing; he wore long, concealing robes. "It is the name my parents gave to me."

He tilted his head slightly to the side, looking at her mostly from his peripheral vision. He looked doubtful.

"I'm sorry to trouble you but I have a problem."

"Your problem. We don't buy problems," he snapped impatiently.

"I don't want to sell you a problem," she protested. What a strange way to interpret what she had said! Although somehow it made sense. She frowned and closed her eyes for a moment, focusing her thoughts. He had asked if she was human. Was he not? He looked normal enough.

She pushed her hair away from her forehead. His large dark eyes fixed on the gem and he reached out and jabbed it with a finger. Phoenix winced and jerked back.

"Phoenix Solara..." he whispered. His eyes narrowed. "The name and the stone... Where do you come from?"

"I come from the desert." She was not sure what he meant by 'the name and the stone'. She realized the dark man was still staring, waiting for her response.

"Ah... I come from the deserts of Silan. The Sangora Desert wherein stands the city of Dunkhar." The man's eyes were still focused on her, unblinking, and she realized that he was listening to her intently. "Also called the Great Barrier Desert?" Still, he did not move. "The sun rises and sets in blood and in between, paints the sky and sand every colour you can imagine. Dunkhar has not seen rain in over a hundred years. Its water comes from down deep in the earth. No horse will abide long in the heat and dryness. Instead, our steeds are spiral-horned, cloven-hoofed beasts. From all around, the people come to seek respite from the desert's burning malice.

"They come to trade, to eat, to drink and more than any of those they come to learn, for we have the finest schools of any land I know. So many colours and tongues among my people..." Her throat was getting tight and though she cursed it silently, it would not unlock. She wracked her mind for more to say. What else did he want to know?

"Tell more!" The man prompted sharply. "Are you the Phoenix? Really?"

"I... yes. Of course I am. I've never had another name." She swallowed hard. "I apologize to you. I have bad news of my homeland. The White Asp marched on Dunkhar and shattered the ancient towers. Like..." She waved her hand in an imitation of the gesture she had seen in the distance before all hell broke loose. "Like brittle bread... they..." She shook her head. Her throat would not let any further sound out. The grief had choked her words entirely.

"Yes!" He seized her wrist and pulled her close. She was too stunned to react. "The name, the stone and the story! You have come!" He grinned like a maniac, heedless of her grief. "Come! Come with me! Sorry, so sorry my Lady, yes come!" He began striding down the corridor to the right, dragging her along behind him. She hardly had time to notice anything but the madman holding her wrist as if she were his lifeline in a sandstorm. "I did not recognize you. You smell like a human!"

He shouted down the hall before him. "It has begun! Spread the news! It has begun! Bring water! Bring fire! Bring food! It has begun!" His voice echoed monstrously and Phoenix felt dizzy.

I smell like a human? What else would I smell like?

The torches along the walls bore the same blue fire as the bowl. They were unevenly spaced, leaving some stretches of darkness interspersed between splashes of light. The scratches in the rock showed where the tunnel had been widened but no thought had been given to uniform measurements. The walls and ceiling bulged and rippled in places and the floor dipped unexpectedly. She had to watch her footing as the man trotted along, jabbering without pause.

"The blue vastness will make us so happy. I can't wait to see real trees with real leaves and real bark and ..."

"What is your name?" she interrupted, having tired of waiting for him to take a breath.

"Dyseris!" he laughed. "I wonder if there are birds up there. Maybe they killed them all! I wouldn't be surprised if ..."

She frowned. No title, no surname, and no explanation; it was the most useless introduction she had ever heard. She stubbed her bare toes on a lip of rock and cursed.

"Where are we going, Dyseris?" Phoenix was beginning to tire and she wondered how many hours she had been awake, struggling against sand,

and wind, and darkness.

"Hanuel under Frozen-Sky," he replied. More gibberish. "You have not been there before? No of course not. You have come to us! Come from far away. The legend told us and we remembered. We have remembered all this time! You will be pleased, my Queen."

"My ... what?" she managed to spit out. Her question was lost under the current of his chatter about the sky and ancient enemies. She gave up trying to follow his train of thought.

What's going on? I am not a queen. Then, she realized the painful truth. *I am the last of my line. I am queen. Of sand and ruins, and nothing.* She felt tears beginning to make their way down her face and wiped at them. Dyseris did not seem to notice.

"We were expecting you but we did not know when. We would have prepared ..."

The corridor widened and curved off to the left, terminating in a staircase. Phoenix scowled. Her legs were already weary but the man did not even slow down as they reached the bottom step. The light grew brighter as they climbed. She could not wait to finally be out in the fresh air.

When they reached the top, she was so stunned by the view that she stumbled up the last few steps. They had not emerged on the surface. The light was neither the sun nor the moon.

Her eyes were wide with wonder. There was an entire city laid out before her, a city built under the ground. They stood on the brink of a precipice looking down on an island-like formation of rock and upon this island stood the city. It glittered with the same eerie blue light like thousands of captured stars. There were massive pillars of solid stone left untouched, twisting and bulging with the natural flow of denser minerals. The buildings simply went around them.

The roofs of these buildings caught her attention most of all: polished mirrors stood and reflected the light of the strange smokeless fires onto the ceiling and pillars of the cavern upon which were painted clouds, stars, the sun, and the moon. A synergy of day and night, dawn and dusk stretched over her head. It was the sky as it was never seen all at one time. Like the memory of a dream where time was as random as the whirlwinds in the desert. The paint itself must have been of some peculiar substance the way it soaked up the light and glowed with it.

She understood, now; this was Hanuel under Frozen-Sky.

Dyseris seemed proud that his guest was awestruck and did not interrupt her gazing. "Do you like it?" he said at last.

"It's beautiful." Her eyes followed twisting pathways, suspended over the rock island like roots of an ancient tree. There were more buildings constructed all along each of these roads looking very much like growths of glowing fungi. The architects of this city had not restricted themselves to thinking only of the surface area of the island but the possibilities that lay in building vertically.

There was a ledge about seven or eight paces across all around the massive cavern. If there were other tunnels leading away from it, she could not see them. She looked over the edge of the precipice and cringed. "It seems to be an awfully long way down."

"It's alright. If you fall, you will surely faint long before you hit the bottom." Dyseris smiled.

"Really?"

"No, not really." He cackled.

She took a step back from the edge. Today, she had experienced all the yawning pits that she ever wished to see in her lifetime. She gestured to the view before them.

"How many people live here?"

"67,459 Ducal; but it changes all the time, so I might be wrong." He disentangled a stray lock of hair from the polished bones on his necklaces. She wondered what creature they had come from.

"Ducal?" she asked instead. "What is that?"

Dyseris frowned. He gestured at himself and at her. "Ducal."

Phoenix shook her head. "A ... duke? What?"

He put his hands on his hips. "Ducal!" he repeated.

"What is a Ducal?"

"A Ducal is a Ducal! It is us!" He waved his hands.

"Is that different from a human?"

Dyseris stared at her as though she had just spouted profanity. "Yes!" He waved his arms again in irritation. "You are not Ducal?"

She flexed her fingers at her sides, wondering if he would become violent. "I have not heard of this word until now. If it is different from a human then, no I am not Ducal."

"You will not fly if I throw you from here?" He pointed at the pit.

Phoenix's insides clenched and she scrambled backwards, down several steps. "No, no. Please do not throw me." What was wrong with this man? Was he mad? She gripped the edge of a stair and braced herself in case he tried it.

"You are a human!" he accused. From his tone, she surmised this must be a crime of some sort. "You are not the Phoenix."

"I am Phoenix!" she protested. "That is my name. I am Phoenix and I am human. Why are you so angry?"

"Because you blaspheme!" He stamped his foot. "You tricked me. You are not supposed to be here."

She crouched lower. Her legs ached. She just wanted to sit down and rest and try to make sense of her life. "Please do not throw me," she repeated. "I do not want to fight. I do not want to hurt anyone. Please do not do this to me." New tears ran down her cheeks and she hated them. She dared not take her eyes off of him long enough to brush them away. "Please leave me alone."

"I will leave you alone," he agreed, his brow wrinkled. "And I will come back with more Ducal. The Regent will say what to do with you. You will wait here for me."

Before she could protest, Dyseris crouched down and his body contorted grotesquely. Bones snapped and popped under flesh and his skin rippled like water. Phoenix clapped her hand over her mouth and turned away, fighting down the bile. When she looked back at him, he had vanished, leaving a rumpled robe, bone necklaces and a large raven.

The bird stared at her for a moment before giving a sharp squawk and taking to the air. Phoenix crept up the stairs to watch it fly toward the city. She sat down on the top step and put her head in her hands.

The temple. I am cursed after all. I have fallen into madness. She despaired. Now that she was not running behind a crazy raven-man, her body had cooled and she found herself shivering. She pulled the robe over herself and huddled under the warm velvet. If she was going to be insane, at least she could be comfortable.

She dreamt of a boy sleeping restlessly. She'd seen him before but never so clearly. What was different about him now? Something focused her senses on him like a lens. Ah, there it was, on his back. Down low just above his tailbone there was a tattoo of a sword. Such a little thing. In and of itself it had no power but somehow it seemed to make her vision stronger. It was like blinking away a fuzzy inkblot to look upon a pristine pin-prick of a star.

His black hair was a tousled mess as if he'd been traipsing through the land of nightmares all night long. His flesh was as white as the sheets he lay on, or maybe even more so. It was like snow compared to paper. Indeed, the vision was becoming clearer: the bluish shine to his hair was more apparent to her now than it had ever been before as was the blue tinting about his lips which made it seem as if he was lacking air but his chest rose and fell rhythmically. The very features of his face were cast in sharp relief by some indoor light. Was there a fireplace that illuminated the room?

I hadn't realized he was so beautiful, she thought idly. From past dreams, she had gathered he lived somewhere in the north, both by the clothes he wore and the scenery she caught glimpses of. Now she wasn't so sure. The place she'd come to could not be any place on Silan, she was certain of that now. What if he lived somewhere far away through the Gateway? She knew it was a childish dream of hers to meet him one day but a special dream nonetheless. Now, everything was becoming more and more impossible to her.

"Help me," she whispered to the sleeping boy. Could he hear her? "Help me find you."

He stirred in his sleep, looking troubled but he did not wake. At first, she thought he wouldn't respond, but after a moment, he mumbled: "Who…?"

She licked her lips, barely daring to breathe. "I am Phoenix Solara."

His eyes flew open, and she was staring into the depths of midnight.

Phoenix winced as she woke, sitting up against the wall with Dyseris' robe over her. She wondered when she had passed out and how long she had been asleep. It took her a moment to remember where she was as the city did not look the same; the blue light was nowhere to be seen and was instead replaced by a warm golden glow. She rubbed her legs under the heavy fabric, trying to ease the sore muscles as she puzzled over the change.

She heard voices echoing but the sound bounced and cascaded off the rock so that she could not tell where they were coming from. After a few moments, her eyes fixed on a small group of people making their way along the ledge toward her. Her first instinct was to hide herself but there were a few problems with that idea: the only place to hide was the tunnel she had just come from and she had no idea where it led. As well, she was also quite sure that they had seen her already.

They were close enough now for her to make out their words.

"Are you sure it's a human?" a man said.

"Yes! It said so." Dyseris snapped. He sounded as though this was not the first time he'd said it.

"I think she is a Ducal playing a trick on you," said a woman.

"If she is, Bowen will be angry. Heresy is not funny," the raven man said. There were mumbled replies.

There were three of them: a tall man with long, rusty hair and pale skin; a woman as dark as hazelnuts with her hair bound in orderly rows; and finally, Dyseris. The newcomers both wore fitted tunics of the same thick velvet as the raven-man's robe. They were green and worked with gold leaf patterns at the shoulders and down the front. Their boots were tooled with the same pattern at the knee. Phoenix supposed they must be uniforms but what they signified she could only guess. Both of them had a brass weapon bearing three curved claws strapped to each thigh. They stopped a few feet away, looking down at Phoenix and talking amongst themselves.

"Well, I see the stone," the pale man said. "Is it really a third eye?"

Dyseris shrugged. "I did not pull to see if it would come off."

Phoenix put a hand over her forehead and drew her knees closer to her chest. "Please do not do that. It is assuredly attached to my skull."

"You did not check! You are an idiot." The man threw up his hands. Dyseris drew up his shoulders again and jerked them up and down like a bird fluffing its feathers in defence. The pale one ignored him and crouched in front of Phoenix. He took hold of her wrist and pulled her hand away from her face. He seemed less prone to fidgeting than the raven-man. He just sat, gazing at the red stone thoughtfully.

She regretted not fighting Dyseris while he was alone. None of them seemed particularly muscular but there were three of them now.

The man took hold of her focusing stone between his thumb and forefinger and tried to jiggle it loose. She winced.

"Aie! Stop it!" She tried to twist her hand out of his grasp and swatted at the fingers on her forehead.

"I think it is attached," he said, putting more effort into dislodging it.

Phoenix yanked the robe off of her legs and brought her shin up against his groin. He fell back with a hiss of pain. Dyseris and the woman burst into laughter.

"I also think it is attached, Adrian!" the raven-man cackled.

"I told you to stop," Phoenix snapped. Adrian did not answer. He rose to his knees, scowling at his companions and catching his breath.

"You said she came from the collapsed tunnel?" the woman asked.

"Yes, and she spoke to me of the desert. She names herself the Phoenix but she says she is human, not Ducal."

The woman pulled her lips back from her teeth and shook her hands as though flicking water from them. "That sounds like Tamiyon nonsense." She pointed at Phoenix. "She is too dark to be of Tamiyon blood."

Adrian made it back to his feet, his stance still betraying discomfort. "It is beyond us to find the truth. We will take her to the Vault Wardens." He turned his glare on Phoenix, sizing her up. "Did you bring me here to carry?"

"Yes," Dyseris said. "I don't want her to see the bridges."

Phoenix squinted at the pit around the island. She could see no hint of anything spanning the distance. How had they hidden them?

"Fine." The pale man moved away a few paces and disrobed. He threw his clothing at Dyseris. "You will carry these back for me. Do not help him, Yarona."

The woman tilted her head. "Why not?"

"Because this is all his fault."

"No it isn't!" Dyseris protested. "I just found her. If you had paid better attention to your guardian duties ..."

Whatever else the raven-man said, Phoenix did not hear it. She clapped her hands over her ears and turned away as Adrian changed his shape. When she looked back, an eagle stood where he had been. It was easily twice as tall as she was and the colour of ash. The bird bent over her, staring with a huge golden eye. It reached out with talons like scythes and grasped her around the waist before hopping over to the ledge.

"No, no, no, no ..." she sputtered. She tried to wriggle out of Adrian's grip but he squeezed her tighter and she stopped, fearful that he would crush the life out of her.

"You can't drop her," Yarona said. "Even though she did hurt you. If she is really the Phoenix, we will not get another chance." The bird made no reply. Phoenix thought it must be impossible to form words with an eagle's beak. Yarona turned to Dyseris. "You must carry my gear as well. I do not want to walk all the way back."

"Hey! I d—"

Before he could finish, the woman's clothing collapsed in a pile and a humming bird shot out of the neck of the tunic. Phoenix stared at the tiny thing flitting around the gigantic eagle's head. She looked like an insect by comparison. She couldn't help but laugh.

Then, Adrian leaned forward and launched himself from the ledge. The maw of darkness below seemed infinite and she would have screamed if her throat were not locked in terror. A strangled whimper escaped her. She still had the robe in her hands. She pressed the soft fabric over her face. She could barely get any air but her muscles were frozen and she could not move it.

This is not real. This is not real. I am on the ground. I am sleeping. Dreaming. This is not real.

The wing-beats jerked her up and down, making her head swim, until the bird settled into a smooth glide. Phoenix's body unclenched itself, bit by bit, until she could finally force herself to uncover her face. Now that they drew close to the city, she could see that the outer edges of it were broad, flat, and free of clutter. There were tall fences of iron separating the landing ledge from the rest of the city.

The eagle slowed, his wings fanning the dust into clouds. Suddenly, he opened his talon and let her fall. Phoenix let out a shriek. She landed on her hands and knees in an awkward half-crouch.

"Bastard!" she yelled. Her legs shook as she stood but she managed to stay upright. She shuffled away from the edge until she was nearly to the fence. Adrian settled on the ground and hop-stepped closer. He stretched up to his full height and spread out his wings, towering over her and displaying his sharp beak. He let out a deafening screech.

Phoenix blinked, fighting with the primal urge to cower in the face of such a display. Her fingers twitched at her hip, reaching for the sword that was not there. She reminded herself of the rusty-haired man on the ground and took a deep breath. She screamed back at him, feral and wordless, and swung at his head with the robe in her hand. The heavy fabric could do no damage to the bird but it did accomplish what she could not from her place on the ground: it slapped him in the face.

Adrian shook his head, dislodging the purple velvet. He crouched and, for a moment, she thought he was going to attack, but he began to shrink instead. She closed her eyes. The snap and crunch of bones turned her stomach but she did not cover her ears this time.

"I will change near you more often, I think," the eagle-man said. She opened her eyes again. He picked up the robe and pulled it over his head. "It disturbs you."

"Maybe you ..." Phoenix swallowed, chastising her shaken nerves. "Maybe you just like being naked next to me."

He rested his hands on his hips, one eyebrow raised. They stood in silence. Phoenix looked down and Adrian began to laugh.

"You're funny, Heretic."

Phoenix had given up on standing. She sat with her back to the massive cage of stone latticework that kept people out of the Vault's courtyard. The carving was beautiful, she supposed. Now that she was resting her tired legs, she could begin to appreciate the craftsmanship. A net of stylized vines formed a dome over the twisted pod that was the entrance of the Vault Library. The building itself looked to be made of the same grey adobe as all the others they had walked past on their way with shiny objects pressed into the mud before it dried. Everything from spoons to gemstones.

Unlike the structures of Dunkhar, there were no square corners or rectangular habitations anywhere in sight. The houses of Hanuel under Frozen-Sky took inspiration from all manner of shapes from lumpy gourds, to ripples of water, to folds of cloth, and even blazing fires. She wondered how the Ducal had managed to get such detail in the forms and how they had baked them to the appropriate hardness without the benefit of the sun.

There seemed to be no designated streets in the city apart from the arms that snaked between the levels of the city. To get anywhere, they had to walk around and between buildings. Everywhere she looked, faces appeared in windows and people stepped out of houses to stare at her. Their eyes fixed on her focusing-stone and they whispered to each other.

All the women she saw had long hair. Some kept it bound, but none had the jaw-length crop that Phoenix did. The short, linen shift she wore was also painfully out of place among the thick robes. She could easily tell why; for such a great city, it was damp and cold.

Phoenix pulled her knees closer to her chest and shivered. Her foot burned where she had scuffed it. She wanted her sandals, her armour, and most of all her sword. She looked around her at the smokeless golden fires and wondered what time it was. Morning? Dusk? If none of this madness had happened, would she be soaking in a bath now? Or perhaps eating dinner?

Dyseris had said that the Vault was 'far down below' and that it would take a while to be admitted to speak with the Wardens. In the meantime, Adrian and Yarona watched over her. Neither seemed concerned with her shivering or rumbling stomach. They talked quietly to each other and ignored her.

This is the worst hospitality I have ever seen. Is this how they treat prisoners? Her father would be appalled. Adrian was back in his uniform and Yarona held Dyseris' other robe. Phoenix leaned forward and tugged at the spare garment. The humming-bird woman looked down.

"What are you doing?" She removed it from Phoenix's grasp.

"I want to wear it."

"Why?"

"Because I am cold and you are not using it." She frowned. She wondered if the woman was stupid or just cruel.

Yarona shook her head. "It belongs to Dyseris."

Phoenix took a deep breath and let it out again, a technique she had learnt in sparring with her father's weapons-masters. She could only win this argument if she keep her temper in check.

"He let Adrian wear it."

"Adrian is not a stranger." Yarona smiled.

Cruel. Definitely cruel. "But I am under guard," she protested. "I will not run away with it. You can watch over it while it's on me."

The two Ducal looked at each other, contemplating. Adrian shrugged.

"Get it if you can!" Yarona wadded up the material in her hand and held it up high. She shook it over Phoenix as though teasing a cat. The pale man laughed.

Phoenix felt her face heating. She gritted her teeth. *What kind of ridiculous game is this?* Neither of them seemed likely to come to their senses, if indeed they had any. She looked the Ducal over. She was too tired to fight and this woman was armed.

Ah, yes. Armed. Phoenix reached up and grabbed both claw weapons. She did not know how to draw them out of their holsters and probably could not have done so from such an angle, but the motion succeeded in its aim. Yarona squawked in surprise and dropped the robe, slapping her hands down on the blades to keep her from stealing them.

Phoenix picked up the robe, struggled to her feet and pulled it on. It was too long for her. The sleeves were snug in her shoulders and upper arms. Dyseris did not have as much muscle as she did, though he was taller. As ill-fitting as it was, it was warm. She hugged the fabric around herself and glared at the Ducal. Adrian just laughed harder as his companion scowled over her ruined game.

They all turned at the sound of the gate. Dyseris stood between two Ducal in pale grey robes. Their hoods were drawn up over their heads, partly obscuring their faces. The one on the right pointed at her.

103

"You, come in." He pointed at Adrian and Yarona. "You two go away." Phoenix expected them to be insulted at such an abrupt dismissal but they bobbed their heads and left, Yarona casting a final glare over her shoulder.

Phoenix followed the hooded Ducal into the Vault. The entrance was really just that; a single room with a staircase spiralling down out of sight. Stairs. She rubbed her aching thighs and wondered if there was any way she could convince one of them to carry her. None of them looked strong enough.

They said nothing to her as they descended.

Dyseris watched the human as the Wardens looked her over, puzzled by her appearance. Phoenix had short hair like a royal guard and the muscles to go with it, yet she had no weapons and seemed to know nothing of the Ducal or Hanuel. The questions they asked of her frustrated her and her answers were mostly nonsensical to them.

She seemed to know nothing of the Upperworld. Even its name, Anemo, meant nothing to her. She only spoke of a place called Dunkhar in the desert and a world called Silan. The Wardens had never heard of either of these things before. Nevertheless, her coming matched the prophecy: the Phoenix would arrive 'ignorant as a hatchling.'

Warden Harkeen, a Ducal of middling years, left the alcove and approached Dyseris. The metal beads at the ends of his coppery braids clacked together as he walked. Dyseris stood and waited to be spoken to. The Warden leaned in close and spoke in a low voice even though the alcove was all the way across the reading room from them.

"The magic I feel in her is not ours," he said. "It is hungry and grasping. Difficult to get hold of. It shifts and changes quickly." He sighed and rubbed his temples.

"Is she the Phoenix?" Dyseris pressed. His heart raced.

"We think yes."

He was stunned. The joy at having been the one to discover her returned to him and he grinned. If the Wardens thought she was the firebird, then she had fit the description and met all their expectations. All except one: she was human. His grin faltered.

"The Tamiyons were right," Dyseris said at last.

Harkeen nodded. "They will crow about it endlessly. Their heresy is not heresy. It is truth." He looked back toward the alcove. Phoenix was gesturing irritably at the three Wardens who were speaking to her.

"Will the Vault remain closed to them?"

"That is for Regent Bowen to decide..." Hakeen lifted his chin at the other Ducal. "...or the Phoenix, if she passes the trial."

Dyseris clasped his hands together, fingers twitching. He had never before considered whether it might be possible for the Phoenix of the prophecy to fail. If she did, would that mean that they would never again return to Anemo and fly in the sky?

"We have waited so long!" he said, louder than he had intended. His voice echoed off the bookshelves.

Harkeen motioned for the others to approach and the three remaining Wardens led the girl towards him. Her feet shuffled in the too-big slippers that had been lent to her; yet despite it all, she managed to do so with her head held high and her back straight.

"Go and stay with Dyseris," Harkeen told her. "Until the Regent summons you. Rest well. If you want the regency, you will have to seize it in the way of our people."

"Which is?" She set her hands on her hips and wrinkled her forehead. Her eyes were fierce, like a hawk ready to stoop on its prey.

"Prove yourself his better. He will pick his champion and you will show him how well you wield your claws."

"And ..." She swallowed. "If I don't want the regency?"

"Then you will have a problem. We do not allow your kind to live down here, Human. Not without good reason."

Phoenix was still, the bravado knocked out of her. After a moment, she raised her eyes to look at Hakeen again. "If I claim the regency, what happens?"

"You will be queen of the Ducal."

She hesitated again. "Do the Ducal have a standing army?"

Dyseris and the Warden glanced at each other, not understanding. "Standing ...?"

"Soldiers at the ready," she said through gritted teeth. Dyseris wondered why she was so angry all the time. "Ducal who can fight and use weapons. Ducal who carry their own weapons."

"Oh!" Hakeen smiled. "Yes, a few thousand here. It is the same with other cities of Hanuel."

At last, a look of grim satisfaction settled over her face. "Good. I will fight this champion."

Chapter 6: The Sapling Soldier

Damon stood in his stirrups, hoping to see the topmost towers of Emmesford over the trees. Despite all the chaos, he looked forward to seeing the city from which King Harlon ruled his lands. The market was enormous, selling goods from the far reaches of the Middle Kingdoms. His favourite memories of the city were the shop that sold flat-cakes with spiced apple jelly and the storytellers that would take turns standing up on the stage at the end of Market Row to regale passers-by with fantastic tales. Though he'd visited times before, the capitol continued to awe him.

By evening, the Stonehearts would present themselves before Harlon in answer to the call-to-arms and be added to the armies already gathered. Though they were still a ways from the city, a massive network of tents, men, horses, and supplies surrounded them as they rode. Silhouette snorted, unimpressed with the din.

"Sit down," Sunev snapped, bringing Torrent up on his right. "Want to fall off?" Damon did as he was told and frowned. He wished she'd have a little faith in him.

The coming winter had already sapped the colour from the world and taken the leaves of all but the golden birch and the ghostly white of the steelwoods. In contrast, Emmesford was built of a rosy-coloured granite that was common in this area. Not only was it colourful, it made the local fortifications particularly sturdy. To his knowledge, there had been several times in Emmesford's history when the city had been besieged and none had breached the walls.

However, he wondered how they would hold against magic. Would it matter to a sorcerer if the walls were granite or limestone? Not if what he'd heard was true. If one man could fell the great palaces to the south with a wave of his hand, surely little Emmesford would not pose any difficulty. Still, in comparison to other cities, it still felt huge to him.

As his excitement settled, Damon realized he was nearly falling asleep in the saddle. Though he had slept for the duration of the night he was still tired. It was the dreams. He was honestly beginning to wonder if it wouldn't have been better to just decline the trial and not touched that damnable stone at all. Sunev kept reaching over and fixing this strand of hair or that fold in his cloak. She said he looked like he just got out of bed, causing him to sigh; his older sister always looked perfect even in her light green tunic and a dark divided riding skirt.

The dreams of battle were the worst. He wondered if they were better or worse than the real thing. They frightened him but still, beyond the fear, there was this strange, boiling anger within him that was easily roused, often forcing him to get up and walk for a bit as if he'd just had a heated argument.

And then, there was Phoenix. He still hadn't told his father about that dream yet. It had been such a bizarre sensation, like he was going to fall out of his dream world into the abyss if she didn't catch his hand. He had felt his Reflection there, as surely as a breath against his cheek. How could he convince Erik that she was not dead? Then again, he wasn't even certain of that himself.

Silhouette kept cocking his ears backwards even though he hadn't said anything to him. Was he worried? Difficult to interpret the expressions of a horse.

The tattoo on his back itched a little but it was healing well. The tunic was light and quite loose so he didn't have much trouble with it rubbing on the new marking. It was more his breeches that were annoying him. It didn't really matter if he had clothing fit for nippy autumn winds. After all, what was temperature to him? He could feel the cold, but it didn't discomfort him.

They were well within the gates of Emmesford by now but his nerves prickled as he glanced around. The streets of the city were choked with armed men but they pressed themselves back against the walls to let the Stonehearts through. Their cold eyes followed the train as they passed. He was used to the attitudes of outsiders. They were wary of the ill luck that dogged the steps of all Northmen. Still, he wondered how they would fight side by side with such a lack of trust. He made sure his cloak wasn't hanging over the crosspiece of the sword. It wouldn't do for it to get caught if he had to unsheathe it.

To Damon, a hundred people together felt like a lot, whereas this place had thousands that he could see all at once. It was more than a little overwhelming and Silhouette, laying his ears back, seemed to think so too. "There there," he said to him. "It'll be alright. Father will get us a quiet stable somewhere away from the mob"… or at least he hoped so. It looked like there were more people here than when he'd last visited. It was somewhat unfortunate that when the population of Emmesford had increased over the years the architects had decided to build up instead of out. It was a good deal of trouble to expand the main walls, Damon supposed, but there was little space to walk between the tall buildings, some of which were three, even four stories high.

He peered down at the faces as they passed, fascinated by any that were old, full of wrinkles, wreathed in white hair. The old saying "no old men in Glasshammer" was depressingly true. The north was hard on a man. Damon had never seen a Stonehart older than his early forties. The "Ice Kingdom" always found a way to cut them down before the grey could set into their hair. The benefit of the Stonehart Curse was that they held the North uncontested. After all, what was the use in snatching a kingdom only to die before one's eldest was old enough to rule? Damon loved his homeland, but for anyone other than a Stonehart, the price of living there was too high; paid in years, not gold.

"Refugees," Sunev said, looking around grimly.

"What?" Damon was startled. He looked again, this time focusing more on their clothing of the people sitting to either side of the street. Most showed signs of heavy wear.

"Refugees," she said more clearly, obviously thinking he hadn't heard her properly. "War's coming. Everyone's getting behind the walls."

Damon frowned; it was a discouraging thought. He looked around himself with new eyes. There were always beggars on the streets of any large city but there were many more here than he's expected. Most of them children and elderly people. King Harlon must have been very serious about the "every able-bodied person" part of his call to arms. The beggars did not put out their hands to the passing Stonehart train. They looked up at them, eyes wide and wary.

"They really think we carry the Curse with us, don't they?" Damon said to Sunev. His sister just grunted irritably in response. "What? What is it?"

She turned her gaze to him, thinking for a moment before gently pressing a palm to the side of her horse's neck. Torrent obligingly sidled closer to Silhouette so they could speak more softly.

"Not just that," she said. "You're of an age to learn about more than just banners and borderlines. There's more to war and politicking than just maps. Understand?"

Damon nodded, leaning close so that he might hear better.

"A thousand or so years past, it wasn't Harlon's line who ruled the Middle Kingdoms. Highseat wasn't Highseat; it was called Tallor, and Emmesford was just a place to cross the Emmes River. The real seat of power was in Glasshammer. The farther back in the past you go, the more land we held. Once, we had everything under our thumb from the tip of the White Blade all the way to the Great Barrier Desert. Now, they didn't just *give* us all that land, Damon, we conquered them. These people don't forget. Especially, not this far north. We may have gotten quiet but we never went away. I think if it weren't for the Curse, they'd push our southern border up clear into the mountains and wipe us out, just to be sure."

"Sure of what?" Damon's discomfort with the stares of the refugees had become much more poignant in the last few minutes. "Weren't' we good rulers?" Sunev was silent, returning her attention to the road. "Sunev?" he pressed.

"Depends on who's telling the story."

He decided not to ask any more.

They did not stop at any of the blocky-looking inns on the way through town but made their way straight to King Harlon's castle. It was a tall and narrow building shaped more or less like a T with its main doors located at the end. The guards stopped them at the gates, eyeing them suspiciously. Damon had never seen so much armour. It seemed people around here were very fond of chain mail. He watched their eyes alight on the crest of the winged horse adorning the cloak pins of his kinsmen. The colour dropped out of the guards' faces.

Erik pushed his hood back and leaned down to speak with them. "We have come in response to the call-to-arms issued by his majesty King Harlon. Three hundred and six souls. We wish to fight under his banner—" The guards moved aside and pushed open the gates before he even finished speaking.

"You'll be fighting under your own banner, Lord Erik!" One of the guards said, bowing. The other jogged a short distance into the courtyard and shouted to the men at the inner gates, announcing their arrival.

Through the open gate, Damon saw twelve banners on display. He recognized two from the myriad of devices that his father had taught him: The blue field with the white cup and swans that was King Harlon's and the red field with a golden swallow that belonged to Lord Foster. The others he did not know and realized, belatedly, that he ought to have studied a bit harder.

The guard waved them through. "Come in, Sir. We'll have your horses stabled and—"

"We will stable them ourselves if it's all the same to you." It was Erik's turn to interrupt. He said it with a smile on his face and the guard smiled back nervously.

"Eh right... Stonehart horses. I forgot, sorry." He eyed the glittering metallic hooves of their mounts. "Well the stable's just that way." He pointed in the direction of a large out building off the right hand side of the castle. "Plenty of hands in there to help you if you need it."

Erik nodded his thanks. As they passed into the courtyard, men unfurled the Stonehart banner. Its grey winged horse and blue ring stood out crisply against the black field. Damon smiled, feeling his excitement building; they were officially counted among the defenders now. He looked to his father but, although Erik rode with his back straight and his head up, his expression was troubled rather than proud.

He felt Silhouette's steps pick up as they neared the stables. He was probably looking forward to some good rest and some food. He patted his neck.

"We'll soon be there. Then I'll give you a good brush down. Would you like that?"

The horse bobbed his head enthusiastically. Damon chuckled. He wondered how other horsemen managed to talk to their horses while their heads were trapped in those bridle-things. Then again, he'd heard that other horses were rather dull-witted and had never seen any but a Stonehart conversing with his mount. They also tended to make other horses nervous. It was not unusual, when let out to graze, for the Stonehart equines to browse at their leisure while the others crowded into one corner and watch them suspiciously, refusing to approach them.

The stables, he found, were rather roomy. He had to warn a stable boy to stay clear of his mount despite his willingness to help. Silhouette's idea of a warning could sometimes consist of taking a few fingers off a person. It just wasn't good practice go to about crippling one's hosts. He made sure to tend to his horse properly and pamper him just a bit before leaving him to return to the main body of the Stonehart contingent.

It was getting on in the afternoon with the sun well down from its zenith. Sunev was tapping her foot as usual, probably irritated at his slowness. Well, if he wanted to spoil his horse that was his affair. He'd had a long, hard ride and would probably have another one before they actually reached the battlefield.

At least that was what he told himself before he reached the little knot of people standing around his father. There was a man showing Erik all sorts of maps and reports. His eyes lit on an encampment that was marked with a snake. It was far closer to Emmesford than he'd thought.

Aervie help us. They're almost on our doorstep! How could they stop such a force? How had they gotten there so fast? His gut felt heavy; it seemed impossible that the White Asp could have already decimated so many forces already, yet no one had even managed to slow him down! For the first time a sense of true hopelessness settled over him. He understood the look he'd seen in the eyes of the people: the world was ending.

While his father went to speak with the king, Damon and the rest of the party were shown to their rooms in the castle. They were not very large but there were enough for everyone if people shared rooms. Lucky they were all of the same clan; the looks the Stonehearts had received riding through town told him that things would be unpleasant if they mingled with others. He was to share a room with his father while his sister would sleep with friends.

Damon curled up on his pallet on the floor but sleep would not come. He got up and leaned against the slit they called a window and looked out at the sliver of moon he could see through it. The moonlight made silver of his pale skin. Far off in the surrounding fields he noticed colourful pennants and fenced-off areas. It hadn't occurred to him until now that there was usually a local tournament at this time of year to celebrate the end of the harvest season. Would they still be holding it despite the situation? It seemed both ridiculous and appealing.

It was late into the night after the moon had set when his father came in. He stopped in the doorway looking surprised. "Damon, I thought you'd be asleep by now."

He smiled and shook his head. "I can't sleep."

Erik sat down on the bed. "Well then, what are you going to do? Want to talk about it?"

"What is the plan? What did the King say?" His private concerns seemed petty where there were greater concerns at hand. Besides, if he at least knew what the future had in store, he'd be less likely to worry. That was what he thought anyway.

"Well..." Erik sighed, looking weary. "Lord Foster has contributed three thousand men. Lord Sergio, just over a thousand ..."

"But—" he interrupted.

His father paused, lifting his eyebrows.

"Westhold is a lot larger than ..." Damon faltered, trying to get his thoughts in order. "I mean not larger than Glasshammer but ..."

"Yes." Erik sighed. "He has a lot more men at his disposal than we do. He sent us a thousand with his Marshal, Ragi. He didn't come himself. It seems that few wished to travel this late in the year. Most of the responses to the call-to-arms stated that more forces would be sent in the spring."

"But … sorry. Don't we need them *now*? We need *everybody* in the Middle Kingdoms to throw him back, everybody who signed the Treaty of Emmesford. The White Asp is already … I mean he is nearly here, isn't he?"

Erik lifted his hands, a sour expression on his face. "Indeed he is, and yet this is what we have. Aside from Harlon, myself, we have Lord Foster of Spearfeld, of course." Damon remembered his father telling him about the lords of that landholding and their ardent loyalty to the crown. They would never fail to come to Harlon's defence. "There's Sergio of Westhold, as I mentioned, and if he doesn't want Harlon to reconsider Duke Astor's request for more farmland on his northern border, he'll do himself proud on the field. The king is already steamed that he sent his Marshal in his stead." He shook his head with a growl of disgust.

"We have Duke Bearhelm of Clowry and he's given us a bit over a thousand swords. That's some good news. Clowrymen are hard fighters. Duke Astor of Stelduran is here and he's pulled every last man he's got. His forces are pretty heavy on the bow. Not much cavalry or dedicated swords. Lord Stanin refused to answer the call. Duke Dagar has given us about five hundred..."

"What?" Damon interrupted. "But that's the Duchy of Rufield right?" He struggled to remember the maps in Stonehart Hall. Erik nodded. "Rufield is huge! It's, what, four, five times the size of Highseat? He should have beaten King Harlon's standing army four to one at least."

His father smiled and wrapped an arm around him, giving him an affectionate squeeze. "You understand my frustration better than I thought you would. Shall I give you the rest of it?"

"May as well, Da." He patted Erik's shoulder, wishing he could be of more comfort.

"Duke Eliason the Younger of Elston gave us three hundred. Duchess Scarlet of Harrower gave us six hundred. Dukes Freston and Jeuller were pinned between the civil war that I told you about, down at the Silver Ring, and what we think was the White Asp's vanguard. Foster gave us two hundred and Jeuller scarcely over a hundred."

"Wait a moment." Damon struggled with his memory, wishing he had the map in front of him right now. "Duke Freston is ..."

"Of Boarsback. Jeuller holds the Duchy of Shirbrook."

"I thought Duke Welland had Shirbrook?" he said.

Erik sighed. "He did. The Asp slew him." They sat a moment in grim silence while Damon digested the ill news. "King Dulmir, King Regaid,

Lord Crowerly, and Duke Heldor all failed to respond to Harlon's call. Interesting enough, we have two popular militias from Rell and one from the Duchy of Seaview led by Marshal Sharon and Marshal Duemor respectively. The tale they tell is a bloody one. I'm not sure if the war down at the Ring is still going on, but if it is, it's with far fewer men. The Asp absolutely devastated the kingdoms down there. There's a rumour that King Regaid is dead but it seems a rather fantastic tale to me. They're saying his castle collapsed, crushing everyone inside."

"Siege engines?" Damon asked.

"Magic," Erik clarified. "If the Asp actually commands that much power, we are in serious trouble. We are to move out in a few weeks and make a permanent camp some miles south of here. That is where we are planning to make our stand it seems." It sounded grim to Damon's ears. "As you know, there are some dense forests to the south of here. That is where we will meet the forces of the White Asp."

"A battle in a forest?" He furrowed his brow.

His father shrugged. "Reports say that is where he is camped. Something wrong?"

"It's just not what I envisioned when I thought of battle. I thought they always took place on an open field." He frowned deeply, thinking of the visions of the stone and the dreams. "I… well maybe that's what he wanted. Our horses won't be an advantage in the woods." He looked up to find his father staring at him quizzically. "Did I say something odd?"

"I hadn't expected you to be such the strategist." He reached over and ruffled Damon's hair. "You never cease to surprise me."

Damon smiled, though inside he felt discomforted. Why was it such a surprise? Horses were big and the spaces between trees were often awkward. Why should it be odd that he knew this? It was, somehow, apparently. Everything made him question himself these days.

"I think I can sleep now Father, Thank you for telling me what's going on." He smiled and went back to his bedroll but didn't sleep for a long time. Indeed the first hints of light were beginning to tint the horizon by the time sleep finally snuck up on him.

Damon's dreams were troubled. All around him, the clash of blades was deafening and he wanted to put his hands over his ears but they moved so slowly. He looked down at the mess that had been his haubrek, his intestines drooping off the sides of his legs into the mud. Numbly, he tried to put them back where they ought to be. They kept sliding through his fingers. Would he sit there forever, trying to hide his innards from the cold rain?

There was something terribly wrong about all this but he couldn't figure out what. Something heavy struck him in the back of the head and there was darkness.

He woke to the sound of his sister's voice berating him. "Hey! Get up!" He eased his eyes open, still trying to grasp at the threads of his dream as it faded from his mind. There had been a girl with dark hair and she had said something but the words were gone now. There was an obnoxious amount of sunshine stabbing in through the window, making his head throb. He didn't know that the sun could penetrate so deeply into the room through such a narrow slit.

"Sunev, why are you in such a huff?" he asked, rubbing his eyes and sitting up.

"Been calling you for five minutes now." She stood there, fully dressed, with her hands on her hips, glaring at him.

"If you're worried about the coming fight, don't take it out on me," he grumbled, stretching his arms above his head. His remark had more effect than he'd intended apparently, because the color drained out of Sunev's face. Her mouth became a tight line and she crossed her arms defensively.

"Just get up," she said finally and stalked out.

He hadn't known that she was really that concerned. It struck him that perhaps he should have been more considerate, but then he had also just been woken and he shouldn't really be expected to be a diplomatic person. He rested his chin on his knees and covered his eyes for a moment. Surely the world could wait for a few moments?

An image came to him. Had he fallen back asleep? Perhaps the girl would return and he could hear her message again? But no, this was not the same dream. A youthful face with a cascade of curly golden hair falling over it lay in trampled grass. Its expression was one of shock, terror, and pain. It was attached to nothing more than the bleeding stump of a neck with no body.

He cried out and leaped up, grasping the wall. He looked around. There was no trace of blood or anything amiss in the room. He waited until his breathing slowed before he moved again and when he did he dressed as fast as he could. He hoped it was a memory from the crystal and not his own mind conjuring up horrors.

Sunev was just coming back to his room when he stepped out. Her blond brows raised in surprise. "Well that's a first, thought I'd have to come back and wake you again." She smiled but her face was tight. Sunev didn't like it when someone else's tongue turned sharp and shrewd but he knew she'd forget his early rebuke in a few hours.

He shook his head, not returning the smile. He felt sick. "Let's go," he said after walking several paces past her. Then, with a commanding voice: "We are needed." She caught up to him and fairly trotted beside him, a quizzical frown on her face. Perhaps it had been an odd thing for him to say but he felt it, deep in his bones. The glass vial of the charm around his neck clinked against the clasp of his baldric as he walked and his feet made a sharp rapping noise as he strode down the narrow stone corridors.

He walked straight past the dining hall before his sister caught his arm, bringing him up short. He shot her a look.

"Damon, breakfast?" She jerked her head in the direction of the door. He could hear his clansmen clinking silverware and cups. His stomach turned. All he could think about was the gore he'd seen minutes ago.

"No," he said simply and kept walking. She was forced to let go or be dragged.

"What's wrong, Damon?" She asked, trotting after him.

He reluctantly turned back and waited for her. "I had a dream... sort of. It's put me off my appeti..."

Sunev's face went grey and she took hold of his arm again, holding herself upright with difficulty.

"Oh," she choked out. "So young."

He realized, with a jolt, that she was seeing it too at that moment. He steadied her shoulders with his hands.

"You see it?" he said. She nodded quickly, staring at his chest. "How?"

"Don't really know. The Link maybe." She forced herself to look at his face. Her nostrils flared ever so slightly and he realized she was fighting to maintain her nerves. "You send things all the time. Pictures, feelings, stuff. I thought you meant to do it."

He stared at her. "I've been sending... I didn't know I was doing it!"

She shook her head. "Sorry, Damon. I know you're not malicious. It was wrong of me to think of you that way."

"Well that explains a lot." He pulled her into a tight hug. "I'm sorry too, Sunev. I really didn't mean for you to see anything at all."

She patted his back. A passing guard whistled at them teasingly.

"She's my sister, you pigeon-poacher," he snapped before Sunev could even open her mouth.

"Hey!" The man stopped on his patrol, forcing his compatriot to wait for him. "Don't you..."

He stopped as his fellow guardsman tugged on his braid. "He's a Stonehart," the other man said quietly. The guard took in the cut of his tunic and the crest on his cloak pin. There was a moment of silence before the first man ducked his head sheepishly.

"Sorry. Um... sorry." He trotted back to his route and continued on his patrol.

Damon watched until he was gone. Sunev gave a nervous chuckle. "Odd."

"Nice to know I'm a scary monster," he said, still looking after them. "Really though, do I send thoughts all the time?" He looked back at her, searching her face.

"Just when you're upset, usually. I see images, feel things, and even hear things sometimes." She stuck a finger up in the air as if something had just occurred to her. "Like when you stopped by the shop in Butherfort. You were getting a stone out of your boot and I yelled at you to hurry. I swore you roared at me. Just like a lion. But I was looking at you and your mouth didn't open. You just gave me dagger-eyes."

He furrowed his brow. "I was irritated, I didn't mean to do it." He felt embarrassed. "Thank you for telling me about this, Sunev." He squeezed her shoulder lightly. "I'll try to make it stop. We'll figure something out. I just..."

"Want some fresh air." She finished his thought for him. She nodded and indicated the doors in front of him with a small smile. "I know. Go."

He was grateful that she didn't follow him out. He needed to be alone for a while; though perhaps not entirely alone, he knew a certain someone he wanted to spend some time with.

He strode into the stables, giving a curt nod to the stable boys who greeted him. He marched straight into Silhouette's stall and put his arms around the stallion's neck. The horse stood still and nickered at him. He felt a nose on his back, rubbing. What a smart creature he was. It comforted him, whether Silhouette knew it or not. He suspected he did.

"We have to go, Silhouette," he told him earnestly. "The castle is nice but I'm going to lose my mind if I stay here all day." A heartfelt sigh escaped him. "What am I going to do? Sometimes things make sense to me. Strange things that shouldn't. And then when I really try to think about them I get lost again. I'm so confused. And now it's leaking out onto my family." He leaned on his horse for support. Silhouette seemed happy enough to lend it. He stroked the long graceful black neck. He must have really given him a first class rub down last evening. He was fairly gleaming. "Bah, let's go see if that tournament is on or at least what there is to be seen in the market."

It was easier to ride in town than he'd thought it would be; well, easier and harder. People pushed themselves back against the walls to make way for Silhouette but they held him with their eyes. Damon was beginning to feel that if any more people stared at the crest on his shoulder that it would burst into flame. He finally gave in and pulled the cowl up over his head. It cut down his field of vision and concealed his face from them. Somehow, it was easier just being 'a Stonehart' than Damon Stonehart.

As he neared the tournament grounds there were more and more soldiers in the crowd. Some were outfitted with the tabard and colours of their respective lords but the vast majority of the ones he saw were without uniform. There was a wide variety of weapons and armour to be seen and clothing that was rather strange to him. Most of the tunics he saw barely came below the waist. He understood, then, why his own garments got him odd looks. *Well it's not my fault if none of them have the good sense to keep their backsides warm.*

He hopped off Silhouette near where the other horses were tied. He looked over the line of equine heads lashed to the posts by their reins and rolled his eyes. Were they really stupid enough to wander off?

"Stay here, my friend," he said. Silhouette simply nodded and began to browse the ground at his feet to see if any grass was to be had.

A peddler passed him, pushing a cart of tools, dried meats and other goods. He flagged the woman down.

"Is there a tournament going?" he asked.

"Well yeah..." She turned, got a better look at him and made a gesture that might have been a brief curtsey. "Yessir. Annual Blades n' Bows Tourney. Ya come to compete?" Her squinty eyes were fixated on the winged horse on the crest. Damon wondered if he should take the thing off, but knew doing so would only upset his father.

"Eh, not really," Damon replied, apologetically.

She nodded, pulling her woollen shawl up around her neck. It was dyed a nice ochre with an orange fringe. He was about to compliment her on it but her next words stopped him. "For the best. Ain't fair having Northland sorcerers coming down and killin' all our good men afore they even see the battle."

He stared at her and she shifted uncomfortably. Was she trying to compliment him? It didn't feel that way, especially with the way she stood defensively with the cart handles in between them. *Perhaps she didn't mean it. Da said something about old people and some sickness they call ... senile was it?* He frowned and she backed up a couple of steps, wary of him.

"Um ... I just wanted to ask, isn't it a bit strange that the Tourney should go on at a time like this?"

The peddler put a hand on her hip and straightened her back. "Nah. Folks is enjoyin' it. Soldier lads get a good exercise of it. Brings in all kinds of money and believe you me, we need it to feed all these extra mouths."

Damon pursed his lips in thought and let the woman be on her way. *A diversion? Harlon must be a terrifically smart man.*

The tournament grounds were muddier than usual due to the unseasonably warm autumn they were having. He walked between the rings of combatants pausing now and again to peer through the spectators at a wrestling match but it was the ringing of steel that drew him. He meandered toward the signs marked 'Live Blades' and 'Mixed Arms'. Here the betting was furious. There were men, and a few women among them, waving coins in the air and shouting at their chosen fighters.

At one of the Mixed Arms match, there was a larger gathering than the other rings. He gazed at the man, who had a messy mop of red-blonde hair he could see standing on the podium. He thumped his chest and bellowed obscenities.

Damon threaded his way between bodies until he could get close enough to the front to observe.

There was no podium. The warrior stood as flat on the ground as everyone else, only he happened to be head and shoulders over even the next tallest man.

"Casey the Giant! Yeah!" the crowd shouted.

"The Giant to win! Ten silver!"

The man stood there grinning, apparently lapping up the attention. He had two simple staves with iron banding crossed over his shoulders. There was no one else in the ring with him yet; so he stood there, waiting for a challenger, his grin never budging. Would no one fight him? Two men near Damon shoved each other.

"Go! Go fight!"

"Fuck no! He'd cave my goddamn head in!"

They both laughed.

Suddenly, another shout rang out from the crowd and people quieted somewhat. It came again and this time he could understand what was being said.

"Staruff! Staruff the Mad! Twenty silver!"

"The Giant! Thirty-"

"Forty on the Madman!"

Damon blinked at the excited chaos that descended as a slender man stepped into the ring. He pulled his long blond hair back and bound it with a strip of leather, seemingly unconcerned with the mountain of a man. He yanked off his tunic and tossed it on the ground. Any doubts Damon had held about this fellow being a warrior evaporated as he took in the scars on his torso. He stared hard. Was he older than he looked? He must have been no more than twenty or so but the marks spoke of far more experience.

Staruff unsheathed the two daggers, almost long enough to be short swords, and sauntered toward The Giant. He grinned brightly, his pale eyes wide. Damon shuddered. He certainly *looked* mad. Casey, for his part just grinned right back as merrily as though he were going to dance a jig with him.

When the betting settled, the two squared off. The Giant took the first swing and Staruff ducked easily under the staff's arc. He rolled to the side as the other staff snapped under the first in the opposite direction. He was fast. By the gouge one of the staffs left in the dirt, that would be all that would save him. The smaller mercenary circled the Giant, both of them grinning like this was the greatest thing in the world.

Casey didn't move much and nor did he need to; the twin staves gave him complete reach of almost the entire ring and Staruff dodged him like a hunted rabbit.

Suddenly, he mis-timed a jump and Casey swept his legs out from under him. Damon winced and closed his eyes for a moment, fearing that this was the end of the crazed fighter. When he opened them again, Staruff had rolled to his feet and resumed dancing around the Giant as though nothing had happened. Almost. He was favouring his right leg a little.

Staruff darted in, holding both daggers in reverse grip. He ducked under one of the staves and slashed at Casey's gut. The big man turned slightly and spun his other staff behind himself catching his opponent in the side. But Staruff was already moving away and didn't so much as wince at the swat. There was a red mark just above his hip though, possibly a welt. With a bit better aim, it would have been a strike to the kidneys. Staruff fled before the next swing. Then he turned, lunged under the staff and kicked his enemy's wrist.

Casey grunted but did not drop it.

"Little fucker!" he bellowed and laughed.

Staruff gave him a sarcastic little salute with a blade. Against all common sense, he stayed inside Casey's swinging range and drove at his gut again. The Giant didn't let him get close. He swung his left staff backward and clouted him in the thigh, forcing his opponent to stagger to the side. Staruff managed to nick the Giant's ribs before Casey brought his elbow down between his shoulder blades and knocked him flat on his stomach.

Damon brought his hands up a bit, intending to applaud. However, it seemed the fight wasn't quite finished. *Aervie be merciful, is this a death match?* He didn't think Harlon allowed such things at his tourneys.

Casey stepped back and to the side to give himself more room to swing down on his prone adversary. Staruff rolled and lifted his blade. The staff came down and snapped the blade at the hilt. It stayed there, locked against the crossguard, sparing the smaller mercenary's life. The madman was still coughing, trying to get his air back after having been so thoroughly flattened. He twisted out from under the staff as the second one swept in to end him.

Staruff skittered backward out of range. Of the two fighters, he looked a lot more exhausted. *He's got to call it soon,* Damon thought.

He did not call it; in fact, he darted in again just as the Giant was swinging at him. He sprang to the side like a surprised cat at the last moment. The staff dug another deep gouge in the dirt. Staruff was still moving forward, though. He jumped again, one foot landing on his opponent's weapon to give him greater height. Casey lifted the other staff but not fast enough. The dagger came down on the side of his neck.

The collective intake of breath around the ring was audible. Damon found he had put both hands over his mouth in shock and couldn't manage to make himself budge them. The Giant clapped a hand to the side of his neck but he did not fall.

"Ow!"

Staruff strutted across the circle and gave the broken dagger handle a little toss. A tiny wedge of blade still attached to the handle was red with blood. He grinned, thoroughly pleased with himself.

Casey took his hand away from his neck and a thin trail of blood could be seen weeping down over his collar bone. It was a small wound, but it was clear that the fight was over. If Staruff had struck with his other weapon, there would be no question of his death. The Giant grinned despite his defeat and nodded at his opponent.

"Next time, use a blade," the blond man advised.

"Pft. No. If I spend time oilin' and buffin' anything is gonna be my cock!"

The rest of their conversation was lost in the babble as the onlookers settled their bets. Besides that, it was hard for Damon to hear anything over the thundering of his heart. He decided it was time to find somewhere quiet to rest and think about what he had just seen. He was at once glad that these men were fighting on the same side as he, and terrified that their foes would be just as skilled. He wondered if there was anyone fighting today that he *could* defeat. His fingers brushed over the leather wrapping on the hilt of his own sword as he moved away from the ring.

Why did I ask for this again?

"I think 'es dead."

An unfamiliar voice spoke nearby. Damon ignored it. The tall grasses were comfortable and the noise of the tournament grounds were muffled by the bulk of the hill he lay on.

"Probably hurt in a fight and wandered off," another voice said.

"Too bad. Real young-lookin'."

There was a twinge of familiarity in Damon's mind; he had heard those voices before, but where? Something warm brushed his face.

"Eeeeh yeah. He's cold."

"It's a good sword. You should take it before someone else comes upon him."

Leather creaked near his head. "Hmm, dunno. He looks like a noble."

"No torque." Soft footsteps shifted in the grass. "No coronet. Not a noble."

"If you say so."

Damon's baldric shifted as his unwanted guests tried to remove his sword. He jolted out of sleep at last, realizing what was going on. His hand darted out and seized the wrist of Casey the Giant.

The cry of surprise he got was quite rewarding. He had not thought that such a high-pitched yowl could come out of a man that big.

"God's balls!" The mercenary shouted after jumping away from him.

Staruff the Mad was doubled over with laughter. Both of them had their shirts back on and their hurts bandaged.

"I'm sorry. Ahaha!" The blond man stamped his feet and wheezed as he cackled. "I saw the crest on the shoulder and I just had to see ..."

"Yeh little shit!" Casey pointed at Staruff threateningly. "Chickenfucker! Yeh knew he wasn't dead!"

Damon stared at them, completely at a loss. "I thought you two were... were enemies."

Casey blinked. Then, he promptly joined Staruff in his crazed laughter. Damon sat up and readjusted his baldric over his shoulder.

"Nah," the Giant finally managed to say. "We're friends."

"Rivals make the best friends," Staruff said matter-of-factly. "You're a Stonehart then?"

"Yes."

"Ahh, I heard one of you looked really strange. I guess it was true."

Damon stared at the madman. He wanted to remark on the man's rudeness but having seen him fight, there was no way he would let the chastisement pass his lips. He shifted his gaze to Casey who shrugged.

"S'true, yeah. Yeh look like a corpse."

Damon sighed and rested his arms on his knees, wondering when these fellows would leave him alone. It occurred to him that he should probably introduce himself.

"So you rigged the fight then?"

Both of them stopped laughing immediately. Staruff went stiff and curled his fingers into fists. Casey shook his head at him.

"Nah. We fight all the time. Sometimes I win. Sometimes he wins. But we both give it our best, ev'ry time." He resumed grinning. "Ev'ry buddy gets a good show of it. Winner takes the loser out fer drinks."

"Yes." Staruff's smile had also resumed. Damon did not like that smile. It showed entirely too many teeth and no warmth. "Loser."

"Oi!" Casey made to cuff his friend but he sidestepped. "Shaddup cockbreath! Let's not ferget yesterday. Good on yeh fer gettin' up this mornin, I thought I cracked yer damned spine!"

"Mhum. Still hurts."

"Perhaps you should see a healer?" Damon asked.

Staruff got a funny look on his face and he thought he was going to be treated to another gale of laughter. However, he managed to restrain himself.

"Bit soft, this one," he said instead.

"Horse shit. If he's a noble I bet he can fight like a bastard." Casey jabbed Damon in the shoulder with his finger. "You a noble?"

"Um ..." He blinked.

"Not a noble," Staruff said.

Damon frowned. "I don't ... well, Erik Stonehart's my da."

"Whoa, isn't that ...?"

"Yes. You just poked royalty." Staruff nodded sagaciously.

"I didn't mean it. Why aintcha wearin' a coronet?"

Damon stared at him. The world outside of Glasshammer was clearly far stranger than he'd thought.

"Maybe he's worried it'd get knocked off in combat? I hear that's rather disgraceful," Staruff offered.

"I didn't come here to fight," Damon protested. They both looked at him. "Er ... not today. Not at the tourney."

"Why not? 's good braggin' rights if yeh win y'know."

"I didn't want to." He looked down at the ground, willing these two crazy men to go away.

"Don't want to or can't?" Staruff asked. Casey sucked in air between his teeth.

"Oh hey ... he's turnin' blue!" Casey crouched down and peered at his face. "Y'aright?"

"Yes. I just forgot my practice sword." Truly, it hadn't occurred to him to bring it with him. He had assumed that now he had a 'real' weapon there would be no more need for the simple wooden one.

"Practice ...?" Staruff crouched down as well. Damon wanted to push the mercenary away but he didn't dare touch him. Not someone dubbed 'The Mad.' "How many times have you actually fought with that?" He pointed over Damon's shoulder at the sword.

"Uh ..."

The mercenaries put a hand over their faces almost at the same instant. Casey shook his head in disbelief.

"Aw fuck me!"

"Not right now," Staruff said immediately. Casey took a swing at him but the other man just sat down, safely out of range. The Giant returned his attention to Damon.

"So yer da brought yeh down here to what?"

"Fight." He looked between them.

"He brought yeh down here t' die is what. This ain't a fuckin' picnic." Casey kept shaking his head. "That ain't right. Yer a kid."

123

"I'm a man," Damon shot back angrily.

"Yer a corpse. An' yeh look like one a'ready."

Damon's fist connected with the big man's jaw before he even realized he'd lifted his arm. He blinked. His heart sat in his throat while he waited for the Giant to flatten him. Instead, Casey grinned and wiped away the blood in the corner of his mouth.

"Sweet swingin' bullock balls; that was a nice 'un. I like the cut 'o you Stonehart princes if yer all like so." The Giant offered his hand. "I'm Casey Baysmuth, frum Dawnshire." Damon shook his hand, bewildered. "This is Staruff Azrum from the nearside o' Hell."

Staruff offered no correction on the introduction. He simply shook Damon's hand too.

"C'mon drinkin' with us! Maybe we c'n give yeh a few pointers on pokin' some guys with a bit o' steel."

"I don't know ..."

Casey stood up and pulled Damon bodily to his feet.

"Yeh wanna live?"

"Well, yes."

"Then c'mon along, Corpse. First we beer, then we brawl!" Casey laughed. With the Giant's arm around his shoulders there really wasn't much alternative.

His father seemed upset about something but declined to say what when he tried asking. He supposed he wouldn't understand it, given that he didn't know anything about war, but it still irked him. Perhaps it was the bruises he'd come back with? When Erik had asked him, Damon had simply shrugged and said "sparring." He was reluctant to admit with whom and he knew that any day now Erik would ask Sunev who would surely say that she had not thrashed him lately. Erik's opinion of men who made a living off of war was not a high one.

When his father came into their room and sat down heavily on his bed, Damon knew he'd finally finished thinking and was going to say what was on his mind at last. Erik had a way of looking at his hands intently when he was going to say something difficult.

"So, Harlon wants us to use magic," he said slowly.

Damon sat down on his own bed and crossed his legs, pulling up a sock that had wandered down to his ankle. "To do what? We don't have any grand sorcerers anymore to give him."

124

"Oh I'd say our magic is still what it once was. We just don't know how to use it." He chuckled. "Magic doesn't really go away, people do. I've been talking to Lorne and he says he knows of a spell that will help protect us from the enemy. You know, make us harder to hit or our armour stronger or ... something. He has to research it more thoroughly though; it's written in an old language."

Damon sat up. He knew why his father had come to visit him. "You want me to help him."

Erik blinked at him like he had two heads. "How did you know that?" There was a moment of tense silence before Damon forced himself to laugh and slap his father on the shoulder.

"You're so transparent Da! It's that tone you use when you want me to do some chore."

The tension melted from his father's face. He didn't want him thinking he was filching things from his mind on a regular basis. The truth was, he hadn't meant to, it just popped out at him. The desire for him to try and aid Lorne with his mysterious power just presented itself as plainly as if he had written it on his forehead.

"I wouldn't mind giving Lorne a hand." He shrugged. "Even if nothing comes out, you know." He made a gesture around his temple, indicating thoughts coming forth. "I'm sure he could use an extra hand or a pair of ears." Truth be told, he wanted to stay hidden for a while. He felt a little ashamed at not wanting to socialize, but the people were so *rude* here.

Erik smiled. There was still some tightness around his eyes. Damon gazed at him, quietly. He could see in his father's mind a man with a chestnut beard and curly brown hair. Stately robes. The king? It was strange. The vision was superimposed on the face of his father. *I will not say anything. I will not. I will let him tell me. It's going to frighten him if he finds out I can see what he's thinking.*

"Also, the king wants to see you." The words came out all in a rush that left Damon blinking in confusion.

"See *me?*" He frowned, eyebrows drawing together. "Why does he want...?" His voice trailed off before it hit him. "Da! You didn't tell him strange stuff about me did you?" He stood up and paced to the window to avoid having to look his father in the eye. He was suddenly very angry.

"No, no. Not I," he protested quickly. "Someone else did though. He's gotten a lot of false information about you but some of it's true. It... It would be better if you set him straight."

He looked back over his shoulder. "Oh... well, I guess that would be smart." He flushed. "Sorry. I... that was rude of me."

Erik shook his head. "No, I completely understand; it must be frustrating for you. You've had to deal with a lot of things you shouldn't have to, not at your age." He put up his hands. "And don't go thinking I don't consider you a man, Damon. I gave you that sword and I meant it when I said you're an adult now. That's one of the reasons I want you to speak with the king. I don't want you to feel like I'm withholding responsibilities from you because of your age."

Damon turned to face him fully, his back straightening. "Thank you, Da," he said softly. He felt a warmth in his belly at the look of pride on his father's face. That feeling would surely comfort him, even in his darkest hours.

He felt a little pompous in his dress cloak, especially wearing it in the local fashion of tossing the opposite end over his right shoulder and leaving the right to hang cast over his back, dragging on the floor. He had already decided that Emmesford folk were strange but this really took the cake. Sunev had polished his boots until he could see his face in them. It was silly, really; they were just going to get dirty later, but at least for the moment it would make him more presentable.

He hadn't been to this part of the castle yet and he found it was quite imposing. There were vases the size of a small child, holding bunches of flowers on either side of the throne-room doors. The white lacquered Porcelain was decorated with a dark blue paint depicting scenes of fields and farmers at work. The guards, their royal tabards impeccable, stood at attention all the way down the hall. They bore the blue swan and goblet sigil of Harlon.

Erik had told Damon, after the first day in Emmesford, that there had been great debate among the guards at first as to whether or not Stonehearts would be allowed to wear their swords in the throne-room. Harlon had just rolled his eyes and told them to come in as they were. "If I can't trust the people who come to my aid, all is lost already," he had said.

At last the heavy wooden doors opened before him and the guards waved him through courteously. Damon nodded his thanks to them and stepped inside. His father stayed at his right shoulder, and for that he was grateful.

The room was lit from above, which mystified Damon as he'd never seen windows embedded in a roof before. The king, who sat upon a raised dais at the other end of the room, waited for him to finish gawking before motioning him forward. Damon took a breath and strode down the navy carpet; it was quite worn, and darker at the edges than in the centre.

He put his left hand on the pommel of his sword, which was hung at his left hip for this occasion, and bowed from the waist as he had been told. The sword was too long for him to draw it from this angle but it was customary to wear it at one's side in this place. Harlon allowed weapons in his throne-room but he wanted them where he expected to see them. Such was his prerogative as king.

Harlon was dressed in a deep burgundy tunic, which surprised Damon; he had not expected the king to be dressed in the Northern fashion. His breeches were of a relaxed cut and looked to be made from silk. His boots were a very soft leather, even the soles. His velvet cloak was arranged around his shoulders in the same jaunty fashion as everyone else. He wore a heavy, gold-plated crown which looked rather like a helm to Damon. He couldn't quite see if it covered the top of his head or not. There was a gilded, flanged, mace sitting across his knees. It looked heavy enough to be for more than just decoration.

"Come forward, Damon Stonehart." The resonance King Harlon's voice carried startled Damon so much that he jerked upright. He did as he was told, coming to the edge of the narrow table in front of the throne. "Damon, please come and sit; Lord Erik, I would speak with him alone," said the king, motioning to a chair, much less glorified than the throne but cushioned and comfortable nonetheless.

Erik was rather taken aback by this and it showed on his face. However, he bowed and took a step back. He patted Damon on the shoulder and smiled reassuringly before taking his leave as he had been asked.

Damon settled himself into the chair. He didn't like the idea of being alone with the king. He was one of the few people he'd ever seen with a beard. He felt like he was facing down a lion.

"Do you like tea, Damon?"

"I do, your Majesty." He had not expected such a question.

Harlon gestured to a servant standing against the left wall. "Tea. One of the lighter green ones."

The young woman bowed, putting her hands against her apron and departed quickly.

"Do you know why I called you here, Damon?" The light grey eyes rested on him again, making him feel heavier. He cleared his throat.

"To defend the land, your Majesty."

The king nodded. "How do you feel about that request?"

Damon thought for a moment. He had to be careful about what he said. "Frightened, your Majesty." He pressed his lips together. He'd meant to say 'honoured' as he knew he should have but the truth slipped out instead.

The king's face took on the ghost of a smile. He said nothing about the mistake. "Your father tells me you have never been to war before," Harlon nodded, auburn tresses falling over his shoulders. "A shame." He paused. "Not that you have never fought a war, but that this one, a most difficult one, will be your first. Do you think you will run away?"

"No, your Majesty."

"You can be honest. I will tell no one." The king smiled a little more.

"There is nowhere to go, even if I wanted to, your Majesty," he said. The visions he'd been having would surely haunt him even if by some miracle the White Asp left them alone and went home. Wherever such a monster called home.

Harlon frowned and closed his eyes for a moment. "That is unfortunately true. They told me you were bright for your age, that you inherited your father's pragmatism." He opened his eyes and smiled again, a little more thinly. The tea arrived. The cups had little plates underneath, and Damon wasn't sure of their purpose. All the porcelain had the same dark blue painting style as the vases outside. "I get a little tired with all my daily duties. I find tea helps." He shrugged and smelled the delicate fragrance.

Damon thought it was too bad that the cups were so delicate they needed handles to be picked up without burning ones hands. Couldn't the king afford more robust craftsmanship? Maybe it was a matter of style. "It smells wonderful, your Majesty," he said. He sipped it, feeling the warmth glide down his throat.

The king looked surprised. "You don't find that terribly hot?"

Damon shook his head. "Sorry, your Majesty. Was I supposed to wait a little?"

"Most people do." He set down his cup, looking very amused. "No don't be embarrassed. I am most interested. I was told that temperature didn't bother you."

"It's true, your Majesty," he said, feeling that he ought to answer. Who had told him all of this? He was going to have to make a polite request of his relatives to keep their mouths shut.

"Is it also true that you can become a shadow?"

Damon shifted on his chair. "Yes, your Majesty."

"Show me." Harlon inclined his chin and Damon realized he was being tested. The king was a skeptic; that much he had been told already. He should have expected this.

"It is a little too bright in here, your Majesty."

He clapped his hands together, startling him. The servant came forward again, bowing.

"Close the drapings."

She bobbed brusquely and trotted over to the corner. She retrieved a long brass pole with a hook on the end and set about pulling curtains of thick fabric across rods placed on either side of each skylight. It took a few minutes but the room darkened noticeably except for a few shafts where the light peeked through.

"Is that suitable?"

"Yes, your Majesty," he said, feeling sullen. He had hoped he wouldn't be forced to call on his power just now. He hadn't had enough time to work at controlling it.

"So, do whatever it is you do." He gestured for Damon to go ahead.

He closed his eyes, trying to calm himself and seek the darkness that enveloped him from time to time. He let himself feel the fear that usually accompanied it. Fear that he would fail was very prominent in his mind, fear like he'd felt at the angry bear in the woods and like he'd felt when he tumbled from the roof of Stonehart Hall. He could feel the tingling rush all through his veins. *Yes. I'm going to do it!* He drew more heavily at the memory of the headlong plunge, the nearness of death and the whistle of air when Casey nearly brained him with a mace during their scrum.

He heard a slight *whuff* like a candle being blown out and suddenly he was weightless. He was looking down at the king, who was startled by his sudden disappearance. He realized he made the chair vanish as well. *I hope he's not upset about that. What if I lose it?* He managed to sort out what was chair from the rest of his self and dropped it. It clattered on the floor louder than he'd intended. He floated over the table, feeling the warmth of the tea pass through him. Harlon gingerly reached out toward him. He let the hand pass through him. It didn't feel like much, just a temperature change and a motion like stirring water.

The man shuddered and retracted his hand, rubbing it. *I must be cold to him,* he thought.

"Can you hear me like that?" he asked timidly.

Damon thought for a moment. He couldn't speak but he could change his shape surely enough. He swirled around the tea pot for a little while. Then he gathered himself and bobbed up and down, much like a head nodding. Harlon seemed to understand.

"That is... really something." The king looked at a loss for what to say. "Can you pick anything up?"

He wondered about that. He'd never tried. He moved down over his tea cup and tried to wrap himself around it. It was hard to do without passing *through* it. The cup vanished. *Whoops, absorbed it I guess.* He sorted it out with some difficulty and put it back again. It dropped onto the tray from about two inches in the air. It spilled the tea but the cup was unharmed as much as he could see. The paint had become swirled and indistinct. No longer a picture at all.

Harlon picked it up and turned it over in his hands. "Oh my... this is exquisite. Did you mean to do that?"

Damon shook himself from side to side with, trying with some difficulty to indicate 'no.' *Well, at least he wasn't angry about it.*

"They say you can change into a wolf. Is it true?"

He hesitated. He'd only done that once, and it wasn't on purpose. Who *had* been telling the king stories about him after all? Nevertheless, a little pride was beginning to well in him and he found himself wanting to impress. He moved himself over the floor, shifting his form into something vaguely wolf-like. Four feet on the ground, a tail, pointed ears, long muzzle. It began to become clearer in his mind. He would have frowned if he'd had a mouth to do so. It was hard to focus like this. He could make himself walk around on four feet and wag his tail but he currently remained spectral and indistinct.

He tried thinking about how his fur had felt and how he'd smelled. He felt air on his face and opened his eyes. His ears twitched. He looked down at himself. Bits of fur appeared and disappeared in the swirl of shadows. It was hard to tell where fur ended and shadow began, given how dark he was. Try as he might, he could not make himself completely solid. He sat down and issued a plaintive whine.

"Well, never mind that," the king said quickly, seeing his distress. "I can see that it's true in any case. Just change back." He looked more than a little disturbed.

Easy for you to say, Damon thought as he released the shape gradually. He floated for a time, resting from his efforts. Harlon was starting to look impatient. It couldn't be helped; he was too exhausted from the form-shifting to speed things up.

"Are you alright, Damon?" he said after a minute or so.

He nodded for him but was too tired to try to communicate anything else. At last, he managed to bunch into his chair and solidify into a human being again. He gripped the armrests of the chair, trying to figure out how air went in and out of his lungs again. His vision was mostly black except the occasional pin-prick of light dancing around in front of him. He felt the room lurch and fought to keep from going shadow again. Then, he fought to keep the tea from coming back up on him.

"Are you sure you are fine?"

No, he wasn't sure of that at all. He held up a palm to stay any further questions until he had found which direction was the ceiling and the floor and put them in their proper places. At last, the rhythm of his heart calmed. His breath came easier and he rested his back against the back cushion of the chair.

"S-sorry, your majesty," he said, a shudder disturbing his speech.

"It is I who should ask forgiveness," Harlon said quietly, splaying his hands. "I know very little of the nature of magic. I didn't know it would cause such hardship to perform."

"Still hard to do it when I want to," he managed to say. His tongue felt a little rubbery.

"I must tell you the truth. I do not care for magic." He sighed and leaned back on his throne. Damon watched him trace his fingers over words etched in the handle of the mace on his lap. He couldn't read them form this angle. "I would not have troubled the Stonehearts for anything were it not for the direst of circumstances."

He could see what he was getting at; the king was afraid of magic, though it was inappropriate to say such a thing out loud. Damon knew not how to reply, so he kept silent.

"The abilities of your people are remarkable, Damon. In this dark time, we need them to repel the threat of the White Asp. You know this?" He waited for Damon to nod his head. "Your father and I have always been on good terms. I have bought many horses from him. My father owned a Stonehart horse that lived as long as he did. Died on the same day, in fact."

The lifespans of Stonehart horses were indeed long, adding to their price. Harlon's father had lived to 67 years of age and bought the horse when he was 20. He had read the log books over many times to keep track of where the horses he was helping to raise might end up. What was Harlon trying to get at? They had been called. They were going to fight. They weren't going to turn around and ride back to Glasshammer any time soon, at least now with the threat of the White Asp hanging over them.

"I want our friendship to remain strong, Damon. Do you understand what I mean?"

"Ah..." He hesitated. "I don't think I fully understand, your highness, no." He shrugged helplessly.

Harlon smiled but it was not a happy expression. "Has your father mentioned my daughter Emma to you?"

Damon cast his eyes upward as he thought. He probably had a few times in passing.

The king seemed to misinterpret this as some kind of answer. "I see. He has suggested that you two would make an excellent match when all this is over." He waved his hand vaguely in the air.

He laughed, he couldn't help it. "Hardly! I was born on a farm."

"As was I." There was no humor in the king's gray eyes. "According to your station, you *ought* to be wearing the coronet of a prince."

Damon bit his tongue. Staruff and Casey had said the same thing. Apparently it was true. "I didn't know. I'm sorry, your majesty. I didn't mean-"

Harlon held up a finger. "It's fine. I was born in Tuador. I moved south because..." He sighed and looked away "...You see, up there magic is wild." His voice was soft now. "It's in everything: the people, the horses, the animals, even the food. I want my daughter to... have the chance to grow into an old woman. Have grandchildren of her own." He looked at Damon out of the corner of his eye.

He understood now. He was afraid that the marriage issue would be forced and he would have to let Emma go to Glasshammer, and the early grave that entailed.

"There is one woman for me," Damon said at last. The one who stretched across vast distances to touch his dreaming mind. "She's not in this world."

The king's face twisted in sympathy. "I'm so sorry." He shook his head. "So young... That really is unfair."

"Though if you want good friendship, you might consider sending some of your soldiers north to help with the bandit problem."

Harlon seemed to think this over. "They would not appreciate being put in such a position, but for you... Well I think if we could arrange to have rotating posts, and they were made to stay in lodgings no further north than Tuador, it could be done."

He hadn't really expected to be taken seriously, but it felt good all the same.

"You have given me hope today, Damon. I will make sure that gift does not go unrewarded." He sat up straighter. "In fact..." He waved the attendant servant closer. The girl looked like she'd really rather not be any closer to Damon but came as she was commanded. "Bring me a torque, new and brightly polished."

He had no idea what this might be, but the king didn't seem inclined to say anything else to him until she returned. It seemed an eternity of strange silence before she reappeared holding a fine circle of braided silver. The king took it, leaned forward across the table and put it around Damon's neck. He bent the metal slowly so that it retained its circular shape and in no danger of falling off him.

"This will mark you as a noble among my people, at least until I can have a circlet made for you."

His mouth dropped open and he spluttered incoherently in protest.

"I asked you to prove yourself to me today, Lord Damon. You did so promptly, selflessly, and without question." Harlon tapped his own crown with a finger. "Once I recognize your rank as prince, you will have nothing to prove to anyone within my borders, and for a good space outside them."

Damon didn't think he'd ever seen his father's face that red. He listened to the entirety of Damon's account of what had happened in the throne room with his mouth in a hard white line. At first he was afraid he'd done something wrong, but then Erik just stormed on about how dangerous it had been to force him to display his magic like that without any other Stonehearts present.

"I knew there was something amiss when he asked which one of us had the most powerful magic!" As grateful as he was not to be the focus of his father's anger, he decided he'd had enough after "collaring my son like a dog." He rose to his feet and cleared his throat loudly.

"It's called a torque. I think he meant it as an honour." He smiled and put his hand on his father's shoulder. "Please don't be so upset, Da. I'm fine. Just tired. I think I'll just go help Lorne for the rest of the day. I'd like to be somewhere quiet."

Erik rested his hand on top of his. "Just don't do anything..." He gestured vaguely "...you know."

Damon shook his head. "No more magic today. I don't think I could anyway." He squeezed his shoulder. "See you later." He turned and walked out of the room before any other discussion could occur. He had had quite enough of feeling like being a pawn for one day.

The library was on the upper floors. He had heard that it had been moved from the basement due to some mold problems. The window fixings had been reworked extensively to ensure that the air currents travelling through the upper floors were as dry as they could be. Harlon had spared no expense in bringing in architects from far away. The air that greeted him when he opened the thick wooden door reminded him of hunting in the lee of a mountain, save for the smell of paper. He smiled. It was silent save for the quiet rustling somewhere far off.

The shelves were tall and made of hardwood. Probably oak by the smell and look of it. The floor had fleeces thrown all over it to cushion footfalls. It was a good thing, too, as the vaulted ceiling echoed the smallest of sounds. He was able to pinpoint the rustling of pages after only a few seconds.

Lorne had folded himself into a chair, legs crossed, elbows on his knees, and was reading a worn but well-preserved book. He was a Darkblood of some calibre himself. He was among the few Stoneharts who could still do such things as lighting fires without tools, cleansing diseases from plants and people and, purifying water. His natural aptitude for learning and articulating knowledge compelled him to spend most of his time either reading or penning books himself. Damon rather wished he didn't live so far away from him. Lorne's pallor made him look less out of place, but only a little.

He took a quill from behind his ear and made a note on a piece of paper sitting on the table in front of him. He looked up when he heard Damon approach and smiled, pushing strands of black hair out of his face.

"Damon, hello. I was hoping you could make it today." Lorne's quiet voice sounded huge in the acoustic atmosphere. He seemed to think this too, casting his eyes upward in annoyance. His soft, thickly-woven black robes had narrow accents of burgundy; something to relieve the monotony of librarian attire. He had been in charge of the Stonehart library since he had come of age fourteen years ago. He adored his job and took it very seriously. He spent hours and hours in Stonehart Hall restoring old books. It was a good thing that the doors of the Hall were imbued with magic. Otherwise, a skinny fellow like Lorne would never be able to open them by himself.

"You alright? You look sleepy." He played with a tassel on his belt, twisting the strands around each other.

"It's strange sleeping in a new place," he said with a shrug. "You know how it is."

"Oh, do I ever." He rolled his eyes. Lorne had a rather dark shade of blue to his irises though not quite so dark as Damon's. He stretched out his legs and shifted himself on his chair.

Damon plopped himself down in the chair beside him. "Can I do anything to help?"

"Sure. Translating this book is tricky." He motioned to the book in front of him. "The language is old and it has a lot of funny little quirks about it. Sometimes a word works completely different than I expect it to and I have to go back and muck about with pages of poorly-interpreted work." He sighed and rubbed his temples.

"What is the book about anyway?" Damon canted his head to the side.

"That's just the thing." He picked it up and closed it partly, keeping his fingers in the pages he was working on. The leather cover was so worn it was impossible to tell if it had ever had any colour. The lettering on the front looked much like the designs carved into the walls in the Hall, only simplified. "It says: The First Book of Higher Knowledge. I have the Second here as well. It makes me wonder how many there are, or were. This book makes mention of things that need further research. The Second picks up on those things and expands on them. Some questions that pressed the writer of the First were answered in the Second, but the Second brings up new questions... you see what I mean?"

He nodded, trying to keep up with Lorne's train of thought.

"In any case, I had expected it to be a great long list of spells. You know, components, how to set it up, perform it, and what kind of precautions to take; but no, that is only a small fraction of the pages' contents. Most of it is a discussion of the theories behind the workings of magic and, deeper than that, spiritual matters. They call it 'metaphysical' things." He paused, seeing Damon had raised his hand.

"Just let me think about that for a moment." He dissected the word in his mind. *Above the physical?* Lorne waited patiently while he sat, counting his eyelashes for all he knew. "Alright. I think I understand so far."

He laughed. The sound boomed in the vast space and he cringed. "Yes, just stop me like that if your brain needs a rest. But, continuing, I'll give an example of why you cannot hope to perform the workings without understanding the theory. There's a long talk about the origins of magic. You know, where we draw it from to do things. It speaks of the Dominions of Earth, the Air, the Fire, the Water, the Blood, and the Void. There's questions about whether these are all separate sources of power or spaces to work in, or if they're all faces of the same greater source. All these notions are correct in their own respect."

"Wait, back up a moment." Damon shook his head. "What do we *do* with these Dominions?"

"We summon them and wield them to do our bidding, or at least I'm pretty sure that is what this is telling me." Lorne tapped the cover of the book with his fingertip.

"So ... hurling a ball of fire?" He mimed tossing something.

"If you can figure out how, please tell me." His cousin laughed and winced as the sound echoed. "But yes, presumably, we would be able to do that. Just like the sorcerers of old. The book says they were called 'Stormforges'."

"So, weather magicians?" Damon asked.

"Yes, as far as I can tell but ..."

"What about the Blood? And what is a Void?"

Lorne lifted his palm like a serving platter. "And there you have it. Sometimes I think I have it figured out only to have things like this foul up my ideas. The passages I've been studying seem to suggest blood is connected with healing but I can't see how it fits with the Earth and Air and such. And as for the void, it seems to be nothing."

"Nothing?" Damon frowned.

"Emptiness. Darkness." He gesticulated vaguely.

"How is 'nothing' supposed to be useful?"

Lorne shook his head. "I have no idea. The chapter I've been trying to grind through on the subject gives me headaches. I think it has something to do with some kind of meditation that the book keeps making reference to.

"It's a bit like staring into a candle flame. There's power in an 'undivided mind.' The book says that is a mind that doesn't take an 'either this or that' approach but accepts all possibilities as viable. So it's a sort of exercise to open one up to more possibilities than one would normally see for any given situation."

"That... sounds pretty hard to translate." Damon scratched his head.

"Yes, now you see why I'm taking so long about it." He sighed. "We don't have as much time as I'd like. We must find out how it works - magic I mean - and figure out how to explain it to the rest of the Stonehearts before the White Asp is on our doorstep."

"It's not something one person can do?"

Lorne flipped the pages to one he had book marked with a bit of ribbon. "No. See here..." He traced his finger along a line of symbols. "It says it needs a host of people to perform. The more the better."

Damon frowned. "Oh... well what is it we're trying to do?"

"It explains the working as a way to obscure our forces from the sight of the enemy. It doesn't right out say it makes us invisible but it... well right here: 'confuse and confound the eye of the foe from marking one's passing, and to increase the time needed to detect movement.' Essentially, it makes us wickedly hard to hit."

"That *would* be quite an advantage."

"Yes, which is why we need it." He looked at the page, his face sullen.

"How long does it last? And does it work for more than just the people doing the working?"

Lorne shook his head. "Now, you see my problems. I'm trying to figure that out right now." He handed over a stack of papers. "Here, have a look at my notes. You can start figuring out the language. Maybe you'll see something I haven't."

"Can I look at the other book while I do it? It might help to see the original stuff."

Lorne laughed. He canted his head in confusion. "Sorry, I was about to hand it to you." He set down a worn, gray-looking book before him. "Stop reading my mind eh?"

Damon elbowed him. "I'm not that powerful," he teased. At least, he was hoping he wasn't. Perhaps he should hope he was? They had to defeat the White Asp somehow.

He picked up the book and inhaled. He was dizzy all of a sudden. *Oh don't faint. How embarrassing.* Fortunately, his vision didn't completely blacken; instead, he was looking at some other place. It was as if he'd fallen into a dream. It solidified until he could see it clearly. A person writing with a feather quill. At first he thought it was a woman but when the figure stopped and read back a paragraph aloud, it was a light tenor that came out. There was an opaque veil over the lower half of his face, concealing all from the nose downward. His eyes were like green fire, like a cat's eyes, running over the words. His hair fell around his shoulders in waves of black silk. His breath made clouds in the air and all but the tips of his fingers were concealed in fine wool gloves. *It must be very cold.*

The book... yes, it was the one he held in his hands. Black when it was new. Glossy. He could smell the cured leather. Smoke as the candle went out. He watched the man slowly replace the candle in its holder and put his fingers on either side of the wick as if to pinch it. He felt the stream of magic in his mind. *"Karinate,"* he heard the murmured word and saw the wick light. It seemed effortless, natural.

The green eyes turned to look at him, black brows drawing together. He said something in a language he didn't quite understand. Then, the vision broke and he grasped the table in front of him for support.

Lorne was holding the book as if he had just taken it. Damon blinked at his cousin. "Sorry."

"Don't apologize. I thought something must be wrong when you wouldn't answer me." He set the book down in front of himself. "Something peculiar happened, did it?"

"I... um... saw something strange. I'm not sure it was real." He put his heel on the seat of the chair and rested his chin on his knee to think. "I think it was the person who wrote the book. He had black hair, green eyes and lit a candle with his fingers."

Lorne drummed his fingertips on his bottom lip. "That makes sense. Perhaps he left an imprint of himself on the books to help us read them?"

It seemed impossible to him that someone, even the sorcerers of old, could have that much foresight. Then again, his clan had always been heavily invested in the future. He picked up Lorne's quill and his cousin immediately put a piece of paper in front of him, watching while he tried to put down what the wizard had said to him.

"Im... no... Inbatre nazin?"

"Um... that is a question. Questions end in 'in'." Lorne shuffled through his notes. "Inbatre... um... ah yes, 'why do you call?' I think. Did he say that? The wizard?"

"Yes. He turned and looked at me and said those, but then you took the book and I was here again."

"I'm so sorry for breaking your vision." He looked down, a curtain of hair hiding his face. "I hope it will come back later and we can learn more. Your father will kill me if I push you too hard."

He nodded. "I'll just look over your notes for now. We can try again tomorrow." The look of excitement on Lorne's face was priceless. Damon smiled. He could fully understand. There was a mystery to be solved, and now he finally had something to do.

Chapter 7: The Owl's Call

Dyseris' house was shaped like two bubbles, one atop the other. The upper floor was mostly taken up by a large, round, nest-like bed with high sides. Some backless chairs and small table had been pushed up against the wall giving Phoenix enough room to throw a few pillows on the floor and make a place to sleep. It was not the most comfortable sleeping arrangement, but after her previous ordeal in the temple it was good enough.

She wasn't surprised to rise from her slumber feeling quite stiff.

She made her way downstairs – or rather, 'stairs', as it was really more of a ladder with thickened rungs than anything else – into the main room. A large fireplace stood in the centre of the room with a crescent table huddled around its contours. Apart from a few squat stools placed around it, nothing sat flat on the floor, not even the stove or the cupboards. She wondered why, but more importantly she also wondered what Dyseris was cooking: the raven-man sat crouched in front of an open stove grating, prodding at the flames. He turned a grin on her.

"Sleep well, my Queen?"

The appellation jarred her. She instinctively rested a hand on her hip, wishing for the comforting presence of her blade. "Like a stone." She watched as he took a tray of sweet-smelling cakes from the coals and tapped them out on a towel. "Thank you," she added belatedly. He simply nodded and handed her a cup of steaming tea indicating that she should sit. She settled on a stool with well-stuffed cushions that cradled her comfortably.

Dyseris arranged the cakes in two bowls and drizzled some kind of warmed syrup over them. As soon as he handed her a bowl, Phoenix picked up one of the cakes but had to juggled it back and forth between her fingers, blowing on it. She realized that she should probably wait until it had cooled a little more but her stomach all but demanded sustenance after so long without fuel. Biting in she discovered there was some kind of cream on the inside. She couldn't decide if it was a custard or cheese. Nevertheless, it was delicious. She wondered if such sweet foods were standard fare for the Ducal? It seemed more like a dessert.

Now that she had had a chance to eat and rest, she burned with questions, but which to ask first?

Dyseris beat her to it. "The Wardens say that you have firebirds in your homeland. Is it true? What are they like? Do they fly in the sky?"

She remembered the phoenix of her homeland. She had been named for the magnificent birds in hopes that she would grow to be as resilient and intelligent as they. Phoenix closed her eyes, remembering seeing the birds in action. Her sister had taken her along on a hunt and had spied smoke upon the savannah. They rode out, gripping the long spiral horns of their sabok, desperate not to fall off in the rush to see the great sight that Darsa had said was waiting for them there.

Their feathers shone scarlet, orange and gold against the pale, dusty sky. Their black heads glittered with hard scales to protect them from sticky guts and fire. Phoenix and her sister had stood upon a knoll, partly concealed in a thicket and watched. The fire was far off and the wind was pushing it steadily away from the foothills and over the flat plain. A phoenix landed in the grass atop a pile of splintered rock, seized a shard and began striking it vigorously against the others. After a while, it dropped the shard and began pulling up and shredding tufts of dry grass with its talons which it placed around the rocks like a mock nest. Again, it began to strike the rocks together.

They watched its struggle in silence. It began flapping its wings as if something on the ground had startled it. It did not take off, but kept flapping and striking, flapping and striking, and finally raking up more dried grass until there was a visible fire which quickly rose from a smoulder to a cluster of flames, licking hungrily at the surrounding plant stalks. The phoenix stayed with the fire, nursing it and encouraging it higher and brighter. The fire took on life and vigour, racing along with the rising wind and eating through the broad plain. Small animals rushed out of the path of the blaze to be scooped up by the sharp-eyed phoenix overhead.

Some of the birds went before the fire, some after it, scooping up the creatures that had not been fast enough to escape the blaze. "This is the king of the desert," Darsa had whispered to her. "The highest of all animals, of all life. When nothing is left but death, the phoenix eats death. One day, the phoenix will catch the Old Man in his fires and eat him, and death will be no more."

Phoenix nodded, shaking herself out of memory. "Yes," she said. "They are beautiful, resilient." She swallowed, feeling the corners of her eyes prickle. *Am I as you wished me to be, Mother? Father? I am trying.* "They are carrion birds."

Dyseris made a disgusted face as though she had said something obscene. "A carrion-eater cannot be ruler of birds!"

"The last living thing is king by default though. The strength to survive is the finest quality one can have. Is it not so?"

The raven-man chewed a bit of cake, his face thoughtful. "It's heresy but it makes sense," he nodded and pursed his lips in thought.

She moved to the side of the bed and clasped her fingers together. "Sorry if I have said something offensive."

"And if you haven't?"

"I'm sorry?"

"You are still sorry if you have said nothing offensive?"

She stared at him, perplexed. "I'm... sorry for uttering a heresy. That's what I meant to say."

"Ah, then say what you mean the first time," he advised her in a sagely way that made her want to scream.

"Yes. I'll try to do that from now on. So... because I have the name of the Phoenix, the stone on my head and the story of the desert, I am the queen?"

"I said so already." He frowned.

"Yes, I'm sorry. I didn't understand properly." How could she get the proper information out of him? He didn't seem to understand a lot of what she said the way she intended it to be understood.

"You know of the phoenix too. Are there no Ducal who change into this kind of bird?"

Dyseris shook his head. "No, no, no, there is only one Phoenix: the prophecy is clear."

She nodded. "Even though you have none in Hanuel, tell me about the phoenix as you know it, please." She leaned forward. Perhaps if he kept talking she would get the information she needed?

"The phoenix..." He sat back and stared at the velvet canopy. "I will tell you the legend of the phoenix. You were not a fledgling among us so you did not have it told to you in the nest.

"Long ago, the sun became angry with the ways of the humans. Day by day it circled the globe, watching the destruction they wrought carelessly. So it began circling closer, punishing all of life with its heat. Mankind did not listen to the warnings. The birds begged the sun to reconsider its cruel onslaught, for we too were dying.

"The sun realized its foolish course of action. For it could not pick and choose what it would kill. However, it could not reverse its pull toward the world. At last, when all life was in grave danger of being extinguished a great golden bird flew into the sky. She flew high into the blazing heat. She grasped the sun with her beak and flapped her mighty wings. All the birds feared for her. We could not go to her aid, for none but she could stand the heat of the sun. All that could be seen were her wings, afire and beating above the bright circle.

"At last the sun returned to its place. The bird fell, exhausted. An osprey managed to catch her and help her to glide to safety. We saw that her face and head were no longer golden, but blackened like obsidian. Hardened and polished by the fire.

"Forever after, she was called the phoenix, as were all her children, for they too bore the charred heads of their mother. The fire of the sun is a holy thing, it reaches through generations and touches all."

Phoenix sat in silence for a long time, pondering the story. "What a magnificent act of sacrifice," she said finally, feeling that Dyseris expected some kind of response from her. He looked pleased with her reaction and sat back, with a satisfied look on his face.

Changing shape was a feat she had never heard of a Solara being able to perform and she thought better of pointing this out; there was already enough trouble and uncertainty surrounding her presence here. If she judged the Ducal right, only those they called the Tamiyons were pleased that she was human, and 'Tamiyon' seemed to be synonymous with 'heretic.' She wondered what it would mean to the Ducal if their one and only Phoenix could not fly.

"We must go." Dyseris stood and washed his hands in a basin of water. "You need robes and slippers of your own. Mine do not fit you."

Phoenix would have preferred armour and a sword but she supposed she would have to take one step at a time. Her rank as a Solara meant nothing here. She could not simply requisition something made and she had no money. *If I succeed in seizing the regency, I will have anything I desire. If not ... Well, it's all or nothing. I must gather my courage.*

The image in the mirror rocked and swayed as Lyre gazed into it. No horned Arcana this time, but rather a man in the belly of a ship. It was difficult to gauge his height, given that the other man was holding his own mirror in his lap and looking down into it. His thumbs appeared as giant blobs along both edges of the images.

Captain Broghan bared his teeth in a grin, almost as yellow as the blonde beard he sported.

"Makin' lan'fall 'n two deys, M'lord," he said. The accent was a little hard to discern but not impossible. "We git yer payment fer the last raid almos' three weeks early an' I thank ye kindly."

"When all is ready, stay your blades until the time I call on you to strike," he instructed. Broghan scowled but he did not ask questions. Good man. "The Stoneharts must be afield and mired in blood before ever you strike at Glasshammer. You must give them not one grain of time or they will round to the north and drive you out."

"I git it good, M'lord." The smile was back on his face. "Ye go hit 'em in the mouth and we come hit 'em in the arse."

Lyre allowed the corner of his mouth to lift slightly. "As you say it, so it shall be. Have you aught more to say?"

"Nay." Broghan lifted a scarred hand and clinked his thumb on his helm. "Blood on yer blades, M'lord."

The sorcerer nodded grimly. "And yours." He waved his hand before the image and it was gone, replaced by his own reflection.

He knew it galled Broghan's raiders to have to sit and wait, they loved to attack when they were still hot-blooded from the rush of pulling up onto enemy shores. The less time they spent waiting the less chance they would be discovered and set upon by the inhabitants of the land. However, while the Stoneharts seldom slouched with their patrols, Lyre knew full well they had a lot of ground to cover and few people to do it with.

Every piece in its place. Every last piece.

For weeks now, he had been casting transport arrays and sending contingents of his soldiers northward, making them vanish and reappear in strategic locations. Some of these operations were surprise attacks on major cities hewing down kings and lords who would not yield to his ultimatum: surrender or perish. When reports of these strikes began circulating, the missions became hunts through the countryside, taking down fleeing monarchs and laying waste to whatever backwater town or village they sought to hide in.

Lyre's men were under strict orders to leave all messengers unmolested. They did the work of spreading terror and despair without wasting any of his resources. In all his long years of life, of struggle and conquest, he had learned one thing: in war, he who controls information, controls the field.

Through the pocket-mirrors of his captains, he watched the dance of the mortals. *So predictable.* Whenever a sanctuary harbouring a local ruler was burnt to the ground, the people inevitably began giving their once lords up in exchange for their own lives. News came to him more and more frequently of men riding out to meet his soldiers under flags of truce, ready to swear fealty to their new lord. Peasants were ever under the thumb of one master or another. Why should they care what his name was or from whence he came?

Of course, there were leaders that inspired love and undying loyalty in their men. Such situations were unfortunate for all involved. The White Asp did not negotiate.

Lyre rose from his cushions, smoothed down his robes and made his way to the outer flaps of the command tent. The Az Taeorans were practising near the walls of Dunkhar just as they had every day since he arrived. Since he had begun sending his strike forces into the Southern and lower Middle Kingdoms, the fanatical devotees of Ostarok now outnumbered his regular army.

Lyre closed his eyes and waited for the memory of the falling towers of the palace to pass. After it faded, he secured his veil in place and stepped out of the tent. Soldiers and servants alike stopped and bowed as though he were a passing breeze bending stalks of grass. When Raach walked with him she liked to make a game of trying to spot any fool not paying attention and failing to show respect. Such displays of discipline were rarely necessary but they kept order.

For his part, Lyre simply enjoyed the meditative bubble of quiet as voices hushed. Conversation was never more than in the periphery of his hearing, in his presence there was only room for business. At the moment, the only sounds he heard were the small chimes at the edges of his sleeves jingling with his movements.

It is well. This, my longest and greatest campaign need not be made longer still by idle chatter.

He stood at the line of stones that marked off the practise area from the rest of the camp and watched his latest weapon at work. The Az Taeorans nearest to him faltered and stopped. They made to turn and bow to him but he lifted a hand and gestured for them to continue.

The long, curved scimitars flashed in their hands, winking with the desert sun. Their armour was light and the threaded, linen veils covering the lower half of their faces, which they only wore in combat, shifted with each breath. Leather, cloth and a little brass lamellar about the torso was all that stood between an Az Taeoran and his foe. The rest was all wits and skill.

One of the men twisted away from his opponent's blade and slapped it downward with the dull-edge of his own. Their sandals carved intricate patterns in the sand as they circled one another. Neither wasted much energy in blocking blows. They concerned themselves instead with simply not being there when they landed. It was much like watching skilled dancers. The way they twisted their bodies, quickly changing configuration or direction, even in the air.

Lyre's attention divided itself between watching the technique and going over the tables in his mind of all the gear and provisions they would need. The desert had sculpted the Az Taeorans beautifully. However, the cold of the North was going to be a shock to them. His thoughts wandered from the travel logistics to the threads of weather magic reaching out northward. The Arcana confirmed that it was still warm enough to keep the passes open. When it came time to face their foes, however, he was going to have to relinquish control on the climate to conserve power. The Az Taeorans would loathe the cold, no doubt, but better to face discomfort than leave the army unprotected.

One of the fighters snagged a bit of loose cloth in his opponent's shirt and yanked him closer at the same time as he swept one of his feet. The imperilled swordsman dropped to a knee to stop himself from being forced into splits. He lifted his blade and turned away an overhand slash, straightening quickly so that he brought his forehead up into his face. The man clapped a hand over his injured nose and barked a curse; he did not otherwise move, there was the sharp edge of a scimitar laying against his neck.

The fight was over. Both combatants turned and bowed low to Lyre. He nodded to them and they retreated, cycling out for fresh fighters who waited under the shade of the tents along the edges.

Wisely, the matches were brief as the Az Taeorans didn't dare risk exhaustion. There was a good deal more leaping and flourishing in their style than he thought necessary but the drills they had run earlier against his own soldiers had pleased him well.

"Intimidating," Emeka had said. He understood the value of intimidation. Minimal effort, maximum impact.

He turned from the training field to see his general approaching in long, easy strides. Emeka planted the butt of his spear in the sand to steady his pace but he was too proud to lean on it. The priestess Ndiro hobbled along in his wake.

When the old woman spared a moment to look up from her footing, she smiled brightly at him and pulled the scarf from her head and let her hair hang down around her shoulders. Lyre squinted his eyes but did not actually bother to smile under the veil. He hated her smell, that combination of ointments, medicinal teas, and a weak bladder. Perhaps he should replace her with someone younger?

Not yet.

"High Priestess Ndiro wishes a word," Emeka announced as he came to a halt.

Lyre simply nodded. The sounds of combat had grown fainter and he could suddenly feel the dozens of eyes on him.

"You honour me greatly, Ostarok, Most High One." She shifted to her knees in front of him and he repressed a sigh as he waited through the formalities. "We have gone to the temples in the desert to seek out the holy relics You described to us, O Lord."

Lyre smiled.

"They are as You said, and where You said they would be. Do You wish us to bring them to You?"

He shook his head. "No. Leave them to their places. They are like unto the points of the compass. Confound them and I shall be wroth with you."

Ndiro nodded her head, the motion rattling the beads around her neck and wrists. Sweat made her face shine in the sunlight.

"Is there aught more you have to say?"

"No, Lord."

"Go and gather to you five of your best wielders of power. Rest yourselves well until the evening and come to me as the morning star kisses the horizon."

The priestess beamed. "Yes, Lord. It will be as You command." She struggled to her feet and set off to do his bidding. Emeka watched her go. Lyre turned back to the fighters.

"You will set up the array tonight?"

"Yes."

"I don't like this. Is it really a good idea to pick up so many men and drop them kingdoms away?"

Lyre smiled at the worry in his general's voice.

"A year and two moons you said it would take to march them. Too long, and I have sent my harbingers before me already. You know the cost of driving men afoot such a distance?"

"Yes." He frowned.

"Therein lies your answer."

The soft robes swished around Phoenix's ankles as she walked. The weaver had insisted on a dark green to compliment her skin and because she 'had the look of a soldier.' Such a thing might have been insulting, except for the admiration in her eyes when she said it. All the same, Phoenix wished she could have one of the uniforms she had seen instead of this garment. Robes were difficult to fight in. The fabric was warm and the slippers were soft and comfortable. On top of that, Dyseris had paid for it so she had no right to complain. Perhaps that admiration would lead to the procurement of a sword for her? She could only hope.

She spotted a large dome of stone latticework that enclosed several buildings and a good deal of space around them. "What is that?" She pointed and Dyseris followed her gaze.

"Ugh, Tamiyon Nesting." He curled his upper lip and her curiosity spiked.

"What are the Tamiyons? People keep mentioning them." She began walking toward the enclosure, threading her way between buildings.

"They are a family of Ducal."

After a dozen paces, she realized no elaboration was forthcoming. "That's it?"

"What's it?" Dyseris trotted to catch up with her.

She took a deep breath, reminded herself that she was talking to a bird and continued. Speaking to a Ducal was like speaking another language. Even though the words were all the same, the way they interpreted them was quite different. "Give me more information about them. The most important bits."

"Oh!" The Ducal smiled. "They are powerful shamans. Their magic is the strongest in all of Hanuel. They are also heretics." Phoenix frowned, navigating around a star-shaped building decorated with spoons and bits of blue glass.

"The Wardens said something about me being human and the Tamiyons being pleased."

He did not answer and she realized that she had forgotten to phrase the question properly. "Why are they heretics?"

"They believe the prophecy of the Phoenix tells us that the Phoenix is human." He nodded gravely.

"What does the prophecy say?"

"'I say this to you, so listen well: 'One day the wings of the phoenix

147

will descend from above. Be kind to the bearer, for this bearer shall be but a hatchling. Heed her well, for the hatchling shall give us back the skies'." Dyseris recited as though he had done so a thousand times before.

Phoenix frowned. "I don't hear the word 'human' in there anywhere," she admitted. "Why do they think as they do?"

"Because, since the Surface War, no Ducal have lived in the Upperworld. Only humans." The raven-man gestured at the rock ceiling far above them. "If the Phoenix comes from above, they think she must be human. How such thoughts anger us! A human would never give us back the sky because it was the humans who drove us down to Hanuel in the first place."

She pondered this. No such war had taken place in her memory and she couldn't remember having read about it in any book. Nevertheless, having finally prodded Dyseris into speech, she was afraid to stop him with a question. She decided to just let him chatter and see what she could glean.

"The humans decided that we were dangerous. Ducal magic, dangerous! Well, it is but only if you make us angry," he grumbled. "Stealing our land, polluting our water, pressing us to tight places while they take up all the space. We were there first! We wrote our first books while they were still living in trees and flinging their own shit at each other."

Phoenix had never heard of a human living in a tree. What was he talking about?

"They were stupid creatures but they bred so fast. *So* fast! They covered the world with their children and we fought them. They were eating everything. Making everything dirty. We fought them but they made us sick. So very sick …"

Instinctively, she put a hand on his shoulder. He sighed, the anger leaving him in a rush. He sagged and lowered his head, watching his feet as they walked.

"I have not heard of this war before today," Phoenix confided. "We must be very far away from Dunkhar. Farther than I thought. Let me assure you that my father would never do such a thing. We are not land-thieves and we are earnest in our preservation of the water and soil. We must be. The desert is not kind. We drive out bandits but not law-abiding citizens, and most especially not those who have a talent for magic. It is not done."

Dyseris faced her and smiled. He put his arms around her. She patted his back, not quite sure what to make of the embrace. When he released her and they resumed their travelling, his step seemed lighter. He said nothing further until they reached the gates of the Tamiyon Nesting.

The opening in the latticework was guarded by two Ducal in the same green uniform Adrian and Yarona wore. They did not stop Phoenix and Dyseris from entering, though they did peer curiously at the focusing-stone on her forehead.

The Tamiyons' houses were laid out in an obvious pattern. There were two crescents made up of tidy rows of houses facing each other with each house shaped like a tear-drop and painted a uniform white. No objects were stuck into the mud and the only adornments she could see were delicately shaped grates over the windows. After the chaos that was the rest of Hanuel under Frozen-Sky, Phoenix appreciated the subtle elegance of the craftsmanship.

A few Ducal wandered the courtyard formed by the two crescents. Most of them wore rich blues or pale greys and Phoenix wondered if there was some significance in colours among the Ducal. There were benches placed around a central fountain which was laid out in many basins of varying heights. After a moment, Phoenix realized that the sprays and falls between basins were not water, but the same blue fire she had seen before. Dyseris nodded, noting the direction of her gaze.

"It's amazing, isn't it? They make things like this and they don't share their secrets."

"Is that why you don't kill them even though they are heretics?" Phoenix made her way to the fountain to look it over more closely.

"Yes," he responded simply. "They do things we cannot, so we don't kill them even though they are so human-like." His lips twisted down in disgust. "Unless, of course, we catch them practising human magic; *then* we kill them, or put them in the eggs."

"Put them in the wh—"

She looked up and cast her eyes around the courtyard. She felt as though the air around her had thickened somehow. Her breath caught in her throat for a moment as she spotted a white-haired man sitting a few benches away from where they stood. One eye, grey as dust and half concealed by a fall of long white hair, peered out at her. She had only seen the White Asp, as the Gatekeeper had called him, for a few moments when he attacked, and from a distance. *But his eyes were green ... weren't they? Think! They were piercing green, but what if they are not like that all the time?* The Solara focusing-stone, after all, only glowed when in use. She felt her heart seize in her chest shuddering and striving to keep its rhythm despite the muscles squeezing tight in fear. She didn't move; she was scrutinized by him.

He held a book in his hands but he was not reading it. His skin was very pale, even more so than Adrian's, and she had the notion that if she touched it, it would be soft like down. He wore a plain white linen shirt almost like a shortened tunic. It had no buttons and the neck was open almost out to the shoulders. His breeches were equally plain and were a very pale blue and on his feet were a pair of faded calfskin sandals. With only a few changes, he could have stepped right off of the streets of Dunkhar. The whole impression of him was one of stillness and dustiness, though he looked perfectly clean. He was no older than herself from the look of him. His features were fine, even delicate.

Not the Asp... no. He was older, was he not? Her thoughts felt sluggish as if they were reluctant to materialize. From what she had seen of this world, white hair and a youthful face were just as uncommon as they were in her homeland.

He rose from his seat and walked toward them slowly, stopping just a few feet away. He stared at her without speaking. His grey eyes moved over her, as if reading words upon her skin that only he could see. She wanted to put her arms around herself, to somehow stop his searching gaze, but could not make her hands move.

"Who are you?" he said finally. It was like a sudden clatter of pigeons taking wing. His voice was soft but somehow, looking at him, she hadn't expected him to say anything.

"Phoenix..." She paused. *He was older wasn't he? No? Surely he would not simply speak to me if he were sent to end me?* It was useless. She hadn't seen enough of the White Asp to make a good judgement. Nevertheless, she left off her surname. "Who are you?"

"Kael," he said simply, not offering any further means of identification either. He turned back to his bench as if to retreat back to his seat in solitude, but paused before reaching it. So still he became that the faint blue hint of veins branching off to his fingers was the only indication that he was not in fact a statue.

Phoenix made to step forward but though her knee bent, her foot remained on the ground, half lifted. It was as if any greater movement would break whatever spell had descended upon them. Had time stopped? Had he cast an enchantment?

She found herself wanting to go to him, to ask him what was going on. Just as she'd worked up the courage, however, he moved. He didn't look at her but half turned his head. His hair concealed most of his face but she could see his lips as he spoke.

"We were right."

Then he was gone, striding away across the courtyard. The air felt normal again.

"Damned shamans and their tricks," Dyseris muttered. "Later, I will take you to meet his father, Wester. For now, I want to get out of here."

The sigils drawn in the sand were illuminated by candles. Lyre traced his fingertips over the map spread out in front of him, pausing at the points where the temples were. The "holy relics" he had sent with his people centuries ago formed the charged focal points for his array. His soldiers knelt by their packed gear and waited. Creaks of leather and quiet coughs told him of their impatience and uncertainty but they did not give voice to such feelings. They stayed outside the circle of candles twenty meters away.

Six priests of Ostarok, the High Priestess included, knelt around him. Their white cloaks spread out on the ground, beautiful in their purity. Of the six, only Ndiro had any hair to speak of. The other three women and the two men were still shaved bare. No matter; there was plenty of time for the others to honour the new covenant.

"Draw up your hoods," he told them quietly and they complied. When he was satisfied their faces were hidden from him, he drew six arrow shafts from his sleeves. The colourful wrappings around the wood stood out brightly against his skin. He moved to the stave driven into the ground and held up the barbed tips to the mirror that hung on it. "Be as stone until I move you, my faithful ones."

He received a mumbled "Yes, Lord," before they fell silent. The night outside the circle seemed to blur as he focused on the mirror. The only sound was the jingle of the chimes on his sleeves as he lifted his arms. Around the edge of the mirror, the delicate script he had written shimmered into a brilliant light. A mask peered back at him, distantly, vaguely, floating in the blackness.

"Vigmaacher, I call you. Greater Arcana of sky-roads and the doors of the Void. I beseech you for your aid this night."

The white, expressionless mask approached and the beast forced its head out of the mirror to loom over him. The soldiers quailed at the sight of it and one of the priests fell over in his haste to move away. Lyre pointed at the vacated place in the circle and waited until the frightened priest shuffled back into position, never once taking his eyes off the Arcana. Above the mask stood a bony frill that reminded him of a plough, only inverted. It slewed its long, sinuous neck back and forth for a moment before flicking its tongue over his shoulder.

"Your call is loud, is your need so great?"

"The sigils are all round and about you. I will not give insult to your eyes and mind, for already you know my intent."

Vigmaacher's breath made his head ache as though the air were suddenly too thin. He glanced behind himself and noticed two of the priests swaying slightly, similarly affected.

"You do not have the strength to pay me." The long, forked tongue flicked from under the chin of the mask again.

"I do, if you will take it in portions. You will have the full ere you leave me."

The gusts of air that boiled out with its rasping laughter burned his lungs, but he did not move. Finally, the Arcana bowed its head.

"Do it; succeed or fail, it will amuse me."

Lyre removed the veil from his face. If the disgusted look there showed, the Arcana did not seem to care. He turned his back on the beast and tucked the arrows away, all except for one. He put a hand under the chin of the nearest priest and lifted his head. The young man had enough time to blink in surprise before he drove the point of the arrow through his throat. The other five, obedient to his command, stayed motionless with heads bowed. Under their hoods, they could not see what had become of their brother. Even the nearest ring of soldiers stood too many paces away to see what he was doing. By the time they realized what exactly the ritual entailed, it would be over.

He tilted his victim forward and lifted the silver chalice under the dribble that ran down the shaft of the arrow. The man's mouth opened in a scream but no sound came out.

The priest tried to move, to lift his hands to the wound but merely twitched, gurgling in confusion. Lyre brought the chalice to his lips and drank. The infusion of power immediately crashed into him and he shuddered, closing his eyes. When the chalice emptied, he looked down on the priest's ashen face. The green radiance of his eyes had grown such that it lit the bowed figures in front of him like twin stars. He reached down and pulled the barbed arrowhead free of the flesh. The dying man sagged.

Lyre bent and put his mouth over the priest's, drawing the last breath out of him. The empty body slumped, forehead on the sand, in a last act of devotion. He looked down at his hands, watching as the brilliant light travelled through his veins and flesh. He sighed and savoured the tingle of power for a moment.

The White Asp turned back to the Arcana and pulled his robes away from his neck and shoulders. Vigmaacher hissed and moved its mask over him. Two long fangs extended below it and he almost mistook them for part of the mask, though only for a moment; there was no mistaking them after the pain of them stabbing down just behind his collar bone. He gasped and held onto the staff. The light faded from him as the serpentine thing pulled it from his body. As stars danced before his eyes, he wondered if it was going to break their agreement and simply consume him.

Release me. It is not finished.

As if it had heard the thought, Vigmaacher raised his head, let out a sigh and the sound made his head ache. The slits of the mask glowed brightly.

"Yes. Go on."

Lyre turned to the next priest, and so it went.

When Ndiro's body went limp in his arms, he turned again to the Arcana. It did not drink from him again but tilted its mask toward the sky.

"Haaaah," it breathed. "Now cast."

The sigils in the sand wicked into bright green flame. The candles swirled, stood taller, and taller still, until they stretched to the heavens, anchoring themselves in the stars. The ground vibrated under his feet. The Asp lifted his palms and began the incantation. "*Stellus hikagni meitan. Ofora, karapo magnius amachi ...*" In the distance, rays of light ascended from the temples, stretching a net over the sky and over his army. He closed his eyes, a smile of triumph spreading over his face. "*Karapo doros in inferni as deli hela yurustai ...*"

Weightlessness hit him at the same time as the cascade of energy poured down from the Arcana overhead. It stretched its long tail out of the mirror and encircled his troops. Sounds of panic reached him over the torrent but he could not bring himself to care. A great roar sounded like the sky itself gasping.

Then, there was nothing but bare sand where there had been troops, tents, and slain priests. The White Asp and his forces were very far away.

Chapter 8: Dreams, Drinks & Disobedience

At first, Damon thought that it was a dream. The vision flickered and jumped forward as if he were opening and closing his eyes. There was a giant eagle, a yawning chasm, and a subterranean city carved out of rock and with strange glowing lights.

He momentarily lost the thread; but when it returned, Phoenix was sitting on a bench watching a fountain spouting blue flame. He was amazed by the clarity of it all: the rustle of cloth as a robed man walked past, the brilliant white of the dark man's smile as he sat down beside her, and the clink of the bones in his jewelry.

It was the first time he had been able to contact her while she was clearly awake and he wasn't sure what to make of it. He was reluctant to break the silence pervading the dirty alley but he knew the vision wouldn't last forever. He needed to make the most of it.

"Phoenix?" he said softly.

The vision rippled like water, drifted like smoke. She frowned and held up a hand to stop the man mid-sentence. By the way her dark green eyes scanned the courtyard, he knew she could not see him.

"It's Damon," he whispered quickly.

She relaxed and dropped her hand. As his sight cleared, he could see her smiling.

"I dreamt of you earlier. Are you well?" he said.

"For now. This place is dangerous. Everyone is mad here."

The dark man stared at her. "Who are you talking to?"

Phoenix sighed. "Just a moment, Damon. If I do not explain, he will think I am talking to no one."

Damon nodded, realized she couldn't see it, and said "Yes."

"Dyseris, I am speaking to a friend of mine. He is in another place but we dream of each other." She watched his face. The man's dark eyes widened with wonder. "Does that make sense to you? Do you understand?"

"Yes. Yes!" He bobbed his head, flashing another bright smile. "You can far-speak?"

She wrinkled her nose. "Far-sp … yes." She nodded. "Yes I suppose that's what it is. How strange … I seem to have learnt how to do it after all." Phoenix pushed her hair away from her face and leaned toward

Dyseris. "Is it glowing?"

The man peered at the stone in her forehead. He put a hand against her face to block the light of the fountain. Amid the shadow he cast, it looked like a small glowing ember resting on her skin.

"Yes! Oh, that's pretty." He clapped his hands. "The Tamiyons will be interested in that!"

She did not answer him. "Damon, are you still there?"

"Yes." He tried drifting closer to her. It was even harder to navigate than when he was a shadow. He gave up and stayed still.

"These people, the Ducal: they're bird people. They have a prophecy that says that I am supposed to return them to the surface but I don't know how. They want me to fight their champion and take the kingship from their leader."

"Regency," Dyseris corrected. The vision wavered as she turned to him.

"Shush! This is difficult."

Another prophecy, Damon thought. *Fantastic.* "Bird people?" he said. "You mean the eagle was real?"

"Yes, they change from birds into men and back again. You saw that?"

Damon frowned. "It was a man? I didn't see the whole of it. It was... splintered somewhat. I cannot explain." Inwardly, he marvelled at the young woman who stood up to the bird, larger than she was, without so much as a weapon. He wished he had that kind of inner strength. Perhaps he didn't wish that he could be at her side so much as he wished she could be by his.

"Damon, do you have news of the White Asp?"

He was a bit taken aback by this, but recovered quickly enough. "He is on his way to Emmesford. Do you know where that is?" She was silent for a moment. Lines appeared between her soft, black eyebrows.

"North. Too far north. How can he move so fast?" The vision rippled again, more violently.

"Be calm, Phoenix. You'll disconnect us." He watched her chest rise and fall slowly as she breathed more deeply. The courtyard became sharper. It was less like a dream now, more like he was really there. He could smell something spicy cooking.

"What is the date? The full date of today."

"By Common Counting, the date is 1782. Month is Asen... though I think in the south they say Asham."

"Ausham, yes," she corrected.

"Ausham, sorry. The day... ah... it was Lovers yesterday; so, the Priest by now."

"You have different names for your days than we do." She frowned again.

"Ah... sorry. The Lovers is the twenty-first day of the month. The Priest is the twenty-second."

"I thought you meant that when you said Priest. Ours is the Mystic."

"Well, it's the Priest if you're from Glasshammer, or Tuador, or thereabouts but anywhere further south, like here in Emmesford, it's the Old Woman. There's a tournament that starts on the Old Woman of Ausham."

Phoenix looked troubled. "Much time has passed since I came here."

"Phoenix... I have to know, what happened to the Solaras? We got word that something terrible..." He almost lost the vision for a moment. It had become hazy and hard to see.

"I cannot..." She swallowed and shook her head "...not right now; please, the grief is still too raw for me."

"I'm sorry."

The vision dissolved and he was left to curse his insensitivity until he fell into other bizarre dreams. Foggy breath in the cold air. Bright green eyes focused on the page the quill scratched its way across. The symbols were not those he had grown up reading; but watching them form through the writer's eyes, he could begin to understand their meaning.

Damon woke slowly, stretching out on his pallet. By the brightness of the room, he guessed it must be near midday. That was odd; usually Sunev would be shaking the life out of him by now just to get him up. He shrugged and started pulling his clothes on. He mulled over the conversation he had had with his Reflection. He was sure now that Phoenix was the one. He couldn't help but wonder how much stronger he would become when they finally embraced. In fact, he wondered how strong he was now, without Phoenix's help.

Perhaps Lorne would know of a way to test himself? He was more familiar with the old ways. At least as much so as anyone could be these days. He stepped out the door, putting his amulet around his neck and nearly bumped into his sister.

"Sorry."

"You're up! Good." She smiled at him. "Was coming to see if you wanted food."

He frowned at her.

"What?"

"You're being awfully nice to me this morning."

"Afternoon," she corrected. Then she shook her head. "You were talking in your sleep earlier. Sounded like serious negotiations."

"I'm glad you didn't wake me." He smiled.

"Will you tell me what you dreamt?"

He smiled and shook his head. "No." When his sister frowned, he said the first thing that came to his mind. "It's embarrassing."

She blinked. "Oh ... well." She looked away from him. "See you in the dining hall ..."

Damon put a hand over his face and shook his head when his sister had gone; he lied, but it had gotten the job done. He was hardly in the mood to explain another strange ability of his, especially when it involved speaking with someone presumed dead. Well, at least she didn't *look* dead.

He decided against going to the hall, and instead sought a breakfast with his newfound friends; if he could find them, that is. *As if one could have trouble finding a giant...*

Still, it wasn't long before he found them in the same tavern they had visited a few days earlier. Casey had a room in the inn upstairs while Staruff usually slept in whomever's bed he ended up with at the close of the night.

Damon had not yet told his father about the mercenaries; Erik's grumblings about 'paid criminals' rather put him off the idea. He knew full well that if Erik knew where he was spending his days, he would demand that Damon stop seeing them. Though, regardless of his father's opinion, the bruises and cuts from their practice sessions told Damon this friendship was something he needed; a warrior had to know how to handle his weapon and Staruff would never fight him with anything but live steel.

"The enemy won't use practice swords," the madman had said to him. "If you keep blinking like a slapped puppy every time my blade-tip comes near your face, you'll miss the moment of your death completely."

Casey spotted him from his place at the bar and waved. The giant man had pulled a table over to sit on as the stools would not hold his weight.

"Corpse! Get over here, yer drink's gatherin' dust."

Damon grinned and threaded his way through the crowded room to them. "Bit early for getting into it isn't it?" The giant responded by glaring at the man on the stool beside him until he vacated it. Damon blinked and sat in the offered seat; no point arguing.

"Never too early, nor too late," Staruff responded casually. He leaned an elbow on the bar and reached back over his shoulder with his mug to clink it against Casey's. The giant heartily obliged. "Come to get your ass kicked again?"

"Haa, yes." Damon looked down.

"Masochist."

"Massive what?"

Staruff looked back over his shoulder at Casey and let his tongue loll out the side of his mouth. "Told you." They both dissolved into laughter.

Damon frowned. He wasn't quite sure what the joke was but he knew it was at his expense. "You don't have to teach me if you don't want to. You have been kind enough to me ..."

"No, no." Staruff waved a hand between them. "I love teaching you; only time I get to beat up a princeling without getting my hands cut off."

He sighed and ordered himself some bread and cheese. He picked up the mug that Staruff offered him and took a sip. It was a bitter, acrid flavour and slightly metallic. Damon stared at the mug and put it down, wishing he could wash his tongue.

"This juice tastes bad."

Casey broke into noisy guffaws as the barkeep glared daggers.

"Juice?" The barkeep brought a hand down on the bar on front of Damon, making him blink and shrink back a bit. He was a bulky, bald-headed man with scars on his face from dealing with unruly patrons. His face flushed in anger and suddenly, Damon understood the reference on the tavern sign to The Scarlet Bull. "Juice?" he repeated. "You call my house wine 'juice' you pale-faced little wampyr?"

Damon wrinkled his nose. He knew he'd given offence but wasn't quite sure what it was.

"Easy Mor," Casey tapped the bar. "Lad wants a stronger drink. I'll buy 'im a blindy an' we watch 'im fall off his stool. How 'bout it?"

Mor looked down his nose at Damon, considering.

"What's a blindy?" Damon looked up at Casey but the giant just snickered. The barkeep barked a laugh.

"You nobles don't know shit. I'll give yeh my strongest and if ye puke, yer cleaning it up." Mor ambled off and began hunting in cupboards.

Staruff sighed. His brows were drawn together and he crossed his arms.

"What's the matter?" Damon blinked. Now that his heart had slowed to a reasonable pace, he was pleased that Mor had looked squarely at the

Stonehart crest and treated him just like any other surly customer.

"We won't get to fight today," Staruff replied. He took a sip of his drink. It smelled sweet. Probably mead. "You're going to get shitfaced and then we'll have to carry you home. Damned wasted day."

He frowned. "It can't be that bad."

Mor returned with a mug of something clear. It bore a certain permeating scent that Erik often described as "smell-it-in-your-eyeballs kind of stink." It reminded him of the solution that Autumn used to clean his healing tools. He shrugged and took a swig.

"Pah!" Damon stuck out his tongue and the bartender immediately roared with laughter. "Tathe like fire," he managed to utter. The tearing of his eyes made it a bit hard to see as the acidic burn scoured his tongue. He picked up a shank of bread and chewed it for full a minute to rid himself of the taste.

Mor snorted. "I betcha never--"

"Okay." Damon picked the mug up again and gulped down the rest. He coughed and thumped his chest as the obnoxious brew hit his gut. "Faugh! Bloodythowtis!"

"Did you just say bloody sow tits?" Casey had mastered himself enough to say something.

Damon blinked at him. "Yeah." The giant clapped him on the back and he smacked his chest against the bar from the impact. "Ow. Yes. It's ... wow. What's it called?"

"Moonshine."

He raised an eyebrow at Mor. "That sounds peaceful and lovely. I was expecting Wrath of the Heavens or maybe Fire in a Cup." The bartender's ire seemed to have abated but it was replaced by something like a glaring scepticism. He eyed Damon keenly. "What?"

"Well good for you, yeh haven't fallen off yer stool yet. Ya want another?"

"Um, how much for a cup?" Erik hadn't given him much in the way of spending cash. In fact, as far as he knew, his son was still in the castle somewhere.

"Ten silver."

Casey slammed his fist down on the bar, making all the mugs jiggle. "*How* much? I'm not paying that!"

Mor leaned over the bar and grabbed hold of the giant's jerkin. "You damned well better! Yeh don't go 'round giving my booze away to children."

Damon gritted his teeth. What could he say to calm them down? He didn't want to get his friends thrown out of the bar. Staruff leaned over and whispered to him. Damon blinked. He held up his mug between Mor and Casey, drawing their attention.

"Staruff says you like to gamble, sir?" He managed a smile for the barkeep. The skepticism was back on Mor's face.

"Yeah?"

"I uh ..."

Staruff leaned over and whispered again, prompting him.

"I bet I can 'drink you under the table'?" he repeated dutifully.

Mor stared. Then he laughed. "Of my own brew? You're fulla shit."

Well, at least he was smiling now. That was an improvement. "Uh, if you win, I'll pay for all the drinks between you and me. If I win, my friends and I drink for free today.."

The barkeep passed a hand over his scalp and thought about it. "I shouldn't but this is gonna be the funniest damned thing I seen all week." He stuck his head through the doorway to the rear of the bar. "Bailey! C'mere. I'm takin a few hours off. Cover for me."

A woman with short-cropped red hair emerged and set down a cask of rum. "You playin' games again?"

Mor pointed at Damon. "Noble brat needs teaching some manners."

Bailey looked him over, her eyes lingering on the Stonehart crest at his shoulder. "Yer an idiot Mor." She walked over to a patron who was waving for service.

The barkeep poured a couple mugs of moonshine and saluted Damon with his. "Bottoms up boy."

Casey roared with laughter as they walked down the road to the tourney grounds. He had a liberated cask of rum on his shoulder. Staruff, behind him carried two bottles of mead and a smile that nearly split his face.

"What the hell kind of magic was that?" he looked up at Damon who sat astride Silhouette.

"Magic?"

"Yeh mighta noticed Mor the Bull laid flat onna floor a'fore we left yah? Where the shit you put all that?"

"Stoneharts don't get poisoned," Staruff put in helpfully. Damon glanced at the smaller mercenary.

"Well, we can; but it depends on how much of a Darkblood you are."

"So, jus' ones what bleed blue like you?"

"Sort of." He thought for a moment of how to explain it to them easily. "The darker a Stonehart's blood is, the more power we possess. My cousin Lorne, for example, has really dark blood. I think he's the closest to me in the family. My sister Sunev has very ordinary-looking blood, just like yours."

"Fuckin' weird."

They settled on their customary hill near the tournament outskirts and Casey got to work on opening up the cask.

"I don't really *wield* magic most of the time, it just kind of happens." Damon shrugged and hopped down from the saddle. He gave Silhouette a pat on the neck. "Usually when something scares me half to death."

"Excellent!" Staruff had his unpleasant grin back on his face. Damon frowned. "I'll try to scare the piss out of you today. Maybe you'll do something besides eat dirt."

Damon suppressed a sigh and drew his sword to do some warm-up swings. *He's right, but at least I'm getting better.* Staruff took a couple quick strides forward and roundhouse kicked Damon's wrist, forcing him to drop the sword.

"What was that for?"

"No weapons this time. We're drinking."

He lifted an eyebrow. "Didn't you say that you could kill a man with your bare hands?" Staruff just grinned in response. "So, grappling? I guess that would be easier."

The mercenary pushed his hair back out of his face. "If I can drag you to Casey, I win. If you can drag me to that rock over there, you win." Damon looked back over his shoulder to gauge the distance to the rock. When he looked back, Staruff was beside him. "Come along, are you going to wrestle in this?" He seized the loose fabric of his tunic and lifted him on to the balls of his feet.

"No. Just ..." He struggled. "Let me put my sword away, alright?" Staruff released him and stalked around impatiently. Damon unpinned his cloak and removed his baldric. His tunic had a lot of spare room in it, given that it was made to be worn over a chain shirt, but he wasn't about to go riding around town in that. *Maybe I should have.* "What kind of rules do you want to play by? Torso strikes only? No kicking? Open hand ...?"

"Just win, idiot."

Damon turned to face the circling mercenary, bracing his feet as he moved closer. Staruff darted to the side and aimed a fist at his face. It smacked into Damon's open palm making him hiss in pain and scoot backward. *At least I blocked it.* His hand tingled. Staruff wasted no time in following him, trying to drive him toward Casey. The giant, for his part, sat placidly in the grass enjoying his rum.

Damon tried to circle back around his opponent. The mercenary was having none of it and moved with him every step of the way. Staruff reached out and seized Damon's wrist, twisting; the savage grin on his face never faltered. This close, it was like having a wolf bearing down on him and Damon half-expected to smell blood on his breath. With little choice, he moved into the twisting. Though it wrenched his elbow and he gritted his teeth, he was able to plant the elbow of his free arm into Staruff's gut. It bought him a little more space, but Staruff never eased his grip.

Just win, idiot. He pressed his lips together and delivered a kick to Staruff's ankle. The steel-plated toe of his boot rewarded him with a gasp and a sudden release of his arm. Damon did not let his new freedom go to waste. Staruff knew no mercy and would not stop until the battle was won. He lunged forward and aimed his knuckles at his opponent's face. Staruff stepped back and grabbed the offending arm with both hands. He stuck his hip against Damon and suddenly he was upside down and airborne.

He supposed he ought to be grateful that the ground wasn't frozen yet. It was hard to be grateful for much with Staruff sitting astride his stomach with both hands squeezing around his neck. Staruff always said to aim for the face first. It was good sense, except that he couldn't get a decent shot from an arm's length away. Damon struggled for breath and dug in his heels, trying to buck him off. Staruff rode out his thrashing like a man enjoying a trot on a spirited pony.

Just win.

Everything was starting to turn grey. His fingernails left bloody tracks on the mercenary's forearms but Staruff just stuck his tongue out and let out a bestial growl.

Hallowed ancestors, I think he's enjoying this. I swear if I ever get up I'm going to...

He had a thought. Damon shifted to his right and drove his fist into Staruff's groin.

"Son of a whore!" The madman rolled off and came to his knees a few feet away. He panted and remained bent in pain, giving Damon a chance to get up. When he could hear something other than his own heart in his ears, he realized Casey was whooping and cheering. He shot the giant a look but

162

it didn't seem to affect his good humour.

"He tried to kill me! What are you so—?"

"Yesss!" Staruff licked his lips and grinned up at him. The curtain of blonde-hair half shrouded his face, making him look all the more wild. Had he stopped smiling once during the entire fight? Damon couldn't quite remember. Staruff bull-rushed him. Damon braced his hands against his shoulders and planted his feet. His adversary was strong, but Damon was accustomed to pushing horses around and did not give as easily as Staruff would have liked.

The mercenary grabbed his belt and lunged to the side, then he swept his leg across Damon's and shoved him to the ground. Once again, there were stars before his eyes and Staruff was sitting on him, this time, on his back. He tried to turn his head to the side to draw some air without getting a mouthful of grass. The torque around his neck was wrenched and twisted around backward. Staruff yanked back hard on it, cutting off his breath.

Damon struggled to get to his knees, trying to buck him off. He reached back, fingers tangling in the fall of hair and he pulled hard. Staruff swore at him but did not let go.

Why? He wanted to ask. *Why? You are my friend, aren't you?* Staruff always took fights with deadly seriousness but wasn't this a bit too much? A cold fog drifted into his senses and clouded his eyes. He let go of the hair and reached for his arm instead. Maybe he would let him go if he tapped him? Small hope, Staruff wasn't much for rules, but he had to try something.

Suddenly, the pressure slackened and there was no weight on his back. Had Casey pulled him off? Damon blinked, trying to clear his vision. Staruff sat a short distance away, intent on his own forearm and the giant was peering over his shoulder at it.

"Well I'll be a sow's left titty! That's fuckin' frostbite! How the fuck did yeh do that?"

Damon pulled on the torque, straightening it enough to breathe properly. "Is the fight over?" he managed to force out.

"Yeah! C'mere and look?"

Warily, he shuffled on his hands and knees over to his friends. There was a brilliant white handprint on Staruff's arm, the edges of it going an ugly dark reddish-purple. It was indeed frostbite. Damon glanced behind himself at the Damon-shaped frost patch on the grass and slowly sat up.

"Oh ... I didn't meant to use—"

"Do it again!" Staruff looked elated.

"What?" Damon stared at him. If he had any lingering doubts that the man really was insane, they evaporated.

"Do that," Staruff enunciated more clearly and pointed at him. "Every time. It's mind-fuckingly cold and really hard to move."

"I don't think I could do it again. Not on purpose."

"You need me to strangle you again?" He raised a hand and Damon flinched.

"No," he said quickly, rubbing his throat. It hurt to talk.

Casey leaned forward and clapped him on the shoulder. "Staruff, open one 'a them bottles. We gotta have a toast!"

Damon's gaze drifted from one to the other. Had Staruff hit him in the head? "Why?"

"Cause yeh might just live!"

Here, now, he understood, was something he could use on the battlefield. Something to give him a hope of besting his enemies. Survival: yes, that was something to drink to.

Casey lifted up the uncorked bottle. "To Corpse! Stay alive you summbitch!"

He smiled, he couldn't help it. "You two are crazy." But he drank and saluted both of them with the mead. Staruff had given him a precious gift, albeit not how he wanted to receive it.

"Damon! What happened to you?" The waspish tone of his father's voice in the doorway brought him to a halt. He paused in the folding of his cloak.

"I was just doing some sparring."

"With *what*? A badger?" Erik gesticulated at the torn knees of his breeches.

Damon looked down, unwilling to meet his gaze. "Couple mercenaries." His father made a disgusted noise and crossed the room to him, his boots making sharp clacks with every step. He seized Damon's chin and made him look up. Damon winced as he investigated the split in his lower lip.

"You smell like hard liquor. What in the hells have you been doing?"

Damon studied the lines in his father's forehead.

"I met some mercenaries. They're helping me learn how to fight."

Erik took a deep breath. He could tell he was angry, furious even; but strangely, he also felt relieved. *Furious enough to send me home and out of this insanity? I should be so lucky. What was I thinking?* He frowned. That alien anger was beginning to boil up in his gut again. *No. I want to fight. Despite the fear, I want to...*

"Damon?"

He blinked.

"Did you hear anything I just said?"

He peered into his father's eyes at last, searching the grey-blue depths for the train of thought. He caught it and blessed the Link. Images of gore and ugly men in animal hides grinning as they slaughtered passed through his mind. *I forbid it! Never again!*

"Um ... forbidden to see them again?" He drew his brows together and took a step backward. The motion pulled his chin free of Erik's hand. He shook his head. "No."

"What do you mean, 'no'?" Erik rested his hands on his hips. "I'm telling you not to associate with those people. You can't trust a man who sells his sword for money. There is no honour in that. They will only get you in trouble and abandon you when you don't amuse them anymore."

"You don't know that!" Damon protested. "You haven't even met them. I haven't even told you their names."

Erik's eyebrow arched. "Would I like them if I knew them?"

Damon hesitated. Staruff's unpleasant grin filled his head. The hesitation was all Erik needed.

"Promise me you won't associate with them again."

The words crackled in the air between them and Damon felt the small hairs on the back of his neck rise. *Is it really so important to you that you would oathbind me, Da?* He said nothing in response, thinking. Erik waited patiently. Once an oath was made, a promise given, it could not be disobeyed, not by any Stonehart. Damon thought it perhaps the most damnable curse of their magic.

"No," he said finally.

Erik blinked. "Damon, I'm your father. You will do as I say."

"Yes, you are my father. And I'm sorry." Damon shook his head. "You don't know the future. Whatever kind of people they are, we're fighting on the same side. I can't *not* associate with them."

The lines in Erik's forehead deepened. "You know what I meant."

"I know what you meant but that's not what you said."

"Don't mince words."

"I'm not." Damon took a deep breath and sighed. "I'd like to live my life with the only oathbind I have being the Code of Valour." He put a

165

hand behind his back, knuckles grazing the area of his sword tattoo.

Erik seemed to contemplate this. He turned away and gazed out of the small, high window. "Fine. Stay in the castle, though; you're not to go out by yourself."

"So I *am* a child after all?" He scowled.

Erik rounded on him. "No, but you *are* a subject of your chieftain and I'm telling you to stay put and obey."

"Yes, *M'lord.*"

For a moment, Damon thought he was actually going to strike him, but Erik channelled the white-lipped frustration into thumping his fist against the wall. His father was not a man to go into long tirades and this time was no exception. The hurt in his eyes as he brushed past was enough of a lecture. Damon watched him go; there was no point in arguing.

You don't understand. He shook his head. Well, that was unfortunate. He had no intention of obeying. Not with so much at stake.

Things just weren't making sense today. Damon sat reading over Lorne's notes, a sullen expression on his face. At least the library was within the boundaries of his new confinement.

"You make awful faces when you're studying," Lorne said. He was laughing at him.

Damon smiled. "Sorry."

"Is anything wrong?"

He put down the paper he'd been reading. "I've been thinking about how to test my magic, to see exactly what it can do; but I still don't know how to use it properly. I was wondering if you knew how it's usually done."

Lorne sat back and adjusted his legs. He was not fond of putting both feet on the floor, no matter what sort of dirty looks he got from the cleaning staff. Well, it wasn't as though he'd been walking around outside.

"That's a problem there, lad." He frowned. "The old ways tell us that you have to find a mentor, someone stronger than you, or a peer if no one is. Problem lies in the fact that no Stonehart even comes close to your abilities." He splayed his hands helplessly. "I know that seems pretty useless but you must understand, the laws weren't written for such a small population."

He'd been afraid of this, but something still didn't add up. "What happened to the strongest Stonehart? How did he practice?"

"Up until you were born, the strongest was always a twin; in the rare cases where they weren't, there was always the person's Reflection to study with." He sighed and shook his head. "I'm sorry Damon. I don't really know what you can do. We were all mightily confused when you were born alone." He left the part about Damon's Reflection to hang in the air, unsaid. It was understandable; it would not have been proper to address the matter unless he said something first. It was such a delicate topic. Once again, Damon was struck by the strange paradox: being held in awe for his power, and then treated so delicately, as though he would break from any sort of shock.

He laughed; it was just so ridiculous.

"What?" Lorne looked perplexed.

"I'm sorry. May I see the book again? Same one. I want to see if I can talk to him." With his cousin Lorne, it was best to interest him in something else, or he would keep asking.

He placed the book in front of him this time. He briefly considered what he would say. The memory clearly was not in his native tongue. Well, there were other ways to communicate. He steeled himself and placed his palms on the soft leather cover.

It was like yielding to a powerful wave of sleepiness. His eyes closed and his body relaxed. The figure sat in the same place as he had before. Black and grey furs wrapped around him. It seemed to take him a minute to notice him. He turned, as he had before, looking at him expectantly.

Damon tried lifting a hand in greeting, not knowing how to tell him 'hello'. The writer responded in kind. "I am Damon," he said, resting a finger on his chest. The writer canted his head to the side.

"Hieben Illtharen."

"Illtharen?" Damon asked, pointing to him and mimicking what he had said to the best of his ability.

He nodded his head. Damon smiled and bowed slowly to him. His heart beat quickly with the thrill of speaking to an apparition that was thousands of years old. He approached him, and looked down at the pages that were being written. They were different from last time: there was a diagram on the left where there had only been plain text; a human body with curved lines drawn through it. He could recognize certain connecting words in the sentences and some nouns but not much else.

"Inbatre nazin?"

He thought carefully about how to try this. Would Illtharen be upset if he didn't speak his language? There was only one way to find out, but did he really want to upset a sorcerer? Lorne had said that it was probably only an imprinted memory, a ghost at best; but who knew how powerful a wizard's ghost could be?

"I'm sorry. I don't speak your tongue," he said slowly. The man canted his head to the side, seeming confused. He looked him up and down and made a curious noise but Damon couldn't interpret it. After a long moment of silence, the apparition held out his quill and pushed a blank sheet of paper towards him on the desk.

Damon frowned at it but took the pen so as not to be rude. Did he mean for him to write out his question? He couldn't write the language any better than he could speak it; still, he could try to convey *something*. He dipped the quill and tapped it gently on the lip of the ink well. He sketched a tree. A pine because it was easier to draw. This, he did at the bottom of the page; on the right edge, he drew drops of water; on the left, a rudimentary candle; at the top, a cloud. He hesitated over the middle, then just drew an empty circle. How did one convey the concept of the void? Below the empty circle, he drew a knife with a soiled and dripping blade. Lorne had said that these were the powers one used to make magic. The fundamental building blocks of a spell. The book called them "Dominions."

He pointed to the book Illtharen was working on and held out his palm, a questioning look on his face. The sorcerer handed it over. He kept looking from Damon's face to the paper, as if seeking to pull some kind of meaning out of them together. The preliminary notes were still fresh in Damon's mind and he flipped to the front of the book. He knew the preface spoke about the intention behind the book. It was designed to preserve knowledge and to teach others. His midnight eyes raked the lines, searching for the phrase he wanted; if only he could pull the right word from it.

He was fairly certain that *dukha* was the word for "teach" so he wrote that above his empty circle. He handed it back to Illtharen to see if he understood.

The wizard looked at it and laughed quietly. "Dukhal miyadet." He crossed the word out. Damon's heart sank. Would he not teach him? "Opanat," he clarified and wrote the word beside it. "Dukha." He gestured from himself to the book and made a writing gesture with his pen. "Opana." He made a gesture from his face to Damon's.

"Ah!" He nodded vigorously. So the words had two different meanings! Lorne was going to be unhappy about the mistranslation.

168

Illtharen rose from his seat and walked slowly to the fireplace. He sat down on the rug and tucked his robes around and under himself. He held out his hand and Damon went to him. He folded his legs and sat facing him. The sorcerer pointed out the tree on the paper. "Mokhast," he pronounced carefully and waited for him to repeat it. He took Damon's left hand in his right and placed his left hand on the floor, closing his eyes.

It seemed to him like all motion had stopped. There was an overwhelming sense of serenity permeating his body. He felt roots extending from his spine and legs down into the earth. Not like they had just grown now, but like they had been there all along and he had only just noticed them. The energy moving through him was like a great slow dance, strong and steady. He would have happily stayed in its embrace forever if Illtharen had not let go of his hand.

Damon nearly fell over. The wizard watched him as he steadied himself. "Mokhast," he said, repeating the word he had heard. He had the feeling that the man was smiling; his green eyes crinkled at the corners.

He pointed at the rain drops. "Aulnhast," he said. He took Damon's hand again, and dipped the fingers of his other hand into a wooden bucket in front of the fire.

This time there was constant motion. Drifting up, falling down, slow, fast, still, back and forth; it was dizzying. There was the glitter of droplets disappearing into the air one by one. The artistry of ice congealing on the side of the bucket furthest form the flames. Snow falling outside in endless prisms. Further away the tide was pulling and pushing in a hypnotically sensual motion. He could feel its caress, the motions deep below the surface, and the currents within his own body. Flowing wherever it was needed, constantly refreshing itself. Compliant and forceful by turns.

A sigh escaped him as his hand was released once again. He realized he was rocking back and forth and put his hands on the floor to stop himself. He was a little embarrassed at how aroused that energy had made him feel. He felt as though he was disconnecting from his body to experience these things; yet, at the same time he was more one with himself than he had ever been before. It was a paradox and a powerful one at that.

Illtharen was flexing his fingers, showing his displeasure at the cold water. He seemed to be alright, though. He pointed at the cloud on the paper. "Likhast." He took hold of Damon's hand and raised his other into the air.

Everything faded, everything except the sensation of his breath, moving in and out of his lungs. He tried to take deeper breaths to feel more of the energy. It would not stay put, always rushing out again when he exhaled, but it did leave tickling bubbles of itself to chase each other through his veins. He laughed, he couldn't help it. There was the most wonderful sensation of flying. Streaming through clouds, pushing on the wings of birds, darting in and out of people, trees, animals, the water, the fire, ripping joyously across fields and between branches, carrying all manner of things with him: laughter, song, dust, flowers, a sheet, the rain.

His hand was released and Damon was back in the room. His teacher was laughing but there was no mockery in his voice, just beautiful, careless joy. Damon joined him. He hadn't heard laughter like this since he was a small child. It was strange how much he had missed it.

When he'd calmed himself, he moved on to the left side of the page. "Katarhast," he said. Holding hands once more, he stretched his left hand towards the crackling fire in the hearth.

He had a sudden, overwhelming sense of being hungry. *Seek, consume, grow, and stretch for the sky.* Anger and a dislike of confinement. Envy of the sun and the other greater fires of the sky. He had the knowledge, deep within, of ever fire's will and potential to be more. *Erase all else, until there is nothing but shining golden glory.*

Illtharen let go. He seemed to be less comfortable with that one than the previous three. Just the way he looked sideways at the fire, suggested to him that he was making sure it wasn't doing anything it shouldn't. Damon could understand that. He'd been told that fire could be a form of renewal, but the fire itself didn't seem to care about that, or even seem aware of it. There was a unique sort of power in that, he supposed. Something that could go forward without looking back. Something totally undistracted from its goal. Still, he rubbed his stomach. It must be awful to be so hungry all the time. He did not think he would make much use of that Dominion.

The wizard's wool-clad hand reached forward and took Damon's hand away from his belly. He shifted forward and took his other hand. After a moment of confusion, he got their fingers laced together, reaching one hand towards the fire, and one up in the air.

He gasped and jerked but Illtharen's grip was surprisingly strong and he held him fast while the torrent of energy raced through him. The air rushed through towards the fire and the flames stretched longingly towards it. Cords of power crashed together in his chest and wove themselves around each other. He became a conduit for them. Fire shot from the fingertips on his left hand, a torrent of air blasted from his right. He felt the fire's joy and satisfaction, the air's excitement. It made him feel so small, as if he were merely an intersection through which golden chariots raced on their important duties. Whatever pathways inside him they travelled along were stretched with their passage. He felt they would burst like a pipe with too much water forced through it.

When his hands were released at last, Illtharen kept hold of his wrists and guided his fingertips to the floor, pressing them there for a moment. He felt the sparks and pangs of energy left disconnected inside him percolate down into the ground. He sagged in the wake of the powers, panting. The sorcerer held his shoulders gently, making sure he didn't fall over, and let him rest. This was the most intense lesson he had ever learned, without question. His teacher had hardly said anything at all, but he had learned such profound things. *I must remember this concept of 'opana'. To show knowledge. Convey it face to face like this. It's so much clearer than just telling about it.*

Illtharen was fishing around in his robes for something. He came out with a tiny mirror, smaller than his palm. He moved a finger in front of Damon's eyes, watching him carefully. He covered one of Damon's eyes, then the other, still moving the finger around. Whatever he was doing, he resolved to just let it be done to him. The wizard had not failed to explain himself thus far.

He handed the mirror to him and positioned it between his thumb and forefinger, up in front of his right eye. He tapped the outside corner of his eyebrow and then pointed at the mirror.

"I understand," Damon told him; or at least he hoped he did. He stared at the reflection of his eye while Illtharen held his other hand. At first, not much of anything happened. He just looked at the familiar blue, almost black, iris and wondered about how his ancestors had produced such a fine quality looking glass. Then, he noticed his pulse. It seemed louder than anything else in the room. He could almost feel it carrying the life through his body. He could see the veins under his skin, glowing an uncanny shade of blue. Brighter and purer than anything he'd seen before. He was attached to everything around him, yet somehow, singular and apart.

Never before had he felt so strong. He knew without a doubt that every bit of the energy he felt came from himself, and nowhere else. *If I could use this, I could do such great things. What if I really can save us all?* His heart surged with hope.

It took him awhile to come back from his reverie, but Illtharen did not take the mirror away until he put it down on the rug. He smiled and patted

Damon's shoulder. "Tananehast." He reflected that *'hast'* carried a great deal of meaning. He wondered if there were more *hasts* than just the six he knew about, but there was no way to ask; not without knowing more of Illtharen's language.

The sorcerer slowly rose to his feet. Had he forgotten about the last one? Or perhaps he was not going to teach him about the Void? He decided to check. He picked up the sheet and pointed to the empty circle.

"Illtharen? Um... nazin?" He had wanted to say 'what' but all he knew how to ask was 'why'.

He stretched, putting his palms in the small of his back. "Omhast," he said simply. Then he walked over to the window and began untying the heavy drapes that covered it. Damon had never seen such drapes. They were made of several layers of dark, heavily-woven fabrics. In between the layers, and on the outside of the last layer facing the window, was a lustrous black fur. As soon as the drapes were open, he could feel the draft of cold air stealing across the floor. They seemed to keep out the chill quite well. He wondered if he could make some for his own home.

Illtharen fiddled with the latches until he managed to push the frozen window open, letting in a blast of icy wind. He motioned for Damon to come to him, and hugged his robes around himself.

Looking outside gave him quite a shock. He was fairly sure that what he was seeing was the very same moor land that stretched out below the cliffs where old Stonehart Hall stood. The face of the land had changed a little, but... yes, he was quite sure now. *I'm home.* There was a pang of longing twisting in his chest that he could neither explain nor brush aside.

The writer tucked an arm around his waist, though there was little danger of falling out of the window. It was set quite high in the wall. He stretched out a hand towards the glittering night sky. Damon did the same.

It pulled at him. The yawning blackness opened above him like the maw of a giant snake. He was paralysed by fear. Surely, it would swallow them both! Any power paled by comparison. His own, or the tiny pin-pricks of fire in the heavens. The very ground he stood on was inconsequential. He resisted the strong arm around his middle, trying to edge back from the window.

Then, Illtharen began to sing. The haunting voice, a smooth and even tenor, soared out into the night. It echoed eerily off the frozen landscape like the call of a wandering ghost. Though he couldn't understand the words, the key and the intonation told him it was a lament. *We still sing them the same way, even after thousands of years.* This land had always known grief, profound and lasting sorrow that nothing could erase; nothing, but the dark reaches of time.

The empty space between the stars drank it in. It did not waver or complain. It did not desire more, but was ready to take should it be given. The lonely sound vibrated in the void, just once, before evaporating into nothing.

He stood still for a long time after there was silence. It was only when he realized Illtharen had begun to shiver in the cold that he stepped back. "Omhast," he said to the sorcerer. The man nodded, his wide eyes seeming to hold just as much awe as he felt. Damon helped him to close the window and get it re-fastened and draped. He could understand the numbness of his fingers even though he didn't feel the cold the same way.

"Thank you for teaching me, Illtharen."

The sorcerer, settling himself on his chair again, looked at him quizzically.

"Um... Opana..." He finished by just bowing his head and shoulders in thanks.

"Ah, atane." He made the same gesture.

"Atane opana," Damon repeated.

He chuckled and waved him off. The motion made him remember where he was supposed to be. *Oh Aervie, how long have I been here? Lorne must be itching to find out what I've learned. But how do I get ba...*

He found himself staring at the book under his hands. The sound of Lorne scratching away at his notes was strangely comforting. He watched his cousin writing for a moment, then cleared his throat. Lorne jumped at the sound and his pen rolled off the table.

"Oh you're back! I thought you'd fallen asleep." He frowned. "Your eyes are terribly bloodshot. Perhaps you ought to rest after all?"

"I will, but I have to tell you... no..." He corrected himself. "I have to *show* you what I learned."

At once, through the Blood Link, he felt Lorne's heart leap with excitement. "Show me? What do you mean show me?"

"We've been missing the whole point of the words, Lorne. This has to be taught face to face, mind to mind. Give me your hand. Let's get started!"

Chapter 9: Hatchling

Dyseris' hand on her shoulder shook Phoenix from her memories. "We can go in now," he said.

"That was quick."

"He is interested to see this human who would be Queen." He shrugged.

Her mouth fell into a grim line. *I am Queen, birdman.* She knew he meant no disrespect. He couldn't possibly understand, but every time these Ducal failed to call her 'Princess' it felt like an affront against the royal house. She hadn't realized how much she had invested in the title until it was taken from her.

"Ready?"

"Yes." She moved to his left side, instinctively leaving her hip open to draw a blade if she had one. She wondered what manner of swords the Ducal could forge with their keen appreciation of beauty.

Even if such beauty could sometimes be eccentric, as the displays of polished serving spoons lining the entryway to the Regent's palace proved, there was no doubt these people were master craftsmen.

Guards, dressed in heavily adorned maroon tunics and breeches strutted about the halls. Their behaviour contrasted starkly with the stoic, understated presence she was used to seeing in her father's house; though, she was beginning to grow accustomed to the way the Ducal comported themselves. As long as she reminded herself that she was looking at birds, not people, everything seemed to make more sense.

Above, the ceilings were high and buttressed but the most fascinating thing about them was that they were covered in tiny pieces of coloured glass with lights drifting behind them.

"Magic," she whispered in awe, but Dyseris offered no explanations in response. He simply cast a glance up at the multi-coloured rippled surface and nodded. That alone made the tiny hairs on her arms stand up.

The guards, for all their proud strutting, eagerly bobbed their torsos in her direction and helpfully pointed out the way to the Regent's 'Hearing Room' as they called it. They had not understood the meaning of the words 'throne room' when she'd asked the first time. They'd simply replied: "But we have chairs in many rooms! Which one do you want?" They meant, of course the raised, rounded contraptions filled with soft pillows where one sat with legs crossed in relative comfort. While Phoenix felt that they were more like small nests than actual chairs, they were quite pleasant as long as she remembered never to lean backwards.

"Why are they so polite to me?" she asked Dyseris after a couple passed them by.

"You are the Phoenix," he said.

She frowned. "But I still have to fight their champion?"

"Yes." He nodded.

"Why?" she pressed.

"Because no one may rule without first grasping the perch of the Regent. Hanuel is not forgiving. We don't need a weak Regent."

She pondered the implications of this. What of Bowen's sons and daughters? Did they have to prove themselves by duelling their Champion of Law, as they called him? Perhaps it was just a ceremonial duel? The royal line could not be very stable if every Regent won the throne by fighting to the death.

The door to the hearing room was smaller than she had expected. Given the size of the place, she had rather envisioned large double doors instead of the single, narrow-topped one they faced. Then, she remembered the Ducal's irritation with cold draughts and saw the sensibility of a smaller entrance.

She approached the door slowly. The guards looked at her with interest but made no move to open it for her; doing so amongst the Ducal was often taken as an insult to a person's strength and competence, and they had no intention of offending her.

She pushed the door open and walked inside with Dyseris following placidly behind her. Inside, the room was large and long. Tall brass trees set into the wall along its length. High above their heads, the branches met and crossed. The leaves were cut from thousands of pieces of translucent green glass. Lights winked behind them, giving the illusion of a lazy summer twilight.

The windows between the trees were a hazy violet glass with swirls of ground mica making eddies of fog across their surfaces. The floor was a distracting mosaic of abstract orange, gold and red bits of tile. The scavenged pieces progressed gradually through the colours of the rainbow as they walked toward the Regent's dais. Phoenix was struck by the patience and care implicit in the crafted beauty all around them.

At the front of the room was a raised dais, higher than any she'd seen before in a king's chamber. The Regent's comfortable padded seat had gnarled animal feet for legs, the toes of which were level with their foreheads. She took a moment to consider this. The man sitting cross-legged in the chair did so with his high-ground uncontested by any possible higher perches. Most of the seating she had seen was very low, almost right on the ground. Head-height was very important to them.

Bowen regarded them in silence. His straight, black hair hung long about his shoulders, like raven wings. His eyes were equally dark and seldom blinked. His skin she might have described as sun-kissed, if indeed any living Ducal had seen the sun. The clothing he wore was cut from glossy black silk and he had an eye-catching red sash tied around his waist. The tall leather boots, like all the other shoes she had seen here, had soft soles.

"Why do you not speak?" The Regent said at last, making her jump slightly. His deep voice betrayed his annoyance and the resonance afforded to him by the rippling glass all around made the echo all the more penetrating.

"I was waiting for you to speak first." Her voice wavered with uncertainty.

"Why should I speak? It's my Hearing Room." Bowen tucked one foot under himself and let the other dangle over the side of the chair.

Phoenix took a breath through her nose. She let it out slowly.

"It is good to size up others upon first meetings."

Bowen nodded, pursing his lips. Apparently, the response had pleased him.

"Do you want to sit in my chair?" Another test. Phoenix did not like the half-smile that wrinkled his upper lip, baring his teeth. This was no act of hospitality, no courtesy. The Regent, it seemed, was in no way gentle or subtle about his assessments of others. It was unfair. She had been trained in political manoeuvring, but not this kind. Ducal diplomacy was something perplexing, even to her.

"I think... I should sit beside you." Phoenix chewed the inside of her cheek, watching the Regent's face. There was no help there. Just dark, sparkling eyes, boring into her. "I may need some extra pillows though."

"Ha!" He clapped his hands together and jumped up so suddenly, he startled both of them. Phoenix forced herself to let go of the side of her robe where she had reached for her sword hilt. "It will be done. Chair! Twelve..." He looked back at his own seat. "Fourteen pillows! Bring them now!" There was the sound of running feet and scrabbling. In a moment, brightly clad servants in yellow and green robes were setting up a seat for her. When they finished, they vanished back into whatever hiding places they had come from.

Phoenix leaned over and whispered to Dyseris. "Should I ask for one for you?"

"No," he whispered back.

"Do you wish him to sit at your feet?" Bowen regarded them sternly again. It seemed that nothing escaped those eyes and it was slightly unnerving. He watched every slight motion or gesture and every time either of them shifted weight from one hip to the other, as if reading whole pages of a manuscript. His face betrayed so little. She cursed her gross disadvantage once again.

She cleared her throat. "He will do as he will do. I think he will be no disruption."

Bowen nodded and returned to his chair. He seemed unembarrassed by the whole interaction. He simply swatted the cushions of the chair beside himself and waited. Phoenix walked around the dais and found steps going up the back. She climbed them and seated herself comfortably in the small nest of cushions. Her head was higher than the Regent's. It was only a few inches difference but it spoke volumes more than any retelling of their ancient prophecy.

The Regent reached out and touched her hair with his fingers as though assessing the quality of a bolt of silk. She jumped involuntarily. "You are beautiful, just as they told me," he said, his voice a little softer than previously. "Even if you do style yourself like a soldier."

Phoenix's cheeks reddened and she covered it by rearranging her hair behind an ear, taking it out of his grasp in the process. "Thank you."

"Why did you walk here? Much quicker to glide over the buildings than to walk between."

"Oh I can't fly," she laughed nervously and crossed her arms over her stomach.

"Surely, it is possible for you. You are strong. You have magic."

"I don't know how." She cleared her throat again. She was starting to feel like a piece of suspicious merchandise and she did not like this close scrutiny. Her scarlet face said as much.

Bowen closed his eyes and returned his hands to his lap. "I wish you had grown to maturity among us. Your mother would have taught you such things." The weariness in his voice was a startling change from the harsh, probing countenance she had faced only an instant ago. Were all his shifts in emotion so abrupt? All the Ducal seemed to be quick to anger and just as quick to forget. Perhaps this was why they all seemed so unhinged.

"Ah... well, Dyseris has adopted me. I am not Ducal but... magic is strong among your kind isn't it? Could he teach me?"

A dark eyebrow arched in her direction and the harsh, testing stare was back as though it had never wavered. "Any Ducal could teach you flight. It remains to be seen if you can *learn* it. For that, you need a teacher of more skill."

Phoenix looked down at her lap. The silence stretched on. It was clear that she was supposed to say something but what? "I honestly don't know," she admitted.

"Yes you do," the Regent contested. "Do you fly in here?" His finger darted out and poked her square in the forehead just above her focusing stone.

"Whe... I..." She blinked at him and rubbed her head, wishing that he would stop touching her. "Well, I dream about flying..."

"Then you fly." Bowen sat back, his face victorious. "Flying is flying. In the mind or in the sky."

"But if that were true, then everyone could fly; there wouldn't be any stairs in the Upperworld!"

"You speak nonsense!" He threw up his hands, rolling his dark eyes toward the ceiling. "You say you are an Upperworlder but you have magic! Ducal magic!"

"I *do* come from the Upperworld," Phoenix contested. "The only magic I have is this." She pushed her hair aside with both hands to show her stone. "And it was given to me just after my birth."

"That does not matter! Born with power or acquired power. It is in you. Use your eyes! Your brain!" Bowen got up and stalked around his chair erratically. "It is like you open your mouth and shit comes out!"

She rose to her feet. "Hey! You're the crazy one here! I think I would know if I could throw fireballs. Believe me, it would make life much easier."

"That's human magic," Bowen scoffed and waved his hand in front of his face as if dispelling a smell. "We do not touch that."

"What? Why?" She had thought that these "Upperworlders" had no magic. Now, she was confused.

"That is not important now!" The Regent grasped her by the shoulders. "I can see our power in you—Ducal power—as clear as water, even if you say you have different magic. I feel Ducal magic in you." He let her go. "I can't tell if you are lying about it or if you are simply ignorant."

Phoenix focused on her breathing, trying to suppress the anger that was beginning to burst. She wanted to shout at him, badly. Fortunately, she had the self-control to keep her thoughts to herself; her mouth would stay shut until she had come up with something sensible to say.

A curious notion bubbled up in her mind. She glanced at Dyseris and back at Bowen. The vast majority of the Ducal she had seen were of dark complexion but all of the ones she had seen in the Tamiyon Nesting had been pale. She wondered if there was a connection.

"How can you sense what manner of magic I possess?" she asked.

Bowen sat back and she could see that she had surprised him. The rapid-fire back and forth of Ducal conversation she had experienced thus far came to a halt.

"It is a talent of mine. Many Ducal have the same." He crossed his arms and frowned. Phoenix knew that face. Human or Ducal, he was warning her to drop it; she didn't.

"You are strong with magic? Are you of Tamiyon blood?"

The last word had barely passed her lips when he lashed out, a stinging crack against her cheek. She put down one foot to keep herself from falling off the chair and raised a hand to ward off any further blows. He did not strike her again.

Bowen paced along the edge of the dais. "Take her to the heretics," he barked at Dyseris. "Let them sort out her mystery. I do not want to see her again until she faces Sora's blade."

Sora? Was that the name of the champion? She froze as the Regent rounded on her. He pointed toward the door as though dismissing a dog. Phoenix clenched her teeth, reining in her temper at the insult. She stood and hopped off the edge of the dais, not wanting to be near him any longer than she had to be. She ignored the hand Dyseris tried to rest on her shoulder and saw herself out.

Phoenix sat with her arms wrapped around one knee. She was still seething from her meeting with the Regent. Wester, the head of the Tamiyon clan if she understood it properly, had been most courteous to her, giving her the highest and most comfortable chair in his house and having sweets brought to her. While the other Ducal were merely polite, the Tamiyons called her Queen without exception, at least from what she had seen so far. They didn't seem concerned with the fact that she had not yet had her duel with Sora.

Dyseris fidgeted as she waited for whomever they had chosen to be her teacher to arrive. He reminded her of a hen fussing over a brood. She supposed maybe he did think of her as his protégé if not child; he *had* found her and taken her into his home after all. She sighed.

"Dyseris, I am sure it will be fine. I have taken up so much of your time already. You have work to do, right?"

The raven man smiled. "Yes."

At this moment, Phoenix lacked the patience to wander through the Ducal's dance of conversation. "Please just ... go." She didn't want to snap at him. It wouldn't be fair to take out her frustrations with the Regent on him.

"Alright!" He stooped and put his arms around her for a moment. She was startled at the sudden gesture but he was so quick about it that she had no time to respond. "Learn quickly!" He waved his hand, bracelets clacking. Then, he was off.

Not a moment after he exited, another Ducal stepped through the door. The hairs stood up on Phoenix's arms.

"Oh, not you," she muttered.

Kael crossed the room and bowed. "You need training. Let us begin," he said without preamble. Of all the Ducal in Hanuel who could have taught her, they chose the one that made her skin crawl. She rose to her feet and stepped to the side, intending to pass by him. She assumed he meant to practise outside given that, if she actually did manage to do something like conjure fire, she could make a mess of Wester's main hall.

The shaman moved into her path and raised his hand to her face. For a moment, she thought he was going to strike her in the same place Bowen had. However, the hand simply hovered there, a thumb's length from her skin, as he looked over the bruise. She tried to turn away from the scrutiny but found that she was stuck yet, even though he did not touch her, it was impossible to move. Whatever this power was, it had no visible manifestation and it wrapped her limbs in the softest of embraces. Soft, but strong as spider-silk around a fly. Kael, for his part, frowned at the injury.

He took his hand away and she staggered as the hold on her suddenly let go.

"Don't do that to me!" she snapped.

"Become strong enough to stop me," he said, unruffled. He folded his arms. Aside from the rise and fall of his breath, he might have been a statue.

Phoenix gritted her teeth, resisting the urge to hit him. "I don't know how."

"I will show you," he said and put out his hand again. This time, there was a violent shove against her chest and she toppled onto her backside. She yelped and scrambled back to her feet. She skirted around the edge of the room, fearful of the unseen power. He followed her calmly.

"What—"

He interrupted her by giving her another push. She bumped against the wall. The pressure did not stay, did not hold her there, so she moved closer to the centre of the room, having no interest in being battered against hard surfaces.

"What am I supposed to do?"

"Fight back with whatever comes naturally."

She realized, then, that he was making some kind of assessment. With the amount of force he delivered and a lack of any ability to counter it, he was certainly capable of hurting her, but refrained from doing so.

"What comes naturally to me is a blade!" she protested.

Kael paused. "What kind of blade?"

"A sword."

He nodded once. "Stay here." Then, he turned and ascended the stairs to the upper levels of the house. She watched his back until he disappeared, perplexed. She found herself wanting him to come back. He had provoked her ire and left her alone to stew in it.

When he returned, he tossed her a short sword in an ornate scabbard. She caught it and drew it out, frowning. It was a good quality weapon but not as long as she was accustomed to and straight instead of curved. At least it was something; any blade at her hip was better than that disorienting emptiness.

"It will have to do for now."

"Are you still angry?" Kael asked.

Phoenix took a moment to make sense of the question. "Yes." Somehow, the Ducal bluntness sounded strange coming from him. Perhaps it was his stillness, the subtle differences in the way he moved, that made her assume he would be more human.

"Good. Now, attack." He stood with his hand extended toward her, palm up, his demeanour just as tranquil as though he were on an evening stroll.

She stared. The hand was empty. Surely, he couldn't be serious? Then again, she was quite aware there was more to this Ducal than met the eye.

She felt the weight of her blade. The sword was much lighter than she

181

would have wanted. She held it in her right hand, with the scabbard reversed in her left for balance.

Without hesitation, she darted forward and swiped at his hand, testing him. Kael met the blade with his fingertips. He brushed the steel in a light caress. The hilt jarred in her hand so hard she almost dropped it. It swung out wide as though he had kicked it with all his might.

She stood, brow wrinkled in confusion. Through her apprehension, a spark of curiosity flared.

"What—?"

Phoenix's question was cut off as he stepped forward again. She met his hand with another swing. Kael brushed the back of his hand along the flat of her blade and it was shoved sideways toward the floor. She had to change her footing to keep from falling. When she recovered her balance, she lunged and thrust the blade at him. It was, after all, more suited for stabbing than slashing. The shaman moved his arm under the blade and it slowed to a halt. He tilted his wrist and the weapon twisted with it. Phoenix tried to fight the turn, tried to withdraw but it was stuck in that damnable enchantment.

The steel clattered to the floor and she threw up her hands in frustration.

"Are you going to explain how you—?"

He curled his fingers, stepped in and aimed a blow at her face. She hastily brought up the sheath to block it and felt Kael's knuckles tap against hers. There was no burst of pain, but rather a persistent pressure between their hands. She stared. There was a finger's width of space between them and though she could see the tendons standing out on his wrist, he advanced no farther. She pushed on his hand and felt the same sluggish clotting of the air radiating around her fingers. He pushed back, shoulder flexing. The air between their hands shifted and compressed but did not yield. Kael withdrew his fist and the congealed air snapped back to normal so quickly that it blew back her hair and rippled the edges of her robes.

Her heart thudded and she broke into a grin. She could not hold him, trap him the way he did her, but if she tried hard, she could push back. The shaman did not smile.

"That was Ducal magic. Why do you not use human magic?"

Phoenix bent and retrieved her sword. "I told you, I don't know how."

"What you react with naturally should be your own magic."

She sheathed the weapon. "Sorry." She wasn't; inside, she was celebrating her small victory. Kael put out his palm again and she jumped, bracing against the push, but he did not bring his power to bear against her.

"Just push back," he said. "As you did."

Phoenix cautiously put her palm to his. It was not hard to focus on her intent. She really did want the vexing bird-man away from her. The pressure built between them again, keeping their hands apart. Kael's brow furrowed. He put his other hand behind hers as though he were going to grab her wrist but he only held it there. Whatever magic he was using, it did not feel quite the same. It alternated between a warm breeze and a sticky pulling sensation like removing partly dried glue from the skin. She concentrated on it.

He pulled the hand away. "Interesting." He did not look pleased. "Your power is mimicking mine. You are not doing it purposefully?"

She shook her head.

"We must stop this. I need human magic, not Ducal."

"You need …? You are already powerful. Dyseris said you are the strongest."

"I am," he said, still regarding her critically. She had not expected him to answer but, once again, he defied what she knew of the Ducal. "I have all the magic Hanuel has to offer. That will not give us back the sky or it would have done so already. The Phoenix has human magic. That is why I must use you to fulfil the prophecy." He turned and began climbing the stairs to the upper level again. Phoenix tightened her fingers around the scabbard.

"You speak of me as though I am a weapon."

He did not look back.

"Yes."

Alsteh, oh noble Goddess, preserve my mind and give me strength. I will end that man.

Bowen looked down from his chair, annoyed with the Ducal who stood before him. He usually didn't let Tamiyons in his Hearing Room at all but Kael's request pertained to the Phoenix. It was important enough that he couldn't decline.

"I want to train her," the shaman said.

"No."

A small line appeared between Kael's eyebrows. He gave no other sign of anger. Bowen had never seen him wave his arms or shout as a Ducal should. Instead, he stored it away, remembered the affront. Unpleasant things happened to those who upset him, but he never seemed to have anything to do with it. Regardless, Bowen thought his behaviour obnoxious and, now that he had seen the way Phoenix acted, very human. *Doubly* obnoxious.

"Why?" he said finally.

"Because she has not defeated Sora yet." Bowen sat back, flopping one leg over the rim of the chair. "I will not have her learning from our strongest shaman before she has taken her proper place." Though the scholars of the Vault had no doubts, he was not completely convinced that this was, indeed the Phoenix. There was still a chance that she could be false and he was unwilling to empower a human impostor with Ducal magic.

"What if she cannot defeat Sora as she is?" Kael crossed his arms.

"Then, she dies." He threw up his hands. He had thought the answer quite obvious.

"There will only be one Phoenix, according to the prophecy. You cannot kill her."

He supposed not. Then again, it would be Sora who would end her. If this really was the Phoenix, then this was just another step on the road back to the sky. It was necessary for her to occupy the position of Regent to order the Ducal and they would not follow her if she did not take it legitimately. If she was not, then this simply eliminated the problem.

Bowen said none of this. Kael had not asked a question and thus wanted no answer.

"At least order the Vault Wardens to release to me the books I will need to teach her with."

"No."

Again, the small line creased his brow. "Ducal magic is not right for her. I need human magic to instruct her. How do you expect me to do so without them?"

"I don't know. I am not a shaman." Bowen levelled a finger at him. "You might have been correct about the Phoenix, but human magic is still forbidden. If you are caught studying it, you will be put to death. As it has been in the past, it is still the same now."

"This law no longer makes sense. You must change it."

"I will not." The Regent inclined his head. "If the Phoenix defeats Prince Sora, then she will change it herself when she takes my seat."

Kael's nostrils flared as he let out a breath. Any other Ducal would have protested, or scoffed, or at least sighed at such a flat refusal. The shaman's face remained blank. He bowed, hair concealing his face.

"When she kills your son," he said, his head still bent. "There will be a place for you in the Tamiyon Nesting, Cousin."

Bowen stood, knocking the pillows from his seat in the process. He wrapped his fingers around the claws that hung at his sides, cold silver pressing into his palms, and he stalked to the edge of the dais.

"Get out!"

The walls echoed with his roar. Kael bobbed once and rose from his bow. His hair lay flat against his shoulders again as he turned to go. Bowen thought he saw the ghost of a smile on his lips. He shook with rage.

"*Out!*"

The shaman continued to the door, his pace never quickening. He exited the Hearing Room without a word or backward glance.

Chapter 10: A Giant among Men

Damon fidgeted with the hilt of his sword. It sat in its scabbard across his knees while he waited for his kin to gather. Today, he would begin putting the knowledge that he and Lorne had gleaned from Iltharen to work.

His cousin stood by his shoulder. *At least I don't have to do this alone,* he thought. *Though it would be better if Casey and Staruff were here. I'm used to working with them.*

They sat in a cleared section of the tourney grounds. Damon had worried that they would have problems with people crowding around to watch, but once it had been announced that the Stoneharts would be practising magic, the area very quickly became vacant. Erik had allowed him to leave the castle but only for this specific purpose.

In front of Damon, there were four large stone basins. One contained water, another sand, another a small fire crackling away on a couple of hardwood logs, and the last with a censer of sweet sage letting off a curling trail of smoke into the air.

"Alright, everyone please assemble," Lorne called. "I think I need not tell you how little time we have and how important it is to get this *right*. Damon is not accustomed to teaching so please have a care. We will need to work on this together."

Strangely, Lorne's quiet voice seemed to reach all of them, or perhaps it was just the air of anticipation that settled over the clearing and brought silence.

Damon rose slowly from the camp chair and stood between the basins of water and fire. He clasped his fingers together and took a deep breath, looking around at the gathered Stoneharts. Erik and Lorne had selected thirty of the strongest darkbloods they had with them for this initial lesson, hoping that they would propagate the teachings throughout the rest of the Glasshammer army and ease Damon's task of teaching them.

Seeing them all together like this, he was struck by their similarities in appearance. Their hair was almost universally black or very dark; their skin, pale.. On their own, he might not have noticed, but in a group, he could discern a slight darkness around the lips and eye sockets. Each and every pair of eyes that gazed back at him were blue. In their battle dress, long relaxed tunics, comfortable breeches, high boots, and thick black cloaks, they looked like a murder of ravens standing around a prospective meal. They left off their steel gauntlets and chain neck guards for the practise but the effect was still intimidating.

Let us hope the enemy thinks so too.

Damon smiled at them. *These are my kinsmen,* he reminded himself.

"Hello. Ah, well this is all very simple," he gestured at the basins to either side of him. "Rather, the basic ideas are. Doing more complex things with those ideas obviously makes for harder work." He looked around to see if they were understanding so far. He got a few nods. Heartened, he continued. "Um, well there are six forces we use in Stormforge magic. We call these Dominions. There are only four bowls here because um, well ..." *I have got to stop saying that,* he chastised himself. *I sound like a dolt.* "You cannot really contain the Void and I'm not about to fill a basin with blood because ... yuck."

They laughed and to Damon, it felt like an old cobweb snapping, the tension in the air dissipating. He realized then that it was not only his own nerves he was feeling, but theirs, through the Link. Curiosity, impatience, mirth, and excitement: he had a multi-hued buzz of emotions and thoughts going through his mind.. *Aervie, how am I to do this without getting distracted?* He wondered. *Will it be like this always? This will make family gatherings difficult...*

"Our tools here are the Earth, the Water, the Fire, and the Air. We can accomplish things by making any of these move and change. We just have to reach out to them and give them a tug."

"What about the Blood and the Void?" one of his kin spoke up. Damon paused, following the spike of curiosity to the speaker. A Stonehart probably only a couple of years past his own Eve of the Sword with long black hair falling over his shoulders from under his hood.

"Um, sorry I'm forgetting your name."

"Gavin." He smiled.

"Right, sorry, Gavin. I will get to those after these four because they are a little different." Damon cleared his throat. "But perhaps it will help you understand what we are doing if I explain what makes them different. With these four, we reach outside of ourselves for assistance to do what we want." He put out his hand as though trying to grasp something. "For the Blood, we reach within ourselves to draw forth power." He put his hand to his chest.

"And the Void?" Gavin prompted.

"We don't reach out to the Void," Damon said. "The Void does not give. It takes."

"Why would you want to use something that *takes* power away from you?" Gavin wrinkled his brow and though Damon could feel the ripples of irritation from the others at being held back, he also felt not a small amount of curiosity being stoked. Others had this question too.

Lorne stepped forward and rested a hand on Damon's shoulder. "Gavin, why don't you help Damon with his demonstration? We have learned that it's much better to see and do than to just sit around while we talk about it."

The young man nodded brightly, very much liking this idea. He moved in front of his kinsmen held out his hands. "What would you like me to do?"

Damon smiled his thanks up at the librarian and returned his attention to his new assistant. "Alright come around to the bowl of sand here." He sat down by the stone basin. "Everyone please position yourselves so you can see. The people closest to me, maybe you should sit so those in the back can see?" He waited for them to arrange themselves while Gavin settled down on the other side of the basin from him and took his leather gloves off.

"Most of us who wield magic often do it without thinking," Damon explained. "Keeping rust off our blades, or making sure the forge fire stays at a constant temperature ... keeping water out of our boots or from leaking through the roof, casting infection out of a wound ..." He shook his head. "The point is, we have assumed that these are just the gifts we were born with. We have assumed that magic is growing weak just because we have such lackluster talents to boast of."

He put up his hands to ward off the protests he could feel boiling just under the surface of stung pride. "It's not true. The truth of the matter is, we are all reaching out to the Dominions without knowing it, wielding rather complex magic without understanding what it is we are doing."

Damon let that sink in for a moment. Around him, the Link was awash with fascination and curiosity, the other emotions having died away. It felt strangely hungry. He fed it.

"What I want to do with you today, is help you understand what we've been doing all along, breaking it up into small bits so that we can use these tools to do different things. Things we're not accustomed to, things we didn't think we could."

He let his hand drop to the sand, raking his fingers though the small white grains. "I can command this sand to do anything I like, but it won't move until I speak to it in a way it understands. I don't use words. Rocks don't talk. I have to feel the power it emits and I have to listen to it. It is not something you will notice until you bend your mind to it."

He reached out to his assistant with his other hand and the young man clasped it, frowning at the chill temperature. Gavin put his other hand to the sand, imitating Damon.

"What does it feel like to you?" Damon asked.

"Feels like ... sand?" Gavin frowned. "What is it supposed to feel like?"

"Focus on the Link and I will show you what I feel. Then you will know what you're looking for." Damon let his eyes drift partway closed, letting the bracing strength of Earth cradle and support him.

"Oh!" Gavin exclaimed. "Oh that's ... it feels still. Very still and ..." He struggled to find words. "Solid. Safe." He stared at the sand as though it had suddenly become the most interesting thing in the world. Perhaps, for him, it had. "I can feel it under me too. Feel everyone standing on it. Walking. The fighters in the tourney scuffling ..."

Damon moved his fingers through the sand, turning over a handful of it. Gavin nearly fell over and grasped the edge of the basin in a panic.

"Aie Lanvie! What was that?"

"That was Earth moving." Damon smiled, unable to help himself. "Very stable, very strong. But when it decides to move, it moves with great power." He released Gavin's hand. "Would you like to play with that for a while?"

The spark of curiosity was back and the young man grinned. "Yes!" Damon rose and left him to toy with the basin while he moved on to the next one.

"Who would like to learn about fire?"

No one moved. Lorne pointed at a tall, broad-shouldered man Damon recognized as Harl the smith from Autumn's stedding.

"I'm not sticking my hand in that." Harl crossed his arms defiantly. "I'm not stupid."

Damon smiled. "Oh, you don't have to. I will." He pulled back the sleeve of his tunic and put his hand into the crackling flame. It felt warm to him, certainly, but it did not burn. "Please, no one else try this. I burn like a frozen swamp-log. The rest of you probably don't have that luxury."

Harl sat down quickly, radiating alarm and inquisitiveness in equal measures. "Alright, fine. Let's do this quickly. I've heard of your luck, Damon but I'd just as soon see you not cook your hand like a sausage."

"Quick is alright," he agreed and took the smith's hand. "Fire is very

189

quick. I don't like it much, personally. Fortunately, neither does the enemy. I haven't found a person yet who likes being on fire."

Harl chuckled, his nervousness easing a little. He stopped laughing when the energy borne of Fire raced through him. Immediately, he began to sweat. He grew so silent that Damon began to worry.

"Are you alright?" he asked, fearful that he had pumped too much power through the Link and hurt him somehow.

"You mean to tell me this is how my forgefire feels all the time?" the smith said, his voice suddenly small.

"Yes."

"It's plotting to *eat* me?"

It was Damon's turn to laugh. "Ah, yes but don't take it as a personal affront. It plots to eat everything. Not just you."

"To wield the Dominions, must we have something of that Dominion nearby or can we summon it out of nothing?" Harl asked.

"You mean, can you make fire if you haven't got any already?" Damon tilted his head to the side, frowning. Harl nodded. "I have no idea. I know that isn't a very useful answer but consider how rarely we are without any one of the Dominions. We are never far from the ground, or the air, or the water, or even fire. I would have to wander quite far from the camp to find myself without fire."

"You could try swimming down into deep water and see if you can bring forth air?" Gavin suggested.

"How kind of you to volunteer," Lorne quipped. "I'm sure we can find you a lake that isn't frozen over yet."

There was laughter all around. Damon felt it through the Link. It bubbled through his skin, tickling as it went. It was quite pleasant.

"Well, beyond throwing rocks or fire at our foes, there is more we can do with the Dominions by combining them. They are like strands of a tapestry for us to weave as we desire," he explained. "For example ..."

He reached out toward the bowl of sand and the bowl of fire. A slow trickle of sand grains followed his arm like a march of ants. At the same time, a thin line of flame crawled up his other arm, close enough to his sleeve to make the moisture in it steam. The sand and fire swirled around each other in front of him, spiralling slowly, then faster. The Dominions blurred together like an angry orange eye.

When it slowed again, it had changed. Damon let the spherical lump of glass fall into his palm.

"Holy Aervie ..." Harl breathed.

Damon looked up at his kinsmen, smiling at the wonder on their faces. "So ... who wants to learn about water?"

Every last hand went up.

Damon's bones ached as he sank down onto his bedroll and leaned his back against the wall. It was his third day teaching his kinsmen the ways of the Dominions. They were learning well and quickly with all the enthusiasm of children at a Springtide fair. Though, chanelling so much energy for them was starting to eat at him.

Most of the Dominions were fine except where it came to Blood magic. Pulling power from oneself to give to another taxed the body heavily. He told them each and every time to use extreme care when wielding it. It was the most potent of all healing energies and the most volatile, even more so than Fire.

Today, he had demonstrated the potential dangers of the Blood. He and Lorne had devised the lesson ahead of time but it had still made him nervous. His cousin sat on some thick furs for everyone to watch and Damon had very carefully exerted some control over the blood in his veins. He slowly pushed the blood down and away from Lorne's head, seeing his face go grey. Then, the librarian swayed and fell over on his side.

As soon as he had released the pressure, Lorne was fine, of course, but the lesson had struck a chord with his kinsmen.

"If you feel your own body," Damon had explained. "If you are aware of yourself, you can easily defend against anyone trying to meddle with you in this way. If you are distracted, it may go ill for you. However, I also want you to know that it is easy to harm yourself while trying to do something as simple as stop bleeding or reduce swelling. If you do not have a head for healing already, and unless you will die otherwise, do not try healing yourself. Get to a healer if you can. Bandage, close a wound with sutures, put cold water on a burn, and wait for help. Too much blood, or not enough, in the wrong place and you will kill yourself."

Despite his stern warnings about the delicate nature of that Dominion, Damon was sure they were going to return home with more healers than they had left with. Many of his kinsmen were showing an unexpected aptitude for it already. The thought cheered him.

Taking stock of himself, he realized he had a lot of residual Fire magic and a bit of Air milling about in him. He settled into a comfortable posture and focused on dumping the excess into the Void so he could relax.

"I haven't seen much of you lately," his father said, interrupting his meditation.

Damon blinked up at him. He yawned and stretched. "I've been teaching."

"I know that." Erik sat down on the edge of the bed. "But we've got enough Stonehearts working on spreading your discoveries around."

"What do you want me to do? I'm not allowed outside." He fixed his father with a glare.

Erik scowled back. "Not if you're going to be consorting with mercenaries, letting them fill your head with nonsense."

"Like survival strategies?"

"I've taught you how to fight. Sunev trains with you."

"You've taught me how to *spar*. I've told Sunev not to bother. She won't turn live steel against me. It's useless." Damon stared at the ceiling, willing him to go away or release him from his imprisonment in the castle.

"Do you want me to speak with her about it?"

"No." He continued his refusal to look at his father.

"I'm not letting you go to them, Damon."

"I can bloody well see that."

Erik grunted in annoyance. "I would appreciate you showing proper respect, Damon. I understand that you are angry, but this is getting foolish."

Damon made no answer.

"I must go speak with the other lords and delegates about the battle. You should come with me."

"Why?" He turned to look at Erik at last.

His father regarded him with the hard expression he wore when Damon had gotten into mischief. "Because you are my son and it is your right to be involved in the planning process, even if only to watch; though, you should know what we are planning so that you can work on the proper magic."

"If you can't trust me to choose good friends, don't trust me with saving our world either." He resumed staring angrily at the ceiling. After a long moment of silence, Erik stalked out of the room, shutting the door with a curt click.

It was inevitable. Damon told himself that as he stood in the hallway, gazing past the guards at the pale autumn sky. It was unfair to simply vanish without so much as telling Casey and Staruff, especially not after all they'd done for him. *I'll at least give them an explanation. Perhaps directions to write to me?* He remembered then that Casey was illiterate and he had no idea if Staruff could read. His heart sank. He shook his head and squared his shoulders. *They deserve a farewell.*

It would be difficult to get past the guards. His father was hardly an idiot, despite his recent bull-headedness, and he would surely have instructed his men to prevent him from leaving. However, there was nothing a man could do about shadows moving across the floor.

Damon smiled grimly and waited for his chance. The cloud cover was spotty today and he had to wait until the courtyard was shielded from the sun before heading out. He pressed his back against the cool stone wall and concentrated. The elusive wisps of his magic were becoming easier to grasp since he'd begun sparring while using it. He was getting used to catching hold of them and making them do what he wanted. Only simple things for now, but trying to do anything complex during the heat of a fight was nonsensical anyway.

Finally, he felt himself melt into the shadow, like a sigh with his entire body. It was relaxing, certainly and he would spend a lot more time like this if he wasn't terrified of getting stuck that way.

Damon cast around the hall. No one was acting out of order. Good; he hadn't been seen. When the sun hid its face at last, he made a beeline for the stables. Travelling in a straight line was hard and he kept wanting to double back to make sure he hadn't lost any of himself. It was silly. In fact, he could feel every inch of his shadow form keenly. He swirled around the horses' hooves, searching for Silhouette's stall.

The stallion was quite out of sorts and looked as though he hadn't been groomed in a couple of days. *Of course. I bet you wouldn't let anyone near you, hum? Did you bite Sunev?* The thought made him smile.

He focused on returning to his proper shape. It seemed to Damon that the first thing he always felt when re-solidifying was his feet pressing against the ground as his weight returned. He always compared it to pulling himself out of the water after a long swim.

Silhouette pinned his ears back and gave Damon an accusing look. "Sorry," he whispered to the horse. "Da wouldn't let me go anywhere. I'm still not supposed to be here but there's something I have to do." He picked up the brush and began tending his horse. Silhouette stood still for the most part, brooding. Occasionally, he bumped Damon with his shoulder to let him know all was not forgiven just yet. Damon sighed. "You'd rather I sneaked out sooner, hum?"

The horse whickered quietly. A stable hand walked by and Damon stepped behind the stallion until he passed. He didn't know how much his father talked with the servants but if Silhouette turned up missing, they would be the first ones he asked. Though, with any luck Damon would be back before anyone noticed.

He saddled his horse and swung up onto his back. The ceiling supports obliged him to keep his head low but once he was out into the sunshine it was clear sailing. Damon drew his hood up over his head. He gave Silhouette's sides a squeeze with his legs and the stallion lunged into motion. Up ahead, he could make out sentries posted at the gates. This would be interesting.

Damon kept one hand up, holding his hood down so it would conceal his face. The two guards closest to the castle gates glanced back and looked to each other. They could see the Stonehart crest on his shoulder and they could certainly see the flash of his mount's steely hooves. Damon's heart rose to his throat, eyeing their halberds uneasily, but Silhouette didn't slow or even break stride.

The polearms did not cross in front of him. Instead, the guard on the right stepped back a pace to give him more room. To them, he was not Damon, he was "a Stonehart"; or more probably "a bloody Stonehart sorcerer." He smiled under his hood, satisfied with his escape.

Only in front of the inn where Casey stayed did he let down his hood. Mor, of course, was not happy to see him.

"You fuckin' tricked me!"

Damon looked down at him from Silhouette's back. The horse showed teeth and stamped a hoof.

"Where is Casey the Giant, please?" he asked politely, instead of responding to the accusation.

Mor eyed the charger in front of him with caution. "Tourney. Where the hell d'you think he'd be? He doesn't sulk in his room all day ya know?" He was about to say something else but Silhouette had already begun to walk away. Damon put a hand on the side of the horse's neck, guiding him toward to the street he needed to take. Likely, the barkeep knew nothing of how much the remark stung him but it did all the same. He wasn't interested in playing word games with people today, only his errand concerned him.

Casey was not hard to find, all one had to do was look over everyone's heads for a mop of rusty-blond hair. The mercenary was treating a cut on his forearm from a recent bout. Staruff, standing by his side swatted the giant's arm and pointed at Damon.

He dismounted and went to them, feeling shy now that he had found them. He cleared his throat.

"Sorry I haven't been around."

The giant blinked at him. Staruff's expression was inscrutable.

"Thought we scared ya off? Kicked yer ass real nice last time eh?" Casey chuckled.

The sound warmed Damon and he found himself smiling as well. "Yeah well, my da found out what I was doing and wouldn't let me leave the castle." Silhouette rested his chin on Damon's shoulder. There was a melancholy sag to the horse's posture. Damon petted his nose.

"He grounded you?" Staruff spoke at last. His pale brows drew together.

"He what?"

"Grounded. Like when you tie a falcon's foot to a post until it calms and stops misbehaving." The smaller mercenary put his hands on his hips.

"Uh, yes." Damon nodded. "I guess so."

"I thought yeh said ya were a man, not a kid." Casey tied the bandage ends and tucked the loose tips into the layers.

Damon frowned. "I am. You've seen my sword."

Staruff snickered. Damon didn't see what was so funny.

"What?"

"Both of them, yes," the madman elaborated.

Damon stared, uncomprehending for a moment. "Oh, you mean the tattoo."

Staruff gave him a wide grin. "Yes. Sure, the tattoo." Casey elbowed him and joined in on his private laugh.

Damon reflected that his friends really were quite strange. "Anyway, I wanted to find you two and tell you that I'd come see you again if I could. But I'm kind of trapped and I don't know when da will let me go about my own business again."

"That's horseshit!" Casey declared. Silhouette made an annoyed grunt but the giant paid no attention. "He can't do that."

"He can, actually." Damon frowned. "Even if I'm an adult, he still outranks me."

"Fuck that!" Casey put his hands on his hips and put his shoulders back. His shadow nearly encompassed both Damon and Silhouette with the sun ambling toward the horizon. "You stay with us. We'll show 'im."

Damon shook his head. "You could get in a lot of trouble for tha-"

"I said fuckit!" The mercenary cut him off. "Gunna give 'im a gift, an' he'll like me."

Did the giants of Dawnshire form the same gift-giving relationships as the Northmen? He thought not. Damon frowned as

Casey's grin was back on his face.

"We'll make a gift for 'im. You an' me an' I'll bring it to 'im. You'll see."

Damon nodded reluctantly. It was worth trying, he supposed. He was already in about as much trouble as he could get into.

Damon was having second thoughts when they crossed the treeline. The forest was about a day's ride from the city. Casey sat astride his gigantic yak he called Boob, so named for the large dark spot in the middle of his pale fluffy head, while Staruff trailed behind them on a grey mare; he did not have a name for her.

"Aright! Now let's get drunk! I need to find a pig!"

He stared at Casey's receding back for a moment. *Strange request indeed.* He shrugged and followed.

"What are we doing?" Damon asked, looking up at the thinning golden leaves over his head.

"You? Prolly nothin'." Casey swatted a branch aside. Boob grunted at a root he was obliged to step over. The lazy creature was clearly not impressed at this walk through the woods. "I'm gonna get a pig."

He blinked at the giant's back. Then, he glanced back at Staruff. The blonde mercenary just shrugged.

"There's no ... wait, you mean a boar?"

Casey laughed. "Yup. Piggy pig. Good eatin'." He nodded to himself. "Saw one out here yesterday. Good idea t' keep these things in yer head fer later in case rations get cut."

It was then that Damon realized the giant was serious about giving his father an actual *gift*. He had assumed that Casey meant to pull a prank on him. Perhaps the giant knew something about Northern etiquette after all.

"Don't you want to leave it for later then?" Damon scrunched his nose, still trying to get a handle on the fact that the giant just decided to go take on a very dangerous beast without much preparation.

Casey reined in his mount and looked back.

"This's important to ya right?"

"Well, yes but not if it gets you killed. My father loves boar but-"

"Then I'm doin' it. We're friends."

Silhouette whickered and bobbed his head, ears flicking around. Damon leaned forward.

"You smell it?"

The horse bobbed his head again and turned it, looking fixedly off to the left.

"How far?" The stallion danced under him a bit but quickly settled. He pawed the dried leaves under his hooves. "Not far? Two minutes?" Silhouette kept pawing. "Five minutes? Seven?" The horse went still. "Okay about seven min ..."

Staruff whistled.

"What?" Damon turned around in the saddle.

"Smart horse."

Damon regarded the grey mare standing docile and looking for nourishment on the forest floor. Did he mean she couldn't do that? He felt bad for Staruff, having to ride an idiot horse.

"Aright, you two wait here. I'm gonna go get it." He took a heavy club from the side of Boob's saddle and sighed. "Someday, I'm gonna have a real nice spear." With that, he nudged the yak off the trail and into the bush.

Staruff and Damon waited in near silence, straining their ears for any sign of Casey's efforts.

"What will you do if he fails?" the mercenary asked. His gaze lingered on the trunks of the trees in front of him.

"If he doesn't bring back the boar?"

Staruff barked a laugh. "He will bring it back." He shook his head. "If your father does not take the gift well."

Damon brought his shoulders nearly to his ears with his shrug. "I don't know. In fact, I don't really understand why he's doing this."

"Let me tell you something." Staruff took one foot out of his stirrup and crossed his leg over the front of his saddle, sitting haphazardly on the grazing mare. "When we first arrived here, some of the locals got pretty uppity at us; not pleased at hosting so many mercenaries, that sort of thing. It seems mercenaries are known for having less *honour* than men who fight for one lord their whole lives." He rolled his pale eyes and shook his head. Damon winced. He'd heard just about the same words from his father. "Casey's often the one who gets picked at the most when people don't know us. Local idiots come around and fluff their feathers, trying to impress each other.

"This one fool came and stood in front of Boob in a narrow street. Wouldn't let us pass. Casey got down to see what his problem was."

"Was he by himself?" Damon interrupted.

Staruff laughed again and let his gaze drift up to the branches overhead. "No, they never are." Damon reflected on the truth of this statement. Staruff continued. "He was just mouthy, you know. Trying to get Casey to swing first so he'd feel justified ganging up on him. He insulted Casey, called him 'ugly.' Casey just said 'yeah? And what?' Little shit, said Casey's mother was a whore."

Damon gasped. "Aervie, he must have killed him!"

The mercenary shook his head. "No. He just said 'I dunno, an' she's dead now so she can't hear ya.' So Little Shit decides to insult Casey's homeland and upbringing and just about anything he can think of, really running out of things to say at that point. Casey just told him to go down to South Dawnshire and tell them all that. I expected all this to be quick so I stayed on my horse. Little Shit points at me and asks Casey if his 'girlfriend there is too much of a coward to come back him up.'"

Damon stared. "Did *you* kill him?"

Staruff pinched the tip of his tongue between his teeth and grinned his unpleasant, manic grin. "Didn't get a chance. Casey picked him up by his head and threw him up on the roof of his house. At least I think it was his house. Threw him two floors, anyhow, and yelled like a bull while he did it too. It was great!"

He frowned. "I don't understand. He loves you more than his mother?"

"Casey values his friends and chooses his loyalties carefully; and when he does, he sticks to them. As his friends, you and I, we have the privilege of knowing his highest loyalty."

To hear it articulated so, Damon finally understood why he had to disagree with his father on this matter. "You have a knack for saying things no one wants to hear, even if they're true."

Staruff bared his teeth at him. "Of course: that's what madmen are for."

A thrash in the bushes followed by a series of annoyed squeals ended their conversation. Casey appeared and dropped a hog-tied boar in front of them. Staruff jumped off his horse, which had begun to sidestep nervously at the sight of the boar. Silhouette, for his part, just lowered his head to sniff the struggling animal.

Casey pulled a sack and other wrappings out of Boob's saddle bag.

"Are you going to butcher it right here?" Damon asked.

"Nope." The giant jabbed a finger in his direction. "You are."

He frowned. "I don't know how to butcher a boar."

Casey laughed. "No Corpse, ya don't know how t' cut anything up fer shit; but thas the point. Git out yer sword."

He curled his fingers around the grip of his sword, reluctant. "With my ... I don't want to cut up an animal with my sword! That's what hunting knives are for!"

"Swords're fer cuttin' meat, thas all." Casey snorted. "Don' tell me yer one of those who names his sword n' thinks it's sacred 'r some shit?"

Damon sighed and released the handle. "It hasn't earned its name yet."

"You haven't killed anyone yet!" Staruff exclaimed. The mercenary grabbed him by the shoulder and pulled his sword part-way from the scabbard to examine the blade. Damon ducked his head forward, wary of the potential for accidental harm. "How the hell can you be a man without having killed anyone?"

He pressed his weight onto the balls of his feet, keeping himself from toppling over while Staruff jostled him. "That isn't how it works among the Stonehearts. We become a man or a woman when we come of age to properly manage a household."

Staruff shoved the sword back into the scabbard, forcing Damon to rock onto his heels to keep from falling backward. "Ridiculous."

Damon's brows drew together and he felt his belly clench a bit. He didn't like it when the madman was upset. "Anyway, I don't have to kill someone to have my sword named. It just has to serve me in combat where my life is threatened."

"I've tried to kill you before, let me name it." Staruff put his hands on his hips, ignoring the boar wriggling in the leaf litter at his feet.

He hesitated. Though he burned to have the honour of a named weapon, he didn't exactly trust Staruff the Mad to give it a good name. At the same time, he didn't want to insult his friend by saying so.

"What? Is there some rule against that too?"

"Um ... no. You just have to be of age and have five years of combat experience."

Staruff nodded curtly. "I qualify."

Damon pursed his lips for a moment. "Hang on, how old are you?"

"Eighteen summers."

"You've been fighting since you were *thirteen*?" His jaw dropped; it was hard to imagine such a thing.

The blonde mercenary tilted his head to the side. The subtle curve of his lips betrayed a mild amusement. "Before that, even. You thought survival was so much easier south of Glasshammer?"

Damon sighed, recovering from his shock. "Fine, fine." He drew his sword and held out the blade to Staruff. "Name it, then. We'll see if it accepts the name."

The mercenaries both peered at the glistening steel.

"Yeh mean it c'n say no? I never heard it talk ..." Casey tapped the flat of the blade with his fingertip.

"My Da says you can feel it when the sword takes its name." Damon shrugged. Just another facet of Stonehart magic. Once again, he was reminded of just how few people actually possessed such power anymore. It was a little disconcerting.

Staruff leaned over the blade, examining it closely. The only sound now was the exhausted grunts and shuffles of the bound boar. He bent closer still until his lips were almost touching it and whispered to the steel as though sharing a secret. A sudden vibration shooting up the weapon almost made Damon drop it. The mercenary straightened and looked at him. He seemed to perceive the change in expression on Damon's face because he smiled.

"It accepted it, didn't it?"

Damon looked down at the sword, scrunching his forehead in concentration. It felt different somehow. Perhaps heavier. Perhaps more alert and alive if one could say that of an inanimate weapon. "Yes?" He turned his wrist, rotating the blade slowly back and forth. He recognized the subtle blur of blue around the metal that marked his blood magic. Staruff moved up next to his shoulder to look at the blade from the same angle as Damon. "Yes. What did you say to it?"

The mercenary leaned close to him and murmured in his ear.

"You can't call it that!"

"Why?"

Damon took his hand off the hilt and rubbed the bridge of his nose. "Because most Stonehearts take the name of their sword as their middle name."

Staruff burst into laughter. Casey looked between them with a confused, lopsided grin.

"What?"

"It's perfect!"

Damon let out an aggravated growl. "No, it's not! Why would you think that was a good name?"

"You can change its name?"

"*No.*"

"What did he call it?" Casey leaned forward as though expecting a good joke.

Damon glared at both of them, very much regretting letting a madman name his sword.

"Misery." The glow flared as the blade took note.

Casey joined Staruff in his mirth. "Yeah! Corpse Misery Stonehart. Perfect! Yeh got the best name ever! C'n I get adopted inta yer family? My weapons're called Fuck You and Ha Ha."

Damon made to sheathe his sword but Casey put out a hand.

"Wait wait, yeh gotta do the pig."

The boar renewed its struggles as he approached it. He took a deep breath and let it out, trying to quell the burn of anger in his chest.

"Fine; but while you take the meat to my father, Staruff is going to find me an engraver." He turned to the blonde mercenary who was wiping tears from his eyes and mastering his laughter. "And *pay* for it as well."

Staruff sobered. "Engraving on blades is expensive."

Damon gestured at him with this sword. "You're a man. Apparently more of one than I am. We know and accept that there are consequences for our actions."

Staruff contemplated this for a moment, casting his pale eyes up at a leaf as it twirled through the air. He nodded.

"Great. Now give me some space so I can give *Misery* its first kill."

Erik looked at the hunks of boar meat the mercenary presented him. The man was huge and if he guessed right, he would say he was a Giant from the south. He wasn't sure exactly how many people it would take to throw the man out.

"What is this, then?" The chieftain indicated the partly unwrapped chunks.

"A gift, like I said, M'lord." The Giant, Casey Baysmuth smiled proudly. "I'da brought yeh the boar whole but we butchered it fer yeh 'nstead."

Erik frowned. "Butchered?"

"Yes, M'lord."

He watched the cold blood from the meat dribble from one of the wrappings and begin soaking into the stone floor.

"It looks like it was taken apart by a child with a hatchet."

Instead of being offended, the mercenary burst into a peel of laughter. It was painfully loud indoors. Erik narrowed his eyes, waiting for him to be finished.

"It was, but with a sword." Casey indulged in a few more guffaws before explaining himself. "But I think you an' yer kin decided he was a man, M'lord. I dunno if that was a mistake 'r not."

Erik stiffened like a listening hound. "You know where my son is?"

The Giant scratched his chin. "Either getting some engraving done or at the inn, I think. I dunno. Wherever him an' Staruff decided t' go. He c'n come back to yeh whenever he wants."

"I have had my kinsmen looking for him all bloody day and you are trying my patience." Erik pressed his knuckles against the table he was leaning on. He pushed down until the strain on the joints started to ache. He was determined not to assault this man. Erik Stonehart was above brawling with hired swords. "What do you want?"

"Nothin' much. Jus' let 'im keep trainin' with us. We like 'im. He's a good man, a good friend. Jus' needs some 'elp with the ..." He made a gesture like executing a few overhead hews with a sword, brushing his fingers against the ceiling as he did so. "Business o' makin' the other fella dead while not gettin' dead hisself."

Erik glared. "You're the ones who have been beating him up?"

Once again, the big man let loose a bark of glee. "Yeah! Wipin' the fuckin' floor with 'im! But really, look 'ere." He raised his bandaged forearm. "Startin' t' give back. Not as good as 'e gets yet but we're workin' at it. Good job 'e c'n throw magic n' shit around. Really gives 'im a leg up."

For a moment, the anger melted a little in the face of his surprise. "He can ... throw magic? Explain?"

"He not been tellin' yeh all about it?" Casey looked confused. "Huh. I'da thought 'e'd be proud as a foot-long cock t' show ya what 'e can do!"

Erik winced at the colourful image the mercenary presented him with. "No. We've not been ... things have kept us occupied. Fighting an invasion is no small matter." He crossed his arms.

Up to that point, mobilizing the army had been a thing of nightmares. The vast majority of their scouts failed to return and the few that did were shot full of arrows. With so little information on at their disposal, Harlon's men were blind in the face of the enemy. To say that tensions were high

202

would be a gross understatement. The last meeting among the lords nearly devolved into a fistfight.

Duke Astor had gone so far as to declare he was turning his men homeward before the snow came and had to be threatened with a trade embargo before he grudgingly agreed to stay.

We are the few, the disorganized, and the unwilling. Aervie help us all.

"Well we oughta fix that." Casey nodded sagaciously, bringing Erik back to the matter at hand. "If 'e can teach the rest o' yer kin some o' that, I think we might be alright. Then again, from what I hear a fuckin' swarm o' the Asp's army jus' came up outta nowhere little while ago so I dunno. Here's hopin'."

"He's been practising magic with you." It was not a question.

"Well yeah, M'lord. It'd be pretty shit if 'e killed one o' you nobles. Whadda yeh call 'em? Darkbloods? Yeah. Couple o' mercs, not so much, eh?" Casey spread his hands. The wide hazel eyes looking down at Erik were guileless as a lamb, in spite of his filthy mouth.

"Awfully selfless of you," Erik said, the skepticism leaking into his voice.

"Bullshit!" The Giant put his hands on his hips and stretched his back until it gave a satisfying pop. "Men o' the sword gotta look out for each other. I do this now n' maybe he saves my ass later. 'nvestin' in yer comrade's never a wasted thing."

Erik rubbed his temples. It was true that his son was awfully green to combat and the proof was in the badly hacked boar in front of him. He sighed. He had to at least figure out what sort of nonsense these yahoos had put into his head. "Well, this is clearly more than I can eat," he said at last. "Why don't you tell Damon and your friend ... Starup?"

"Staruff."

"Staruff. Yes. Tell them to come to the dining hall at dusk. You may dine with the rest of our family and we will see what they have to say. Perhaps the wisdom of the other family heads will prevail on him where I cannot."

"Fair 'nuff." Casey nodded. "Right nice o' yeh t' invite us teh dinner."

"Yes, well, bring your wits as well as your appetite. If the answer is 'no,' you will respect our wishes and keep away from Damon."

"Sure! I'll go tell 'em. Good meetin' ya, M'lord." Casey turned and waved over his shoulder as he ducked out of the room.

Erik sighed at the badly-butchered meat and resigned himself to seeing what the cooks could make out of it.

Chapter 11: The Birds Beneath

Phoenix's fight with Sora, the Regent's champion, was to take place in a prison where the Prince was stationed as head of the royal guard. This had at first made little sense to her, but when she saw it, her confusion changed into awe: this was nothing like any prison she had ever seen. There were no bars, no holding cells, and no buildings to speak of. Instead, there were great stone eggs sitting up on their wide ends.

Dyseris had mentioned "The Eggs" earlier, but she had not understood what he meant. She had thought it was simply a colloquial term for cells but she might have known better: the Ducal were a very literal people. These were enchanted things made to encase the criminals of Hanuel under Frozen Sky. There were no doors or latches on them and no openings that she could see. She had asked, when they first arrived, how the incarcerated managed to breathe. Dyseris had simply said "they sleep," and would say no more on the subject. Phoenix was willing to cast a wager that the Tamiyon had something to do with their creation.

If duals of succession were always fought here, she could see why: except for the orderly, smooth rows of the Eggs, there was nothing here; nothing that could be damaged, at least.

She stood in the centre of a roped-off area at the base of a short stair leading up into the main prison area, trying to struggle into some borrowed armour before she faced her quarry. She had not expected the Regent to force her into her duel with Prince Sora quite so soon and she did her best to ignore the crowds of staring Ducal. Many had transformed to their bird shapes and perched on nearby rooftops where they could afford a better view.

Phoenix tossed the leather chest guard aside and settled on a plain white shift and pair of breeches. While the Tamiyons had provided her with a decent sword and the finest armour they could muster, it seemed that the shamans were lacking in the way of true battle garb. She supposed it was fair for such powerful magic-wielders to rely more on their abilities than their physical prowess in the heat of a battle, but she still considered it something of a failure to put too much stock in the arcane when a sword would do just as well.

Sora stood at the top of the stairs, watching her. His pale eyes, hard as diamonds, followed her every movement as she prepared herself for combat. Phoenix felt a strange sensation in his presence. His calm was so unlike the other bird-men it disturbed her; yet nothing about his countenance was all that menacing. On the contrary, he was rather handsome. His pale blonde hair was cut shorter than most others and he had fair skin, like his father's.

"A Tamiyon," she said.

Dyseris, at her side, cringed. "Don't say that out loud!"

She ignored him, raising her voice a little. "I would say that he and Kael must be at least blood-kin if not brothers."

The prince's eyes narrowed and she knew she was right. The Ducal around her chattered and the air was full of fluttering and bird calls for a moment. Sora lifted his hand and silence descended again. If Bowen was here, she could not see him. He could be any one of those birds and she would never know.

"Tell me again what I am supposed to do?" she asked Dyseris.

The raven man smiled and placed his hands on his hips, giving a little jerk of his chin toward Sora. "Go and touch one of the Eggs behind him."

Phoenix looked over her shoulder at him. "I thought you said this was a duel to the death?"

"Yes."

"If I touch the Egg, he dies?"

"No."

Phoenix drew her sword, letting the shush of metal and the weight of the blade calm her. Dyseris' eyes locked onto the blade.

"Explain the rules to me," she demanded, extending her sword towards him. "I cannot afford to make a mess of this."

"He will die before he will let you touch one of his charges." The voice that spoke was not Dyseris' but rather Kael's. Phoenix turned around to look at him.

"How long have you been standing there?"

"Long enough." The shaman pointed at the prince. "Go and challenge him formally. I wish to begin your training as soon as possible."

She glared at him. When she turned to approach Sora, she realized he was levelling the exact same gaze at Kael as well. A smile tugged at the corners of her lips and she pressed her lips together to hide it. She walked up to the base of the steps and lifted her blade straight up.

"I am told I must fight you, Prince Sora. I do not want to."

"Then go away."

She had not expected such a response and it took her a moment to think of something to say. She looked down at his hip and realized that he wore a sword as well, not claw weapons. The sight of such a familiar setting slowed her racing heart enough to let her mind work again. He had not spoken the words rashly or even rudely; it was simply a suggestion.

"Is there any other way to lead the Ducal? Can I convince you step down or forfeit?"

"No. No."

He rested his palm on the pommel of his sword. It was a relaxed gesture. She wondered if she would ever feel so comfortable in front of so many people.

She took a deep breath and let it out slowly. The muscles in her gut refused to unclench. *Waiting will not make it any easier. Let us do this and be done.*

"Very well then, Ducal Prince. I challenge you to a duel."

Sora drew his sword.

They stood for a long moment, assessing each other. Phoenix felt he blood throbbing in her chest and she fought for calm. Her knuckles whitened on the grip as she remembered the reassuring weight of the blade. She turned to the side, making herself as small a target as possible. Sora did not have this advantage. He was forced to stand squarely before the Egg to keep her from getting past.

If I can overpower him, there will be no need to slay him.

He moved first. The Ducal's glossy boots clacked on the stone as he leaped from the top stair. Gravity sped his charge. She watched his blade glitter through the air, sweeping left and right, as if it were trying to draw an eternity symbol but had somehow forgotten the rest of the pattern. It was almost too fast to follow. She moved to block on the right only to realize it was nothing but a feint.

Phoenix turned quickly, sidestepping, but pain still blossomed up her left side. She danced off to the right glancing down to see the damage. There was a shallow slash up the left side of her ribs; harmless, but it would bleed profusely if she weren't careful.

Sora did not attack again right away. Instead, his pale eyes studied her intently. She read the signs on his face. The small lines deepening between his brows. He was displeased. *Did he expect to finish me immediately?* If he had, his confidence would not be quite so steady now.

Phoenix reset her stance and tried to circle him. He sidestepped, dutifully keeping himself between her and the prison.

This is unfair, she thought. It was always harder to defend than to attack. Always one other thing to bear in mind. She was free; only her own life was at stake. Perhaps, she could forfeit and walk away unscathed but her pride said otherwise. Even if she could postpone this, it would only give her more time to worry about it. She smiled grimly. In this cold, bizarre world, here was something she understood at last. *The time is now: this is my forte; I will not fail.*

Phoenix brought the blade around and stepped in. She swung at Sora head-on, wanting to see his reply. Solaras never toyed with opponents but reading their movements was essential to victory. The Ducal met her strike with assurance. He turned her blade aside and stepped in, driving for her chest. Despite his swiftness and obvious lethal intent, he did not quite manage to twist it out of the lock of her cross-guard. She pushed his sword up and away from her. Steel ground together, sending reverberations through her hands. He grappled for a moment, but she kept turning the crossguard against his movements and he could make no headway.

Sora took a couple of steps backward, trying to free his blade and reset his stance. She realized that he was either holding back, or that she had the upper hand in strength. He did not seem to be able to wrench his blade down and away safely. Her mouth pulled upward at the corners. He was obliged to yield precious meters of ground to her. One more pace and he would have to step up onto the bottom stair. The space he had gained by his initial leap down on her would soon be lost. She lashed out her leg and kicked him in the shin.

He sucked in air, wincing in pain, and moved to return the favour but she stepped back and disengaged. Though his teeth were bared in discomfort, there was little other indication of disquiet about the Prince. He did not seem worried, but the lines about his eyes suggested otherwise; even if he had was frightened, she refused to underestimate him. *Fight every battle as if faced with a master swordsman.*

Phoenix closed the distance again. She feinted to the left, spun, and brought her blade up from the right. He shifted quickly and the blades clashed again. She was forced to brace herself on one knee for a moment. Her muscles flexed. Despite his weight bearing down on her, she was able to rise to her feet and block his kick. His boots gave him much more protection than her slippers but she was not sure if he had as much traction. He set his heel on the step and moved backward out of reach.

Sora was sweating slightly. *Already?* She felt her spirits rise. He seemed to favour very short clashes. His aim was vicious but there were strikes he did not take when he could. Nevertheless, she was quite sure that he did not fear harming her. The blood soaking into the fabric of her pants told her that much.

She half-circled him in lazy crescents, looking for an opening. He was obliged to continue moving back and forth to hold his guard over the prison.

It was time to test a theory. *Who is stronger, Ducal? I think I know.* She moved in, blade parallel to the ground, pommel tucked in nearly against her belly. She sidestepped as Sora stepped forward, but it was only a feint. Her blade came around and clashed against his. She did not waste time on locking him up and getting close. Instead, she stepped back and brought her blade around from the other side as she came forward again.

Her deep green eyes went wide. They soaked in every last piece of information she could glean: his attitude, the posture of his body and his movements. *There!* His shoulders rocked noticeably in their sockets when she struck at him. He was quick, that was for certain but his strength, did not match up to hers and he was beginning to suffer for it.

Again, he moved up the stairs. She did not let him disengage but followed him. She brought down blow after blow. *I will chip at you until your arms go numb.*

She twirled her sword around his, trying to loosen his grip. Abruptly, she changed direction. He moved to step back and regain his balance. In that window, she jumped forward and lashed out with her leg. She did not manage to strike his belly, he twisted too quickly for that, but she landed a solid blow to his hip. He staggered and almost tripped. He jogged up the last few steps sideways. It was an awkward move and she had gained the stairs, but she could not fault him for it. It was too dangerous to face her on unstable ground.

They were now only a few meters from the Egg. Sora's attacks became more ferocious. He deliberately struck for her head and belly. Phoenix met him boldly and blocked every attack. Her arms were steady, her grip sure. She swung up from the left. The Ducal guarded it and their hilts locked again. His face shone with sweat and he shifted his weight in anticipation of another kick. Phoenix judged the way he moved his feet from side to side to indicate his wish to retreat; but, they both knew there was nowhere left to go.

She squeezed her left hand tightly on the grip of her sword until her left arm alone held his blade from coming down on her. It was time to make a gamble.

Her right hand came off of the hilt, balled into a fist, and drove upward into his gut. Sora's eyes went wide as he tried to take a breath. For an instant, his grip loosened. It was all she needed and she twisted the weapon out of his grasp. It clattered on the stone behind her, far out of his reach. The Ducal bent as he tried to retrieve the knife from his boot but she brought the flat of her sword down on his shoulder. He grunted and rolled backward out of her reach.

She knew the knife would not be much good for blocking but it was light and could be dangerous if he could get around her guard. All the same, Phoenix knew her gamble had worked. He was less sure of himself without his blade. The left shoulder—the one she had struck—hung lower than the other. She could not tell if it was dislocated or cramped. If he had to grapple, the match would likely go in her favour and he seemed to be well aware of this. His eyes kept flicking to the discarded sword. His weight shifted from leg to leg.

Thinking of how to get around me without exposing the egg. She darted in and swung. He ducked and tried to lunge under her guard. She brought her hilt down hard on his hand. The knife fell but with his left hand, he grasped her cross guard. The arm was not injured at all. *Damnit!* They struggled for the weapon. She did not let go. *I have been too long without a blade. I will not let it be taken from me now.*

Sora thudded to his knees and for a moment, she thought he had fallen. He rose quickly, throwing his weight against her midsection, and lifting her off of the floor. She writhed and kicked. He grabbed her wounded side and she gasped in pain. Her vision fogged but she kept thrashing. He would not get the clean throw he was looking for if he could even keep his feet. Phoenix was not quite sure if she was upside down or not but the wild slash she delivered earned a scream. She smelled blood.

In an instant, she was in the air, head over heels and striking something solid and unforgiving. There was a deafening crack, as though she were flying through a thunderhead. Then, she hit the floor.

She stared up at the egg as bright golden tendrils snaked across its surface. Her focusing stone felt like it was about to explode, or perhaps shoot backward through her skull. Pain wracked her body. She was sure it had nothing to do with the fall, for the golden lighting raked over her as well. The egg began to split down the sides. Huge pieces fell away. She could not move. The only thing left to do, was watch the smooth, heavy stone pieces of shell come down on her as the light within sprang forth from its prison.

Hazy shapes moved across her vision. At first, she thought it was fire, but the colour was all wrong. White and ethereal. It wasn't hot either. She turned her head slowly and looked at the rough stone wall beside her. No, not a wall, she remembered now; it was a fragment of the egg. Quickly, she turned her head the other way and was rewarded by a sharp jab in her skull and the lights lurching and swimming all around her. She swallowed hard, praying for the bile to stay down.

When her sight began to clear again, she saw him. Kael knelt in the rubble beside her. The bright tendrils of light flowed and twined around him. He was looking over her to something beyond.

"I said stay back," he said. His voice was quiet but full of venom.

"Kael." Phoenix coughed and he looked down at her for a moment. She wiped a hand across her face, trying to clear some of the dust away. Her other hand still gripped her sword. "Kael, what are you doing?"

"Guarding, until you awaken."

She smiled. "Thank you."

"It is my duty. My life is yours. You are Queen." His pale brows were drawn down as if in anger. He did not look at her. "Order them back."

Phoenix blinked slowly. "Order?"

Kael jerked his chin. She slowly rolled onto her side, wincing in pain. Gripping the fallen chunk of egg shell, she managed to lever herself into a roughly seated position. Her head swam. She took deep breaths through her nose and tried to keep the nausea at bay.

Sora held his sword, point downward a few meters away. Dyseris was beside him. His dark face was creased with worry.

"The fight is over," she said. She swallowed and sat still for a moment. This was no time to be making errors of judgement. "Sheathe your blade and stay back."

The Ducal prince's eyes narrowed but he looked more hurt than anything else. He did as he was told. Phoenix could see blood on the legs of his breeches but not where he was hurt. Why wasn't he getting himself to a healer? The spectators simply stared, their chattering soft and urgent.

She opened her mouth but Kael shifted behind her and grabbed the back of her head. Light filled her vision. Loud grinding and popping noises reverberated inside her head. She couldn't hear anything else. She may have cried out, but it was all silence.

How much time passed before she could see again, she could not tell. Sora still stood where he had been before. His face was white with rage and every muscle in his body seemed to be clenched. Dyseris was touching his arm, and murmuring to him.

"All is mended now," Kael said.

She turned sharply to look at him. There was no pain. She looked down at her wounded side and found it barely deeper than a scratch. She returned her gaze to the shaman.

"Are you alright?" she asked.

He stared at her. His pale eyes were blank. She frowned at him. Didn't it tax him to wield such magic? What was it about the Upperworld that made such power inadequate? She wondered, now, what made her his weapon of choice for the conquest he planned. *I will find out soon enough.* She had won, and now her training could begin. *So, you would wield the fangs of the desert, Bird-Man?*

"Say 'thank you'," Phoenix said.

"Why?" Kael sat back on his heels, his lips pursed.

"Because I deserve it." She stared back at him, refusing to blink.

"Thank you." There was neither gratitude nor irritation in his voice. Phoenix could not decide which was more annoying: this expressionless mask he presented to the world, or the flailing and squawking that Dyseris and the other Ducal engaged in when upset.

She stared a moment longer. Then, she rose to her feet and extended an arm toward Dyseris. "Give me my robe, please." He threw it to her promptly. Now that the fight was over, she was cold. She turned it in her hands, deliberately swatting Kael's shoulder with it in the process, and put it on. She began to pick her way through the rubble towards the other two Ducal.

"This fight is ended," she said again to Sora. "What will you do now?"

Sora's eyes kept shifting between her and the shaman behind her, wary like an animal. He shook his head.

"I will seek reassignment," he said at last.

"You will not pursue revenge? You will not attempt to end your life? Explain."

"I have failed in my duties," he said. "I have guarded my post to the best of my strength. It was not enough. There is nothing here for me to protect, save yourself, your Highness." The quiet chatter of the Ducal around them rose until it was hard for her to hear his words. "I am alive by happenstance. It happens sometimes. There is no need to pursue further

211

action. My death now, after the fact, would be meaningless."

She nodded, satisfied with the answer. "I will see the Regent now. There is much to discuss." She looked over her shoulder. Kael stood quietly amid the stone shards. He looked unperturbed, as if all of this were perfectly normal. She looked around, wondering which of these noisy avians was the Regent. "I will go to the Hearing Room."

She was not sure if she was now qualified to order Bowen to do anything but she left the suggestion that he join her there hanging ambiguously in the air.

"Kael, come with me," she said. The authority in her voice surprised her a little. *Well, better that than weakness.* She turned and began walking away from the crowd, away from the bloodied ground and broken Egg.

Phoenix resisted the urge to look over her shoulder to see if he was following. She heard nothing from Dyseris and Sora except footsteps when they had gotten further away from the prison. The smart clack of the prince's boots had become something of a shuffle. *I got him in the leg then. How badly?* There was no time for regret. She had allowed herself to hope and that hope had filled her with urgency.

Their passage through the city streets caused much activity, bordering on panic. The Ducal all seemed to recognize Kael. She wondered if he faced this kind of annoyance wherever he went. Were Tamiyons allowed to wander freely in Hanuel under Frozen Sky? She had never thought to ask.

It didn't matter now. All that was about to change. Ever since the White Asp had lain waste to Dunkhar, disorder and upheaval had dogged her steps. She saw the opportunity to grasp some kind of control and she aimed to do just that. Anything to stop the wild spiral of chaos that her life had become.

Phoenix ordered Kael to walk two paces behind her right shoulder so that everyone would see they were together. No one accosted him though it did not stop the cacophony of chatter produced by the onlookers. Kael remained quiet, his face unreadable. Sora trailed behind them.

The guards were equally perturbed by the appearance of the white-haired shaman. They shifted and glanced at each other, fingers flexing on weapons. Phoenix nodded to them. She reached back and grabbed Kael by the wrist, yanking him physically through the doors of the palace. He blinked at the handling but did not resist. No doubt he would rather be seized by her than the guards and he seemed to sense that her patience was at an end.

She stopped before the regent's Hearing Room door. There, she faced her new teacher. Kael regarded her calmly. His face was partly hidden by the framing of long hair. For a moment, he looked small to her, delicate even; but only for a moment.

"You know how to take back the sky, don't you?" she said, her voice low. She knew the answer.

He nodded slowly.

"You know how to return me to my home as well, don't you?"

A hint of a smile tugged the corner of his mouth. He nodded again.

"You know what I want. I know what you want. We will combine our strengths and we will have what we desire. Do you agree to this bargain?"

His head bobbed again and she reached out and grasped his throat. His dusty eyes widened for the first time.

"No double-crossing, no loop-holes, no twisting my words. Speak your agreement aloud and swear to it. I will make of you a new sheathe for my sword if you fail me."

Kael was silent for a moment, expressionless. She felt him swallow under her hand. "My life is yours, Queen. I must obey whatever you say. What bargain can there be between master and slave?"

Phoenix narrowed her eyes. "I do not want a slave. I want a general, a mentor. I will give you your life when we are through."

The guards by the door glanced at each other. She could see them in her peripheral vision. She knew she had said something dangerous. How much of this foreign culture had she grossly misunderstood? There was no time to grasp it. She might spend her whole life trying.

"The deal is struck, Phoenix Solara," he said finally. "I will do as you ask, all that you ask. Leave it in my hands and it will be done. The conditions will be met. This, I oath by the highest authority I know. I swear it by the name of the Phoenix. Command me."

She stared at him hard, trying to detect any hint of dishonesty in his gaze. It was like staring into frosted glass. It would have to do. She took her hand away from his neck and pushed open the door. Kael, still lead by the wrist, trotted after her.

"Regent!" she called. "Speak with me. And get off of my chair!"

Chapter 12: Serpent's Strike

The Stonehearts enjoyed the boar. At the dinner, Staruff had about a quarter pint of cider and immediately switched to beer, being unable to finish the strong drink while Casey, on the other hand, had taken no such precautions and praised the brewing talents of the clan heartily. To Damon's immense relief, neither of them had challenged each other, or their hosts, to a fight.

If Erik had hoped that the rest of the family would support his decision to ban Damon from associating with the hired swords, he had been sorely disappointed. He failed to take into account that the Stonehearts not involved in the war council had been actively visiting the tourney grounds and had seen the two mercenaries fight. It was evident from these brief encounters that their skill was undeniable, leading to the eventual decision that Damon would be permitted to continue his training with the mercenaries but only while under the watchful eye of a fellow clansman.

Damon asked Casey what he'd said to his father when he delivered the boar meat but the Giant claimed he didn't remember. In any case, the days of their private scuffles had come to an end. Too many of his kin were interested in watching the training and, moreover, learning how to wield magic as Damon did.

It was nice, he supposed, having the added responsibility of teaching. His cousins looked to him to bridge the gap between dusty tomes and reality. It was rewarding to see pebbles dance around their fingers, candle flames tie themselves into knots, cups of water freeze and boil in seconds. The Link had become stronger as well. They practices sending simple images and sounds to each other at points all over the city. At the end of the day, though, he was simply glad to return to the quiet of the library.

He found Lorne at their usual table, searching through a stack of papers in an agitated fashion. When he looked up, his expression brightened. "Damon, did I give you my notes on herbal enhancements of the blood?"

"Yes. Just a minute." He took the books out of his bag one at a time, looking through the pages for where he had put them. Lorne was a little obsessive about fraying the edges of his paper. 'Good knowledge is wasted when the medium is destroyed,' he would say. The librarian had fairly glowed the first time she heard him say so. Damon suspected she was sweet on him but his cousin remained oblivious.

At last, he returned the notes to him, in the book on the very bottom as luck would have it. Lorne seemed distracted, and more than a little waspish. He chewed the inside of his cheek while the book was checked over for signs of harm.

"Did you make any progress on the levitation spell you were working with last night?" he tried.

He was rewarded by the mood vanishing like fog before the sun. "Yes, actually. The balance of the aspects is different for each material. If I want to lift something, I have to know what it's made of, otherwise I could break it. Living things I wouldn't even try yet. I mean, I suspect it takes the aspects of earth and water, and perhaps blood as well. But if I tried, I might pull all the blood out of someone's body via their ears or something horrid like that."

Damon shuddered. "Please don't practice on anyone until you're sure eh?"

He laughed. "Not a chance. I'm curious, not reckless." He adjusted his legs, massaging the stiffness out of them. "However, I *can* lift the air around an object. That seems to work fine if I don't constrict it too hard. I'll show you later; right now I think your father wants a word."

He turned and saw Erik striding between bookcases, looking for them. He hesitated, but Lorne put his hand up and waved to attract his attention. Spotting them at last, he quickened his pace to reach them.

"There you are. How do you find your way through this maze? It seems to have no order whatso-"

Lorne gestured for him to be quiet. Erik looked around for the librarian.

"Eh, no order my unenlightened mind can pick out." He didn't fancy any scolding. "I was wondering if I could have my son to myself for a few minutes."

He rolled his eyes. "Must you?" Chuckling and gathering his papers together, Lorne extricated himself from his chair. He gave his legs a shake and walked stiffly off to one of the narrow spiral stairs to the second level. Damon and his father sat in silence until he had climbed to the narrow gallery that stretched all the way around the room and began browsing the books up there.

"Damon, did Sunev bring you the message?" Erik winced.

"If this is about the mercenaries-"

"It's not," he interrupted. "We move out at the end of the day, marching under the cover of darkness. We'll pitch camp sometime late morning tomorrow."

Damon swallowed hard. *So the orders come at last.* He knew they would, but still; to think that his quiet days in the library and outings to the tournament with Casey and Staruff would come to an end so sharply was a shock. Then again, there was a war on their doorstep: he had to remember that.

"I'll go find my friends." Then an idea presented itself. "Maybe I should stay with them while we're in camp?"

Erik looked skeptical. "I'd really prefer you stay with the Stonehearts, Damon. I like to keep an eye on you."

"If I'm not safe in camp, I'm not safe anywhere," he reasoned. "And if fighting breaks out, I'd rather fight with my back against someone I know. Besides, is it a good idea to keep all our magical protection cluttered up in the same place?" He slapped his father's arm lightly and let his eyes plead a little bit.

"You know, that is something I wasn't thinking of..." He frowned and stroked his beard for a moment. "You may be right about that. We should spread the Stonehearts around the encampment, in case something happens." He grinned. "I'll speak with the others about it and see what's to be done. You're right; we should be protecting everyone, not just ourselves." Erik clouted him on the back.

He felt a little dumbfounded but allowed himself to be hugged and made much of. As he excused himself and began his trek through the castle, he began to wonder if he *wasn't* inherently good at this battle business. He hadn't seriously intended to suggest that they change their camping plans, but it was a reasonable idea; a good idea, even. But it just seemed like common sense to him, not any sort of mystical inspiration.

Outside was a flurry of activity. He had to stick to the walls or risk being trampled by men, horses, and carts being moved out. It seemed that some units were already on their way and a flash of panic hit him. *What if Casey and Staruff are already on the road?* He picked up his pace, boots rapping against the cobblestones. Despite the business of the mobilizing army, anyone who saw the coronet on his brow nearly threw themselves out of the way. Damon wondered what sort of recourse he would have if anyone barred his path. The locals seemed to think it was fairly serious by the way they jumped about.

His worries evaporated when he cast his eyes on the huge wooly yak, Boob, still hitched to the parking rail outside Casey's inn. There was some congestion in the doorway with people shouting instructions to those inside and others trying to get out with bundles of gear slung over their backs. They stood aside for Damon as he squeezed himself through. His gigantic friend was sitting at a table in the middle of the room, casually sipping a mug of black tea. Staruff sat at his right side, eating a bit of bacon.

"Corpse! Hey!" Casey bellowed as soon as he saw him.

"Da says we can camp together. Took some convincing but I think he's coming around."

Staruff flashed a line of straight white teeth. That disturbingly wide smile. "Oh don't worry. I won't go easy on you for it. I enjoy spanking you in the ring too much for that."

"Hey, one of these days I'm going to beat you. You'll be walking funny and for no pleasant reason!" He shook a finger at him and his friend laughed. "Don't laugh too hard. You'll see."

"It's not that. Just how you said it." He shook his head, grey eyes dancing with mirth. "We've robbed you of some innocence I think."

"If anyone has, it's you, not me," Casey declared over his tea mug. "Yer more of a dog than I'll ever be. Yeh'll find a good time with anything tha's still warm."

"Tch." Staruff rolled his eyes. "Doesn't have to be."

"Ah stop!" Damon covered his ears, not wanting to hear any more disgusting stories. He didn't know if his friends made up these perversions to entertain themselves with his reactions but they always seemed to get him going. Casey, he knew, joked about a lot of things that he'd never do, but Staruff he wasn't so sure about. He had a good betting face.

"So you're travelling with us right?" Casey canted his head to the side. His large, blunt finger followed the mug's handle around and around, making it spin slow circles on the table.

His brow furrowed. "Well, I didn't exactly tell my father that..."

"Bah! Your pa has a battle standard. You can find him anytime you need him. We got nothin' but stinky old Boob."

Damon laughed. "I guess you're right. He will worry though."

"He'll worry if yer right beside him too. Difference is, yeh'll have to hear 'bout it." Casey's simple logic was difficult to argue with. He kneaded his temples.

"Okay but you have to come help me explain why I just vanished the day of the exodus."

"Fair 'nuff." Casey leaned back and stretched.

"I would be delighted." Staruff folded his hands under his chin and sat his elbows on the table. "Meeting the king of the Stoneharts was an

217

incredible experience, I think."

"Um... well you shouldn't call him 'king'," Damon protested, suddenly worried about what his friends thought of his family. "He doesn't really think of himself as one. I know he *is* one, as most laws say but... well he doesn't want to be called that."

"I heard about that. It is a subject that many gossip about. Not within your hearing of course." He nodded his head in Damon's direction. "I wouldn't be offended if I were you. The lore of a people is its soul after all. Sometimes battles are won on reputation alone."

Once again, Damon found himself without a suitable answer. Staruff often said things in such a way that one was almost sure they understood what he was talking about, but not sure enough to reply at the risk of feeling foolish. He always made him think, though. Were people afraid of his father? Did they think there was something wrong with him for not wanting the title of king?

"Staruff, stop talkin' up yer nose." Casey gulped down the last of his tea and licked the back of his hand to get the stray leaf bits off his tongue. "Yer confusin' 'im. We'll meet up with Erik and he'll be how he is. Even if e's an ass, e's Damon's pa and we gotta make nice. C'mon Damon." He stood up, dodging the overhanging lamp with practised skill. "We'll grab yer horse and yer stuff and get while the gettin's good."

His long-legged strides left Damon and Staruff trotting to keep up. Once outside, he was suddenly scooped up and placed on the back of the gigantic wooly yak. "There! Now we'll not lose ya. Star, you want up?"

"Thank you, no." His savage grin again. Boob's sheer bulk and novelty of such an animal in this part of the world prompted people to move aside for him. Despite the animal's size and gentle nature, he would be glad to get to the stables and sit astride Silhouette once more.

The other soldiers on the road travelled in groups, laughing and talking. Now and then, a few strains of a bawdy song rang out. From the stories Damon had read, he had expected orderly columns of marching men but, while the personal guards of the nobles kept in formation, everyone else did what they wanted.

Casey and Staruff, being part of Marshal Deumore's militia, followed more or less behind the red pennant bearing two bars. They told Damon that they had been designated "Company Number Two" to distinguish them from Marshal Sharon's men who carried a blue pennant with a single bar. Deumore's men, dissatisfied with such a banal name, had taken to calling themselves "Shitstorm Company" and refused to answer to anything else.

The giant and the madman had changed companies twice. Sharon had offered them a higher price for their services after which Deumore was obliged to outbid her to win them back. This was not an unusual occurrence for any of the sellswords of notable talent, and while it aggravated the marshals, the mercenaries didn't seem to care; it was all business to them, after all.

The militias were originally supposed to be leading the way to the camp, given that they were the most expendable, but Duke Astor had kicked up an unholy fuss about having "nameless bastards" at their head. To placate him, the war council had decided to put Astor and Duke Bearhelm's forces in the vanguard with the mercenaries following behind him. Duchess Scarlet, Duke Freston, and Lord Sergio's marshal came after that. Damon wasn't completely sure of the order, but he knew the Stonehearts were in the rearguard alongside King Harlon's men.

Despite maintaining a quick march, Damon was obliged to ride more slowly than he wanted to, given that a good portion of the militias were on foot. While the dukes and lords could afford to furnish most or all of their men with mounts, the mercenaries were left to their own devices for transportation. The foot soldiers kept in a tight knot in front of their mounted counterparts so as not to be outpaced. Silhouette was not fond of being made to walk when he would much rather a cathartic gallop.

The stallion had developed a habit of leaning over and sniffing Boob, as if he hadn't quite figured out *what* his travelling companion was. The grey mare Staruff rode interested him not at all. He thought he even detected a bit of disdain for the other horse.

I didn't know horses could be so snobbish. Maybe the mare just has a weak personality?

The cool, crisp air filled Damon's nostrils, and he found himself taking deep breaths as they rode further and further from the city.

"Excited?" Staruff heeled his mare to make her keep up with Silhouette. Damon shook himself a little to break his reverie.

"I suppose. I'm worried though."

"Don't be." He smiled, tight and close-lipped for once. "If you die, you won't go alone. It's the best thing you can hope for."

He was reminded again of just how different people's cultures could be. Even without knowing very much about it, he was sure he could never understand Staruff's beliefs.

He noticed that his friend was wearing a thick, fur-lined cloak, held closed by robust clasps of leather and steel. It must have been heavy, given that the metal clips were each as wide as his index finger was long.

In fact, the entire crew of twenty or so Shitstorm mercenaries was bundled up in warm clothing. Damon felt a bit embarrassed by his light tunic and cloak.

"They must think I'm crazy," he nodded to the three men riding a few yards ahead of them.

"Oh yeah," Casey piped up. "Everyone thinks yer right out yer tree."

"Thank you." He rolled his eyes and sighed.

"Hey now. So long as they think yer batshit, they'll steer clear of you. Won't make yeh angry or nothin'. Trust me, it's better." He clouted him on the back. Damon gripped the saddle-horn to keep from falling off. "Lots o' crazy stuff goes on in camp when folks're bored. All sorts of horseplay. Don't be the focus of it if yeh c'n help it."

That gave him pause. He nodded. He couldn't help wondering if this wasn't some convocation of village bullies from all over the world. Compared to the war stories of old, the nature of this defence felt somewhat reluctant. Damon had imagined uniformed, regimented lines en masse to repel the invaders. In truth, such a sight would have reassured him. *This is all we have left.* The idea sat in his stomach like a cold and heavy brick.

"Do you think we can win?" he said, more to himself than anyone else.

"Absolutely." Staruff's grin was back in full force. He was looking to the horizon like a dog lusting after a steak. His hunger was shocking. Damon wondered if he'd ever become accustomed to it. "We have an excellent chance of throwing him back, for a number of reasons."

"Such as?"

"Such as the old magic returning to use." He held out a gloved hand, indicating Damon as his example. "Strong warriors from diverse origins." He angled his hand towards Casey. "And we know what is at stake should we fail. Besides, the terrain is different than what the Southern armies are used to. It is hard to fight in the cold if you are not accustomed to it. Between you and me, I think he is slowing down." He lowered his voice and winked.

"Why'd ya say that?" Casey shifted in his saddle and Boob grunted sleepily.

"Well, think about it. How old is this Asp fellow?"

Damon frowned, scrunching his nose in deep thought. "There are tapestries in Old Stonehart Hall that show him. They're hundreds of years old but the legends of the Asp go back further than that."

"Probably thousands of years if we estimate fairly?" Staruff looked satisfied at the judicious nods he received. "Well, what is he living on? It must be special, otherwise everyone would live forever."

"You think he's some kinda demon like the stories say?" Casey lifted an eyebrow. "Eatin' souls? How the fuck d'you even *do* that? I dun think I believe that kinda shit."

"Well, he *could* be a pretender taking the mantle of the legend to frighten people..." Staruff sniffed disdainfully. "But surely he couldn't plough through entire continents on a simple story? No one is that powerful, or gullible. If Casey doubts it, imagine how many more do as well!"

"But if he *is* the real White Asp, I might as well sit on a sword!" Casey protested. "How d'ya fight legends?"

"With other legends." He inclined his chin to Damon.

We're all going to die. He looked up at the pristine sky, far away as his hopes, and prayed to the Aervie for a miracle.

The camp was restless. Though he stood still and quiet with his general beside him, Lyre felt ill at ease. A faction of Raach's berserkers were preparing themselves for the battle that was to come when morning lit the sky. He intended to place them at the front of the skirmish that they might suffer the brunt of the Stonehart attack.

They shall live long enough to do my bidding. He sat down on his plump cushion. He knew the legends of the Stoneharts, but what manner of men were they now? From what his scouts had told him and what he could glean by scrying, their numbers had diminished more that he'd thought. This gave him little joy, if any.

He watched the women as they donned their war paint and began their incessant drumming. Padded and weighted mallets pounded on robust hide-covered drums. The sound vibrated in his chest.

He had intended to punish Raach by having a portion of her warriors slaughtered, but she took it as an honour. She could be unfathomable sometimes; for a band of savages, their code of behaviour was oddly complicated.

Regardless of how she felt, he needed to find out if the power of Glasshammer still ran strong in the veins of the Stonehart clan. If it did, then all his work would soon come to fruition; or, to a catastrophic end.

Give me eternity, great men of the north. His eyes narrowed and Emeka shifted uneasily at his side. *I shall slake this foul thirst at last and see Death on his knees. No more shall it plague my horizons, and all my tomorrows.*

Emeka crouched down beside the painted map. Though it was usually spread out completely, affording a complete view of the known world, it was folded over to show only the Middle and Northern Kingdoms. The General's adjustments to the positioning of troops were smaller now. He had succeeded in harrying the enemy, keeping them on their toes with attacks on random targets.

Even now, Lyre watched a contingent of twenty men entering the camp from their raid on Sharherd, a small village to the east. Or at least it had been. Emeka had ordered them to burn it to the ground and a column of black smoke rising into the chill air told of their success. With the weather taking a turn toward winter, they could not afford to feed any more prisoners than they already had. Any refugees fleeing the slaughter came upon a line of severed heads mounted on stakes long before they were in any danger of stumbling into his camp. It was easier to warn them away than to waste efforts on putting them to the sword. The General called it "keeping things tidy." Emeka fastidiously kept the bloodshed exactly where and when he wanted it.

The White Asp lifted his hand slightly and the nearest servant jerked forward, arms up near her chest like a startled squirrel.

"We captured a seer in our quelling of Ulthar's Rest. Bring her to me."

She swallowed quickly, a flash of motion in her delicate throat. It was the only betrayal of her thoughts. She bowed and trotted quickly back into the camp proper. He was pleased. Good servants said nothing of his dealings with magicians. Poor servants did not live long enough to make the same mistake twice.

His tent was placed near the front of the camp. Three sides were open to the elements, but the back wall was closed off. He needed a place to think without the noise of his men distracting him; that, and to be seen by his troops as little as possible. His absence kept them aloof and wary as most of his men weren't sure of what he looked like. Instead, their imagination often turned him into something fantastic and with that all it took was the occasional display of his powers to keep them in their place.

Lyre had selected a wide, open clearing with plenty of flat ground for his troops to set up. It was surrounded by a wide swathe of pine which were mostly bare up the trunk until the very top. The fallen needles provided cushioning, insulation from the cold ground, excellent fire-starting materials, and made the soil unsuitable for all but the most determined undergrowth. Those of his troops who could not fit in the clearing found good accommodation among the pines.

While he could have moved in closer to Emmesford, he had chosen to stop here. His scouts had reported that the terrain became much rougher north of the clearing. There was a broad stand of poplar, birch, and steelwood between his forces and Harlon's city and these made the forest floor a damp chaos of detritus. Thickets of rhamnus, blackthorn, and holly competed for the space between the leafy trees; the enemy would have to push through them to mount an assault, or come down the road and risk ambush. Neither would go well for them.

The meadow beyond this thorny barrier was rocky and uneven and much too small for his army. He decided to let Harlon's men squabble over the few decent places to pitch a tent.

He heard footsteps and sighed. Good servants walked too softly to hear; she had brought the seer. Sure enough, a few moments later, his girl appeared, leading the fortune-teller by a rope which bound her hands and forearms together. She cursed viciously at the servant and pulled the bindings back against her heavy skirts, trying to throw her off balance.

The servant paid no attention. She came to a halt a few paces away and pushed the woman down on her rump with a good kick to her middle. Emeka chuckled, his scarred face wrinkling.

The woman kept trying to kick her with her narrow, flat-bottomed hide shoes but she couldn't reach anyone from her place in the grass. The cowl about her head was coming loose, spilling curly black hair shot with grey about her face. She would have been beautiful if it hadn't been for the angry scowl.

"I will tell you nothing, bastard!" she shouted at him.

Lyre sat quietly and folded his hands across his lap. He spent a few minutes observing her in silence before he waved Emeka forward. With a few quick strides, he was at her side. He lashed her legs and knocked her down to her knees. She shrieked with indignation as he hobbled her with a length of rope.

"Calm yourself," the sorcerer said smoothly. "I have use for neither your body nor your words." He stood and walked to the struggling woman. She looked up at him, throat flexing as she swallowed.

"What do you want?"

He leaned down and loose plaits of glistening white hair fell forward over his shoulders. He stared into her eyes, motionless.

"A travesty. You failed to foresee your fate."

"Don't mock me, pretty-boy," she shot back at him. "I see what God wills; no more, no less."

"So it must be. He would have you die by my hands?"

"You won't kill me." She looked away from him. "You'd have done it back in the village if you wanted that."

He said nothing in response. He straightened up and adjusted his cloak over his shoulders. Instead of seating himself back on the pillow, he busied himself with a chest at the back of the tent. He fished several long strips of green, black and gold. He sat down with a slender shaft of wood and began carefully weaving them around it.

She looked confused, but refrained from questioning. She occupied herself with trying to get more comfortable but it was not easy with her legs tied up. She reached up to fix her hair and realized that the rope binding her hands was looped around the one hobbling her.

"Oi! At least let me retie my shawl?"

He ignored her.

"You bastard. This is improper!"

Lyre's eyebrow cocked at her. His fingers, however, kept moving.

"Your vanity is unfounded."

"I don't care!" The red tinge that came to her face said otherwise. "A woman is to cover her hair. No one's to see it but my husband," she snapped.

"Your husband is dead." He returned his full attention to the wooden shaft in his hands. The braided cloth was two thirds of the way down. "Who issued the mandate?"

"What?" She was caught off guard by the question, but when he didn't repeat it she gave it more thought. "God says so."

"What is His name?"

She hesitated. "Sanwel."

"Sanwel was a prophet. Three of a hundred and three of ten years passed." He paused for a moment. "Three of ten and four years now." His fingers resumed their weave about the shaft.

"But He was His form in this world."

Lyre laughed. The sound was hard and cruel.

"Speak to me of a God you have seen with eyes and touched with hands. A fleshless face and an empty voice are bereft of meaning."

He could tell that she was fuming but she closed her lips and said no more. He finished his braiding in silence. At last, he fitted a silver arrowhead into the notched end of the shaft and began attaching his fletching to the other end.

Now, her face hardened. "You didn't look to me like a fletcher," she grumbled, clearly unnerved. He couldn't fault her. With her simple world-view, a king performing such an apparently menial task was out of the question. If she were willing to give her life to him, as the priests had been, he would have no need of such implements. No matter, he wouldn't have to deal with her silliness for long.

He finished with the feathers and rose from his seat. His hand delved into the trunk once more and brought forth a smooth crystal chalice. It was well made and he had commissioned the shape specifically to remind him of the sacred womb.

Fingers clasping the fluted base, he tapped the rim lightly with the head of the arrow. A single, pristine note rang.

"Holy vessel from which springs all life. Give to me existence unending as the heavens. Power boundless as the stars in unity."

The woman was staring at him with a peculiar expression on her face. He could see the whites all around her irises.

"You... will end this world," she said in a hushed voice.

Lyre pressed his lips together tightly. No matter how many seers said such things to him, it always unnerved him.

"So they say."

"But I don't..." Her chest heaved as he drew closer to her. "I don't think you wish it."

He folded his legs and knelt smoothly in front of her. He stared at her, but her gaze didn't falter. She had the clear eyes of one in the throes of *seeing*.

"No," he whispered. "I wish it to go on."

"If you break your oath, you won't-"

"No," he said again. "That I cannot do. To fail is impossible."

She knew. She knew everything in that moment, and he could see it by the tears forming in her eyes.

"C-cover my hair?"

He smiled gently and lifted her head scarf over her curls. His grip tightened on the arrow shaft and he drove the silver wedge up into her chest. Ignoring her sharp cry, he held the chalice under the fletching, catching the rivulets of hot blood. The enchanted shaft bindings held her as still as a statue. There was no pain, if only she held perfectly motionless.

She tried to move once, but only once. Her face went grey with a groan.

Quickly, while she still lived, he drank from the vessel. Hot, metallic liquid sluiced over his tongue and down his throat. The onrush of magic hit like a punch to the chest. He tilted his head back, reeling slightly. He could sense her muscles twitching, trying to keep herself still. Trying to avoid that terrible pain. The shaft twitched with the shuddering of her heart.

She groaned again as her muscles trembled and jerked involuntarily. Then, she slumped. It was the moment he had waited for. He tilted the head of the dead woman and pressed his lips to hers. The explosive exit of the escaping soul rocked him but he kept the seal tight and swallowed it down. Warmth spread through him, suffusing his limbs.

He rose from the ground and shook himself. It was complete. His powers would last awhile longer, along with his glorious immortal life. He sat on his cushion, pupils dilated and robes spattered with dribbles of stray blood. His servants knew enough to leave him alone when he was like this, so exhilarated and so terribly sickened.

Around him, the Az Taeorans standing guard shimmered, their heat shields renewed against the steely cold of the north. Overhead, the snow was beginning to fall.

The defenders set up camp within sight, but out of bowshot of the treeline. Standard-bearers staked up the banners of their lords and their companies.

So many people, Damon thought. His heart rose a little. Surely, an army of thousands like this could repel the Asp; especially because a great number of their forces were trained mercenaries. It was one thing to be the honourable man fighting for his home and his lord; it was quite another to wield the sword as a profession.

They had little idea of the enemy's strength; too many scouts failed to return. At least they could spot movement from among the trees. The autumn had stripped away much of the concealing foliage. The enemy was stalking them, watching from the underbrush. Damon felt a shudder pass through him and the cold, cloying fear settle heavily in the pit of his stomach. It was like being stalked by a mountain cat. Being thought of as prey was rather unsettling.

The bray of a horn was the first thing that alerted him to danger. The red banner of Lord Foster with its bright gold swallow swayed and hit the ground. Casey and Staruff, having politely disregarded Erik's suggestion to camp well back from the outskirts of the camp if they were staying with Damon, were now poised to have a good view of the chaos erupting on the encampment's southern edge.

 Casey dropped the tent pole he had been setting up and yanked out two long iron rods, each with half a cross-piece on it. Damon recognized these as the infamous "yak-whackers" that had been banned on the first day of the tournament on account of their tendency to break bones. Normally these tools were made of wood but the Giant never intended to use them for herding; when they were in his hands, he meant a different kind of business.

"What's that?" Damon called to him over the growing noise.

"That's the fucking enemy catching us with our pants down."

"*What?*" He didn't think it necessary to mention that this was distinctly against the rules of war.

Staruff drew his daggers and leaped over his tent, making for the knot of struggling fighters at the edge of the field. Casey followed close behind and Damon stayed as near to him as he could without the danger of getting clouted in the head with a whacker.

The Blood Link was alive with confused chattering and churning emotions. He stopped running for a moment, letting the Giant go on ahead.

We are under attack!

His thought blasted through the Link and silenced everything except a soft fuzz of underlying confusion. He had forgotten that his signal could be so loud and clear. He hoped that he was not hurting any of his kin.

He moved carefully, picking his way toward the fighting, trying not to fall over anything while he focused on conveying clear messages to his fellow Stonehearts.

South and east of us. Lord Foster is imperilled.

Damon frowned. He looked toward the east. He did not remember having seen anything amiss in that direction which was why the proclamation took him by surprise. Indeed, smoke billowed from the tents on the eastern edge of the camp. *Those are not cooking fires.* The strange anger that bubbled up in him was colouring his thoughts as he sent them. He did not have time to analyze or try to subdue it. If the defenders could not collect themselves when it mattered, he wasn't going to be able to think about anything much in short order.

Their attackers seemed to be women wearing hides and bones. From the livid slashes already riddling their exposed flesh, they must have charged through the mess of thorn bushes. *Are they mad?* Their piercing battle-cries made his chest squeeze tight in fear. He unsheathed his sword as he fed the image into the Link.

Come quickly!

A red-haired woman spit flecks of foam as she screamed, plunging her daggers into the soldier before her. She got him in the neck and armpit where his chain shirt did not cover.

Casey, visible over all the other men swung out with one of the yak-whackers, catching the woman in the side of the head. She dropped onto her side and did not move. The Giant did not stop, but kept wading into the thick of the charging berserkers. A rallying cry came from his right and suddenly the green and blue tree banner of Duke Bearhelm was there, his forces slamming into the line of crazed fighters.

Damon cast a panicked glance over his shoulder, trying to see everything at once. It was hard to see over the mass of soldiers. They were bunched up too tightly for him to be able to get in between them, and certainly too tight for a longsword to be of much use. Bearhelm's men were outfitted with short swords and kept their shields locked together. It was a good formation but it denied those with larger weaponry the chance to do anything but watch and wait for an enemy to break the line or leap out in front like Casey. Damon nervously resigned himself to the former.

If only I could see what was going on. There were plenty of defenders who could rise up against the attack but they were scattered throughout the camp, some still trying to sort out supplies. He looked around for a tree to climb to get some sort of vantage but there were none he could reach without running all the way to the rear of the camp. Then, he had an idea.

Lorne! Come to me, hurry!

He felt an inquisitive but inarticulate thought lift its head. He hoped that was a 'yes.'

Casey let out a roar and hurled a struggling body into the air.

They're flanking us! East side!

"Damon?"

His heart shot to his throat as Lorne stumbled from between two tents.

"Aervie, stop pulling! I'm here."

He rubbed his temples and winced.

Pulling? There was no time to contemplate his strange choice of words.

"Lift me up! I need to see more!"

"Lift ...?"

"The levitation spell. Quick!"

Lorne paled. "I can't do that! I could hurt you!"

More berserkers burst from the treeline, but the way the terrain sloped up toward the enemy camp it was hard to tell how many. Granted, they hadn't had much choice in the matter, but setting up on the low ground had been a mistake.

The shield wall was beginning to give ground. Step by step, they were being pushed back into the tents and camping gear by the force of the assault. One of the soldiers stumbled and a dark-haired woman leaped between his comrades and hurled the torch into a nearby supply waggon.

Lorne drew his blade and moved to place himself between Damon and the warrior. A pale-haired figure vaulted over the heads of the defending soldiers and tore after her, screaming like a banshee. This berserker did not run at them but rather sunk two daggers into the first warrior's kidneys and bore her to the ground. The axe fell and buried itself in the half-frozen dirt.

Staruff lifted his face and gnashed his teeth at the sky. He was spattered and smeared with blood but still recognizable. He planted his boot on her spine and pulled the blades free. His tongue dragged along the flat of one of the daggers as he watched the twitches of the body slow, the steam of one final breath fading into the cold air.

Shock rooted Damon to where he stood. He could only stare as his mad friend returned to the fray. At last, he managed to swallow the bile in his throat.

"I trust you, Lorne. Please, let me see what's going on so the people who know what they're doing at least have a chance to do it."

His cousin cringed. After a moment, he nodded and rested the tip of his blade on the ground, eyes closed in concentration. Damon felt the Dominions pull and twist around him. The air thickened and he choked. Lorne's brow furrowed in concentration.

I can't breathe ... Panic fluttered in his stomach. The shifting air did not yield. The magic faltered and Lorne looked up. Damon realize he had projected the thought by accident. *Keep casting dammit!*

He reached out for the Dominion of air and seized the threads of his cousin's spell. He spun and wove them outward from his face, forming a narrow tunnel. The air pooled in around his face, letting him breathe. The spell constricted around his body and he felt his feet lifting from the ground. The rippling cloud around his torso and limbs squeezed him painfully. He pulled the pool of uncompressed air downward from his face, widening out the small pocket. He began to push outward against the force holding him aloft. The light refracted all around him and his ears popped with the change in pressure.

As the stars hovering in his vision began to clear, he saw that he was several feet above the ground. It was hard to see through the mass of unnaturally thickened air. He lifted his sword very slowly, having to fight against the pressure the entire way. The blade ignited with a dark blue fire as he stretched out his power. The tip caught and sliced the air over his head. He rotated it around, carving off the top of the bubble that encased him.

Lorne squinted up at him. Beads of sweat rolled down his face in spite of the cold. He lifted a hand and Damon saw the confusion on his face as he tried to cope with the changing shape of his spell.

Keep casting. Don't let me break your net.

His cousin let his gaze drift back downward, focusing on the hem of his robes as he worked at maintaining the magic. Damon looked down over the battle. Lord Foster's banner had been lifted up again. Duke Bearhelm had been joined by Duke Astor and the latter's archers were firing into the trees. The berserkers did not retreat, but no more were forthcoming from the forest.

Casey had cleared a space around himself at least fifteen feet in all directions. A warrior charged him but he braced his shoulder and thrust out with the long end of a yak-whacker. It caught her in the gut and she dropped. He pivoted the weapon so that it spun full circle once and brought it down on her skull on the second pass. A second berserker moved off to his right, trying to get around him. He slammed the long end of the whacker against her blade, snapping it, stepped in and punched the short end into her throat.

Damon winced. He looked eastward again and caught his breath at the sight of the destruction. Soldiers were desperately trying to beat down the flames. He could not see the enemy but he could see the defenders falling as they were hewn down.

Where the hell are they?

He squinted. A man thrashed a burning wagon with a soaked blanket. Suddenly, a blossom of red opened up in the centre of his back and he fell. All while apparently standing alone.

What the hell? Damon reached out his hand toward the fires and squinted. No, there *was* something there; a shape garbed in a muddy mixture of greys, browns, and greens made it hard to see until the bright arc of a scimitar heralded oncoming death. What manner of creatures were these? Ghosts?

The White Asp...

He took a breath. Another soldier died, his head rolling between burning tents. The figure that had ended him turned, stooped, and vanished again into the smoke and chaos.

Ghosts do not kill people. These must be men, though they move like snakes.

He concentrated and projected the thought into the Link.

The foes to the east are hidden from the eyes. They blend with the earth and leaves. Look low and watch for their steel. I think they're crawling in the grass. The fire is spreading. We have to put it out!

A garbled response made it back to him, which reasoned as "trying." The soldiers could not hope to extinguish the flames while under attack from a force they could not see. If they did not do something quickly, there would be no saving the camp. A weak scattering of snowflakes drifted down from the heavens, not nearly enough to help quell the fires.

We need rain.

He closed his eyes and projected the sight of the heavy gray clouds overhead.

My kinsmen hear me! Call it down. Call it all down. Right now. We need rain!

The resounding "Aye" almost startled him out of casting. The deep bowl of concentrated air that he sat in squeezed painfully on his legs. He forced it away again, giving himself some more space. Dividing his focus like this was exhausting. He held on, for in the sky all around him he felt a change. A sense of purpose. The snow thickened and began dumping out of the clouds like a torn pillow shaken by manic hands.

Damon let his attention wander back to the fire. He lifted his sword and directed the wicking blue flames toward the orange blaze. The Dominion of earth in its sluggish, interlocking matrices began to permeate his vision. He reached deeper and pulled at the tendrils of water, of frost. The ground heaved and rippled, tossing clods of dirt into the air. The soldiers turned and fled from the fire and the unseen foes. If there was a horn call to retreat, Damon did not hear it.

Shit. No, not earthquake. Dammit, keep focus...

An inquisitive curl went through the Link and he realized he was still sending.

Sorry, keep channelling; I'm doing what I can.

He reached out and grasped at the heat of the fire instead. The roaring hunger nearly overwhelmed him. He had to release it and renew the pressure outward to keep the air pocket from crushing him. Again, he reached out. The flames would not obey. Either the Dominion of fire did not respond to being told to snuff out or he simply did not have the skill to do it.

He pulled at the water in the earth again. This time a mist exploded up from the ground, hissing violently against the invading fire.

A wave of dizziness washed over him and he curled in on himself slightly. *Snow.* It was too cold for rain. If only some of that abundant heat chewing through the camp and its supplies could be made useful rather than destructive.

Damon blinked. The idea was a strange one but perhaps not impossible.

I can't know unless I try.

He extended his sword again toward the fire. The wavering threads within that Dominion swayed toward him eager and responsive now that he was not trying to stifle them. He reached his other hand upward tangling his fingers with the whorls of the air Dominion. The mixture made him light-headed and ravenous at the same time. The bowl of air that upheld him squeezed in again as he lost his focus on it. He ignored it.

Can't do everything. Just have to hold out long enough to do this.

The fire leaped and stretched toward the onrush of wind from above. Damon lifted his sword and directed the heat of the fire at the clouds. He pulled the water in the heavens downward at the same time. There was an explosion of steam. Still, snowflakes fluttered down around his head. Damon wiped at his nose and his hand came away a dark blue.

Augh, nosebleed. Aervie, my head hurts. Come on, please. I can do this.

He extended his hand again and the blood began to mix with the churning mist. He frowned and tried pushing the power in his blood into the sky. The cords between the sky and the ground pulled taut and a torrent of water poured down over the camp. It was a strange sensation, rather like his fingers were connected to the water itself. Indeed, there were runnels of it following the line of his arm and soaking his tunic.

The sound of twanging bowstrings crept into his awareness. In the deluge, he was able to pick out the blue banner of Duke Astor. The duke had moved his forces from the southern edge and swung around to rain death on their unseen foes. The creeping men in their strange garb screamed as they fell to the barrage.

Something snared in the threads he was pulling from the sky and the earth. It lashed out and severed some of them. The Asp was reacting, countering the magic with that of his own.

Stop it! He pushed against the snake-like shadow that was weaving itself into his spell and tangling it. Whatever the apparition was, it turned on him and the world seem to darken suddenly. His mind was filled with a vision of vivid green eyes. He recalled that unholy glow from the black rider he had seen in the crystal when he reforged the Blood Link. This time, there was no grotesque helm. No white horse. The eyes pulled back from him. For an instant before it vanished, he glimpsed a face of remarkable beauty and long, ornate robes of white. The delicate jingle of wind chimes lingered in his ear for a few moments after.

The next thing he became aware of was the crushing pressure of the air holding him aloft. Either his focus was too divided or he had exhausted his energy to cast because he could not for the life of him strengthen the outward push against it.

Lorne, stop casting. I can't keep up.

Alright. The voice in his mind was faint. He wasn't sure if his cousin was having difficulty sending through the Link or if he was passing out but with the darkness crowding the edges of his vision, he was betting on the second. *I'll lower you, hold on.*

Just drop me. Please.

He found himself abruptly on the ground, blinking as the rain threw droplets of mud against his face. Damon couldn't stop shaking. People were grasping his shoulders. Shouting, laughing, someone was weeping. His eyes were locked on a woman's head. It was separated from her body. The muted light filtering through the clouds made the blood glisten where part of her face and scalp had been torn away. She had curly red hair.

He couldn't remember feeling cold like this before. His hands and feet were numb. The ground was rocking under him. His tunic was too tight all of a sudden and he pulled at the ties at the neck.

Casey's face swam into his field of vision. He had his big hands on either side of his face, forehead against his. It was the only way he could make himself heard above the din.

"You did it! They're runnin' like piss in a gutter!" He hooted back over his shoulder at their retreating foes as they tried to make for the road before they could be shot down from behind. "Run bitches, run! Next time bring yer balls with ya!"

Damon couldn't stop staring at the severed head. Red hair, like the boy in the vision he'd had back in Emmesford. What was it that plagued him about it? Was he having a vision now? He felt like he would fall over if moved. No, that was preposterous. He was already lying down.

"Casey," he said. He wanted to cough but his tunic was squeezing him too hard.

"What's wrong?" His friend shouted back.

"I can't breathe."

In a moment, the world lurched and he was being carried. He was seated on the mercenary's broad shoulder. An arm was wrapped around his thighs, and one hand held onto his wrist on the other shoulder. They sailed through the crowd like a tallship. Lorne trotted behind them, holding up his robe with one hand to keep from tripping on it. All around them, men were vanquishing flames with sodden blankets and tarps, calling for healers, recovering supplies, and beginning to set the camp to rights.

Casey stooped near a fire pit and thrust him into a large tent. Damon recognized the crest of the winged horse displayed on a shield that was hanging from the central post. *My father's tent.* The Giant stalked back into the sleeping area. When he returned, he started wrapping him up in fur blankets.

"That won't make me warm..."

"Don't matter. I seen this before. No worries." He received no other explanation, only the strong arms wrapping around him.

"I can't..."

"Shush. Look at that lamp there." He pointed at the wrought-iron lantern, candles flickering behind blown glass. "Take a breath with yer nose, slow."

He did as he was told, fixing his gaze on the warm glow.

"Breathe out long n' slow with yer mouth. Slow now. Don't blow out the fire."

He obeyed the absurd command. In the back of his mind, though, he was afraid of extinguishing that light.

"In through yer nose," Casey said. "Say: 'It's gonna be okay,' and let it out again."

"It's gonna be okay..." The words came in a whispered rush.

"Do it again. Nobody needs yeh for nothin' right now."

"It's gonna be okay."

"That's right. Again."

"It's gonna be okay."

His heart was starting to slow down and he found he could hear more clearly now.

"Yeh got all the time in the world."

"It's gonna be okay."

He didn't know how many times he said it, or how long Casey held onto him but after a while, the dark fog cleared from his thoughts and he could feel his limbs again. "I think I'm fine now," he said after a moment of silence. "What was that?"

"Panic attack." Casey shifted so he was sitting beside him. "Happened teh me when I was younger. First startin' this business. Happens to a lot of folks."

Damon pushed the blankets down so he was sitting on them. "Thanks for, um..."

"No problem." His friend grinned at him and swept his hand back and forth as if to swat the gratitude away. "How d'yeh feel now?"

"My chest is still kind of tight." He sighed and wrinkled his nose. "And I smell like sweat."

"Well that we can fix. I'll get some water an' the hero can wash 'isself off."

He grimaced. "I don't feel like a hero."

Casey smiled. "I don' think y'ever will. But take the praises when they come anyhow." Casey pointed at Lorne who sat nearby. His cousin had remained so quiet that he'd quite forgotten about him. "Give 'im a look over eh? Make sure 'e's not really hurt or nothin." He stepped out of the tent before he could answer. Damon shrugged and wrestled his damp tunic off.

The Giant stuck his head back in the tent flaps. "Relax a bit. I told 'em all to fuck off 'cause yer feelin' sick."

Damon smiled. "Thanks." Again, the hand waved his thank-you away and his friend disappeared into the busy camp.

Now he had a chance to think by himself. He didn't know where his father was. Likely doing something important with the other lords and marshals. He sighed heavily. Lorne prodded his ribs carefully, making sure he hadn't broken anything with the air pressure, or the fall.

There was something wriggling at the back of his mind. He tried to think of what it could be. Understandably, seeing the White Asp across the battle field in his stark white regalia had been disturbing. He was... beautiful. He almost couldn't believe he wasn't a woman. It wasn't right that such a terrible fiend should have such a divine face.

The bright green eyes had bored into him, glowing like the sun through leaves. Like the great northern aurora. Like... "Illtharen!"

Lorne blinked at the sudden outburst and stopped dabbing at his bloody nose with a damp cloth. "Damon? Are you alright?"

No! It couldn't be. He would have to be thousands of years old. *Just like the legends say... "The wily old Asp, undiminished through the ages, stealing children from their beds and bringing ruin and woe upon the heads of the people. The demon. The thief of souls ..."*

He lurched forward, meaning to stand. His cousin put a firm hand on his shoulder and pushed him back.

"Stop that. You need to rest. Do you have any idea the kind of energy you were just channelling?"

"Lorne!" He grabbed his wrists. The lorekeeper just stared back at him, uncomprehending. "Lorne! It's *his* book!"

"Who ..." The colour drained out of his face, leaving him nearly as pale as Damon himself. "Oh ... oh no."

Chapter 13: With Talons Bared

Bowen abdicated the regency more easily than Phoenix expected. That didn't mean he was cheerful about it and he was not the only one to share in his sentiment.

There were brawls in the streets and while many Ducal acknowledged her right to rule, some Ducal refused to accept that their saviour had come to them in the guise of a human.

How many prophecies come to fruition this way? Fate had such a vile sense of humour. Waiting, hoping, and searching for salvation was a way of life in and of itself. When it finally came, it was often rejected out of fear; fear of the alien existence that might await on the other side. *Have you Ducal grown so comfortable in your cage?*

Phoenix closed her eyes, listening to two of the guards—*her* guards—shouting at each other just outside the Hearing Room door. Half of them had deserted their post in protest shortly after her arrival. She had a feeling that by the end of the day more would follow.

How can I blame you? I would not accept me as a saviour if I were in your position. She tightened her grip on her sword until her fingers throbbed. *No, I will not let myself think this way. I will not be drawn into the madness. I am Phoenix Solara, Queen of Dunkhar, and this is just a game I must play to return to my people. I will do what I must to escape Hanuel. I will go to Damon. He fights the White Asp. He will help me and I will help him. Any help I give to the Ducal is incidental. I do not care about their destiny. Surely, they do not care about mine.*

She opened her eyes and looked over Dyseris and Sora, standing at the foot of the dais, watching her. Why did it feel like such a betrayal? *You deserve to be free. You deserve to have your home back.* Her gaze shifted to Kael, lounging comfortably on the dais at her feet, one leg dangling off and swinging slowly back and forth. She scowled and her resolve hardened again.

Phoenix rose and hopped down to stand with the raven man and the Prince. "I cannot stay here." She looked between them. They glanced at each other and back to her; no one spoke. "Dyseris. Go and find me some armour as befits my station. If possible, make sure it fits. If not, find someone to fix it so that it does."

He nodded. "Yes! It will shine like fire! I will bring you beautiful armour …" he continued to ramble as he trotted out the door. The sound of the guards shouting grew louder as the door opened. She waited until it was muffled again to continue.

"Prince Sora, gather together those loyal to me and wait for me at the entrance. We march for Tamiyon Nesting."

Kael's head came up sharply. "Why?"

Phoenix turned and savoured the look of trepidation in his pale eyes for a moment before answering. "The former regent and those who support him know this place far better than I do. This is not friendly territory."

"If you vacate the Regent's …" Sora stopped himself and reworded the sentence. "If you vacate your seat here, it may be seen as a concession."

She nodded. "I know. I will have to occupy his position without occupying his perch; it's a fight I cannot avoid. Fortunately, Tamiyon Nesting has something that this palace does not: a surrounding wall."

Kael chuckled. "You are a general's child."

"A *King's* child," she barked. For a moment, there was nothing but the echo of her voice in the Hearing Room. "My father put down uprisings before. I am young, not stupid." Kael remained silent, perhaps sensing that her patience was at an end. She pointed at Sora. "Go."

He bowed and left. Once he had shut the door behind him, she turned back to Kael. "You have lessons to teach me." He watched her, saying nothing; then, at last, he nodded. "And you need the books to do so." He nodded again. "Lead on. I will go with you and ensure that the Vault opens for you."

The shaman smiled and she turned away from the look in his eyes. There was only one word to describe such a gaze: hungry.

Damon looked across the tent at Lorne. The books were spread out in front of him, one near each knee. The small gathering of Stonehart kin, his father included, sat in the cramped space behind Lorne. Despite their efforts to be quiet, Damon was sure he could hear them all breathing. He swallowed hard.

"Okay so..." he began quietly. "Well, you've all been told how this works. I put my hand on the book, close my eyes and sort of... dream for a bit. That way I can talk to Iltharen."

"Or The White Asp," Jae said caustically.

Damon nodded. He pressed his lips together tightly, the pale blue going white for a moment. Then he sighed and made himself relax a bit. "I've

238

never been harmed before by the apparition in the book. It might be that he can't actually hurt me and I hope that that's true but..." He clasped his hands together in his lap, willing them to stop their subtle shaking. "Lorne and I have practised with the books before. He's usually been able to bring me out by simply taking my hands off the book."

"What do you mean 'usually'?" His father piped up. Damon hated the look of concern written all over his face.

"Well sometimes I stay in there regardless but I think it's just because I was really focused and didn't notice." He sighed. "Da, it will be alright. I'm absolutely sure this will work. All you have to do is wait for five minutes and if I don't come out by then, just hit me."

Jae gave a short, sharp laugh.

"Hit you?" Erik raised an eyebrow.

"Yeah, just push me off my chair or something. I know it sounds odd but it will break my concentration for sure."

"The White Asp wouldn't need five minutes to kill you, Damon," Jae told him flatly.

"I know." He looked down at the books, feeling the apprehension sizzling in his stomach. "But we need to know if these are dangerous. After all, we stopped the White Asp with the magic we found in here." He gestured to the book and felt his relatives lean forward instinctively.

Erik leaned back, taking a long slow breath. Then, he nodded decisively. "I give my blessing. Do what you have to do." He looked around. "Jae? What do you say?"

"He's your lad Erik," she nodded to him solemnly. "I'll be watching his face like a hawk though. First sign of anything and I'm popping him in the jaw."

Erik nodded. The corner of his mouth twitched but it didn't quite make it into a smile. He turned to Damon. "Can you ask Autumn? Your Link connection is the best."

Damon nodded and closed his eyes for a moment. Autumn had been left to keep watch over those Stonehearts who could not respond to the call-to-arms. Glasshammer was in his hands while Erik was away at war. He was the only adult Darkblood of the clan not in the camp. Damon had reached him earlier and explained the situation. Now that he was rested from the intense casting during the battle, it was much easier to reach out to him.

Autumn, what are your thoughts?

Autumn looked more tired than usual in his mind's eye. The lines in his forehead were deep and his mouth was set in a frown.

It has to be done. We have to know. He crossed his arms. *Tell your father, I say: we need those books, Erik. They're the only thing that have stopped the Asp so far.*

Damon opened his eyes and related the message. He did his best to ignore the gazes of his clansmen. Even Sunev, for all her stoicism, was more than a little mystified that he could reach all the way to Glasshammer.

"Lorne?" Erik turned to the last of the family leaders.

"You already know what I think." He stared at the books disconsolately. "The only way to fight the unknown is to make it known."

"Well spoken. Damon?"

Damon sat up, feeling anticipation course through his body.

"Do what needs to be done. Be careful."

Once again, he was keenly aware of the difference between himself and the rest of his clan. *I'm the only one who can do this. They're counting on me.* Damon put his hand on the first book and closed his eyes.

Instantly, Iltharen was before him in his familiar tower room. Upon seeing him enter, the apparition put down his pen and smiled.

"Welcome back. What can I do for you?"

After learning a great deal of the language, it was much easier to communicate with Iltharan. Still, Damon realized that he was a bit at a loss as to what he should say. Although he was fairly sure that Iltharen was not a real person, only a memory, he felt rather like they were friends. At least, he had been sure before. Now, he was beginning to question what he knew. He cleared his throat.

"Who are you?" He threaded his fingers together nervously.

"Has your memory failed you?" Iltharen raised an eyebrow. "I am Iltharen."

He shook his head. "No, who are you really? Did you write this book?"

The apparition frowned. "I do not fathom your question. I really am Iltharen. Who else would you expect to find here?"

Damon sat down on the edge of the desk. He kneaded his temples with his fingertips. He had to try something else. This was getting nowhere.

"Who is the White Asp?"

"I do not know." He shook his head, long black hair sliding over his shoulders as he did so. "If you tell me about him, I will remember for you."

"I don't need you to remember for me." Damon was trying not to get angry with Iltharen but it was difficult. He only had a few minutes to get the information he needed. *How can he not know? He knows nearly everything else but he's ignorant of an important ancient legend? Can't be.*

"*Why* do you not know?" He slapped the desk with his palm.

"I hazard the author did not know or did not wish to share that knowledge." Iltharen tucked a foot underneath himself, rearranging his robes more comfortably.

"Alright." He let out a breath. Losing his temper would do no good. The apparition could not be intimidated, or indeed harmed in any way as they had already established. "Who wrote this book?"

"You asked me before, you know."

"I know, but I didn't understand you well enough then. Explain it to me now that I understand your language better."

"I do not have that which you request." Iltharen spread his elegant hands in a helpless gesture.

"How can you not? You're *his* memory! Just tell me who you are!"

"Iltharen is Iltharen," he stated clearly. "I am the book."

Damon frowned in concentration.

"No, you're *in* a book. A book is a thing with pages and writing on them."

Iltharen laughed. The sound was startling in its joyfulness. "Not so! The paper you hold, the words you read are but a preface, a cursory table of contents. A *book* is far beyond that: it is a piece of the mind."

"So... what I'm doing right now... is reading?"

"You are conversing with Iltharen. Reading is something far more mundane."

Damon nodded slowly, looking at the floor. "So, I'm the only one who can converse with Iltharen... with you, out of the Stoneharts alive today."

"So you have said." The apparition stood and walked to the fireplace. His robes brushed Damon's knees lightly. For some reason, it seemed absurd. That a talking, breathing man could *be* a book. Both physically real, and very much all in his mind.

"I am saddened by this," Iltharen continued as he prodded the glowing logs there.

"A book can be sad?"

"You did not find this strange earlier." He put down the poker and held his palms out to the warmth. Seeing that Damon still didn't understand, he smiled indulgently. "Books are both for the moment and for eternity. We straddle the worlds in that respect."

"And you still can't tell me who wrote you?"

Iltharen shook his head. "The knowledge is not with me."

"Why would the author not want to share that information with future generations?"

"I do not know, specifically. But, the most common reason for withholding knowledge was political." He laughed at the noise of disgust Damon made in his throat. "I know, I know: I have explained historical policies and you've proven a naked infant about the whole concept."

"Alright, don't rub salt in it," Damon said sourly. "I'm just upset that some old policies are keeping valuable information from me."

"Is the author really so important?"

"If this is the White Asp's book, I want to know how we got it from him."

Iltharen's shrug was depressingly predictable.

"The last person, before yourself, to access me was over five of a hundred years passed."

"Who was it?"

"He did not speak his name." Iltharen walked back to his chair and sat down.

"Where was he?" Damon tried a different track.

"An alehouse."

When he realized no further reply was forthcoming, he sighed in despair. "I should go."

"Will you return to speak with me again?"

Damon shrugged. "Yes. I have to, or we'll all die."

"I will miss you; as much as a book can." He smiled.

Against his will, Damon returned the smile. "I will be back to dig more secrets out of you." He shook a finger at the apparition.

"I look forward to it. Farewell Damon." He took his hands off the book. His kin were all staring at him expectantly. "Um..." he cleared his throat and swallowed. "Well, it seems that 'Iltharen' is a thing, not a name." Damon looked around at the confused faces. "Ah... give me a moment, I've got to put it back into proper language. It's like... the soul of a book I guess; and this Iltharen has no idea who created him."

Lorne sighed heavily. "Just our luck! A historic manuscript left unsigned." He threw up his hands in frustration. "So it might very well be the White Asp's book and not even know it?"

Damon nodded slowly.

"What are we going to do?" Jae looked to Erik, then around at the others.

"Keep using it." Damon was the one who answered. He fought not to look away from the host of surprised eyes. "A sword is a deadly thing, no matter whose it is. Better that we just stay on the right end of it and hope for the best."

His father smiled, the apprehension melting from his face. "Best advice I've heard all day."

The Vault Wardens watched them with scowls etched deeply into their faces and to Phoenix, they looked like gargoyles. Kael, however, was as smug as she had ever seen him. He still walked with the quiet grace but the blank slate of his face was fixed with an upward curve of the lips.

"Do you know where the books are? The ones you need?" she asked.

Kael preceded her down the long winding stairs. "I have a reasonably good idea."

Warden Harkeen stood in the atrium below, waiting for them at the bottom of the stairs. His hands were folded into the sleeves of his grey robes. His copper braids spilt over his shoulder from under his hood. He barred their path.

The shaman stopped and looked at Phoenix, waiting. She took a deep breath and straightened her back.

"My teacher and I have need of some tomes. Please, assist us in finding them?"

She hated the rise of her voice at the last. It shouldn't have come out as a question or a request; it should have been an order. She could not expect to be taken seriously as Queen if she went about asking nicely for everything. When she had last been in this chamber, she had asked Harkeen and Dyseris if the Ducal had a standing army. That army was hers now, if she could command it.

"I am aware of what he wants. I will not put them in his hands." His voice echoed like a door slamming. The Warden glared at Kael.

Phoenix felt her anger uncoil and rise from the pit of her stomach up into her throat. She curled her fingers on the grip of her sword and Harkeen's eyes were instantly focused on them. Apparently, word of her prowess in the prison had spread. *Good.*

"Is that how you address your Regent?" she asked. She curled her lip, showing teeth. He hesitated.

"No. I just—"

"Then do *not* treat your Queen in such a manner!" she snapped.

Harkeen pressed his hands together. "Please, I am sorry, Highness." He bowed his head, braids clacking. "With all respect, I cannot let this Tamiyon have something so dangerous."

"Am I the Phoenix of your prophecy?" She took a step forward and pressed her weight into the ball of that foot. *Oh Shorah, oh Thero, hear me. Let my father live and breathe in me, if only for this day. Retreat would be the death of me and I do not know if I have the strength to stand my ground.* When the Ducal hesitated again, she shouted at him. "Am I?"

He flinched and she felt confidence flood into her.

"Yes, Highness. We have verified it by our arts and you did pass the trial. Still, I cannot do as you ask."

"Then stand aside and we will find what we need for ourselves."

Harkeen shook his head. Kael, who had been standing quietly at her shoulder, watching, stepped forward and put out his hand. The Warden stepped back, raising his arms to protect himself but he was not fast enough. There was that same terrible feeling of time bending around the will of the shaman. It took an eternity for Harkeen to fall.

A blossom of red spread across the front of his pale robes. He laid on his side, one arm extended as blood trailed from the corner of his mouth. His eyes were glassy, staring at nothing.

Kael stepped back again and everything snapped back to normal. Phoenix darted to the Warden's side.

"What have you done?" She felt his throat, searching for a sign of life.

"He opposed you," Kael answered, folding his hands behind his back. He looked down at the fallen Warden as though he were an overturned piece of furniture. "It is my duty to defend you from traitors and renegades."

"Heal him, you madman!"

"I'm afraid a burst heart is beyond my skills, my Queen." The shaman bowed, his hair curtaining his face. "So sorry." There was no apology in his voice.

Phoenix pulled away from the corpse. She wanted to strike him, to cut him down with her blade. He watched her, expressionless as before except for that damnable smile. She reminded herself that she needed him, that her training was under his control. That he could have done this to her at any time while he was testing her power. Perhaps, as Queen, she could order him to wear a mask so she wouldn't have to look at his face.

"You will need to do something about the opposition to your rule," he told her.

"Shut your mouth!" she snarled. He was right, she knew that, but this was going too far. "You will not execute anyone without my permission. I will *not* have my decisions taken out of my hands! Is that clear?"

"Y—"

"Nod your head! I do not want to hear your voice until I say otherwise!"

Kael nodded.

"Go and send for someone to take care of ..." She gesticulated at Harkeen's body. "...*this*. Then we will get the books and leave this place." He nodded again.

She ground her teeth as she watched him go. She wanted to sit down beside the corpse, to apologize to Harkeen, to do something—anything— but stand there in silence. How many men had died in her father's service? Did it feel like this every time? She watched the pool of scarlet as it spread slowly across the floor.

Chapter 14: Path of the Unseen

"Riding back to Emmesford?" Staruff raised an eyebrow.

"Just fer a bit." Casey stuffed a thick, woolly scarf, into a side-pocket of his travel bag. "'S too much goddamn pressure on the kid."

"Man," he corrected pointedly. Casey looked at the other mercenary, then to the back of the tent where Damon sat. Damon himself had been about to point out that it didn't really matter to him, but he hesitated seeing the serious look on Staruff's face. He was beginning to feel like there was nothing at all that could damage the crazed swordsman's pride but he was not about to test him.

"You think that stinking pot of refugees will make him feel more at ease?"

Casey put down the bag. "Gotta do somethin'. Can't go runnin' round by ourselves. Even with me. I gotta tell sommin' te Damon's ol' man or he'll never agree."

"Don't take him off alone then," Staruff said simply with a shrug.

Damon stared at him. Even though those steely eyes were focused on nothing in particular, they still seemed to pierce everything around them, slicing through the tent fabric. *The eyes of a strategist,* he thought and wondered where that idea had come from.

"You got a better idea?"

Staruff nodded. "Patrols."

"Huh?" Casey scrunched up his nose.

"The other men don't get a holiday - young or otherwise - but getting out of the camp for a while is possible if one goes out on patrol. Observing enemy movements is important and I'm sure it would be easy enough to be added to the regular rotation, especially around the forest. Since the attack, no one's enjoyed going near there but thankfully there hasn't been any trace of those creeping soldiers since then. We can even help cut back the thickets if you've a mind to do some work." He looked towards Damon. "It's a job to be taken seriously, though."

"His da'd never let 'im do that!" Casey scoffed.

"He let him wield dangerous magic easily enough. Did you see some of the other Stonehearts collapse after the working? Even Sunev did and she's no soft-handed one by a long shot."

There was silence in the tent or a moment. Damon cleared his throat and stood up.

"I will ask my father."

Casey made to stand up but Damon shook his head.

"I will go alone. Just... stay here." He straightened the baldric over his shoulder. "If I cannot stand up to my own da, how can I stand up to the enemy?"

Erik, blessedly, had not shouted down his request immediately but that did not mean that he was not set against it.

"Our men have finished cleaning up the camp from the battle," Damon tried again. "You told me to rest and I did; now there's precious little to do. I've seen scouts go into the forest, sometimes alone, and they come out unharmed without so much as an arrowhead launched in their direction"

His father nodded slowly. "That *is* what the reports keep saying but I think it strange. We presume they *have* archers but they haven't made any use of them yet." He rested an elbow on his camp chair and his cheek on his fist. "I wish we knew more."

"That's why I want to go have a look around!"

Erik frowned, his brows drawing downward. "Damon, do you even know *how* to scout an enemy? It's like hunting but different. Your quarry is much, *much* more intelligent and devious; his signs and markings, equally different."

"That's why Casey wants to take me with him," he said. "Please." He spoke more quickly as his father's face darkened and his mouth started to open again. "I know you don't like him much but he's quite used to this kind of life and he's very strong."

"Strong and fearless as a bull and about as responsible."

Damon sighed, feeling the hope he had worked up before approaching his father draining away.

"What if Staruff came with us? Patrols usually go in threes or fours..."

"Staruff the *Mad*," he emphasized the title, "is crazy as a quicksilver-drinking stargazer," Erik said with very little humour in his voice.

He couldn't really argue with that, so he worked around it. "He *has* proved himself useful, everyone says so. He's clever and he's been doing his job for years. If people fear him, it's for good reason: his skill in combat is unmatched." He paused. "Don't tell Casey I said that." Damon raised his hands, staving off Erik's retort. "With his knowledge of war and mine of magic, perhaps we can make some sense out of all this that other scouts haven't. The other Stonehearts have been too busy training with the Dominions to have a look around haven't they?"

Erik shook his head, frowning.

"Isn't it about time that one of us did?" He gestured off in the direction of the woods. "I know I haven't had as much to do with the strategy meetings and such as you'd like." He looked down at the rugs underneath him, cushioning his rump from the hard ground where he sat. In truth, the Lords and marshals had begun asking if Damon would attend their war-room sessions since they had seen him in action on the battlefield. He didn't really feel qualified to tell all these experienced men what to do. "I'll come and talk to them if you want me to."

His father sat back, surprised. "You're ready to take on that responsibility?"

Damon pressed his lips together for a moment. "Lorne keeps putting questions to me whenever we study. Questions that the marshals ask you about what we can do with our magic. How we can help them. Wouldn't it be easier for me to just answer at the meeting than having to wait until the next one?"

Erik smiled. "I've said as much, but you told me you thought it wasn't your place."

He returned his gaze to the rug, disliking having his words tossed back at him. "I've given it some thought; I want to do more but I still need to learn. You, on the other hand, your place here is clear: command. It's not for me."

"Not yet," Erik interjected quietly.

"Hopefully not for a long time, yet." Damon scowled at his father's tacit suggestion. "But there will be no future for me to steer in any way if we cannot break the Asp on our lines. You said yourself, we have stopped him but we have not pushed him back. There can be no victory until we do. The supplies from Emmesford and the lands around here can't hold out forever. Let me do something. Please? Maybe nothing at all will come of it but let me try at least."

His father let out a long, drawn-out sigh. He knew that sound well and his heart leaped in his chest.

"Alright. Many of us are having to learn in the saddle. I cannot really begrudge you some kind of training." He rose from his chair and wrapped the fur draped over its back around his shoulders. Damon had quite forgotten how cold it was. There had been no more snow since the battle but the ground was covered in thick layers of ice from the unseasonal rain.

"Take Staruff with you if you must. He may not have all his proper sense about him but I can't suggest anyone better suited to protect you. He is far-sighted, as you've said."

Damon nodded enthusiastically. Try as he might, the smile would not stay off of his face. "Thanks, Da. I promise."

The silence of the forest gave him shivers as they passed amongst the trees. The bark was dry now, no longer darkened by dampness. If the White Asp's view of the resisters' forces and their excursions along the pathways through the wood was a clear one, he gave no sign of it. There seemed to have been no similar scouting activity among the enemy.

Erik had insisted on them heading out at night to take advantage of its cover. Damon resented being coddled this way but at least he was allowed to go. Perhaps his father would be more confident when he realized that there was nothing to worry about. They had been walking for nearly an hour and seen no movement much less any danger.

Staruff had been surprised at the invitation to escort him through the forest but he had bowed and accepted the honour graciously. Damon still found it strange that his friend so revered his father; then again, he had never really made the connection between his father's rank and other kings.

The smaller mercenary took point, stopping now and again to take a deep breath through his nostrils and let out a quiet sigh. Given the season, there wasn't much scent to anything. Still, a faint whiff of decay was detectable through the cold. The fallen leaves swirled around their feet when they moved. The nearly naked branches made tortured shapes in the dark.

Staruff held a small, well-shielded lantern. Despite the opaque slats all around it, letting out only a single beam in front of them, he kept his cloak over his arm, hovering around it like a wing while Casey grumbled about not being able to "see shit".

"We have a precious charge, Casey. Take this with the utmost gravity," the mercenary admonished in a breathless whisper. He motioned for them to stay still while he darted on ahead, staying low to the ground.

"Does he think we'll be attacked?" Damon looked up at his huge friend.

"Prob'ly hopes so. Crazy wanker." He squinted off into the the dark in vain. He suddenly realized that Casey could not see. He'd forgotten how keen his dark sight was compared with others'.

The wayward mercenary came back momentarily though they did not see him until he was almost right on top of them. He put a finger to his lips, looking around.

"It's fine. I thought I saw something," he whispered. "But that doesn't mean we're alone. You two still need to quiet down." Staruff stood quietly for a moment. The lantern light made his angular cheekbones under the red scarf look like he wore war paint.

"What's wrong?" Damon whispered, leaning forward.

Staruff looked away from him for a moment, when he looked back his eyes were narrowed and even more troubled. He turned his leg to the side and showed a long scratch across the side of his calf. "I walked into a patch of thorns over there. It is harder to see in here than I'd thought. We should have done a better job cutting back the pathways." He shook his head and readjusted his hood. "Well, we must go on. I'll not let this wood make a fool of me."

Damon caught his arm as he turned around. "Let me take point."

"What? I've walked this in the daylight. You don't even know the way."

"I can turn shadow. I may not know how the path goes but, in shadow, branches and traps won't hurt me and I can see better than I do now, just like daytime."

Staruff stared at him, his pale eyes wide. "You can do that?"

"Aye. Just keep the lantern away from me. The light makes it hard to... breathe." He made a face. "I'll explain it all to you later. Just give me a moment to concentrate." He wasn't completely sure he could do it on demand but he had been practising. More than anything he wanted to feel useful.

"Yer gonna make magic?" Casey said, an obvious excitement in his voice. "This's better n' watchin' Boob chase rabbits."

"Boob chases rabbits?"

"Na but it'd be fuckin' funny if 'e did." Casey grinned.

Damon stifled a laugh and closed his eyes. He pretended no one was watching and no one was waiting for him. In his mind, he returned to the night on top of old Stonehart Hall. Falling. Falling through cold air. Falling towards danger; death. A shiver went through him as he remembered the fear and desperation.

"Holy shit." Staruff had completely forgotten to keep his voice down. "Why didn't you do that when we were fighting?"

Damon could not answer, of course. He opened his "eyes" and looked around. The light of the lantern, even sheltered by the mercenary's cloak was nearly blinding. He swirled about their feet and moved in front of them. After a moment, the two men began moving forward slowly, uncertainly. He could not speak to them, but remained out of the lantern light. He had been told that there was a small grove halfway along the path where the patrols typically took their breaks. Meeting up with them there would probably be the best idea.

Flowing between the branches and underbrush was easy. He found he could move faster than he could run otherwise and he was not winded. The darkness soaked into him like sweet nectar. He swirled around the first clearing he came to, finding the arrow stuck into the ground with a red cloth tied around the shaft. This was the shortest of the trails so he wasn'tt really surprised to come upon it so soon. The purpose of their walk tonight had not been to find anything in particular, despite what he'd told his father, but to get Erik accustomed to letting him go about, if not by himself then at least with a small escort.

Damon swirled around the trees on the border of the clearing and ran up against a pair of legs. He coiled back in revulsion wondering why the soldiers had left a corpse here so close to their resting spot. No... This was a living body. Hide hung around her waist and decorative animal bones wrapped their way around her arms, legs and throat. He had seen this attire before needed no second glance to know that the berserkers lay in wait for them.

This is wrong... all wrong. They don't wait to pounce do they? They charge in screaming... they should have... He moved around the clearing quickly. *Six... seven... eight... oh Aervie...* There were too many.

He fled back along the path. There was no time to focus on coming back slowly and neatly as he wanted to. He hurled himself into the beam of lantern light, gasping in pain and dizziness. Staruff stopped immediately and Casey slammed into the back of him.

"Go back!" he hissed. He took a step and lost his balance, falling to his knees. "Go back! They're waiting for us... the-"

There was a savage whoop and cry coming down the path towards them at frightening speed.

Oh no... Suddenly, he realized he had forgotten to check along the path on the way back, so hasty he had been to get back to his friends. Casey swore loudly, pulled out his yak-whackers and turned to face more foes leaping from the trees, unveiling their lanterns. The first one to reach the giant swung her lantern at his face. The hard black iron whacker snapped out from its place along his forearm and smashed it, sending burning oil splashing back over her skin. She screamed in rage and lunged with her dagger.

The dried leaf-litter at their feet caught instantly. Staruff hissed angrily and put himself in front of Damon. An arrow took him in the left shoulder. He snarled like a maddened animal and staggered. "Stay behind me!" Damon did as he was told. He had no interest in being in front of Staruff's blades at this moment. Three came at him at once, swinging heavy maces. Damon was pressed against his back, steadying him and he heard the grind of the arrow head against bone as he raised his sword. He felt ill. Staruff screamed and swept his blade across the eyes of the first one to reach him. The woman went down in a fit of howling and flailing at the air.

Casey knocked into him as he was drawing his sword, trapping him between them. There was not enough space to draw without harming them. Looking back, he could see why the big man pushed so hard against them both. The fire was quickly spreading, hot and bright. On the one hand, it kept some of the women away. On the other, they could not retreat that way, and there was now too much light for him to fade. Damon reached toward the sky but it was filled with only snow-clouds. Not enough unfrozen water and he did not have the strength to remedy this in any way without the help of his clan. However, he *could* call for help and did so emphatically.

Under attack! Berserkers! He sent the message through the Link.

One of the berserkers grabbed for him and fouled up his attempt to finish sending his message. Casey's whacker caught her in the side of the head and the other followed swiftly, gouging into the ribs with brutal, blunt force. A fine, warm mist of blood went up into the air, sprinkling the side of Damon's face and he squinted against it. She went down and did not move.

Staruff, still standing by some unknown miracle forced the two remaining to give ground. The archer, somewhere in the dark, caught him again. This time in the side. A pink froth clung to his mouth and he screamed at them in fury and pain. Tears streamed down his face. His lantern had rolled away into the dark.

"Damon, run!" he called.

"I can't! Too bright!" He thought frantically, putting together bits and pieces of things he had learned from Iltharen. His fear was proving an effective filter, stopping his thoughts from coming to anything useful.

252

Damn you! You will think and you will save them! ... Ice... I can do that.

He lunged in front of Staruff, barely missing a sword-swing in close quarters. He rolled under the berserker's mace and grabbed her legs. Feeling blood and flesh and fluids pumping through the body above him, he hauled his power forth. Forgetting the words of the spell, he screamed at her.

"I will not yield!"

From the dark heart of winter, the dead of the year, the frozen tears of the sky, shards of ice flew from his fingertips. She spouted crazed words in some other language as her whole frame went rigid and whitened. Staruff's sword smashed her head, sending red shards in all directions. The momentum staggered him and he fell on his knees.

"Staruff!"

The mercenary was struggling to rise but another enemy, howling like a mad wolf, darted down the path. She stopped short and hurled something into the air – a net! One of its weights caught Damon on the neck and stunned him. He found himself on the ground beside Staruff who writhed and fought as the net tangled and bore him down to the ground.

He groaned in pain and Damon saw that the leaves around him were beginning to glitter darkly in the firelight. He was bleeding; a lot. The woman leaned back to toss another but at that moment, Casey hurled a screaming, thrashing warrior over their heads. Both women went tumbling into a skeletal thicket. It was at that moment, Damon noticed the arrows in Casey's back; all three of them that he could see. Long gashes showed themselves across his chest, stomach and arms. But the bull of a man would not relent. He charged down the path after them, cursing at the top of his voice.

Damon marvelled that he had not been struck by anything more dangerous than the net weight. Then he remembered Staruff's words before. '*Magic workers... magic workers and those who surrender; they take them to their camp, everyone else they kill.*' They meant to capture him, he realized; that net had been aimed at him. He clawed at it, trying to free the blond man. There were barbs woven into the ropes, and they stuck in his clothing and flesh.

"Leave me..." Staruff growled, between his teeth. "Go. Quickly."

"I cannot..." He looked back at the blazing hell that was the path back and the carnage that was Casey introducing his iron whackers to the woefully under-armored bodies of the berserkers. He coughed in the dust and smoke.

Staruff's hand gripped his wrist, pulling him close. "The White Asp ... will fall ..." he gasped for air, closing his eyes. His hand went limp.

He will bleed to death ... I am no healer ... I must do something ... anything! The last thing he remembered casting was ice. *There is no time ... Autumn could heal him but he isn't here. Lorne could, maybe? He must live long enough to get back to the line.* He put his hands to the arrow shafts. The glistening blood went dull and frosty. The mercenary grunted and his half-open eyes rolled back.

"No!" He turned toward Casey. Several bodies lay strewn among the dead vegetation. But still more came. He could hear the alarms in the camp. *They can't get to us ... Not without going through fire or madwomen.* "Casey! Casey run! Get back to the line! Get help!" *They will take me. Alive. They will not spare him.* Another leaped on the giant, sinking a dagger into his shoulder. Damon lurched to his feet only to be pulled back by his throat.

A lithe, sweaty arm gripped him tightly against a hard body. He smelled blood and burned flesh - one of their wounded. They had underestimated the berserkers; they were not all screaming and madness, they were cunning. Many would pay with their lives for this oversight.

Damon tried to turn but she held him too tightly. He drew the dirk from his boot and thrust it into the warrior that held him. She howled and jerked but her steely grip did not loosen. He was beginning to see stars swimming before his eyes. He twisted the blade and she lurched forward, pinning him to the ground and wresting the hilt from his hands. He could see Staruff, lying so still in the leaves; and then, nothing.

He could hear hushed voices as he came around. Damon eased his eyes open and blinked at the white walls of an unfamiliar tent. There were large, crackling fire-bowls a few feet away and twinkling lanterns suspended high overhead. The flames cast everything in a bloody hue. He was bound hand and foot, lying awkwardly on his back with his knees bent and his hands above his head. He wriggled his fingers, trying to restore some feeling to them. Under his knuckles, the earth was packed hard from much traffic. He did not dare to move enough to look around but he stretched his fingers slowly and felt the thick metal stake that his wrists were tied to. Putting a little tension on the ropes told him that it was driven deep into the ground. There would be no escape by pulling it out, at least not without a lot more effort. He caught sight of a large collection of flowering plants along the other wall, in full bloom despite the season, and stared. Surely, they could not be real?

"He will need healing before we can pull what we need from him." It was a man's voice that was speaking. Soft, as if he were trying not to wake him. Damon turned his head and felt his chest clench tight in fear.

A few yards from him, the White Asp sat on the floor. His pristine white robes were like drifted snow on the dark furs beneath him. He had a hand on Staruff's chest. The mercenary was lying motionless with his arms limp at his sides. If he was alive, he was barely holding on. Damon could not even see the rise and fall of his breath. A woman with long black hair stood behind the sorcerer with her arms folded. By her dress, he could guess that she was a berserker. He didn't remember her from the attack but then, he didn't remember much of it.

The sorcerer was murmuring something quietly and for a bizarre moment, Damon thought he was praying. Then, he felt the magic begin to stir. It prickled in the air around him. His muscles tensed uncomfortably. What was he doing? He'd said something about healing. Damon stayed as still as he could, afraid of distracting him. He did not know what would happen if he interrupted him while his friend's life hung in the balance but he didn't want to find out. Staruff had bravely defended him; he deserved to live.

He watched with eyes wide as colour began to return to the mercenary's skin. He had expected to see the threads of magic weaving through him as Iltharen had described, but either the weave was too fine for him to see or the Asp worked with something other than the Dominions. It certainly felt different; it was neither solid nor airy. The only words he could put to it were 'prickly' and 'sinister' and those didn't describe it particularly well either. It was almost as if he were talking *to* the magic rather than working through it.

The sorcerer pressed his fingertips to his temples and sighed. The woman leaned over his shoulder and spoke softly.

"Need to go bargain with them again?"

The Asp shook his head. "Not this moment."

"I can fetch a priest. We still have plenty."

Damon wrinkled his nose, trying to make sense of the exchange.

"You have awakened."

Again, his muscles seized as he realized that the sorcerer was no longer looking at Staruff but him instead. He turned to the woman for a moment.

"Silence this one. I want not to hear his howling when he wakes."

For a moment, Damon thought he'd meant him, but the woman bent to gag the mercenary who had begun to twitch in his sleep. For the time being, he had eyes for no one but the sorcerer as he approached him. His eyes were such a vivid green, even in the dark, that he could swear they were glowing with a light of their own. Lyre sat upon the floor beside him, tucking his robes around his legs neatly. He was no less beautiful up close than the glimpse he had caught on the battlefield and something about that made Damon angry; what it was, he could not quite put his finger on. All he could think about right now was bracing himself for whatever was to come. His eyes stung with tears but he kept blinking. There was nothing he could do to still his shaking though. The Asp either did not notice or was used to such things.

"By what name are you called?"

What do I do? Damon thought furiously. There was clearly some intention of interrogating them, at least given what he had said about Staruff. *Is it dark enough in here to turn shadow? What about Staruff?* He swallowed hard. The sorcerer's lips parted again but Damon spoke first.

"Where is Casey?" he blurted. His voice sounded thick and choked as if he'd been crying. He hated it and swallowed, trying to clear it up.

Strangely, the man smiled as if he'd said something amusing. "The Iyotan?"

Damon stared at him, wide-eyed. "The ...?" Whatever the word was, he did not know it. It sounded something like yo-tan but he wasn't sure.

"Giant men, I think you call them now."

He nodded quickly. The Asp turned and extended a hand toward the other side of the room. Looking where he pointed, Damon saw Casey lying still on his stomach. His sides moved with breath, though the bloodied tears in his clothing did nothing to ease his worry. He seemed to be sleeping. All around him were pieces of broken chain, some of them flung a good distance away.

"He pulled the chains to bits," Lyre explained. "Many times. Formidable, yes. A wanton waste of good steel and handicraft. I brought him down. When he acts a man and not a bull, I will sit with him, and I will see what news he will tell me."

"Casey?" Damon tried to sit up but the bonds on his wrists reminded him that he was not going anywhere. He struggled but the sorcerer did not touch him or otherwise try to restrain him. "Casey!" he called. "He was wounded! He could die!"

Inexplicably, this was met with light-hearted laughter both from the

Asp and the woman sitting by Staruff.

"He will live." He looked over his shoulder at the still chuckling woman. "At the cause of your empty-headed banshees, Raach."

The woman, Raach, quieted and frowned. "It's not any fault of theirs," she protested. "He had the tattoo. What kind of ass gets a tattoo just because it looks good? They listened well to you, Master. You told them anyone bearing the mark of the sword there was a Stonehart."

"It was a new inking. Fresh."

"How were they to see that in the dark?"

Damon was momentarily flummoxed until he realized what they were talking about. Casey had admired his tattoo in the camp a few weeks ago. Damon squinted at his giant friend's back where the shirt was pulled up. There was indeed a small black sword tattooed there; it was angry red around the edges. *He must have thought it was only a design,* he thought. *Many of the other mercenaries had tattoos of all sorts... Oh Casey what did you do that for?*

"Well I can kill him right now and fix their mista-"

"No!" Damon tried to sit upright. The iron stake jerked and quivered as he pulled on it but it would not otherwise budge.

They both quieted and looked at him. Raach started to speak but the Asp held up a hand.

"No?" he said, canting his head to the side. "Will you speak to me all the things I would know of your people? Of their doings and plotting?"

Damon swallowed hard. "Would you... let us go? All of us?" He felt absurd trying to bargain with a monster thousands of years older than himself. That monster was shaking his head 'no.'

"I will grant freedom to the Giant and the other one. You will die," he extended an arm and tapped a wide, thick wooden bench a few feet off the floor. "Upon this table."

Damon felt his mouth go completely dry. He could not have swallowed if he'd wanted to, though he felt much more like he was about to vomit.

"Swiftly or slowly shall be by your design. Speak, and receive mercy." He held his gaze until Damon looked down, curling in on himself.

Damon concentrated. The terror in his mind was very real and fresh. In a way, it was more so than falling from the tower. *The light might be dim enough. I can fade to shadow. I don't know what's outside this room but if I could just...*

Suddenly, there was a grip like steel around his throat and he flinched. Lyre held him by a single hand but that silken flesh seemed to be all deception; it was as immovable as a pillar. He could feel the sorcerer's power pressing in on him, prickling, jabbing... speaking. Was it? His head swam and he struggled harder. No, it had to be the Asp's voice. But his lips were not moving. He felt himself becoming weightless and for one glorious moment he thought he had succeeded.

The Asp inclined his chin toward Raach. "Take the pay-swords into your tent. Do as you must, but see that they remain upon this side of death."

He could hear Raach laughing and calling for assistance to move the unconscious mercenaries. Damon could not see either of them both because of the position in which he lay and the tight grip around his neck that dulled his vision. He could only hope that they were alright.

The stake that had held him fast to the ground slowly pulled upward though nothing was touching it. Magic. He could not recognize which Dominions were at work but did not waste time trying to figure it out. He pulled at the ropes and tried to roll away. Lyre's fingers tightened on his throat and he felt a wave of thunderous energy roll over him. His sight swam and faded.

Then, his back slammed into a hard, wooden surface. The floor? No he'd just been lying on it and it had been bare dirt. He desperately tried to get his bearings.

The pressure at his throat went away. When his vision cleared, he found Raach at his head, removing the ropes that bound his wrists. He did not remember being unbound or carried though he was sure only seconds had passed. Where were Casey and Staruff? Had she dealt with them already?

This was not the same tent he had been in. That, or it was another section of it because the plants were absent and it was much smaller. He struggled but the berserker cuffed him hard across the face. He blinked while the room swam. He found his hands down at his sides when he came back to his senses. Raach waved an eight inch stake of rough iron in front of his face and laughed. There was a sick feeling in the pit of his stomach that grew until it swallowed up his whole body. To his shame, he found himself too terrified to move at all. He could not even find coherent words to beg her to leave him be.

"To your task, Raach," the Asp reminded her, standing placidly near his feet. Damon realized that, given that he was level with the sorcerer's waist, he was on a table of some kind. "I will crack this cask and pour out its secrets. Make haste."

What cask? He wondered and looked back to the berserker. Damon realized, far too late, that he had failed to notice the hammer in her other hand. There was no time to react. The iron tip touched the back of his hand and she swung down. He screamed and tried to jerk away but the spike had bitten into the wood beneath him. Every strike of the hammer jarred the bones of his arm, paralysing him with pain. As the mercy of unconsciousness rose to claim him, the last thing he could see was the sorcerer's eyes, burning like green fire in the dark.

Lyre pressed the silk handkerchief to his forehead and took a few deep breaths. The binding of a Stonehart was no small task, even as weak and inexperienced in the ways of power as they were in these times. The priests and the seer were easy as an afternoon stroll by comparison. He could feel this boy's magic coursing through the air around him like a rushing torrent. So much power... yet he was too young to lead. No matter, he would use him to find what he needed to know and, given that he was likely a Darkblood, drain him to bolster his power. The Stonehart scouts he had taken already had fortified his strength in a way it had not been in years.

The boy lay upon the table before him, pale and still. Raach had turned his feet to the side and driven two more spikes down through, just behind his ankle bones. If he struggled too hard, he would tear the tendons there. It would not be a problem for long, Lyre suspected, but he'd been surprised before.

A long, narrow spear bound with blue and black wrappings jutted up from the Stonehart's torso just below the sternum. Lyre had woven complex spells in thin white strips around the handle to keep him from dying before it was time. The spear's head was not a single wedge but an elegant two-pronged steel affair, much like a very large tuning fork. The space between the tines was only wide enough to accommodate the spine.

A cold and clammy sweat formed against his skin. Lyre was exhausted, but that was hardly the chief reason for distress. As soon as Raach had brought the hammer down he had noticed it – the colour of the boy's blood. *Blue. Not red. Not merely dark. Blue.* The thought had stilled his mind and body such that he did not even move to assist her with the thrashing boy. He could not seem to make himself do anything but stare. He had not seen such a thing since he was young in times now ancient. Did the Stoneharts of today realize the significance? Did they still use the stones in the temple to measure their blood magic? Surely they had noticed the concentration of power within this single body. *Power unparalleled. You, young one... are you my fountain of youth? I thought not that you would come to me in this manner. I thought to hunt you but here you are before me.*

The deep blue streams from the spear wound rose upward from the motionless body, spiralling around the shaft until it reached the top and twisted back down again to seep back into the flesh. It glittered like liquid sapphires in the torchlight. It was the most intricate and prefect blood-binding he had done in a very long time. He could take no chances, not with a Stonehart and most definitely not with a Stonehart like this.

As soon as Raach had finished, he had ordered her to go to her surviving berserkers and decorate them lavishly with the highest honours they possessed. They had brought him a priceless treasure unharmed. He would make much of them for they deserved it. He had told her to do the same for Feral, or "Staruff" as his friends apparently called him, but she had something else in mind. He hoped it was good, whatever it was. The boy had successfully led their prize right into the berserker ambush, and they still did not know he had betrayed them.

He could not help but smile with pride. *You have done well, my son.*

Lyre trailed his fingertips across Damon's forehead, smoothing away stray hairs. The lad had fainted before Raach had even finished with the first spike. So much the better. He had not been struggling when Lyre had thrust the spear down. Such things were best done slow with surgical precision. The magic of the pinning spear would keep the boy from moving more than any other restraint. Any motion, any at all, caused instant and excruciating pain, worsening each moment until the movement stopped.

Earlier he had doubted, really doubted, that he could complete his quest. The Stoneharts had come against him in force accompanied by men from many lands. The one boon was that he did not have to hunt them on their own lands. Glasshammer was a minefield of magic. He knew the ancient protections laid over it and what great trouble it would cause him to bring them down. He had left it to last. The need to face them alone with the strength of the Az Taeorans at his back was so great that it necessitated such measures. Of course, his plan had also included the benefit of terrorizing them into sending all their Darkbloods to the front within easy reach.

Now, their resistance was over. He held the tool of their demise in his hands.

The boy's eyelids flickered. A grimace of pain etched itself into his face and he tried to turn his head to the side. Lyre heard the choking gasp and watched him open his mouth in silence, too agonized to manage a scream. He went limp again. This had happened several times and would likely continue for the entirety of his stay on the table. Any other torturer, trying to garner knowledge from his victim would think him foolish for having gone to such extremes. Lyre, however, did not need the boy to speak.

He placed his hands gently on either side of the lad's head and closed his eyes. The quiet murmurs of his spell drew him downward. Down into the darkness and twisting nightmares of an unconscious mind. He maintained firm control through the disorientation. Flickering thoughts and memories danced around him in the amorphous mass of swirling cloud and crackling static energy. The pockets in time moved and swam at random. They were like windows looking in on some scene unfolding; those windows had lost their frames and bled out into eternity.

He waited and listened. A scene of hunting in the woods on horseback rippled by and dissipated into the mist surrounding him. Two girls sat in a small kitchen playing at a dice game. The image was clear, if flickering. He reached out a hand and steadied it. Delicate white threads pulled it closer to him. Lyre's mind always tried to supplement this bizarre feeling by telling him he was walking towards the memories he viewed. He knew he was still. He was, in fact, the only thing not in motion here. The chimes at the ends of his long sleeves hung in silence.

It seemed as though the girls were talking to him. He heard the rules of a game being explained by a voice he recognized to be the boy's.

"Isn't that cheating?" The young one with chestnut hair asked.

"No, it's betting. You're not really lying, you're just guessing what dice are under the cup."

"Oh!" She smiled. "Right, it sounds easy enough."

Something banged. The boy's attention turned towards the door and the two girls drifted away. A man wearing a stained work tunic was motioning for him to come.

"Damon, I need you in the barn, quick as you can. Jae's here with a load of grain just in from Tuador. We've got to help her unload."

"Aye. I'll be along."

There was more to the memory but Lyre let it go and pushed it gently away. He had what he needed from it. Damon, was it? He sighed heavily. It was a butchery of a very archaic name, and one he hated at that.

"Damon," he said into the darkness. His voice sent ripples through all that he could see and distorted the sounds into something garbled and alien. He felt a quiver run through the air around him. For a few moments, he remained silent, listening as the mingling voices resolved themselves into something comprehensible once again. "Damon, come," he said. Though he spoke calmly and gently, the mindscape about him jarred as though he had carelessly swung around a hammer. Fear, he thought. The static around him prickled the hairs on his skin. The bright discharges leaped from cloud to cloud with greater ferocity.

Memories were winking out all around him. The glimpses he saw of the ones that remained were of the forest aflame, the giant man Casey, the defenders' camp; all were recent and fresh. Fear sharpened the images to a painful level. He narrowed his eyes against the burning lines but did not look away. He knew terror often etched recollections most deeply and with surreal clarity. It was something he counted on.

Suddenly, there was an image that did not flicker or waver; instead, it moved slowly in the dark miasma. Lyre paid heed to this one more acutely than any others. It was unique in that it was the only image that portrayed the boy himself.

Lyre took a deep breath and focused his energies on maintaining his calm. The soft light that emanated from his flesh grew a little brighter. He lifted his arm and passed a silk sleeve over his face, deliberately obscuring his features. He floated there, hazy and indistinct as something almost forgotten, as the boy made his way toward the beacon in the darkness.

Damon looked confused. *Of course,* Lyre mused. *You are not accustomed to viewing your own mind in this way, outside of dreams.* He called the boy's name again and watched him change course to make for him directly. He was surprised to see the lad wearing oversized, much-repaired working clothes. It confused him as he had seen the circlet on the boy's head when they had brought him in. *Wear a crown while mucking stalls?* He wondered. *I had forgotten the profound strangeness of your ilk.*

The boy stopped a few feet short of him. His arms were wrapped tightly around himself as if he were cold. He squinted up at the glowing figure. Lyre knew he was trying to see through the obfuscation and wondered what face Damon's mind would decide to put on him. Such was the way of dreams. The mind always tried to force them to make some kind of sense. He could not perceive any change yet. Perhaps he looked too unlike anything the boy had ever seen? It was a possibility.

"Iltharen? What are you doing here?"

Lyre felt as though his heart had fallen right out of his chest. The lapse in concentration loosened his grip and he felt himself slipping out of the mindscape. He did not try to recover.

Once again in the tent, he stared down at the young pale face below him. He had never expected such an ancient tongue to come out of his mouth. Iltharen... a concept lost to time. *Long gone,* he thought. That was why his face had not changed. Damon knew it too well. He had seen it elsewhere. A simple clouding would do nothing to obscure what he already had a familiar reference for.

"How came you by my book?" he whispered to the silent body on the table. He stared at the double spiral of blood, twining sinuously around the spear. "And *which* book?" His mind raced. Did they have more than one? Did they have all of them? It was obvious now that they had at least one. It was the only way they could have resisted him so effectively while being so ignorant of their own history. They had thrown his own magic at him.

The boy's cheek was cold under his hand. The berserkers said he had been that way when they took him. The bizarre white hue of his flesh made him look painted, or dead. The strange power he possessed was becoming more of a mystery to Lyre by the moment.

He shook his head. They could not have all of the books. If they did and had figured out how to use them, they would have repelled his forces already, and perhaps even managed to *kill* him. It should have been impossible. He had seen them all safely destroyed.

"I must know," he murmured to no one. Pushing himself away from the table, he went through the tent flaps, heading for his private room. The boy knew too much to do this the simple way. His sudden appearance startled the servant girl and she pulled the tray of food she was carrying closer to her body.

"My Lord..." She fumbled for words as he stared at her. "You... I... sorry, you missed breakfast."

Lyre gestured at the low table in front of his sitting cushions. "Later. Time flies too fast this day. Go to my chambers and fetch my tool chest. I have much to do."

Damon blinked. He had never seen this place before and he turned in slow, shuffling circles as he tried to get his bearings. He was surrounded by walls made of pale, smooth stone. He would have guessed about ten or twelve of him would need to stand on each other's shoulders to reach the top. The wall behind him, closing off the corridor was blank and showed no signs of any kind of door or gate but ahead a path, broad and straight stretched into the distance. He noticed that he was still clad in battle dress, his circlet around his head and his sword on his back.

How did I get here? He wondered. *And where are Casey and Starruff? The forest? The Asp?*

The last thought made his breath catch in his throat. He remembered with crushing clarity that he had been grotesquely nailed to a table with the monster and his warrior woman looking over him. Damon moved closer to the wall and sat down, leaning his shoulder against it. The walls suddenly seemed so much taller and bleaker. He crossed his arms over his chest and curled inward.

This is a dream, he thought. *Oh good and holy Aervie, let me never wake up.* He closed his eyes, resting his face on his arms. His stomach felt like lead. The end of his days playing at being a hero had come. His father would find his body in that small tent, his tunic ripped open and body mangled, his sword gone. Likely, they had given it to one of the soldiers. It was good steel; a fine weapon.

He realized he'd been assuming that the resistance would find a way to stop the invasion and drive off the terrible White Asp. *Did I really have so much hope? How could I be so foolish?* He wondered what they would do with his body.

Damon's grip around his shoulders tightened and he found that he was shaking. The prospect of death had not been real until this moment; not his own death, in any case. The one comfort in his mind was that the pain had not followed him into this dream. He wondered how long it could last.

Swallowing numerous times, he managed to fight down the bile. There had to be something he could do. *No one knows where to find me.* That, however, did not need to be the case. It dawned on him that he did not have to be alone in this place. He could seek comfort if not help from the Blood Link.

His heart hammered in his chest as he tentatively reached out. Instantly, he felt others reaching back to him; searching for him. He focused on his father and put all of his concentration into getting through to him.

Erik's face swam fuzzily in the darkness behind his closed eyelids.

Damon? The voice was distorted at first but sharpened quickly.

Damon! You're alive!

He could distinguish his father clearly now and some parts of the tent he was sitting in. Erik was waving at a couple of marshals sitting near him to be silent.

They've got me, Da, he said quickly. He sounded choked and raspy even in his own mind. *I don't know how long I have to talk to you. I'm trying to stay asleep as much as I can.* The words came out in a rush. He tried to school himself; to make his thoughts more coherent. *Casey and Staruff are here too. They're not doing well.*

His father's knuckles where white where he was wringing his hands just under his chin. He was nodding rapidly. Damon could feel the desperation coming from him as well. Each moment of contact was precious to them both. *We're doing everything we can, Damon. You need to hold on. You have to. We're coming. I promise.* Tears were standing out in his eyes. He paid no attention. *How are you? Are you hurt?*

Nothing managed to come out of Damon's mouth. He did not want anyone to see him like this much less his father, but if he was to be rescued, they needed to know. He needed a healer badly. *Da ... don't ...* He swallowed and looked away for a moment. *Don't break the connection. Please don't. I ... I'll show you - well I'll try to show you - you're not going to like it....*

He pulled up the memories of what happened from the time he had woken up in the tent and fed them through to his father as clearly as he could. Erik's face grew paler as the view moved over Staruff, the shackles, Casey lying still and bloody. The words were slightly muffled but they were intelligible enough, at least as Damon could hear them. The memory flickered back and forth in time twice but he tried his best to keep it a steady stream. He saw the woman lift him in his mind's eye.

The Link wavered sickeningly as Erik struggled to stay calm. A lot of howling and cursing managed to leak through from his mind. The seething rage seemed to help him hold on. The memories became small snips of what he had been able to see when he opened his eyes before the crushing pain had driven him back under. The spikes, the spear, the White Asp standing over him murmuring…

Erik was unable to send anything coherent for a while. Damon persevered through the emotions that rocked him as his father strove to master himself.

I am so sorry. Erik put his hands over his eyes and gave in to tears. His inner voice was still mostly clear but the sorrow and guilt carried by it were difficult to bear. *Oh my son ... I thought ... the legends and the prophecy ... I thought they all pointed this way. I thought we should put you forward in this fight I ... we should not have ... we have wronged you. We have used you. Oh Damon I am so sorry. We will find you. You will be alright. Lorne is already working with the books and he thinks he knows a way. I swear, I will come for you and I will keep you safe. I will never make you do something like this again. I promise.*

Da, he interrupted. Damon put up his hands to still the flow of words. *There was no way to know. I did help a little bit, didn't I?*

Erik nodded vigorously. *A little bit? You did all I could have ever hoped for. If not for you, we would not have had any idea how to use those books....*

Suddenly, an overpowering electric prickle ran up his spine and made him shudder. He opened his eyes slowly, keeping the image of his father in his mind. Erik and the dimly-lit tent were superimposed on the smooth stones of the wall. Satisfied that he had not lost the connection, he turned his head to look down the long empty corridor.

It was not empty. The White Asp stood in his pristine alabaster robes, watching him calmly.

Damon got up and stumbled backward. He backed away from the sorcerer, feeling his way along the wall. The Asp made no attempt to come any closer to him and watched his movements with tranquillity.

Get out of my dream you monster! Damon's back hit the wall behind him. *Why are you here? Leave me be!*

Damon? It was his father's voice. Damon realized Erik had been speaking the whole time but he'd lost his focus. *What's wrong?*

You ... He didn't dare take his eyes off the sorcerer. *You don't see him?*

See ... Erik, now superimposed over Lyre as he came into focus again, squinted. *I see a light blotch. Is that a person?*

He's right in front of me. Damon swallowed hard, trying to keep his heart from drowning out everything else. It was then that he began to notice the strange magic he had felt before. The prickling feeling that had alerted him in the first place was one and the same. If he focused hard enough, he could see the faint ripples in the air around him.

Da, you can't see him?

His father shook his head. *Is it him? The Asp?*

Damon nodded. He forced himself to take slow breaths. How long had Lyre been standing there? He didn't seem to be doing anything but watching him. A terrible realization dawned on him: if the Asp could get into his mind and invade his dreams, what was to stop him from eavesdropping on their Blood Link? Of course Erik couldn't see him. The sorcerer's power vastly outstripped their own. He could shield himself quite easily if he wanted to.

Da, I don't think this is safe. He clenched his teeth. *I think he can hear us. At least... probably me. You mustn't say anything....* He could feel his chest tightening up. His shaking fingers helped him feel his way down the wall until he could kneel on the ground. He didn't think he could stand anymore; not with his legs shaking so hard.

Perhaps this was not a good idea, he thought privately. *But without my father - without the Link - I'm alone here. I don't think I can do this on my own. I can't bear this.*

The White Asp moved then, but only to close his eyes and bow his head. Erik made a startled noise.

I see him! Anger rushed into his voice. *You!* Damon watched his father's jaw work in silent rage before he managed to say anything else. *You must know, you will get exactly the same amount of mercy you give. We will stop you and you will answer for your crimes. Take care with your prisoners!*

For a moment there was silence. The White Asp canted his head to the side but did not open his eyes. *Old and strong powers you toy with, King Erik.* The voice came through with a sterling quality that made everything before it seem mushy by comparison. *Weak are the voices of your kin. Yet, I hear them. Woe to you who stand against me. Strive as you will, you will fall.*

Damon's mind worked frantically. He had said "the voices of your kin." Could he hear everyone through the Blood Link? All the Stonehearts? *No,* he thought. *He can't. He can't be able to do that. Not even we can. Not all at once. Not if we aren't trying. But what if he can? Is there any safe way we can speak to each other?*

Just as he felt his hopes beginning to dim, Lyre's image suddenly went hazy and indistinct. He could hear a woman's voice speaking. That terrible voice. He recognized it from the madwoman who had made such savage use of the hammer and spikes.

"The scouts have reported in as you ordered, Master. The raiders have landed successfully and ...."

The Asp flung out a hand, as if to stop her from speaking but already rippling images were intruding into the air between them. Black-clad brigands leaped from their boats to be greeted by a contingent of grinning berserkers. Damon recognized the shoreline, and the woods they approached.

He realized then what the enemy meant to do. They had been contented not to move or show much aggression to the defenders because they had already arranged the doom of Glasshammer in advance. With all the Darkbloods many days to the south, they could not return in time to protect the kinsmen they had left behind.

Damon felt the strange and terrible wrath he had felt so many times before. The anger that was not this own. *No! This isn't the time to lose my head! I must do something!*

Close the Link.

The voice was not one he recognized, yet it was familiar. Not Lyre's, not Erik's, not Raach's and certainly not his own. Nevertheless, it spoke to him, pressed on him.

Da? Did you see? Did you see what the woman was saying?

Erik made a face. *What woman? Damon? What's going on?*

The White Asp opened his eyes, his image becoming more distinct again. He looked angry. Damon pressed himself back against the wall, wanting nothing more than to sink into it and get away somehow.

Close the Link. This will break the battle line, and divide the Darkbloods. The voice was relentless. That same voice that had spoken inside his mind before. That part of him - or something within him - that understood things he had no right to know. At the same time, he knew it was true. He could see it clearly. The Stonehart line would be divided and broken as they tried to race back to Glasshammer and protect it from the onslaught.

We have all our best fighters with us, Damon pleaded weakly. *Our kinsmen are defenceless.* But he already knew what the voice was going to say. He wondered if all people hated their conscience's voice so very much. He wanted to shut his ears and pretend he didn't understand.

It will end the same for them if the line breaks here. They cannot know. Our only hope is to maintain focus here. The Asp must be stopped or he will march on and seize everything uncontested. We must stand firm.

They cannot know. Damon said the words inside his mind at the same time. His whole body felt weak and battered. His stomach was a tight knot inside him that would not unclench. *Please, spirits of my ancestors,* he prayed. *Let me make the right decision. I don't want to be alone. If everyone dies ... if I make the wrong choice...*

He reached out his hand to his father. The White Asp made a small sound and stepped forward.

Damon? What's going on? Erik reached for him, not understanding.

I'm sorry, Da. He closed his hand and felt the Link snap.

Chapter 15: Cracks

A trickle of sweat ran down her temple. Phoenix knelt on the stone floor of Wester's common room with her hands out, palms upturned.

"Are you certain you are focusing on fire?" Kael rested his hip on a table as he watched her.

She glared at him. He waited.

"Yes." She folded her legs to the side and sat.

"Do not stop." The table was full of books taken from the Vault. After Harkeen's death, the other Wardens had stood aside for them, offering no resistance. It did not make the act any easier to accept.

"I cannot do it."

It was true. They had been working at simple exercises for days and the only magic she was able to wield was Ducal. The fire bowls ranged around the room had changed from their daytime gold to the blue of the night.

"Do not stop," he repeated, his expression unchanged.

Phoenix ignored him. She was beginning to wonder what manner of psychotic slave-driver had trained this man. She pressed her palms to the stone.

"You understand the fundamentals of human magic," he said. His voice was closer now but she did not bother looking up at him. "I have taught them to you."

"If you are so confident in them, why do you not wield it yourself?"

He was silent. After a moment, she heard the sound of pages turning.

"I am Ducal," he said at last. "You are human. It should be faster for you, simpler. I have continued to study each night."

Phoenix looked at him then. His hair shielded his face as usual, but she wondered if perhaps his shoulders hung a little lower than usual. If he studied at night after their hours-long training sessions, when did he sleep?

He wants this so badly.

She warned herself not to ascribe human feelings to the bird man. She crossed her legs and straightened her back.

"I have not yet had my Feast of Life," she told him. "You cannot expect me to be able to wield the power of my ancestors without their flesh and blood to guide me."

Kael paused in his perusal of the book and turned to look at her. "Feast of Life?" He sat on the edge of the table and pulled the tome into his lap.

"This is some sort of initiation ceremony?"

She nodded. "When a Solara is old and ready to leave this life, there is a ritual held in their honour. Three days of feasting when all their friends and relations come to see them and listen as they tell their stories for the last time and their words are recorded."

The shaman closed the book he had been reading and dug out another one from under a stack. He flipped through it, his brow wrinkled in thought.

"And then?"

Phoenix blinked in surprise. She thought he had stopped listening to her.

"On the night of the third day, the old one goes to the temple of whichever God to whom they feel the strongest allegiance. They say their final prayers and the priests slay them."

Kael's hands paused over the book. He closed that one too and set it aside. He made to pick up another, hesitated, and rested his palms on his knees. Phoenix waited for him to say something but he remained silent, giving her all of his attention instead. She resisted the urge to squirm and continued.

"The flesh is stripped from the bones and cooked in special dishes. The bones are engraved with the name of the dead and given to their family members and friends. A man is said to be great or unfortunate depending on how many, or few of his bones are given away. If he has too many friends for each of them to have one of the bones, it is a great honour."

"And the flesh?" He gazed at her with the same intensity as he had the pages of the books. She hated that look.

I am not just another tome, another tool for your arsenal, bird-man.

"It is distributed among the friends and family of the departed. Those who are aged sixteen cycles or more."

"You *are* over sixteen cycles by your count."

"Yes, and no one died last year." She frowned.

"Pity." He glanced at the stack of books beside him. "And I have no humans for you to eat."

"How can you say that!" she exploded. "How can you be so callous? The Feast is a time of grief and honour for all Az Taeorans. It is not some frivolous picnic!"

"And, am I to understand that you care deeply about liberating my people? The Ducal mean much to you?"

"Why should they?" Phoenix struck her fist against the floor, the hard surface scuffing her knuckles. The spike of pain fuelled her anger, making it rise and spike within her until she could hear her pulse in her ears.

It took some time for her to realize that Kael had not answered. He simply sat with a contemplative look on his face, his lips curving up on one side in that annoying half-smile. The silence conveyed all that needed to be said.

Indeed. Why should they?

"Leave me alone," she muttered and turned her back on him.

"Your lesson is not finished. It is not time for sulking."

"I am not sulking," she said and took a deep breath. "I am meditating. I need advice."

"What can you find in your own mind that is not in the pages of these books? You said you had no training."

"I am not consulting my own mind. I am consulting Damon."

She heard the swish of his clothing as he drew closer and willed him away. He stood by her shoulder, arms crossed.

No such luck.

"Who is Damon?"

"A human boy …" She stopped and corrected herself. "A human man. He lives where I came from." She did not care if he believed her. Perhaps if he thought she was mad, he would leave her in peace. He was quiet for so long, Phoenix looked up.

That keen, predatory look was back.

"This man can wield magic, yes?"

"Yes." She leaned away from him.

"Good." He walked back to the table. His fingers tapped over the spines of the books as he searched them.

"Good?" she pressed.

"Yes."

Phoenix cursed under her breath and rose. She could not hope to meditate while she was so irritated.

"What are you going to do?"

"I have not read of any Feast of Life but there are other initiation rites in these tomes." He picked one up and leafed through it. "Several, in fact."

"You mean to use Damon to help with one of these rites?"

"Yes."

Her heart leaped. "Can you send me to him? To the Ice Kingdom?"

He considered this for a moment, eyes focusing on the ceiling as though making some kind of tally in his head. "Yes," he said finally and went back to inspecting the diagram on the page he had paused on.

She gripped his arm. "Why did you not say so before?"

"I did. It is part of our bargain." He ignored her hold on him and skipped forward to the next section of the book.

Her stomach tightened and she felt a familiar chill seeping in. "*Will you send me to him?*" she rephrased her question.

"Is our bargain complete?"

Phoenix let go of him. "No."

The shaman retrieved a piece of parchment from the table and began to write. "You say you can speak with him? See him?"

Phoenix nodded, realized he wasn't looking at her, and sighed. "Yes."

"That is enough." He copied the diagram carefully. The only sound in the room was the scratching of his quill. The feather was of some deep blue bird and it glittered like sapphires.

Like Damon's eyes.

"I will prepare a rite. The next time you reach across the distance, you will lead me to him."

She didn't bother to ask how. Kael did not look to her for an answer and she gave none. Her hand hurt from gripping the hilt of her sword. She flexed her fingers as she walked to the door. The shaman paid her no mind and she assumed that their lesson was over for the day.

You may wield the fangs of the desert for now, bird-man, but you will not be so pleased when they turn on you.

Phoenix turned her head this way and that, eyes closed. At last she shook herself and looked up at Kael. The bird man looked like he had not moved since she'd begun to meditate.

"Something is wrong. He is ... not where he should be."

Kael canted his head to the side. She had been trying to reach Damon for hours. The shaman shook his head and stood up. "You must not fail in this. I need direction. I need to know what you know, and what he—this human friend of yours—knows. Otherwise, I cannot attune your magic."

"As I said, I do not know where he is." She shrugged. "I followed the ..." She thought for a moment on how to put it. "...pathways, that I normally do; but he is not there. To find him when he sleeps is easy. I have done it by accident before. I can find him also when he is awake, unless he is in great turmoil." A cold pit began to form in her stomach. Was he in danger? She knew something of the battles he and his people were facing.

"He could be dead," Kael offered helpfully. Phoenix glared at him. He stared back, expression blank. "Try again. I will help you widen your search." He shuffled around behind her on the bed and seated himself comfortably.

"You can do that?" She craned her neck to look over her shoulder.

A pale eyebrow raised by way of response. "I am shaman. I walk the planes," he enunciated, as if she were simple-minded. "Now concentrate. The sky will not come to us while we wait."

Phoenix closed her eyes and faced forward, feeling chastised. She tried to ignore the bird man behind her and let her mind fall into peaceful contemplation. Relaxation came slowly to her now. She was beginning to tire of this exercise. Past the frustration of her search and the annoyance of the Ducal, there was Damon. He was out there somewhere.

She had just succeeded in forgetting the shaman behind her when she felt his fingers wrap around her neck.

Chapter 16: In Dreams

Lyre stood beside the table where Damon lay pinned, stiff with rage as the boy cut the Blood Link. He let go of his concentration and slipped out of the labyrinth. Kneading his temples with his fingertips, he slowly began to calm his breathing. Such audacity he had not expected in one so young, nor such power, but that power remained closed to him for as long as the boy resisted him.

Nothing important ever came easily, he reminded himself. Lyre meandered around the table. He found himself loathe to go far from the boy who could very well be the reason for his quest. He replayed the moment in his mind: The thick ribbons of blood magic stretching out from Damon like a nexus, each rippling line of blue reaching into the darkness and touching his kinsmen. He had felt old magics in that moment. Things that he had not sensed for a very long time. The Dominions hovered and hummed around him, close, and ready to respond in an instant should the boy but turn his mind to them. There was something at work here, within this small, pale body that defied reason. Such vast strength, yet untrained and untempered; perfect for his purposes, if indeed he was the one.

If this Stonehart was the key to obtaining everlasting life, it would radically alter his plans. If he was not, Lyre would have to move to counter whatever it was that the boy's kin were planning. He knew they were not to be underestimated. He had to know the truth and that was going to take some delicate work.

He could simply capture another Stonehart, it was true, but Damon's connection to the rest of his clan was so clear, so sharp. The kind of information he could get through him would far outstrip the abilities of any other, of that he was certain.

There were slender scarlet threads crisscrossing over Damon. They spiralled out from where they were wrapped around the head of the spear in a wheel-spoke web. This net was secured around the edges of the table with small nails. Lyre reached out and carefully lifted one of the threads so that its looped end came off of its nail. He moved it over two nails and secured it again, distorting the symmetry of the weave. Tinkling laughter echoed distantly as the small glowing eyes of the Arcana raced along the threads, exploring the new weave.

The Asp walked to a nearby cushion and sat, folding his legs under him as he observed his silent captive. Raach had departed at his scolding, leaving him alone; that was just as well, he had a lot to think about. His eyes wandered over the black hair, the blue-tinted lips, the subtle rise and fall of the boy's chest. This was a mystery in human flesh and one he did not have much time to solve.

Who are you, Damon Stonehart? They have flung you upon the field, a wolf in the skin of a lamb. But the wolf knows not what he is and so he goes to slaughter. Fools.

In thousands of years of life, the Asp was seldom surprised. People were the same from one century to the next. They laughed at the same jokes and feared the same shadows. Their children, weak and easily led. This one, however, had set him back on his heels.

Why had he closed the Link rather than warning his kin of the impending attack on their homes? Granted, Damon had done the *right* thing, the intelligent thing, but how had he known to do so? Where countless grown men would have fouled up he had remained steady on course, like a battle-hardened general.

Though Lyre had initially been vexed with Raach for tipping his hand without his permission, he could certainly have worked the situation to his advantage. A splitting of the Stonehart forces could have been a godsend. Instead, Damon had handily slammed that door shut, denying his captor an opening to the minds of the rest of his clan in one fell swoop.

Scouts, he could make use of, of course, but the information they delivered was piecemeal at best. The kind of detailed plans Lyre needed to assure himself of victory needed to be gotten by scrying or peering through the Stonehart Blood Link. He was coming up short on energy for the former, quickly running out of priests to consume for fuel. Unless he wanted to make yet another bargain with the Arcana, he was going to have to find a way to break through Damon's resolve and force him to open the Link again.

He did not want to make another deal. The demands of the Arcana were getting steep and sooner or later they were going to command a price he could not pay. He was going to have to break this boy.

Your valiant choice I admire, young one, but it will be to no avail in the end. You will open my paths for me, even as I shut yours.

Damon stared at the wall that had just swung out in front of him. It had moved of its own accord. On one hand, it created a new opening off to his left. On the other, it barred him from going the way he had intended.

He sank down to the ground and pressed his palms to the stone. Neither direction mattered now. Not now that he knew his adversary could change the terrain at will. He could—and likely would—lead him in circles until he starved to death. *Can someone starve to death in a dream?* There was no answer though at present he was neither hungry nor thirsty, only tired. His one measure of time was that he had yet to fall asleep; although in fairness, he supposed he already *was* asleep.

He had stopped trying to figure out how long he had been there. The exercise had only tied his mind into knots. Time in a normal dream was abstract enough. In an induced dream, controlled by another ... he lacked the knowledge to even finish the thought. It was beyond his understanding. Now, knowing that the landscape could be changed upon his captor's whim, he was fairly certain that time could be equally altered. The thought of spending years in this place that were really only days unsettled him. He reminded himself, and not for the first time, that it was best to not ponder such ideas. *If this continues, I will be able to measure time only by how crazy I am.*

"Damon."

He looked up, feeling his insides grow cold.

"Damon where are you?"

"I'm h—" His voice died in his throat. He recognized his mother's voice and lowered his head.

"Damon?"

"Shut up."

"Damon?"

"Shut up! She's dead; stop it!" He covered his ears. It did not help. He could still hear it in his head. "Stop!" His mother. The bastard had dug through his thoughts and pulled up the voice of his mother. He drowned her out with all the profanity he could recall interspersed with angry gibberish.

The beauty of the garden failed to charm him. Damon sat with his back against a mossy wall, surveying the flourishing greenery. It had the air of a manicured space that was allowed to loosen and swing back towards its more natural state. There were benches and gables in the middle of the large square, set around an old but energetic fountain. Archways were covered with vines and mosses as were the flowering trees that stood in the clear spaces made in the cobblestone.

It is winter, he thought. *You do not fool me, Asp.*

277

After the sorcerer had tired of playing with his heartstrings, with his mother's voice and then –even worse—her face, he had left him to wander alone in the silent maze.

He reached back over his shoulder, fingers tracing idly over the bejewelled hilt of his sword for a small measure of comfort. "It will not help me," he whispered to no one. Again, he despaired. He would be an amusement for the sorcerer until his campaign of terror finally rolled over and crushed the last resistance of the Stoneharts; then, he knew, he would die.

Damon did not bother trying to remember how he had come to the garden. With the way the walls shifted around, keeping his sense of direction was impossible. He suspected that it was also futile. It wasn't as though salvation was waiting for him somewhere within these walls.

"Do you not enjoy the place I have made for you?"

The voice sent a jolt of fear through him. He looked up to find the sorcerer suddenly there, his hands folded serenely before him. The chimes dangling from his sleeves tinkled in the breeze. A breeze that was and was not there.

Damon swallowed hard. From this position, with his sword sheathed and caught between his weight and the wall, he could not draw. Had Lyre been waiting for this moment? It was not as though any of Damon's defences had been successful thus far. He realized that even drawing his weapon was pointless in the face of what he was up against.

"Will you not answer?"

"I might ..." Damon cleared his throat, trying to release some of the tension in it. "I might, if you were not in it."

Lyre's smile came readily enough. He wondered if there was no way at all to offend the sorcerer. He had cussed at him as viciously as he knew how. The young Stonehart's anger only seemed to please him.

"What do you want?" he asked, and not for the first time. "I will not re-open the Link."

"You think I require this of you?" The Asp crossed his arms patiently. He had no need to fear Damon's sword and he knew it quite well. Damon found this galling. "I have already sent all of your kin into the darkness of death. I keep you for my amusement; nothing more."

He felt his heart seize in his chest. The sorcerer watched him. Damon shook his head vigorously.

"No. You lie."

A flicker of interest moved over Lyre's face. "You see? You do amuse me greatly. How long will you deny it, I wonder?"

"You are lying!" He wanted to stand and shout it in his face but the urge to be as far away from him as possible was too great.

"Your anger will undo you, young one. Pity."

There was a bright glint at his side and suddenly a long, curved blade was in the sorcerer's hands. "You resist casting magic against me. Why?"

"A drop in an ocean," Damon retorted, eyes on the sword. His mouth was almost too dry to swallow.

"You used it to great effect before. Quelling the flames, setting your kin on my men like warhounds ... what a skillful murderer you are!"

Damon's muscles tightened until the strain made him tremble. His opponent's brilliant green gaze bore into him as if trying to read by the reflection in his eyes. There was too much light to fade into shadows, but he could feel the cold prickling around him, responding to his unspoken call. Surely, Lyre felt it as well? The sorcerer's chest rose and fell more quickly; he was excited.

"Maniac," Damon spat.

The blade descended on him suddenly. He raised a useless hand against it, waiting for the bite of steel. A loud clash sounded above him. He opened his eyes and blinked in stunned silence.

The sword that had halted the Asp's strike was not one that he recognized, but he did know the young woman holding it. Short black hair cut sharp along her jaw. Her bared teeth were bright against her tawny skin.

"Phoenix!" He could not believe his eyes.

Lyre stepped back a few paces, surveying the armour she wore. Scarlet silk embroidered with a brilliant gold bird across the chest.

The sorcerer dropped his sword and the weapon floated at his side, its single edge pointing downward. He stepped back again. It moved with him as surely as if it were in a scabbard. Phoenix did not move anything but her eyes. She studied her opponent. Lyre returned her gaze impassively.

He lifted his hand and the blade spun out into the air as if he had thrown it. Phoenix blocked and dodged to the side but the floating sword did not move as she expected. It was not constrained by any attachment to a human hand and it pivoted by the hilt around her blade. The tip of it caught her arm and she gasped. Blood spattered on the paving stones and she grimaced but did not drop her weapon.

The Asp watched her fight, unmoving, though Damon could feel the prickling cords of magic dancing and chattering around the sword.

Maybe if I distract him she could ... He couldn't make himself move. Fear held him rooted to the spot and he gritted his teeth in frustration.

The sorcerer's blade flipped itself upside down and the flat of it cracked against Phoenix's knuckles, forcing her hand to release the hilt. She stumbled. Then, she put out her empty hand, just as the Asp's sword swooped at her in a deadly arc.

It halted just before her palm. Phoenix shook hard enough to make her armour rattle and sweat beaded on her face. Still, the blade advanced no farther.

Lyre tilted his head, his lips pursed in an expression of curiosity. "I see. This power is not yours. You have not conjured this protector from your own mind." His sword floated back to his side. "By what art have you come here, little Solara?"

"Are you going to attack me again?" she demanded, not answering his question.

He looked amused. "Attack you? You are between my fangs and my prey. I will harm you not at all if you remove yourself from my path."

"Is that a no? You talk like a damned Ducal."

The amusement vanished. The word was unfamiliar to Damon but it apparently meant something to the sorcerer. Lyre waved a hand over his blade and a sheath materialized around it. He rested it across his shoulders, his face contemplative.

Phoenix set her weapon down and unclasped her breastplate, yanking her armour off one piece at a time. "Damon, have you got bandages?" she asked, not taking her eyes off of her foe. A heavy spaulder fell near Damon's foot with a thud. She pulled off her padded tunic, leaving only a white sleeveless shift. She bent and picked up her sword.

Damon stared. Wasn't she supposed to be a princess? The muscles of her shoulders and arms made her look more like a soldier. He wondered if the Asp would call her 'little Solara' after seeing the cut of her. She could, no doubt, swing Misery about better than he. Suddenly, all of those afternoons of practise seemed like nothing.

"Damon?" Phoenix glanced at him out of the corner of her eye. He realized that he'd been sitting there gazing in awe like a fool while she bled from a gash across her left forearm. The sleeve of the padded tunic was soaked through. He silently cursed himself and began looking through his belt pouches. He produced a narrow roll of linen.

"Bind the wound." She held out her arm, blade still facing the Asp. The sorcerer was paying them no mind and seemed to be searching the walls with his eyes. Damon was not proficient in treating injuries but he did his best. "Quickly. I have my sword now. There's no way I'm letting him away without gutting him."

His fingers stalled, catching in the fabric. "Are you mad? You can't fight him!"

"Well, I can't if I sit down on the ground and cower!" she snapped. His stomach clenched and he felt his blood rising to his face. Phoenix jerked the bandage out of his hands and gripped the hilt of her sword with both hands.

Lyre hummed in thought. He did not respond to her advance. "I see," he mused. She paused. "Who is the third?"

Phoenix did not answer. Her mouth was a grim line.

"I marvelled at the Princess, untrained, opening the way to the mind of another. Who opened the door for you, and why does he hide while I shed your blood?" He received no reply but his opponent's fingers flexing on the grip of her sword.

Damon looked between them, perplexed. He could see no one but the three of them.

The Asp sighed. "I will discover it for myself, then." He closed his eyes and vanished.

As soon as the threat of the sorcerer was gone, Damon was on his feet. "Phoenix! How did you find me?" Abruptly, his smile vanished. He stepped back against the wall again.

Phoenix looked down at the armour piled on the ground. She frowned at Damon.

"You are another illusion, aren't you? Thinking I will reveal battle plans to a face I trust and recognize?" Phoenix put away her sword. She bent and passed a hand over the lacquer of the breastplate, her expression reverent.

"I ... think I am not an illusion," she said slowly, hand raising to rub her neck. "I do not want to know any battle plans. I came to you ... I ..." she stumbled over her words. "I am Phoenix Solara, of Dunkhar."

"And how many minutes ago were you my mother? Hours from now, you will be my father, telling me you have re-established the Blood Link and that is alright to speak with you." Damon looked away.

"I am myself!" Phoenix shouted. The gold-plated claws on her boot struck sparks against the stone.

He stared at the claws. He lifted his gaze to meet hers.

"If you do not know me for who I am, then all is lost. We have spoken many times, visited each other's dreams. Is my presence in your mind no different than the White Asp's?"

His eyes narrowed as he looked at her. His expression softened by stages as he realized the truth of her words. Perhaps the sorcerer could forge faces and voices, but the air around her just felt ... *different*. It did not prickle or whisper. It was warm and crackling with life. He smiled and reached out a hand. She took it. The last vestiges of doubt left him.

"It *is* you!"

"Yes, so I have said." Her sarcasm was ruined by her grin.

"But how? I ... I am trapped here." The joy drained from his face. "The Asp has crafted this prison. I do not know how to escape."

"You cannot."

The voice made both of them jump. Kael was leaning against a stone arch several feet away. His white hair against the verdant foliage made for a stark contrast. Phoenix was sure he had not been there a moment ago. Damon looked between them uneasily.

"You!" Phoenix pointed her blade at him. "What was that about?"

The bird man tilted his head.

"Grabbing my throat while I was trying to meditate! Don't play stupid with me."

"The neck is the best place to access the power of another, short of cutting the body open," he explained. "I thought you might prefer the method I chose."

"You might have told me what you were doing," she snapped. "I thought you were trying to kill me."

"Yes," he agreed.

It took her a moment to parse the response. Damon just stood in silence, thoroughly confused. She growled in annoyance and gestured at the Ducal. "This is Kael Wester, born Kael Tamiyon, of Anemo and the lands beneath it," she introduced him hastily. The Ducal made a face but she wasn't completely sure which part of the title brought on the wince. Likely, he would never tell her. "He is a shaman of great strength. It is he who helped me find you. Kael, this is Damon Stonehart, of Glasshammer."

Kael stared at him blankly. The silence continued.

"Say 'hello,' you horse's ass!" Phoenix gestured at him.

"Hello, you hors--"

"Thank you," she interrupted him and turned back to Damon. "I come here not only on my own behalf, but his. His people have been forced underground while the other people of his world live upon the surface.

They wish to change this and I must help them. In return, Kael has promised me that he will return me to Silan."

"So I can finally stop talking to ghosts?" An attempted smile flickered and died at the corners of Damon's mouth. "How can I help?"

"There are none of my people remaining to teach me to unlock my power." She tapped the stone in the centre of her forehead for emphasis. "I must use my magic to help them. Kael hopes that between you and him..." She splayed her hands, letting him finish the thought in his own mind. Damon nodded slowly.

"There is a problem, I think." The young Stonehart looked down at his boots. "The White Asp; he will come again. He wants something from me, only I don't know what. I think maybe to wear me down, make me re-open the Blood Link to my family." He shook his head. "But I think it's more than that. I don't know why I'm still alive. He surely could consume my life, if what they say about him and the magic users he catches is true. If he could take all my power, I'm sure he could crush our resistance. But ... he continues to play these games." A nagging worry at the back of his mind continued to suggest that it might already be too late. Perhaps Phoenix should stay in that other world, free from the Asp's influence? Perhaps it would be safer there.

"He is testing you then," Kael said without preamble. Phoenix and Damon stared at him in confusion. "Good." The Ducal pushed off of the wall and strode toward them.

"Good?" Phoenix cried. "What do you mean *good*?"

"The plans and desires of your enemy do not matter to me," Kael clarified. "Phoenix needs to spread her wings and learn to fly. You have an invading sorcerer of considerable power to contend with. There is great possibility here."

Damon gaped at him. "You ... mean to use my mind ..." He gestured around at the labyrinth. "As some sort of proving ground?"

"Yes." The Ducal's dusty eyes bored into him. "Now, explain the magic of your world to me."

Phoenix could only stare at the shaman.

"And what about my people? What about our war?" Damon pressed.

Kael heaved a sigh. "If you can manipulate me into accomplishing your goals, then do so; but in the meantime, we discuss magic."

Barely containing his anger and incredulity, the young Stonehart felt himself nod mechanically. He promised himself then, that one day, if he survived, he would live a life where he would have many choices. Destiny, and its love of propelling him down pre-determined tracks be damned. He put out a shaking hand, indicating the fountain.

"What if the Asp listens in?"

Kael shook his head. "I will feel it if he enters this place again; for now, he cannot hear you."

"Let's go to the benches then. And keep your ears open. I'm not repeating anything."

Lyre sank down into the plump cushion that had been set out for him while he was busy in the boy's mind. He felt something wet on his face and frowned. Reluctant to simply wipe at the unknown substance, he fished in his sleeve for the small pocket mirror he carried. There were trails of blood running down from his eyes like red tears. He stared in disbelief. Had the encounter taxed him so greatly? His head was throbbing painfully.

Phoenix was alive and there was another bizarre presence lurking in the labyrinth that he had been unable to identify; likely it was hiding itself until he left. Many things weighed heavily on his mind. What had she meant by referring to the Ducal? As far as he knew, the last of them had died out and vanished from Silan hundreds of years ago.

If Damon was the fountain of immortality he had searched for, then he could consume him here and now and have no need to continue his conquest. He could leave the Stonehearts and the rest of the Northern Kingdoms to their lives, even withdraw from Silan entirely if he so desired; but if he was not, then he badly needed access to whatever plans the magic-wielders were concocting. Another mistake like the powerful weather magic the Az Taeorans had fallen prey to could finish-off his campaign entirely.

This was cutting it far too close. Time and his power were running out and now... this. He curled his fingers into a fist and rested his knuckles on the table. He wanted to strike something in frustration but this was not the place. The balance of magic was too delicate. He composed himself.

Phoenix, Damon, and the unknown one would surely provide all the power he needed to lay the defenders flat, but he had only one of their bodies here and one heart's blood to consume. He could kill Phoenix and the other one, surely, but could gain nothing from their deaths. They were not in his grasp to feed off of.

He sighed heavily and rose from his seat. He needed to rest and time to allow his preparations to unfold. He wandered off to the tent his beloved berserker occupied with her latest plaything.

Raach paced the length of it, her whip trailing on the ground. She studiously avoided the lip of the pit off to the left side of the tent. The deep, sheer-sided, hole had been the only way to contain the Giant. He kept breaking whatever bonds they placed on him.

She turned at the sound of Lyre's chimes as he approached. Feral—or Staruff—as Damon had called him, hung by shackles against crossed wooden boards. Blood dripped down his back, arms, and legs from the lash marks.

"What are you doing?" the sorcerer asked. His nose wrinkled in obvious distaste. "Why are you torturing our son?" he gestured at Feral.

"The giant man hasn't given in to any tortures I can think of," Raach threw her hands up in despair. "Not even starvation bothers him. But, this one is his friend." For a moment, she was all teeth and cackling as she revelled in the deception. "Staruff' had done his job to perfection. Even now, under duress, he faithfully kept his cover. She brushed her knuckles over her victim's back, drawing a hiss of pain from him. "You saw how he went right out of his mind when we chained *Staruff* and the boy." She laughed at the alias. "He may not speak on his own behalf, but the sight of his dear ones in pain sure loosens his tongue."

Lyre pressed his fingertips to his lower lip. He walked around the cross to look at his son's flushed face.

"You think to make him speak like this?"

Raach nodded. Feral took notice of his father nearby and raised his head to look at him. His pale eyes were glossy but showed no emotion.

"We'll toss him in with the giant after I've given him a good treatment," Raach suggested. "Let the big one see his friend like this; let him hear his screams and the crack of the lashes against his body. He might resist a little while, but not forever. He is a big, hardened warrior, but he has a big, soft heart. I've seen it before; he'll fail eventually." She dropped her voice to a whisper, leaning close. "It must be realistic, though." The berserker nodded sagaciously to herself. "The Giant is not stupid."

Only the tightness of his voice and a small line between his eyebrows betrayed his unease. Lyre had never been close to the boy, letting Raach raise him as she wished without interference. She had, indeed, made him into a useful tool. For the most part, the sorcerer preferred to keep his distance from him for his madness rivalled that of his mother.

"Feral ... agrees with this?" This was going too far. As crazed as Feral

285

was, he was forever striving to impress, to prove himself. Raach joined him on the other side of the cross.

"He suggested it." She beamed brightly. Her hand came up and for an instant, Lyre thought she meant to slap the boy. Instead, she caressed his cheek. "I am so proud of you, my son. Fearless and cunning, just like a woman."

Feral recognized the praise for what it was and he smiled. Tears spilt down his face.

"Mother," he whispered.

Raach leaned forward and kissed him on the mouth. Lyre looked away, not wishing to be involved in their private moment.

"If you survive," she whispered to him. "You will become the first man among my berserkers. Your name will be spoken for years to come." She walked around behind him and drew back her whip.

Lyre stood still, watching joy and agony fight each other on his son's face; then, he turned and left the tent. He needed some air.

Chapter 17: The Hammer's Fall

Erik sat rigid on Everlasting's back. His fingers kneaded the saddle's hilt, worrying at the leather until Lorne was sure he was going to make his fingertips bleed. He reached out to the Stonehart chieftain and rested a hand on his arm. Erik glanced at him.

Long hours at study and in the war council had made dark circles around the chieftain's eyes. The strain of Damon's plight was clearly wearing on him. Lorne had never seen a Stonehart look so old.

"Are you sure about this?" the librarian asked. He received no answer.

Erik had screamed himself hoarse in the war council time and again. The other marshals understood neither the magic nor the necessity of his request before king Harlon. In the end, he had told them that there just no other way; they would have to wait for the Stoneharts to win the day. He could tell that they were angry but they would not speak against him. They had seen the first battle, and the second that had boiled up after the chieftain's son had been captured. They knew what the Stoneharts were capable of.

King Harlon admitted Lorne and Erik to his throne room.

"How goes it, Lord Erik?" he said, indicating that Erik and Lorne should sit.

"I do not even know how to answer, in all honesty," the chieftain said. As much as he loved his horse, he was grateful to be able to sit on something not moving. "We ... have found a way to destroy the White Asp." He looked down at his boots.

"That is wonderful news. You seem less joyful in delivering it than I had thought you would be."

Erik raised his eyes slowly. "He has my son," he said. The words did not want to come out but he forced them.

The smile vanished from Harlon's face. "Erik, I am sorry." He dropped the title. "Is he ... do you know?"

Erik shook his head. He could see by the King's expression that he feared the worst. He could say nothing to reassure him. Every Stonehart had felt the Link snap. That hollow apology Damon had spoken an instant before it happened still haunted him. It sounded too much like a goodbye. He shook his head again.

"I know a way to end this, but it will not be easy. It will require everything we can muster and I doubt you will like it."

Harlon frowned. "I would be inclined to like anything that expels monsters from my lands."

Lorne cast a quick glance at Erik but received no answering look. The chieftain plunged ahead. There was no time for delicate words.

"Cede the lands-rights of Emmesford to Stonehart rule."

Harlon opened his mouth, his brow tightening in anger, but Erik held up his hand.

"Let me explain. Stoneharts are most powerful upon their home ground, but the boundaries of Glasshammer end a few days' ride from here. If we extend those boundaries down to the Middle Kingdoms, the Asp's army will be on our land, and much more under the influence of our magic."

"As will we be!" Harlon exploded.

"Only for as long as necessary," Erik put up his hands. "I am prepared to swear an oath to you, and write it as well: when the threat is ended, the rights of the kingdom will revert to you."

The king massaged the bridge of his nose. Erik knew his mind must be churning to a froth. He let him think. If he decided against it ... he didn't know what he would do.

"There is more to this, I assume?" Harlon looked at him sideways around his hand.

He nodded. "We have found a way. It will be the most involved and taxing spell we have ever done ... Truth be told, I don't know if it will succeed; but, Your Majesty..." he placed the title carefully, trying to ease the regent's ire "...the Asp has us in numbers and in power." He did not bother elucidating that the former was an assumption. It would not help his case. "We cannot face him on even footing, but, as Stoneharts, we can call forth the ancestral magics of our land. We can expel all magic that is not Stonehart from our borders. If we can do it, he will not be able to use his magic at all. If we're lucky, we might strip him of his magic altogether."

"That ... would certainly turn the tables." The king took his hand away from his face. He still looked worried, but the way he sat forward on his throne betrayed his interest.

"That's exactly what we intend to do." Erik's fingers curled on the arm rest.

"You know what the people will say." Harlon's eyes bored into the chieftain's. "The Stoneharts and their protectorate nations of the olden days."

288

"I know what they will say," he conceded. "But you and I both know this is not a bid for power. We can do this now, or later. If Emmesford is not ceded to Glasshammer, we will have to wait until the Asp ploughs his way through your kingdom to the true borders of our lands. Harlon," he dropped the honorific, making his plea more personal. "I don't want to wait that long. I am telling you that this is what we're able to do. If you want the Stonehart magics to defend you, this is what we can offer; if not, if you want to use us as general troops, I'm sorry ..." He shook his head. "We will have to pull back into Glasshammer and prepare to make our stand.

But I don't want to abandon you to this fate. That is why we don't simply go now."

"I think you wish to be near your son more than you wish to support me." The king's words cut deep. Erik's jaw muscles jumped in agitation. He knew the shot came from a place of fear but the hurt was not lessened by this knowledge.

"I think my son is dead," he said. His voice rasped but he did not drop his gaze.

After a long moment, Harlon looked away. "I will speak with my advisors. Please, Lord Erik, go and take some refreshment while I decide the fate of my people."

"He has returned." Kael said. He jerked his chin at one of the garden walls. Damon could not have said what direction it was. The sun in this place simply circled around their heads and seemed to switch direction at random. It was better to not even look up. The maze was disorienting enough.

"You should fly over the walls and seek him out," Phoenix suggested.

"*You* should fly over the walls, Phoenix." He crossed his arms across his chest. "We are here for you to learn. Not I."

"You seemed interested enough in learning of the Dominions," Damon retorted.

The shaman stared at him for a long moment. "Thank you," he said, just before Phoenix could say anything. Somehow, the expression of gratitude frustrated him even more.

"If you were here, in body, as my Reflection, this would be easy." Damon rested his chin on the heels of his hands. "An Embraced Stonehart and a Solara ..." He gestured at Phoenix.

"Witch," she finished for him.

"And a Ducal shaman." He gestured at Kael. "I'm sure we could—"

"Die spectacularly," Kael interrupted. "You said you need to be in physical contact for the embrace to happen?"

"Is the Asp moving?" Damon looked toward the wall, wondering what the shaman could see.

"No. He is weaving a spell." He looked completely unconcerned about this. "We are in your mind, your dream: we are not with you bodily. I cannot bring Phoenix across to you from this place."

Kael stood up and motioned for them to rise as well. He lifted his head for a moment, looking at the sky and his brows pinched together in anger. "Draw your blades and follow me." He walked toward the archway leading out of the garden. They had almost reached it when it melded into a solid wall. Kael sighed. "Damon, open this."

Damon stared at the wall. "I can't; I didn't do it."

The shaman turned around and glared at him. "This is *your* mind. Everything here belongs to you."

"But ... you don't understand. Lyre shaped it this way. I don't know how to ... to make it different." He found his words failing him. He barely had concepts to understand what was happening to him let alone ways to explain it.

"Enthralled ..." Kael trailed off, thinking hard. He reached out and put his hand on Damon's cheek. The touch was strangely tender and for that reason, the young Stonehart did not immediately pull away. The shaman stepped in close, holding Damon's face between his hands. He was close enough to feel his breath on his face.

Phoenix stepped forward, unsure of what was going on.

"Hold," Kael said. She stopped. Her fingers clenched and unclenched as she watched them. She thought the position much more appropriate to a lover than a ... what *was* Kael anyway? She would not call him 'friend'; teacher, perhaps?

"Fine bit of work this is," the shaman said after a moment. Damon stood stiffly, not pleased with the continued scrutiny. "Yes, this is a hard bind: physical and mental binding with all the weaving done manually... spell lines just perfectly aligned with your life lines, some of them actually integrated right into them ... and tapped into ley lines at the ends. The threads are crawling with spirits of some kind. Very powerful. Hoo ..." Kael released him at last. "What a master." He nodded appreciatively. "My apologies," he said unexpectedly and stepped back a little.

"What ...?" Phoenix couldn't even finish the sentence. She had no idea what had just transpired.

"It is customary to apologize after touching someone's soul." The shaman explained. "In truth, the custom is to never do it at all. It is something invasive and you can cause serious problems if you are careless and ignorant."

"You risked his well-being for your curiosity?" Her face flushed. Damon blinked at the brilliant twinkle that suddenly beamed out from the gem in her forehead. Kael, did not miss this either. His head tilted with interest.

"Why not?"

Phoenix took a step forward, lips pulled back from her teeth.

"He is going to die in any case." Kael rested his hands on his hips. The anger in her eyes shifted to anguish. Damon looked away, not wanting to see the expression. He had known, in all probability, that this would end with his demise but hearing it stated so bluntly was a heavy blow. "He does not know how to undo what has been done to him. No amount of power he possesses will save him if he does not have the knowledge of how to use it."

"Can you teach him?"

Kael's protracted silence brought Damon's gaze around. Phoenix reached out and grabbed the front of the shaman's shirt. The gem pulsed again, much to his fascination.

"Why?"

"Answer the question."

"I am here to teach *you*." There was no malice or irritation in the Ducal's voice or expression. Phoenix, however, was gripping her sword so hard the leather of her gloves was creaking.

"Answerthedamnedquestion!" she spat at him.

His dusty eyes stared back at her, unphased. "Yes," he said finally.

"Then do so and do not protest. Damon is the reason I wish to return to Silan. My family is *gone*, Ducal; without him there is nothing for me there. If I no longer wish to return, there is no reason for me to help you." She shoved him backwards against the wall. "You can all die in the dark!"

Kael rested his fingers gently on Phoenix's hand and closed his eyes. An instant later she hissed in pain and pulled back. Her glove was smoking. "Your words are persuasive," he said. "Do not threaten me."

The sky rumbled, breaking the silence. Damon realized that he had not noticed the clouds forming above them. He frowned. "I think we're going to get wet." The sting of a hailstone on his thigh put a lie to his words. "Oh Aervie."

Kael was already trotting toward the fountain. The upper tiers of it would not provide much protection, but it was the only thing they had. The archways and benches were too narrow. The delicate trees were already being stripped by the onslaught. The three of them crouched in the water, pressed against the central pillar of the fountain while fist-sized hailstones floated around them. The shaman reached up and put his hand against the underside of the tier above them. It began to crack and warp, sending off gouts of smoke as it wobbled and began to turn itself inside out.

Damon fell flat on his back in the water, dazed by the pain. He could hear Phoenix shouting something. His skull felt like it was being crushed, or possibly pulled apart. As he swung back toward consciousness, he found himself being supported by Phoenix's hands, keeping his face above the surface. The fountain's once-controlled trickle had become an umbrella of shifting water all around them.

"Oh," he said simply. He reached up and touched the translucent wall. It began to turn sluggish and opaque.

There was a loud splash as Kael seized Phoenix by the shoulders and threw her against the fountain's pillar. "Climb! Get out of the water now!" She was momentarily confused before she realized what was happening. Quickly, the two of them found hand holds in the ornate stonework. It was not very tall, certainly not high enough to stand upright under the bowl, but they clung awkwardly to swan-necks and leaping fish designs while the water under and around them froze solid.

The sound of hail zinging off their icy refuge was uncomfortably loud, but the glittering walls did not give. Damon lay encased up to his chest except for the arm he had reached out. He looked around, blinking as his senses returned to him.

"Safe now?" Phoenix said through gritted teeth. She had to shout over the noise.

"Ah ... Damon, have you stopped channeling?"

"Losing my grip." She moved her hand to get a better hold. Her right foot slid off of the stonework and struck the ice. She clung there at an angle for a moment. No doom seemed to be forthcoming so she let go and slid into a seated position on the solid surface. Kael followed suit, seeing that nothing unfortunate had happened to her. She crawled over to Damon. "Are you alright? We have to get you out of there."

"I'm fine," he shouted back. "The cold ..." He flexed his fingers. "It's nothing."

Phoenix remembered, then what he had told her about his friends calling him Corpse as a joke. Whether or not Kael perceived this, she could not have said. His face was as unreadable as ever.

"What did you do?" Phoenix prodded the shaman's arm and pointed up at the warped bowl above them. "Why did it hurt Damon?"

"I manipulated it. It's part of him, part of his mind." He tapped his temple. "I thought it better to hurt him than let the Asp bludgeon us all to death."

"Next time, warn me!" Damon shouted.

"Next time, you will work with me; there was no time to ask." He gestured at the ice walls around them. "Your skill with barriers is good. Why did you not reform the wall this way?"

The young Stonehart blinked at him. "This is just water. It's easy."

"Is it easier to manipulate the Dominion of water than stone?" Kael crossed his arms.

He realized his mistake. Slowly, he began to shake his head. He had just finished telling Kael that all the Dominions were equally easy to work with provided one engaged them on their own terms. If he could move and change the water...

"Perception, Damon," the shaman hammered his point home. "This is your dream, your mind. The sorcerer is powerful, but he engages you on your own grounds here."

"Will he live, now that he understands?" Phoenix asked. She moved closer to Kael so that he could hear her.

Kael shook his head. "It is not enough. The White Asp still has the upper hand in brute force. Even if he had no finesse, he would still crush Damon." He held up his hand to stay her. "You can assist him, if only to fight."

"Why can you not bring me to Silan?"

"I can, but not here; as real as this feels, it is a dream. I cannot place your corporeal body in Damon's mind: you would both die." Phoenix blanched. Damon knew she must be imagining the same gory scene that had just presented itself in his own thoughts. "We must go through the Planar Gateway. The way you came through. Such thoughts are useless now. We are not finished your training, you have not fulfilled your bargain with the Ducal, and even if you could go through a gate right now, it would put you outside of the Asp's defensive lines and several days' ride away."

293

Phoenix cursed.

"Do what you *can* do," Kael said. "Learn from him; attune your power to his; help him wrest control of his mind back from the sorcerer and hope that he has the ability to defend himself once he's freed."

Damon looked away. Kael had seen his predicament. He knew that there was no hope for the captive Stonehart to do anything from where he lay, nailed to the table. He took slow, shallow breaths through his nose and willed himself not to break down and weep. The ice held him tightly enough that his ribs could not accommodate sobbing. *I can stop this game at least,* he thought. *Whatever Lyre gains by keeping me alive will end when I am destroyed.*

"Come, he is distracted and we are protected for the time being," Kael said. "Give me your hands." Phoenix took the offered hand and seized the opportunity to let the claws of her gloves dig in. The Ducal winced but did not complain. Damon took his other hand. It was a little awkward due to the ice but they managed a reasonably comfortable positioning.

"What are you going to do?" he asked the shaman. "You still haven't told me what this 'attunement' is."

Kael considered for a moment. "Phoenix's magic is blood magic, like yours; but unlike yours, it reaches out to learn, to augment itself, all of its own volition. It strives to grow itself, emulating the magics that surround it; it is even trying to emulate mine." He shook his head. "I don't need more Ducal magic: I need human magic."

Damon wrinkled his nose, trying to understand.

"Explain more," Phoenix commanded.

The shaman frowned. "Right now, her magic wanders like an untrained hatch…" He paused and corrected himself. "Like a child without schooling. It may learn a few skills but it will never be a master of anything unless it is anchored firmly and directed along the appropriate paths. Essentially, you will be the latticework for the ivy." He pointed at Damon. "The scaffolding I use to build with. Does this make sense now?"

"I think I understand," he said. "What do you want me to do?"

"Channel one of the Dominions. Focus on attuning Phoenix to it the way you described to me." He nodded toward Phoenix. "This is her power we are striving to awaken. Channel fire, it may help the most. I will do the rest."

Damon nodded and closed his eyes. *Of course it had to be fire,* the one he disliked the most. No sooner had he reached for the hot, crackling energy of fire when he felt a visceral tug hauling him through the air at an impossible speed. He opened his eyes and felt instantly nauseated. The ice still held him fast but his mind told him that he was moving. The conflict between his brain and his eyes was making him ill. From the greenish tint of Phoenix's face, she felt the same.

"Do not move," Kael said through gritted teeth. "Unless you want me to pull your soul apart." He was staring at a point a few feet in front of him. His dusty eyes were wide with concentration.

Damon suddenly realized that there was something there. The bright fibres of energy he had followed so many times in his dreams twisted and writhed before his very eyes. Phoenix's cord whipped and crackled in the air like a glowing, golden ribbon. A dark blue rope hummed and curved sinuously around it. He wanted to smile, but he was too afraid to move even that much.

Kael gazed at the two strands as they wove together tightly. Was he doing that, or were they twining of their own accord?

There was a strange sensation in Damon's chest. The cords had aligned themselves to the centre of Phoenix's sternum and he assumed that it was the same with him. He dared not look down. Trickles of water ran down the icy walls all around them. He realized, then, what he was feeling.

Warm. For the first time in his life, warmth suffused his flesh and coursed through his veins. The light from the crystal in Phoenix's forehead threw shadows against the floor and walls. She had her eyes closed and was grinning.

"Phoenix," Kael said. His voice was strained. "Channel fire. Damon has attuned you. You must reciprocate with some kind of energy. Do what is natural to you."

She opened her eyes and squinted at him. "What ... what if I hurt you?" Her jaw was clenched as if she was afraid to open her mouth.

"We are pressed for time. We will do it this way, in the name of expediency." The shaman's chest rose and fell quickly. The front of his shirt was damp with sweat. "Focus the energy out behind you. I will pull the necessary threads from it to link with Damon."

Once more, she closed her eyes. Damon kept up with the attunement even though he knew that it had run its full course. Kael had not told him to stop and he did not want to foul up his work.

A gentle rain was falling on them as the ice melted more quickly. Damon wondered how long their shield would last at this rate. His heart was so loud in his ears he could not tell if the hail was continuing or not. Phoenix's skin began to radiate a golden light. Water poured down over their heads. Suddenly, a blast of fire consumed the wall behind Phoenix. He closed his eyes against the brightness as he felt Kael's hand clench on his.

The sensation of motion was gone. There was only a firmness anchoring him with the ground, an immovable boulder. It was peaceful despite the deafening roar of flames. The feeling became lighter and lighter until it faded away entirely. The shaman released his hand.

Damon opened his eyes. Kael sat between them on the wet ice. His head was down and he was curled in on himself, panting hard. Phoenix knelt at his other side. Behind her, there glimmered a pair of flaming wings. Though they burned brightly, they were mostly silent save the occasional hiss or pop.

"Kael?" she said. She rested a hand on his shoulder.

"I have done what I can do. You remember your promise to me?" His voice rasped in his throat.

"Yes, of course." Phoenix frowned.

"Good." Kael nodded. The curtain of hair waved back and forth. "That is good." He shifted, as if to sit up straighter but instead fell backward. His right hand was burned from holding onto Phoenix.

"Shit!" Damon placed his hand against the ice that encased him and began channelling fire as quickly as he could. It was messy and there was a lot of steam, but Kael was clearly in need of help on the other side. Phoenix was already cradling the shaman's head in her hands, keeping his face clear of the water. The Ducal remained limp and senseless. The ice was slow to crack. Damon urged the fire faster and the water around him began to bubble and simmer as it ate away the frosty layers.

"Our work is done for us, Damon," Phoenix told him. "His hand is in cool water already." He could not see her face through the steam but her voice sounded like she was smiling.

Vanvie be praised for that small mercy.

At last the ice fractured enough to let him out. He sloshed over to them and peered down at Kael's face. He looked pale and his hand was quite badly charred but he did not otherwise seem to be in any danger. For a moment, there was silence. The hail had stopped. Damon looked up through the rippled window; it was all that remained of the ice wall. Without Kael's insight, there was no way to tell what the White Asp was doing or where he was.

"Can you heal him?" Phoenix asked, looking up at him. She waved her hand through the mist, dispersing it somewhat. The moisture still hung heavily in the air. Damon winced and put a hand on Kael's forehead. His skin felt cool, though he'd always been terrible at interpreting the body temperatures of others.

"I ... I don't know what's wrong with him," he confessed. "If Autumn were here ..." He caught himself, remembering that Lyre was somewhere in the labyrinth no doubt listening to all they said. "I am not skilled in healing magics. I could try ... I don't want to hurt him. Let us just get him out of the cold water first. He might catch a chill."

"Can you catch a chill inside someone's mind?" Phoenix furrowed her brow in thought.

Damon stared at her. "I ..."

After a moment, she shook her head. "Take his other arm and help me lift him over the edge." They dragged him, as gently as they could, out of the deteriorating ice enclosure and rested him against the side of the fountain. With Phoenix's arm behind his head and his burned hand resting in the water behind him, he was as comfortable as they could make him for now. At some point, the flaming wings had disappeared; Damon didn't inquire, she looked preoccupied as it was. He couldn't blame her. Her key to returning to Silan was injured and unconscious. If he perished, Damon was not even sure she would be able to get out of the labyrinth.

Erik dismounted outside of his tent. He had not spoken the entire way back. Lorne did not press him. He knew how much it had cost the chieftain to speak those words aloud. The mantle of leadership had never weighed so much for as long as he could remember. Indeed, Erik's shoulders were bowed more than they ought to be, even with the weight of the sword on his back.

The chieftain raised his head, realizing that the marshals had been informed of his arrival and had already gathered there. Their eyes demanded news, though they held their tongues in check. Erik turned away from them.

"Lorne, go and tell the others. There is much to be done." The librarian nodded and strode quickly away. He was lost among the tents in moments.

Erik ducked into his tent and, for a moment, it seemed as though he was going to forego the day's military council entirely. He re-emerged after a while, bearing a black cloth bundle under his arm. He walked away from the marshals. They followed him, confused, as he threaded his way through the winding path that led to the centre of the camp. He approached the pole bearing the standard of King Harlon and stared at it for a long time. Then, he grasped the rope, untied it, and lowered the flag.

"This is your solution?!" Marhsal Deumore, the leader of the popular militia, exploded at last. He was infuriated, rage clearly written over his face. "Surrender? You could find nothing better? If you think to speak for all of us, I assure you we will not stand down so easily! We will fight whether or not you and your useless kin stand with us!"

Erik folded the flag carefully and set it on the stones piled to hold up the pole. He fitted the black cloth to the rope, ignoring the growing storm of anger and indignation growing behind him. The flag began to rise, unfurling as its weight and the wind pulled the fabric out straight. The marshals fell silent. The sigil of the winged gray horse galloping from a thunderhead lay encircled by a vibrant blue ring in the centre of the black standard.

The chieftain turned to them finally. His eyes were cold. "I *do* speak for all of you. As king of these lands, I welcome you to bow your knee in compliance, or leave." He lifted his arm and pointed towards the forest. Faces paled. There was a tinkling of chain armour as knees slowly bent and rested on the ground. They all knew there was no real option: it was stand behind the Stonehearts, or go south and be shredded on the Asp's lines. Erik turned away from them. "As you wish it. Go to your men and inform them of the situation. You will be given your battle orders later." He did not look at them as they left. He did not need to see the restrained rage in their eyes. *Let them rage. We will need that anger.*

Phoenix came to her feet and drew her sword in one motion. The blank wall that had been an archway, was once again an archway. Lyre stepped through it and the vines hanging there parted as if they dreaded to touch him. There was no scowl marring his features, but his green eyes burned with anger. Burned with a hard, arcane light. Damon hurriedly leaned Kael against the wall of the fountain and stood. He pulled the sword free of his scabbard and moved next to Phoenix, keeping just enough room between them for them each to swing unimpeded.

The White Asp's blade came up. "Banish these guests that come uninvited," he said softly. His eyes bored into Damon. "Lest I destroy them."

Damon did not answer. He glanced at Phoenix, clenched his jaw and raised his blade, pointing it toward the beautiful and hated face. Phoenix shifted her weight forward slightly.

"I see, you fear to die alone," the Asp chided. "And you would bring low the last of the Solara; a terrible waste. You do my act of mercy a disservice."

The young Stonehart gazed at the princess again for a moment but her eyes were fixed on the sorcerer. She was untroubled by his words.

As one, the strange voice inside whispered and he found himself echoing it aloud. Phoenix nodded. Lyre's eyes narrowed for a moment. He looked a little perplexed and Damon wondered if it was his imagination.

Phoenix lunged first and he followed a half-breath later. Lyre blocked both blades in a movement too fast for his eyes to follow. Before they could strike again, he lifted his free hand. A thunderclap deafened them. Phoenix found herself on her rear several feet away. She scrambled to get up. The sorcerer stood, watching them. He still had not even put his other hand on the sword hilt. The blade pointed toward the ground. He assumed no defensive position.

"Magic and swords ..." Phoenix muttered. She moved in again, slowly. Damon followed suit.

"We have the same," he said. "Let us try."

A smile lifted the corners of Lyre's mouth at that. Damon scowled in response. A cold wind began to whip up around the young Stonehart's feet. For a moment, Phoenix was afraid; but then, she realized that he was doing it himself. She felt her skin prickle and heard ghostly whispers begin to permeate the air. The two magics locked and conflicted, twisting around each other and colliding. *This is going to get ugly very quickly,* she thought. She breathed deeply and pulled forth the power that they had awakened together. The light from her focusing stone glinted off of the bared blades and she knew she had succeeded. The heat of the wings burned at her back and she grinned as the dark expression returned to Lyre's face.

The wind pushed the sorcerer's hair out behind him and pressed his robes flat against his body. An eerie glow surrounded him and the wind redirected itself back at them. Phoenix stepped forward and rolled under Lyre's left hand. She brought her sword up while he appeared distracted.

Unfortunately, he had enough concentration to move out of the way and drop his blade, letting it dart straight towards her head.

Metal sang through the air and clashed against the Asp's sword. Damon pushed it away from her and pressed the attack while she rolled out of the way. Lyre defended with a lazy arc of his blade, pushing Damon's out of the way like a tired cat. The arc shifted trajectory, caught Phoenix's leg and left a wicked gash as she made her escape.

She hissed in pain and staggered upright. She took one hand off of her sword hilt and a livid ball of flame danced at her fingertips. She stepped forward and launched it at the sorcerer's back.

Lyre stepped to the side and Damon had only enough time to fall flat on his face to avoid being scorched. The sorcerer regarded them both warily, measuring them up. He returned the floating weapon to his hand and pressed the attack on Phoenix, striding toward her and slashing quickly. She could barely block him. She moved gingerly, hop-stepping with her injured leg.

Damon darted forward, aiming a strike at the Asp's exposed back. The sorcerer sidestepped at the last moment and deflected it. His blade twisted around and used the momentum of the lunge to direct Damon's sword at Phoenix. All she could do was jump back, fearing to harm him.

The smile that had settled on Lyre's face was a grim one. His lashes sat low over his eyes at half-mast and his face was relaxed and unlined. Damon hurled the wind at him with greater force. The sorcerer's free hand moved up and the noiseless thunderclap came again. Damon did not fall this time. The cobblestones around him lurched and kept him balanced as his body was rocked by the impact. The anger etched into the young Stonehart's features only made Lyre's smile more glaring.

Phoenix had no idea how long the skirmish would last. If she stood behind Damon, out of the way, she could not strike without harming him. If she took to either side or behind the sorcerer, he would dodge and force them to parry each other or dodge in turn. Alone, Lyre had the luxury of not having to hold back or look out for anyone else. His attacks were broad and sweeping. Phoenix could not give full force to her newly awakened fire without harming Damon, or Kael who still lay senseless against the fountain.

Suddenly, the earth beneath them shook and Lyre frowned. Damon dropped his sword and fell to his knees. He clutched his head and groaned. The sorcerer paid no attention. Instead, he stared at some undefined point in the sky. Phoenix took that moment to run to Damon's side, supporting his shoulders.

"What is wrong?" she whispered.

"Oh ... oh make them ... stop ..."

"Them?"

"It's too much ... "

"What are they doing?"

"Don't ... know ..." He was panting now, harder than he had been while they fought.

The sorcerer said something under his breath that sounded very much like an epithet. "Pardon my leave-taking," he said and saluted them with his blade. He dropped it and it drifted lazily to his side. "I am summoned." The air around him swam and his image distorted until he was gone.

Chapter 18: Landtaking

Snow was flying thick in the air as the Stonehearts gathered around the large stone vessel. The water in the bowl kept freezing and Erik was beginning to worry that this spell was not going to work after all. This was what they had bargained for with Harlon: if they could complete this ritual to claim the land that had just been ceded to them, it could be the blow that would finally throw back the White Asp. If not, this would all be for nothing.

How much time do we have left? Hold on Damon.

Lorne returned to the centre of the circle bearing a small mirror. "It's not water but it will show an image just the same."

Erik hated having to improvise, especially on something so serious, but they didn't have any other option. The spell that Iltharen had described to them had said that a vessel of still waters was used to claim and dedicate the borders of the land. The last time the rite had been performed was centuries ago and it had been indoors.

Lorne placed the mirror on the ice within the bowl. "Vanvie bless this humble glass. May it serve in your place."

Erik walked around the makeshift tent they had made and pushed down the corner posts. The wind kept trying to tear at the fabric and he didn't want one of the poles coming free and letting it fall down on the candles. "Can you see well enough?" Erik asked. The librarian nodded.

"Tell them to begin."

They had designated four points with which the whole clan was familiar to be their 'four corners' and had set out items to be dedicated to them. Originally, the ritual was performed while riding around the border of the land but there was no time for that. Iltharen had told them that there was great power in innovation. Still, Erik was nervous.

The chieftain took up a heavy war-hammer and pointed it eastward. The circle of Stonehearts around him closed their eyes and envisioned the Aerie Cataract in the eastern ranges where the water thundered down from a terrific height into a ribbon of white foam. Erik held high a hunting horn fitted with brass at the mouth piece and bell. Then, he looked back at the small tent.

"The heart of the east. Do you see it?" he called.

Lorne peered down into the mirror, his brow furrowing. After a moment, its surface began to mist and show him the falls. "Yes!" he called back.

Erik took a deep breath and threw the horn into the air. "To the east we commend thee!" He brought the hammer down with all his might. The horn gave a loud crack as it broke. The chieftain took a moment to regain his balance and lifted the hammer's head off of the ground. The horn was gone and the frozen sod was indented and torn where the weapon had struck. He felt the small crater with his hand. Not so much as a shard of bone or piece of brass remained. He looked around nervously, beginning to feel the thrill of the working.

He walked to the southern side of the circle. An ornate clay oil lamp sat flickering weakly in the wind. There were pheasants engraved into the sides and handle of it. They had not filled it very full lest it start a fire of dangerous proportions; still, he was a little worried. The kinsmen directly in front of it knelt and held a couple old tower shields in place to keep the pieces from flying onto anyone.

He waited while he fixed the image of the Gray Lake Fairgrounds in his mind. Through the Link, he could feel the others doing the same. It grew in clarity and strength as they bent their minds to it.

"The heart of the south. Do you see it?"

"Yes!" Lorne's answer was immediate.

Erik squared his shoulders and aimed the hammer. "To the south we commend thee!" He brought it down as straight as he could manage. Despite their efforts, pieces of hot earthenware flew and bounced away into the frozen grass. They vanished where they hit the ground. He stared in disbelief. The power was growing; it was undeniable. *But will it be enough?*

He walked to the west. A string of pearls sat on a flat rock. There had been some debate about whether or not to sacrifice this precious object. Erik had looked at his kinsmen grimly and asked how much their lives were worth. He aimed his hammer. The old Sunny Eye Port came to mind with its gigantic ruined piers. It had not seen ships in so long that every last bit of wood had rotted away in the damp sea air.

"The heart of the west. Do you see it?"

There was silence for a moment. Some of those present had only been there once and a few could not readily remember it. The next closest well-known point was not close to the boarders of their land and was more north than west.

"Yes, I see it."

"To the west we commit thee!" The pearls shattered under the heavy iron head. Like the other items, they were gone when he lifted up again. The ground under his boots felt like it was humming, singing with power. It pulled at him. He could feel the ebb and flow of his own blood in his veins. If he listened hard enough, he was sure he could comprehend the inner workings of his bones.

He stood over a finely made sword; it lay bare with its point toward the north. The vision was easy to bring. There was a tall mountain with sheer sides that was visible through most of the highlands in Glasshammer. They called it the White Blade.

"The heart of the north. Do you see it?"

"Yes ..." Lorne sounded breathless. His excitement was palpable. The Link sent the sensation through all of them.

"To the north we commit thee!" The blade snapped and there was a bright flash of light. Erik stumbled back, surprised. When he took his hand away from his eyes, the sword too was gone entirely. He swallowed. The air had a bright, bluish glow to it as if a huge piece of stained glass were held between them and the sun. The sun could not penetrate the cloud layer today. Yet, the light remained. "Let holy fire be kindled round and about our land and cleanse it of all ..."

Erik stared, he couldn't help himself. A roaring orange fire raced past the outskirts of the encampment and barreled southward. He was afraid to continue, afraid to speak the wrong words and doom them all. The power was in his voice and in his heart now and he found himself struggling to remember the exact words. *Speak true. Surely I don't speak the precise words of my ancestors in this moment. I don't even speak the same tongue.* He gathered his fortitude.

"Cleanse it of all ignoble hearts, malicious intent, and the powers that be not under Stonehart rule." The magic roared like a ferocious wind all around them. He didn't know if his heart had ever beat so fast. He truly wondered if he would begin floating off the ground at any moment. "By the power of our will and of the sacred Lanvie, we claim this land in the name of Stonehart and do proclaim it the sacred grounds of Glasshammer!" His feet took him to the center of the circle, beside the tent. Lorne stared into the bowl, into the mirror as though hypnotized by it. Erik could see the threads of power then. Moving from each of his kin into the center. Into him, into Lorne, into the mirror. He took his knife from his boot and held it up high. The magic concentrated there until he could barely force his fingers to stay wrapped around the hilt.

"By the blood of Stonehart, it is done." He brought the blade across his forearm quickly. Dark red, almost burgundy splashed out over the snow. He did not feel the pain. The vibration within and all around him was too great. "We have made the holy sacrifices to the Vies and the ancestors. By our toils, we are made worthy. By its bounty, we are made strong. It is done!" He threw the dagger down. It landed point into the ground.

The magic began to smooth and ripple out beyond the circle. Erik knelt on the frozen earth, feeling suddenly dizzy. "By the hallowed void, it is sealed. Give now, unto the void what is its due." There was a rustling as everyone settled on the ground. Then, there was silence. A long stretching absence of sound. Erik did not even dare to breathe. The noises of the camp were gone. Not muffled. They were not present at all. The magic began to pull upward and down at the same time. It thinned until it separated and began to float and disintegrate. Only after he was certain it was gone, did Erik rise. The other Stoneharts seemed contented to stay seated and whisper amongst themselves.

Iltharen had told them that the only true gift they could give to the void was an aspect of its own essence. Silence, darkness, emptiness, the paradox that was the ultimate finality and the immeasurable infinite.

Erik made it into the makeshift tent before his legs refused to hold him up anymore. He was still having trouble feeling normal sensations. He leaned against the stool Lorne sat upon. "Lorne ..." He looked up at the librarian who was still hunched over the bowl. "Your hair ..."

Lorne sat back and scooped his hair away from the candle flames ringing the bowl. "Oh ... I ..." He looked at Erik and his pupils were the largest he'd ever seen. "I saw things ... such things ... I don't know if I was meant to ..."

"Record them," Erik said simply. "They may be important. I ... don't think any of us are fit to fight just now. Let us rest."

The librarian nodded and pulled out the book.

Lyre moved back from the table, balancing his hands on it for a moment. He could tell as soon as he left the trance that something was terribly wrong. He felt drained, more than he should have from manipulating the labyrinth. It was like waking from a long illness after the fever had passed. He felt brittle and his body ached.

Emeka, seeing the expression on his face stepped forward immediately. "My Lord?"

Lyre looked at him across the table. "You ... never call me such." It amused him though he could not say why. It was difficult to think through the light-headedness. He folded his legs under himself and sat with his head resting against the side of the table. There were no sounds except for the trickle of blood as it wound its double helix around the pinning spear and Emeka's boots as he approached.

"Something is wrong," the general said.

"Yes," Lyre replied simply. He looked into the wide, dark eyes of the man who knelt before him.

"Orders?"

The White Asp could not help but smile. "Fetch my chalice; then, ready the troops. This battle is in your care; the dice are yours to roll."

For a moment, Emeka's brow furrowed but at last his eyes crinkled in a grin. "Yes, Lyre." He stood and bellowed for a servant.

Lyre gazed down on the trapped Stonehart. He was certain now. He had felt the well of untapped potential as soon as the boy had brought his magic to bear against him. All that remained was for Emeka to hold off the coming attack long enough for him to take that magic for himself.

Kael sat with his back against a bench, wrapping his injured hand in his shirt. He had woken up a short time after the Asp had left, or at least that was all Phoenix and Damon could guess. They had no way of gauging the time. The shaman had said nothing since he'd woken except that he was pleased with Phoenix's progress.

While Damon wanted to throttle the shaman whenever he spoke now was not the time for that. He wasn't quite as aggravating when he wasn't playing word games but he was still having a great deal of trouble trusting the man. He seemed to have no clear moral compass that he could discern and the way he referred to Phoenix as his "weapon" set his teeth on edge.

What held his thoughts most clearly at the moment, though, were the waves of magic he could feel crashing around him. The currents were so strong and insistent that he felt like he was being physically pushed back and forth. It was getting worse.

The prickle was back in the air, and the whispers. The sensation was no longer subtle but violent. The tickling he had felt before was now a bladed jabbing from all sides, hard enough to make him shiver. He wrapped his arms around himself and drew his legs under the stone bench.

"Damon?"

Phoenix was looking at him over the Ducal's bent head. Her eyebrows were drawn together and she seemed about to rise.

"They're fighting," Damon said. "I think," he added, looking down at the flagstones. He could tell by the slow shake of her head that she could not feel it. "There's two different kinds of magic. The Stonehearts' is all over the place. The White Asp's is ..." He frowned. It was a sensation he did not quite recognize. "It's ... rather like roots going into the ground, pulling up water." He gestured with his hands. "Perhaps gathering for an attack?" His lips pressed together tightly and he glanced at Kael.

The Ducal did not respond. He tucked the corner of his sleeve neatly into the makeshift bandage he had made and admired his handiwork.

Phoenix cleared her throat and nudged the shaman's shoulder. "What do you think is happening?"

Kael glanced up at the sky and narrowed his eyes. He reached back and rested an elbow on the bench, his face contemplative. Finally, he shook his head.

"He is killing you."

Something hard and cold formed in the pit of Damon's stomach. His arms tightened around his body but there was nothing to be done for the creeping chill of fear. In the sky, there was a ripple, stirring the clouds and threading strange colours through the blue. Violet, burgundy, black, shifting even as he watched them twist and leech into the blue expanse above. The clouds began to burn with a livid, searing light. He looked away.

Phoenix stood and turned in a slow circle. "We must do something." She looked down at Kael. The Ducal gazed back at her and nodded serenely.

"Yes."

He pushed off of the bench and got to his feet. He offered her his uninjured hand and returned his gaze to the heavens. They had begun to lurch and twist sickeningly and though Damon tried not to look at the bizarre swirling, he found it strangely hypnotic. He made himself look at Kael instead.

"Open up the channel again," Kael said. "Like you did when I attuned your magic with Damon's. I have need of your power for this."

The fiery aura came easily to her this time. It glimmered over her skin, wisping away to either side behind her in a ghostly suggestion of wings. The shaman's hand did not burn. It was much more controlled now, stable.

"Good." He nodded grimly. Then, he turned to Damon and regarded him for a long moment with his strange, pale eyes. "Thank you for your gift of knowledge."

Phoenix took a step back, realization dawning on her face, but Kael held her hand fast.

"What are y—"

"Farewell, Damon," the shaman said.

Then, he was alone.

Erik sat quietly on Everlasting's back. His hands were folded on the pommel of the saddle and his eyes were focused on the forest before them. Marshal Landholt, Duke Dagar's marshal, was giving some kind of speech to his troops but he wasn't paying attention, not really. At least not until the man turned toward him expectantly.

"Yes?" He inclined his head, even though the other man's horse was shorter than his.

"Would you like to say something to inspire the men before we ride into the fray?"

Erik sighed and looked down at the back of his horse's neck. Everlasting walked out in front of the assembled Stoneharts and assorted mercenaries. He straightened up in the saddle and pitched his voice to carry.

"You all know what we're about to do. What we're about to try." He looked over the faces before him. The young and the grizzled alike. "We must not fail! Fight for your lands; fight for your lives. May the Vies side with us!"

He guided Everlasting back into the ranks of the Stoneharts. Marshal Landholt blinked at him as if to say "that's it?" Erik nodded. Though he had the battle plans ingrained on his memory, his mind was filled with only one thought: Damon. He did not know what had happened to him since the Link between them was severed. He prayed that he would still be alive that he would be alright. But his heart ached in a way that seeded him with doubt.

The army started forward, splitting into three columns to thread through the woods. There was no charge, no point in such a manoeuvre. The trees were a bulwark to both sides. The Stoneharts rode with palms upturned, focused on the shielding spells. Light shimmered and refracted strangely over the condensed air. The bulk of their forces would be the last through the woods. By then, the vanguard of the resistance would be on its own, pitting themselves against the army of the Asp. The prospects were not promising but there were no options left. At least if they attacked they had a chance of survival.

Erik could feel the strain on the spell. The net over the marching men was stretched thin and gauzy. He did not know if it would hold against a serious assault but it would simply have to. He gritted his teeth as he heard the roar of combat beginning at the front. Time slowed. Every breath, every heartbeat seemed to mock his efforts.

He caught the hint of some excited shouting and frowned. It was a sound he had not expected to hear on the battlefield. Lorne, riding in front of him suddenly chuckled.

"What is it? What are they saying?"

Erik stood in the stirrups, trying to see farther.

"It's alright, Erik ... they're saying ..." The librarian squinted and for a moment, they were both silent, straining to catch any clear thoughts through the Link.

Sunev spoke from behind them. "They can see the Asp's soldiers: they're not shielded."

He turned back and there was a kind of savage smile on his face. "The protections over them seem to have failed. It seems that the enemy can die after all."

He felt a surge in his heart. *Yes!* This was precisely what they needed. The narrow thread of hope widened into a stream. Branches scraped against his tunic and pulled at his cloak making Everlasting twitch at the scratching fingers. The roar din of the battle was getting louder. Terrible as it was, threading their way through the bottle-neck of the forest, the protection spells laid over the vanguard seemed to have held out well enough for them to push through the front lines of the enemy. Bright tongues of flame had begun to spring up in the distance where they had managed to work their way into the camp proper.

As the trees began to thin, Erik drew his sword. It was time for fate and the Vies to pass judgement on them. If the verdict was not in the favour of the defenders, he would never know.

The White Asp stared grimly down at his prey. Damon, of course, had not stirred at all. Lyre took the chalice and held it in the downward-flowing spiral of the blood helix, letting it fill slowly. He took a sip and fought the urge to cough. Tiny sparks of power exploded throughout his body. It was inadvisable to imbibe raw blood magic without first weaving the proper incantations but he needed at least some energy to work with or he would not be able to do it at all.

He expected the dizzy sensation to fade almost immediately and leave him to his task but it stayed for several minutes. A smile curved his lips. This was the one; of that there could be no doubt. Such a repository of magic would be the last he would ever need to draw on.

Damon lay on his back watching the sky ripple and change colour. The ground twisted and lurched sickeningly. Every now and then there came the sound of falling rocks as part of the wall toppled.

What would happen when he died? Would it all just ... stop? Go black and silent? Or would he be stuck here indefinitely? Had he already died?

His chest rose and fell, breathing the air that was and was not there. *There has to be something I can do. Something. Aervie, I have to at least try.* Nothing came to mind. Something pulled at his guts and he curled in on himself. He shivered and gasped. *Is this it? Please no.*

The anger, that foreign-feeling rage bubbled up from places unknown and took hold of him. *Fight. Let me fight! Damn you, at least give me a chance!*

He recalled Phoenix standing bold against the sorcerer and held the image in his mind. The surety of failure had not deterred her. She refused to flee, even facing such odds; yet, in the end, she had escaped. He had given her the power she needed and, if she kept her bargain with Kael, she would make it back to Silan and use it against the Asp. He closed his eyes and embraced the thought, letting it stand against the waves of fear.

Staruff would envy him now, no doubt. A chance at a 'glorious death,' killed by the White Asp himself instead of some nameless lackey. Damon wondered where he was now. If his friends were still alive. If that lunatic, Raach, was hurting them. The thought stoked the fires of anger inside him, adding fuel to the voice inside that was crying out for justice.

"I think he is slowing down," Staruff had said. Damon recalled the weariness on the sorcerer's face after he had healed the mercenary. But was he? And did he really devour souls? He wasn't certain, but whatever he was doing made his insides feel like they were being slowly torn apart.

What happens if you miss your next meal, Asp? Can I starve the demon? The idea rolled through his senses like an electric current.

"Well ..." He swallowed. "I can't if I sit down on the ground and cower."

Damon reached up, hands grasping at the boiling sky. Somewhere, out there was a thread of power spiralling upward from his body. He had a decent guess as to where it went. There. Twisting cords between his hands. Gauzy at first, then more tangible. He closed his fingers around them and pulled.

Lyre gasped and planted his palms on the table to keep himself from falling. The chalice spilt and rolled off the table. He did not have the wherewithal to wonder if it broke or not. All his focus was on the serene face of the young man before him. He tried to stand, to pull back, but the force drawing him down was too strong.

The sorcerer found himself standing under an angry sky, his feet balanced precariously on rubble. The labyrinth was a chaotic field of broken and twisted stone walls. One notable thing stood upright in the ruin: the boy, his hand stretched upward as though he would tear the clouds down from the sky. His blade sat in his hand, bared.

The dark eyes met his and Damon lowered his raised hand to the grip of the sword. The tightness of his shoulders spoke of his fear, but his stance was firm. Lyre rarely found himself in such a situation. He knew what a mage was capable of when cornered, all options taken away. If he perceived that this was the end, he would throw everything at his adversary, regardless of whether or not he thought it would work.

The sorcerer lifted his hand and his sword materialized there. The young Stonehart straightened, lips pressed together. He lifted his blade and sheathed it. Lyre narrowed his eyes. Did he mean to come at him bare-handed? Fight by casting only?

No. Damon turned on the balls of his feet and lit off down one of the broken corridors.

He shook his head. *All the better*. He knew the boy lacked the courage to fight him. He stretched out a hand to flatten the walls; he would finish this quickly.

Instead, the ground under his feet pitched and he dropped to his knees, clapping a hand over his mouth. His stomach clenched and shuddered. It was all he could do to keep from retching.

Was this the boy's doing or simply a result of the mindscape's deterioration? He had never been in the mind of a dying victim before, it was unwise. There was the possibility of being dragged down with the death. He felt like his head was going to split in half. It was impossible to tell if Damon was similarly affected.

He followed him slowly, trying to think of what to do. The narrow corridors were made more so by the avalanches spilling over the flagstones. He picked his way through the wreckage. The soft soles of his boots made the sharper bits of stone irritating. He tried to shift his clothing to suit. It should have been easy in a mindscape—a glorified lucid dream—but the resistance was incredible. He ended up having to stop and stand still. Even then, he could only modify the thickness of the leather.

It was puzzling. Even if the Arcana would not heed his call, he should have been able to utilize their dreamworld equivalents here. It did not make sense for Damon to fight so mightily against his will. Unless, somehow, he had found a way to make use of his power.

No. Too young. He paused as a wall toppled in his path. It would do no good to run after the boy; Damon had a head start, he would only tire himself out.

Calm. Let the rabbit exhaust itself in the flight. My thoughts I must keep clear.

He took a deep breath and extended his hand again. The gut-turning pain resumed its assault on his head. He focused on his task in spite of it. The rubble of the collapsed wall shifted bit by bit, rolling back out of the way like a lethargic wave.

He stood panting for a moment.

There. It can be solved. The greater will shall overcome.

Damon pressed his back against a wall, getting his breath back. *Just long enough. Hide and run. I just have to last long enough.* For what, he did not have the presence of mind to think that far ahead. Admittedly, he had expected Lyre to be on him a lot faster. What was he doing?

He risked a glance around the corner. Nothing stirred except the dust that continued to billow and shift in the wind. *Wind? Good I can use that.* He focused on it. The irony of using Lyre's own book against him struck him as funny. He repressed a little hysterical laugh and exhaled slowly, letting the air currents move around him and down his arm. Passing his hand through the space in front of him, he began to illustrate a pattern until the dust and grit formed a murky cloud in the passage behind him.

Heartened by his success, he spread both hands out, stretching the effect over the corridors around himself. It scintillated in the strange, shifting light. Damon set off again, this time at a walk. *Maybe if I do it this way, I can save my energy ... draw it out longer. Maybe he'll get tired and make a mistake?*

He had expected Lyre to clear the fog immediately but he did not. *Something is ... odd.* Why wasn't the sorcerer attacking yet? Perhaps he was readying for something truly disastrous? The waiting was beginning to make the hairs on his neck stand up.

A bolt of lightning lanced through the gloom. The sand it ripped through instantly turned to jagged forks of glass and smashed on the ground. It had come within a foot of his arm. That was not good: it meant the Asp was still close. Damon put a hand over his face for a moment, concentrating. The air around his head expanded and contracted, turning in quick circles until the space immediately in front of him was clear. He wanted to remain concealed and coughing on dust would not help him achieve that end.

This is a dream ... he told himself. *I can do anything I want in a dream, right? Maybe ...* He continued to think hard as he forged his way forward through the storm. He still couldn't believe he had actually pulled Lyre back into his mind. Perhaps he hadn't? Perhaps the sorcerer was returning anyway? But this time felt different; he couldn't put his finger on it. Though he could not say exactly where Lyre was, he could sense him. He knew he was not gone.

Good. Let's keep it that way. Damon took another calming breath. *What if I can do more? Should I attack?* He put a hand on the grip of his sword and considered the possibilities. Even if he couldn't kill him outright, he might be able to hurt him or at least slow him down. *The worst that could happen is, I do nothing, right?* He hoped so.

A slender thread of blue light shimmered over the ground. Whatever kind of trap this was, he didn't intend to fall for it. Damon stepped over it carefully. A pleasant shiver rolled over his skin from his feet to the top of his head. *What is that?* He tried following the light.

The sword slid free of its scabbard as quietly as he could manage. *Even a charging knight can be brought down by a loose stone under the horse's hoof. If I can be that stone, maybe there's a chance. Maybe if I can hold on long enough ... maybe they will come for me?* It was a small hope. Very small. What could they do when they arrived? He was impaled on a spear and had no idea how he was still alive in the first place.

Another bolt lashed out, and another in quick succession. A wall toppled somewhere out in the gloom. It was close, but not worryingly so. Damon frowned as he moved away. It was true then. Lyre did not know where he was. Perhaps his direction, at best. From what he had seen of the sorcerer, he was not one to waste energy.

He considered trying to conjure an attack from a different location to draw him away. It gave him pause. Could Lyre be doing the same thing? Perhaps herding him?

Herding me where exactly? It's my mind. He looked around at the swirling dust and debris. The wind changed, lulling and he knew the sorcerer was starting to pick apart the spell. The clouds overhead were already starting to show their bruised colours. Damon frowned. *A dying mind. This is what it looks like?* Where could he flee to, in that case? He stopped mid-stride, almost running into a wall himself. He turned, to the left, then the right, wondering which way would take him around the obstacle. The line of blue light went right through the stone. Not precisely helpful.

A bolt lanced over his right shoulder and the resulting collision with the stone sent fragments flying everywhere. He winced and skittered to the side as a rock thudded into his ribs and one whisked across his neck. It was like a spark from striking a flint. The anger in him smoldered and caught light.

This way.

He didn't question the curious sensation. The blade in his hands led the way as the dust began to fall away in sheets, hitting the ground with a hiss. A flash of brilliant green showed him the sorcerer's eyes, much closer than he'd thought he would be. *Dammit, I almost walked right into him!* The faint flicker nearby alerted him to another incoming bolt. He raised his sword. Perhaps he could throw up an earthen wall to absorb the shock? No ... earth was stable but too slow.

The sudden downpour of rain startled him. He hadn't realized he'd even been casting. In the blink of an eye the water forked around him pulling the lightning with it and casting it down to the ground. Lyre, for his part, looked just as shocked to be soaking wet. He did not attempt to throw another attack, at least not of that sort. The water smelled acidic with a tang of metal.

The sorcerer lifted his hand and the graceful curved blade at his side floated up. Damon's breath hitched in his throat he stepped forward, both hands gripping the hilt. Though Lyre appeared just as wary, it gave him little confidence. He had seen the way the man had fought both he and Phoenix together. Two blades had not even slowed him down. How could he defeat him on even footing?

Stand firm. Attack. Damon took a few more steps and set his foot down on the line of blue light. The thread became brighter and more distinct. It thickened and he found he could see other brilliant ropes of light stretching across the labyrinth. The thrum of power reminded him vividly of the sacred places in Glasshammer where one could stand and feel the presence of the Lanvie. Damon frowned, trying to remember what Illtharen had told him about such things. *What was the word? Ley lines? Yes that was it. But this isn't Glasshammer. Where am I?*

Steel met steel in a hesitant brush, eliciting the softest of sounds. A flicker of bright cobalt blue made Damon jump back. Lyre scowled, showing the barest hint of teeth. He did not look surprised. The flash had lasted only an instant but twisting, ethereal filaments of blue remained hanging in the air. The line that snaked along the ground between their feet crackled and flared wider.

Damon stepped forward, his blade whipping through the air. Lyre blocked easily but striking flesh was not the aim. He forced his weight against the blade. His grip shook, keeping steady pressure on the dull side of the sorcerer's sword so that he could not wrench it away. Slender fingers curled and uncurled behind the crossed blades and the Asp's eye's narrowed, perceiving the shift in the air. The sorcerer released the weapon and it pivoted to get around Damon's block.

The mindscape shook and swam. A vast gap yawned under him, or at least that was what it felt like. All around was only blackness and ringing silence. Damon did not know where his enemy's blade had gone, but when his sight resolved itself, he was not in the labyrinth. The panicked gasp that sounded in his ears was not his own and he knew he had succeeded.

The mind of the enemy ... any better than my own at this moment? I don't know. Let us see what I can do.

He blinked at the familiar walls surrounding him.

No ... Aervie. It's not possible...

Casey snorted awake and rubbed his aching forehead. Some obnoxious loud noise had woken him from an admittedly fitful sleep. The problem with sleeping with one's hands bound behind the back was that it was very hard to get into a decent position to sleep. He blinked and looked down at his hands. "What in hell ...?"

315

The ropes had let go. The maddening, unbreakable ropes had just simply fallen off as if they'd never been knotted in all their existence. What did it mean? Was the sorcerer dead?

He rested his head against the earthen wall, just listening, feeling the vibrations in the ground. Yes. There it was again. The clash of steel. Something was happening. There were screams and shouts and they were too far away to be Staruff.

"Staruff!" he bellowed. There was no answer. "Staruff yeh stupidfuck! Are yeh there? Staruff!"

Still, nothing but silence in response; and curiously, none of the guards came to quiet him. No spear-prods or rocks thrown down on him this time. Casey stuck his newly liberated hands into the dirt and began digging hand-holds. It was rough going and agonizingly slow. He had no tools at his disposal but he pulled and dug at the hard-packed ground until the holds were deep enough to at least sink a forearm into for leverage. Shoddy work, but it only had to serve him once. Small stones cut his hands and soon, his stinging flesh was covered in a muddy mixture of blood and soil.

Every now and then, he stopped to shout for Staruff. Every failure to reply spurred him. Had they taken him somewhere else? Killed him? Even a stray arrow flying through the tent-flap could mean mortal peril for someone bound and unable to dodge or lie flat.

His knuckles hit a larger rock and he cursed, trying to dig around it. Where was Damon? He'd heard the beginnings of the kid's interrogation but no more from him. He didn't know where they were holding him, or if he was still alive. He could not imagine what Erik was feeling but he bet the rage in the father's eyes would be a sight to behold.

The rock came free and he pulled it out. He'd been about to discard it when he realized it was crudely of a wedge shape. Not fantastic but it was a tool where he'd had none before. He clawed at the wall with it, stuffing his feet into the lower handholds as he went. It was a blessing, he reflected that the soil went so deep in this region. If he'd been stuffed down a shaft of solid rock, he had no idea how he would get out. The partly frozen ground was hard enough to get through.

At last he levered himself up over the edge and rolled onto the floor of the tent. The sight of Staruff seated and bound to the central tent post did not hearten him, especially given that 'seated' in this case was a relative term. He looked like he'd been dropped there and the only reason he was partially upright was the fact he was secured in place by rope. These bonds had not spontaneously let go, it seemed. Casey shuffled over to him quickly, not wasting the time getting to his feet.

He pushed the hair out of his friend's face. The smaller mercenary was unconscious. Casey lightly swatted the side of his head, trying to wake him up. He was greeted with a soft grunt, a twitch, and nothing more.

"Yer alive ... aright ..." The giant let out a breath; one victory at a time. His eyes raked the tent for something to help. He spied a wash basin and made his way over to it. His joints and muscles were stiff from being bound for so long but he forced himself to move. Sitting around coddling a sore body would not aid them in any way.

The basin held some - what he could only have described as - tools. The water was a pale red and had the familiar coppery scent of blood. He scowled and took them out, throwing them down on the rough wooden table. He carried the basin over to his friend and dumped it unceremoniously over him.

Staruff woke with a gasp and promptly smacked the back of his head into the tent pole. He blinked up at Casey with wide eyes. The look gave him pause. Was he afraid? The shock on the man's face twisted up into his customary, manic grin. No, of course not.

"You awake, Sunshine?"

Staruff laughed in response. "I am now."

He moved to untie him. "Where are yer clothes?"

"No idea."

He looked like someone had attempted to take his skin off with an object too dull for the task. His flesh was dappled with bruising and lined with welts and slashes. It looked almost intentionally balanced, like some very gruesome art piece. Casey half expected to have the hand he offered swatted away but Staruff gripped his forearms and shimmied himself upright, leaning back against the pole. He bared his teeth, wincing in pain.

"Anything broken?"

Staruff looked down at himself, appraising. "I don't think so." He rolled his shoulders and began stretching his legs one at a time. Casey looked around the tent for something for him to wear.

"Can yeh stand on yer own?"

His response was a distracted nod; good enough. He walked over to the wooden trunks beside the table and stuffed under it. The first one he opened was full of more metal objects. The function of many of them eluded him but there were several he could guess. He slammed the lid down and opened the next one. He found the stiffness of his muscles leaking out as the slow burn of a good, lasting rage began to build up in his gut. He spotted something draped over a low stool and picked it up: leather trousers, still drying from being cleaned.

He brought them back to Staruff.

"These fit yeh? Maybe?" He held them up to him. "Maybe kinda snu ..."

Staruff burst into laughter. He leaned his head back against the post and cackled madly. "Yes please!" he choked out between gales of mirth.

"What ... the shit is so funny?"

"Her working breeches." He pointed to them. "Perfect. Help me get them on."

Casey obliged, letting Staruff alternately hold onto him for balance and assist with tugging the garment into place. The hips were too ample but the waist was a little too tight so he slit the seams on either side a couple of inches and belted it in place with a bit of rope. The smaller mercenary's movements were recovering dexterity and that heartened him, even as he watched him grunt in pain and stretch his arms up over his head.

"I'll be fit to fight in a few minutes. Check and see if there are guards outside."

The giant blinked at him. "Yeh kind of look like shit ... are yeh sure—"

"Fuck you." Staruff cut him off. "I am not yet dead." He jerked his head at the chests. "All I need is a weapon, as do you."

Casey straightened and found a grin creeping onto his face. "Crazy sombitch," he muttered and peered through the tent flaps. There were a few men milling about outside. *Soldiers.* They stood grouped together, their faces tight and harried. Something was very wrong. One of the *most* wrong things he could see about this picture was that the soldiers were visible. He questioned for the second time if the sorcerer might have met his end. The Az Taeorans were always cloaked in his magic. With that defence removed they would be very vulnerable. Casey's grin widened. He backed away from the narrow gap and returned to his friend who was shuffling sluggishly around the trunks.

"There's some assholes out around front but they're not guardin' us. Somethin's wrong. I can see 'em, real good and clear."

Staruff stood, contemplating a large hook and a straight dagger. He canted his head. "Really? I wonder why? I wonder if it is beyond the camp proper. They usually keep to the shadows like wraiths."

"Dunno. I hope he's dead." The giant took a breath and let it out. Then, he spoke the words that had been on his mind for days. "Where's Damon?"

Staruff shook his head. "He was not in the tent with us when I woke. I haven't seen him at all."

"We should ask."

He was met with a crooked eyebrow. "Of whom?"

Casey jerked his chin at the narrow gap in the tent flaps. There were a couple of armed men approaching. He could tell by the shape of the helms that they were Lyre's men. "These fuckers."

He turned in time to grab the hammer that Staruff thrust his way. The smaller mercenary was obviously still stiff but moving much better than he had been.

"The ones across the way still there?"

Casey nodded.

"First we take the two guards and then move on the other two; let's be quick, we've not much time to make an impression."

Casey stepped out of the tent first, extending a long arm and catching the soldier on the left with a blow to the temple. The man went down in a heap with not even a chance to cry out. Deftly, he pulled the sword belt off of him and turned to hand it to Staruff; but before he could do so, an agonized scream froze him to the spot.

Staruff had thrust the hook up through the soft flesh under the other guard's jaw, its point protruding from his mouth. He planted a bare foot in the centre of the man's chest and forced him to the ground, hauling back on the hook just before he hit. Jaw muscles tore, sockets popped. He drove the dagger in under the throat strap, freeing the jaw from his face entirely and leaving him to gurgle, clawing at what was left of his head and trying ineffectually to crawl away. Staruff straightened, ignoring the dying man, and hurled the bloody jaw at the two soldiers standing across the path. Both of them appeared to have petrified from sheer horror.

"I am Staruff Azrum and I am freed!" He screamed at them "Speak the location of the Stonehart captive or you will be next!"

Casey recovered from his shock, giving an appreciative glance at the foam flecks dotting the other mercenary's lips. He circled round the other side off the soldiers, cutting off their retreat.

"C-command tent," one of them managed to spit out. Neither of them dropped their weapons, clearly possessed of a strong suspicion they were not going to be allowed to leave alive.

Staruff snorted. "Made no bloody attempt to hide him did they? Such hubris."

"There'll be more o' these 'tween us and there," Casey pointed out.

The Az Taeorans put their backs to each other, baring their scimitars. They had forced the two desert men close together, robbing them of much of their mobility. The elegant sweeping strikes of their fighting style would be of little use when denied the space to execute them.

Staruff just nodded, intent on his prey. "First, we dispatch these; then, I will head for the command tent while you find Erik. When you do, meet me there."

The giant squinted down at his friend. "Why? We oughta stick together."

"If they gave Damon as good as me, or worse, he will need healing."

"So you want me te find both Erik an' Lorne then..."

Staruff nodded again. The soldier nearest Casey lunged under his guard and gouged his side, startling him. Casey hissed in pain and surprise and grabbed the man's wrist, holding the blade in the wound and bringing down his hammer. To his credit, the man *had* raised his other blade to block the downward strike but his arm buckled under the force of the blow and he collapsed. The other soldier spread his stance a little more, his back no longer guarded. He was taller than Staruff and could not easily get under his guard.

When, the smaller of the mercenaries darted forward with a dagger thrust, he caved under the attack and rolled backward. He kicked out a leg, actually using Casey's shin to change direction and spin out from between them. He rolled again and dove into the shadows between tents. Staruff snarled, annoyed at being denied a kill.

"Go Casey. Let none stand in your path."

"Take care of that asshole." Casey jerked his chin at the hidden Az Taeoran. "He'll stalk you like a fuckin' cat if you let him have your back."

Staruff just nodded and licked his lips. Casey set off toward the sounds of battle, silently wishing his friend luck.

Staruff watched him go, bellowing the Stonehart king's name. He regretted not being able to witness the carnage the charging giant would bring to the field. Casey would go straight for Erik's banner like a plough through good earth, but Staruff had other business to attend to. He turned and began to walk toward the command tent. Even if he'd not known where it was, he could easily see the standard flapping high above the camp, marking its place.

He went unchallenged. Perhaps it was for the best, given how stiff his legs were from kneeling so long. Still, where was that Az Taeoran Emeka? He longed for the rush of pitting his strength against him. The desert warriors were cunning as well as skilled; the man probably knew that while Staruff occupied Raach's attentions, she was not tormenting any of them. The thought brought a sour taste to his mouth. He fought the compelling urge to deviate from his path and try to find the bastard. His heart screamed for blood. Sounds of battle drifted across the camp, electrifying all his nerves.

No matter. The command tent will be guarded.

It was indeed, but not by who he expected. Raach stood, flanked by four berserkers, looking angry enough to split heads with their fists. Staruff just stood there for a moment, perplexed. They were clearly livid at being held back from the battle. Why would Lyre order such a thing? There was no way anyone was going to get into that tent without being ripped to shreds. The small smile that tugged the corner of his mouth grew until he was baring his teeth.

Ahh, you really, really want no intrusion. What are you doing, Father? Have you killed Damon yet? My dear friend and beloved enemy. I hope he fought you. He has such beautiful anger when cornered.

He approached slowly. The sword that Casey had given him remained stuck through the cord that secured his trousers. He did not unsheathe it. Recognition bloomed in the berserker queen's eyes. He had half expected the others to simply charge him but they did not. They waited, likely due to some previous order, and they were not happy about it. Distantly, he heard a bellow that sounded like Casey. Now, the dance became difficult.

The last command he had received from Lyre was to keep his cover at all costs. It had been an effective technique for interrogation. The giant man had been so close to cracking, if only they had had more time. Now he stood before the sorcerer's concubine, knowing full well that should Casey be successful he could not be seen idly chatting with the "enemy."

"You escaped," Raach said, her voice betraying nothing to him. No hint of what he ought to do. He said nothing. "You are strong," she said at last. Then, "Not strong enough."

The pronouncement of judgement stabbed through him, twisting cruelly in his gut.

"Test me," he said, lifting the hook and knife.

"You are injured. You will not fight well." She lifted her chin. The torches outside the tent made demonic shapes across the sharp planes of her face. He hated that look. *Disappointment.* It made his blood simmer in his veins. He stalked forward.

"Test me, bitch!"

She grinned, then. "Will you die well?" She lifted a hand and the berserkers gleefully surrounded him. Staruff's smile returned. He had risen to her provocation, as she desired. He wasted no more energy responding. Instead, he lifted his weapons and screamed.

"Azrum!" The women stopped moving, eyes wide as he called the name. The holy ancestor, first of the Blood Seekers to die. It was no accident that he had taken it as his surname when he had crafted his alias. He invoked her to witness his battle. He screamed again. "Shoreth! Basalar!" The names of the dead berserkers of years gone by pierced the air. He called them out, from the very first onward and gave them his breath, his memory, their rightful immortality.

They lunged at him, all at once. Berserkers had no foolish notions of the Code of Valour in their heads. No flashy one on one combat while the others politely waited their turn. They came on like a pack of wolves and Staruff would have it no other way.

He jumped over the axe swing aimed at his gut. He was a little surprised at himself. He hadn't expected to be able to get enough height, but having gotten up there, he took the opportunity to drill his foot into the woman's face.

A hot line of pain made its presence felt across his shoulder. He turned without hesitation and drove the hook down through his assailant's hand, forcing her to drop her blade. What kind of weapon it was, he could not have said. His eyes were only for the ones that were still in motion. He pulled and drew himself closer to his opponent, feeling the grind of bones against metal as he used the hook to steer her. Her face was twisted into a mask of pain but still, she lunged with her dagger.

He lifted his own, smashing the dull edge into her thrust and deflecting it over his shoulder. His blade sliced into her throat.

"Camelyi! Dorsa!" he called the names like an invocation, feeling it as keenly as he did when he'd first heard the war drums.

Staruff turned and hurled the lifeless body into the woman whose nose he had broken. Its legs tangled with the berserker with a club and all three went down in a heap. The sapper was up almost immediately and charging again, while the bloody-faced axe-wielder struggled to get out from under the torso of the corpse.

He could spare them no more attention, for the bald woman with two hatchets had ceased to circle him and stepped in to strike. Darsha; he recognized her. How many times had the desire to spar with her crossed his mind? She had denied him, of course; never the time to humour an idiot manling. She deflected the hook, almost taking it right out of his hand. The kiss of steel nicking the inside of his forearm made his blood sing.

Nothing compared to this. Not even when he was drunk. Not even in the throes of carnal pleasure.

Their feet scuffed the hard-packed dirt as they grappled. The head of her other hatchet was firmly couched in the crossguard of his dagger though she kept trying to jerk and twist it free. He moved with her, dancing half circles with her. She kept trying to hook both weapons and spread his arms out in opposite directions, making the widest target she could for the others. The two other warriors circled, hissing and hurling insults at him. They awaited their opening.

"Unworthy!" Darsha screamed at him. He blinked at the fleck of spit that landed on his eyelashes. She dove forward, lowering her head. The head-butt caught him off guard but he had jerked back in time to catch it on his lower lip and chin rather than his nose. A fattened, bloody lip was, by far, preferable to being blinded by reflexive tears. She snarled, obviously unhappy that she had failed.

His peripheral vision alerted him just in time to yank Darsha into the club strike rather than taking the blow himself. The bald berserker screamed profanity and he wasn't sure if it was aimed at him or her sister-at-arms. Probably both. The mistake caused the sapper to back off, but the other axe-wielder was undeterred.

Staruff fixed that. He dragged down hard with his hook, putting pressure on the woman's injured shoulder. He forced her to turn. With Darsha's back facing her, the axe woman had to move to pick a better line of attack. A few more precious seconds of protection to consider his next move.

"Samora! Baliya!"

"Unworthy!" Darsha screamed again. "You are unfit to call their names you miserable cock!"

Staruff felt his fury soar higher. He lashed out, bringing his knee up into her groin with a savage howl. Not as devastating to her as it would be for him but it made her jerk and twist away instinctively. He did not put his foot down. Instead, he planted it firmly just under her kneecap and threw himself backward into a roll. He felt the knee give out and heard her cry of pain. Staruff's grin was triumphant as he rose to his feet. Darsha stayed down.

He had been obliged to let go of his hook during the manoeuvre but it was not the end of things for him.

"Unworthy!"

It was the last thing Darsha ever said. Staruff hurled the dagger at her and watched her clap her hands to her throat as it struck home.

"Kalima! Fastorah! Eikezwi!"

He drew the sword at his hip as the remaining Blood Seekers began to circle him again. They had lost the advantage of coverage with their dwindling numbers but they did not have to worry quite as much about hitting each other. They had more space to move. For that reason, he was glad for the longer weapon.

A new sound seeped into his ears. They were not hissing, nor were they cursing him. They chanted the names of the dead. Chanted it with him, falling into the rhythm of the litany as the dance continued.

Erik squinted into the snow. The mage light kept their visibility well enough to venture into the forest after the Az Taeorans. Still, they weren't foolish enough to press ahead too far. They kept well within the protective wings of the mercenary columns to either side of them. The one to their left was having little trouble, being mostly on the road, but the right was having difficulty keeping up. The left flank of the resistance army slowed to keep formations as tight as possible.

Everlasting picked his way carefully through drifting snow and tree roots. The horses were uneasy making their way through the forest but they did not refuse. It was a good sign.

The Az Taeorans were pulling back. Erik did not know why. Even though the drop in temperature was slowing them them, they were still formidable foes. Their numbers might even be superior. He could not say for sure. Whatever was happening, there was a firm agreement among the Marshals that they would not be allowing the desert warriors to regroup. They would push them southward and reclaim the roads, and the re-supply and trade routes. They would scatter the forces of the Asp if they could.

Erik heard his name being bellowed from somewhere off in front of him. *Who the hell...?* As far as he knew, no one on the opposing side was really acquainted with him. Beyond an opposing Commander seeking out his equal in battle, he could not think of why anyone would be shouting for him from that direction.

The call came again.

"Eeeeriiiiik Stonehaaaaaart!" The syllables were drawn out to carry over a good distance.

I know that voice. He drew himself backward a little and Everlasting paused in his stride in response.

"Casey?" he shouted back. His chest felt painfully tight. If it were truly the giant mercenary, captured at the same time as Damon, he might know of the fate of his son.

"Erik!"

He was close enough now to see shape moving, head and shoulders above the tallest of his company. "It's me y'asshole lemme through!" There was no mistaking the voice now.

"Let him through!"

His clansmen peeled back to either side of the charging giant. Casey looked worse for the wear though his wounds seemed few. He seemed to have lost most of his gear. Everlasting flared his nostrils and sprinted forward to cover the rest of the distance, evidently as impatient as Erik for news.

"Where's Lorne?" Casey called up to him. "Lorne!" He looked around, squinting through the fog of his own breath. "No, stay on yer horse!" He put up a hand as Erik made to dismount. "Stay in saddle, M'lord."

Erik frowned. "Lorne!" he called. To Casey, he said. "What news, man? How did you escape? Where's Damon?"

"He's alive Erik. Get a goddamn healer!"

Lorne emerged through the press of ranks and pulled the bear-skin mantle he was wearing off of his shoulders. He threw it over Casey. "What is this now? You'll catch your death without a cloa... Casey?" He blinked and looked to Erik for some kind of direction. Erik, though, was battling to control the furious hammering of his heart.

"Alive? Where?" he breathed.

"Asp's command tent. Hurry the hell up! If he got anything like me an' Staruff did, he's gonna need a healer real bad."

Lorne winced and looked at Erik. "I wish Autumn was here; I'm not as skilled as he is."

"You're the best we have, Lorne," he said. "We owe this to Damon. If not for him, we'd all be dead and the knowledge of our forefathers lost forever." He cupped his hands to his mouth. "Send for a spare mount! Find the yak or an ox! Hurry!" Erik rested a hand on Casey's shoulder. "Tell me what happened?"

"M'lord, we were separated right quick after they took us. Staruff was hurt real bad in the fight. I wasn't bad but they smucked me in the head pretty nice. 'M sorry."

The chieftain shook his head. "No. Don't say that. There's enough blame to go around. Especially me, bringing a child into battle."

"Yer son's a man, Erik," Casey barked gruffly, startling him. The hard set of the mercenary's jaw silenced any protest he might have offered. Especially when the big man's face lit up and he shouted: "Boob!" Erik stared, perplexed, until he saw the yak approaching, warding away any in its path with a broad spread of horns.

"Sunev!" Erik's daughter lifted her chin and urged her mount forward. The bright scarlet of her skirt showing under her hauberk stood out starkly against the whirling snow. "Take charge for me. The clan is in your hands while I'm gone."

She lifted her sword on salute. "Aye."

Once the giant was mounted, they swung toward the road to make faster progress, leaving Jae in command under the Stonehart banner. The men of Lord Foster's column were confused by the yak-riding mercenary, but did not break formation any more than was necessary to let him through. They were used to messengers ferrying word from the rear to the front and back and didn't even take note of Erik and Lorne riding behind him. There were a few inquisitive calls from the vanguard, as they left the head of the column behind. Lorne turned and shouted something about "preparing a spell" and that quieted them.

When they reached the tents, Casey slowed and halted.

"What are you doing?" Erik protested. "I can see the command tent from here ..."

"Yup. I gotta make sure Staruff cleared the way, like he said. Stay put a sec."

Much as it vexed Erik to be stalled when he was so close to his son, he had to admit that the giant was right. He would be of no help to Damon if he died here due to stupidity. He gritted his teeth and watched the yak recede into the maze of tents. After a few moments of eerie silence, there was a quiet shuffle in one of the tents nearby. Erik drew his sword.

A tall man of the darkest complexion he had ever seen emerged, tucking a flat leather sheaf under his scale hauberk. The lines on his face spoke of age, but his body was hale and strong despite it. He stared at Erik and Lorne impassively and leaned his barbed spear against his shoulder.

"And?" he said at last, his voice grating out like lose shale under a horse's hooves.

"Who are you? What are you doing here?" Erik demanded, his sword point not wavering.

"I could ask the same of you, North-man." He smiled. A gash of white in the darkness.

"I am Erik Stonehart, Chieftain of Glasshammer."

"Ah, the king who will not be king." The man's laughter boomed. It was a deep belly laugh.

How the hell can you be so relaxed at a time like this? Erik wondered, his brow furrowing even more.

"When are you going to find your manhood and step under that mantle?"

Erik growled at the taunt and took a step forward. He could feel the tingle of magic at his back as Lorne prepared to heal him.

"I am Erik Stonehart and I have come for my son!"

"I am General Ingvor Emeka and I am saving my army."

Erik faltered for a moment at the mention of rank. *The General?* "You're retreating?"

"I am an old man, but I am not done playing with you yet." The grin on his face just grew wider. "If we do not meet again, I will surely play with your son after you. He will be less challenging, though. He screams like a monkey in a hawk's claws."

Erik lunged at him. Emeka parried easily, using the barbs to his full advantage. He did not try to trap the chieftain's sword though he well could have. He was like an old cat being pestered by a child. Lazily swatting at attempts to tease him. It only made Erik more furious. It felt like an eternity before the general tired of their game and slipped the spear over Erik's guard. He brought it down hard on his wrists, forcing him to let go with one hand. Then he caught the blade in the barbs, twisted and stabbed it down into the ground, pinning the sword hilt tight to the earth.

The chieftain backed away, disarmed for the moment and reached for the dirk in his boot. But Emeka was already walking away.

"Where are you going?" he shouted after him. "You're just going to leave?" The apparent lack of fidelity appalled him.

"I will not die for the mistakes of my Lord. I only fight to win, Erik the Not-King." He tossed over his shoulder. "Look around you. Only death has won today."

Erik dove for his blade, trying to wrench it out from under the spear, but Emeka was already gone. "Damn it ... Lorne, help me find something to pry this up with."

"Pry what up?" It was Casey who answered. Boob pushed his way between two tents, shaking his massive head and tearing the fabric to clear a path. He grunted in annoyance. The mercenary jumped down off his mount and joined them. "Oi, this 's a good spear!" He yanked it out of the ground. "Way's clear. I thought there'd be more bodies? I dunno what the hell is goin' on."

Erik picked up his sword and slammed it back into the scabbard. Casey looked toward the flicker of movement between tents.

"Who was that?"

"One incredible bastard." Erik swung back up into his saddle.

"Can yeh be more specific?"

"No. Lead on, Giant."

Casey shrugged and turned away from the steely glare. "Aright. Come on, it's quicker through this way."

Staruff grinned at Raach, seeing the expression mirrored on her face. He had his hook and dagger back, the sword back in the sheath at his hip. The berserkers lay dead behind him. They had taken their toll but the victory was his, still standing and breathing as he was. His heart hammered in his chest.

"Are you the last of the Blood Seekers?" he said. There was no need to shout. Raach held two curved daggers in her hands. There was no great length of steel between them as with a sword.

"I am not. The rest have gone with Emeka. Even if I were the last, there are more in the South."

"I will find them."

She smirked. "You're that confident?"

Staruff licked his lips, his eyes raking over her blades. "If my words prove false, I will never know. Let us dance."

She circled him and he followed her movements. He'd taken a bad kick to the ankle and though it pained him to put weight on it, he knew it would hamper him badly when the swelling set in. He had to keep moving it if he wanted it to serve him.

Bless the pain. You are still alive.

She lunged at him and he dodged out of the way, but barely; the blade whipped through his hair, the hilt catching some strands and yanking them out. He hissed. Her blinding movements made a sense of overwhelming pride swell in his chest. There was no wasteful twirling of the blades over and around her hands. She had no one to impress. He tried to catch and grapple her right dagger but she slipped his hold and gouged at his ribs. Had it gone between them? No need to check, he didn't care.

The beauty of it, if we were to fall here together. Mother. Can you know how much I love you? Can you feel it?

The banshee scream that tore out of her throat stunned him enough to make him take a step back. His sinews vibrated with it and the small hairs raised on his skin. He let loose a howl of his own. He tasted blood in his mouth. Whose? He lunged and she deflected his blade upward, pulling his arm high. He kicked the other blade away from his side. His shin connected with her hip and he shoved her hard. She pushed back but he had more leverage and she stumbled backward a step.

It was enough for him to disengage and come in again. She delivered a short, sharp kick to his ankle, the bad one and he was forced to step back again. The pain wasn't quite enough, for when she attacked again, he ducked and hooked her leg with the very same foot. She snarled and lashed out with her left dagger, catching him in the hip before she rolled backward, out of his reach.

The trousers were still held in place by the length of rope but the steel had bitten into them and his flesh. Raach wasted no time and charged him. He felt her right dagger bite into his back, higher than she had intended, for it struck his shoulder blade and slid. He screamed in pain and fury but managed to keep the left blade locked. He swung down with his hook under the meat of her backside and into her inner thigh. He tore it free with all his strength, rewarded with a scream.

She fell and he saw that she had dropped her dagger but it was only a momentary setback; she twisted her left dagger free and drove it down through his ankle.

For a moment, he couldn't see anything. There was nothing but the smell of packed earth and blood. He realized he was kneeling. His own hook was buried under his right collar bone, the tip, sticking back out. When had that happened?

Raach stared up at him from the ground. The colour in her flesh was draining from the wound in her thigh. The tear was too deep to staunch the flow and he knew she would not want to anyway. Her pale lips were peeled back in a savage grin. Staruff swayed, putting his fingertips on the ground to keep from falling over entirely. The hook's tip let a steady drip of blood fall on her chest and neck, she raised her hand to it as though accepting a benediction.

"You know the names ... of the fallen ..." she rasped.

"Yes. All of them." Nothing in the world could take his eyes away from hers in that moment.

"Blood Seeker, I name you. Feral out of Raach."

He did not dare to breathe, lest he miss any of her words.

"Be s...trong. Like a woman." She drew another breath. "To my shame, you were a son. But, you have bled like a daughter. That is my pride."

Staruff covered his mouth to silence himself. The tears stung as they escaped his eyes. They mingled with the blood on his fingers.

"Follow your father. Where he goes, there is death. Die well. Become immortal." She grinned then and chuckled. Her voice rose in peal of laughter that came from the very depths of her.

Staruff—Feral—let his head fall back, ignoring the tugging pain of the hook, the grinding agony of the dagger in his foot and let the sound wash over him. The snow fell in his eyes and made a mockery of his tears. He drew his lashes closed. The howls of mirth died away and he listened with all his attention fixed on the last shuddering breaths.

"Staruff!" He recognized the voice, but he did not answer.

That's not my name. I am Feral out of Raach. I am Blood Seeker.

"Staruff!" He heard the snort of the yak. The thump of heavy feet as the giant dismounted. He didn't look.

Follow your father. Where he goes, there is death.

He felt hands on either side of his face. "Sweet holy fuck ... get bandages! Staruff?"

Staruff, and so I must remain; Staruff, until my father should liberate me from my mask.

"Come on say something!"

His eyes eased open, looking up into the face of his friend. *Friend?* For all the deception, the feelings were real. He smiled.

"I'm here," he whispered. It was all he could force out. "See to Damon. I will live."

"Fuck that! Let the wizards fight the wizards!"

Erik and Lorne glanced at each other. There was hesitation written on both of their faces. Staruff stared back at them.

"Go."

Erik did not need to be told again.

The sorcerer who walked the hall in front of him had black hair. The robes that trailed behind him were scarlet. But he recognized him nonetheless. The shape of his jaw, the slender hand that traced the patterns carved into the walls of Old Stonehart Hall. The words glowed brilliantly under his touch. They scintillated in the stone down the hallway and up the stairs, around the door frames. They burned into Damon's eyes with the fervour of a lover's gaze.

It was a dream; no, a memory. It was sharp and clean as though it were fresh, yet this was an old memory. The sorcerer's face looked much the same when he turned to face him, but the eyes glinted with a purity only afforded to the young. He held a leather-bound tome to his chest with his other hand, his head tilted curiously, seeing something long lost to the passage of time. More years than any living thing had a right to exist.

Iltharen. Lyre.

Lyre Stonehart.

Suddenly, it made sense. He felt a tension in the air around him as though a force was trying to expel him but he held on. He envisioned roots extending down from the heels of his feet, tenaciously binding him to this place. Could Lyre kill him while he was here? He didn't know.

The image distorted and stretched away from him, darkening.

Is this it? No. No!

Without thinking, he stretched out his hand and a bolt of blue light lashed out at the fading figure. He hadn't even realized that he'd used blood magic until he felt the familiar tugging in his veins. The spidery threads drifted and spun in glittering cobalt in front of him. He could not see the sorcerer anymore. He found himself longing for the labyrinth. Though it had nearly beaten him into submission, this was far worse. There was nothing to hold onto. He drifted in a sea of darkness, a host of foreign memories drifting around him like distant stars.

Among the flickering images, he recognized the lines and glyphs of spells, far too complex for him to puzzle out with his limited knowledge. Still, he burned to know. He searched for patterns, anything recognizable, as he tried to orient himself. If Lyre really was Stonehart himself there should be something familiar. Then again, if he was a Stonehart, he was thousands of years old. Would anything be the same?

Damon focused on the image of the tattoo on his own back. That was an ancient tradition. Perhaps old enough? There was a twinkle in the distance. He propelled himself toward it. He focused again, putting mental pressure against it. The seal was much closer now, he could see the detail of the sword in a ring of runes. *So that's what an oathbind looks like?*

He put out his hand to it, more carefully this time. There was no flash of light. The ring around the sword was broken at the bottom and the top. *What does it mean? I thought an oathbind couldn't be broken?* He paused and looked around, turning a slow circle and sending out branches of blood magic. *Are there other oathbinds? Are they broken too?* He looked for any similar shapes. There were a few and they flared brilliantly as the tendrils of the blood magic touched them. He turned to inspect the nearest one and was suddenly dazzled by a bright light cutting through the darkness in a long, straight line.

At first, he didn't understand. He floated there in the half light, watching his enemy's memories drift by. As he turned, he realized it was not a line. It was a circle and the branches of his spell were pushing up against it, unable to go any further. He had sent them out to search for oathbinds and they had found one. *Why ... would someone do this?* The blue tendrils curled back on themselves, having hit the edge of the mind. It struck him, then, the magnitude of the working he was looking at.

Who would do this? Surely not the Asp himself? He felt a subtle squeeze in his belly as he let himself move slowly along the glittering runes. *What oath could he possibly have taken that would encompass all that he is?* He stared into the emptiness beyond the ring and once again felt far out of his depth. Another unwanted thought crawled into his mind. *How great would be his power if he were unbound?*

He put out a hand and touched a rune several times larger than himself. It was cold to the touch and unyielding, much like steel. He tried to pass under the ring, then over it, but to no avail. *Oh well, with my luck I would probably just fall back into my own mind. If it even still exists.* The thought made him queasy. *If there's nowhere to go back to, am I now but a dream in someone else's mind? Should I hope that my enemy survives?*

"There you are."

Something tangled in Damon's blood spell and yanked. The fibres tore and he screamed at the pain that burned through his nerves. He curled in on himself, feeling as though he'd been skinned.

When he could see again, the Asp was in front of him holding onto a fistful of blue tendrils. This was no memory. He was exactly as he remembered him, white hair and long chiming sleeves. Dozens of inky black shapes swam around the sorcerer, peering through the eye holes of blank masks and laughing. The sound hurt his head and made his body prickle all over. The masked creatures held chains that glowed with the same livid green as his eyes. They were affixed to a steel collar around the Asp's neck.

Damon tried to pull back away from him but Lyre squeezed his fist tighter on the branches and he gasped. He gritted his teeth, struggling to keep his senses as his veins twisted and seared.

"You leave yourself a naked infant in the hands of your foe." The sorcerer shook his head, amused. "Fool. Such power is wasted on you." He turned to the nearest creature. "Great Arcana, Shargus, grant to me the strength to snuff out this life."

"What do you offer in exchange?" A deep voice, like the growl of a bear, answered him. "Nothing is for free."

"I have need only of his power." Lyre extended his free hand toward Damon. "The rest of his soul you may consume at your leisure."

Again, the creatures' laughter crawled over him. "Acceptable." The chain between them ignited. The sorcerer smiled, his face blissful for a moment. Then, he drew his blade. It was bright with green fire.

Aervie ... I have to do something. Now. I can't get away. I can't move! Damon struggled but the tendrils of blood would not retract, would not dissolve. The ripping sensation reminded him of the spear that held him pinned somewhere in the waking world. *Damn you, I want to live!* He drew his sword and prepared to defend himself a final time. He wanted to blast through this man, this demon who had taken him from the life he loved. *I just want to be free.* His blade bore no enchantment, no light of its own.

Lyre pulled him closer, tugging on the branches.

Damon took a deep breath and looked to the void beyond the confines of the mind. There was no solace there, no amnesty from the torment. "Misery," he whispered. The darkness slithered down the edges of the steel. He swung his sword and the Asp brought up his blade to parry -

but he was not aiming for his enemy. Instead, he hewed the chain the Arcana held in its claws. It sliced through it like water. Shargus howled with laughter as it drifted away into the dark. Lyre froze in shock, staring at the severed links. By the time he looked back, it was too late. Damon swept his blade through the blood tendrils and cut himself free.

He was looking at the ceiling of the tent. There was excruciating pain in his chest and it was only when he remembered how to breathe that he realized he'd been pulling against the spikes driven through his limbs. He willed his muscles to go slack and the pain died. He remembered this feeling. The sickening way his diaphragm pushed against the forks of the spear when he inhaled. The burning pressure of the spikes. He immediately wished he had not woken at all.

No ... no, I'm alive. Still here. I must open my eyes. While there is breath there is hope.

There was a sound off to his left. He made himself turn his head and spots and bursts of light danced in front of his eyes. The lines of agony radiating out from the spear very nearly forced him to stop. He managed to glimpse a pool of hazy white and focused on it. The sorcerer's green eyes met his, still livid in their pale frame. But the Asp sat on the floor, his shoulders shaking as though he would fall over at any moment.

"Damon!"

He blinked. His father's voice? Surely the pain was making him hallucinate? Or was this another trick? The sorcerer letting him think he'd been defeated to gain a footing in his mind while his guard was down?

The corner of Lyre's mouth curled up slightly though there was no joy in the expression.

"Thank you," he said softly.

Thank you? Surely, he'd misheard him? But the sorcerer vanished, a crossbow quarrel striking the ground where he'd been only a second ago.

"Damon! By all that's holy ..."

Damon turned his head back to the prescribed position and the spear stopped torturing him. He realized he'd been holding his breath. Erik came into his field of vision and he blinked his eyes, trying to clear them. His father was pale, his face pinched with fear. Damon tried to smile for him, but the spear pulled the lines of his face back and he did not have the strength to fight it.

Erik was speaking but it passed in a haze. There was someone else. Threads of magic moved around him, brushing his skin, abrading the spear's careful weaving. It didn't occur to him to rejoice that freedom might be imminent. In fact, not much occurred to him at all as his thoughts sank into a gentle haze.

"Now?"

Now ... what? He was about to open his eyes again when something very abruptly ripped him in half. The spear's spell lines unravelled rapidly, spooling out in all directions and puffing out of existence. Strange glowing eyes and ghostly forms flew out in all directions from the red threads as they snapped. They chattered and laughed as they went and disappeared through the roof of the tent.

He didn't know how much time passed between the spear being pulled free of him and when he began to think again. He did not even mark its absence until his back arched off the table.

Now, only the spikes held him in place but pulling on them only brought pain. He made himself be still.

"Damon, can you hear me?"

He took a breath, then another. At last, he made himself open his eyes and look up at his father.

"Yes." His voice came out in a rasp.

"Lorne is healing you. You're safe now. I'm so sorry."

"Where's the fuckin' Asp?"

A smile formed on his face at the voice of the mercenary.

"Casey?"

"Yeh."

Damon turned his head, marvelling at the ability to do so after so long being restrained. Casey sat just inside the tent flaps, cradling Staruff's head in his lap. He frowned.

"What happened?"

"Staruff bein' Staruff. He said we gotta heal you up first." The giant smiled though his concern was clear. "Too bad we can't heal stupid, eh?"

Staruff mumbled something that sounded like "shut up."

"He was ... just there." Damon meant to point but the spike through his arm reminded him of its presence. He winced. "He vanished."

"We will get him, Damon," Erik reassured him. He stroked his hair lightly. The gentle, painless touch was suddenly the most fantastic thing he'd ever experienced. It struck him, then that this was real. That he was truly not going to die. The twin helices of blood no longer twined above his body. He felt a tickle on his face and realized there were tears there, creeping along the lower lids of his eyes and escaping along his temples. He started to shiver and could not make himself stop.

"I'm s-sorry," Damon whispered.

Erik shook his head. "No, this is all my fault. By all the bloody hells, I will find that demon, and when I do—"

"Erik, stop cursing and help me cast a sleep on him."

Lorne sounded exhausted.

"Sleep?" Erik blinked, clearly perplexed.

"He's already in shock and these spikes need to come out before I can heal the rest ..."

Damon felt new spell lines falling over him, light as a dusting of snow, piling on heavier. The drowsiness began to outweigh the discomfort. *This is alright,* he thought. *Yes. Safe at last.* He idly reached up a thread of his own power, lending strength to the spell. Lorne took the errant strand and wove it into the others before he realized what it was. The web swelled with energy, becoming less of a gentle tiredness and more of a hammer-like introduction to unconsciousness.

He had enough time to hear "Oh wow—" before the spell abruptly dropped him into oblivion.

Chapter 19: No Horns Sounded

With the coming of the snow, the covered waggon that had borne him homeward had been switched out for a sleigh. Blessedly, it was also covered. It wasn't that the cold bothered him, but rather that Damon wasn't ready to see anyone just yet. However vexing the looks of awe and expectation had been when he'd first ridden to battle, he was certain the looks of disappointment would be worse. The poorly-masked anguish on his father's face was more than enough for him.

Lorne, the only one he would let attend to him, tried to tell him of the success of the Stonehart spells. He told him of the knowledge he had gleaned from Iltharen, and the workings the clan had done together to turn the tide of the battle and keep their men alive.

"If not for you, all would be lost."

The words echoed in his head again, but this was not how things were supposed to be. There was no blood on his sword. He was not quite sure how to feel about that. He had not vanquished his enemy, or had he? He was not foolish enough to think that he could face down the power he had seen in the sorcerer's mind and best him at his own game.

What did I expect? To bring him down in glorious combat? Perhaps he had, and why not? It had been everyone else's expectation as well. *Perhaps, they will stop talking about heroes and legends and prophecies now.* That thought settled much more kindly on his mind.

He had forcefully denied King Harlon' request to see him and Erik upheld his wishes, much to his relief. The chieftain simply signed over property rights of Emmesford to its rightful owner without ceremony and pressed on for home. He hadn't spoken to the king since then.

Damon ached to see his house again. He wondered if the raiders had caused much damage and prayed that the kinsmen they had left behind had been enough to defend their lands. He said nothing of it to anyone and refused to open his mind to the Blood Link even now that the danger had passed. He wondered if his failure to warn them had been the right decision after all. If it was not, could he ever be forgiven?

He concentrated on the smooth gait of Everlasting and Silhouette and pretended to know nothing.

Phoenix paced the length of the room while Kael sat in the nest-like bed reading a book and occasionally taking notes.

"I should not have chosen you," she said, placing her hands on the frame of the bed. "There have to be others powerful enough to assist me."

The pale eyes lifted for a moment, pen poised. He took the pen away from the map that sprawled across his lap and slowly hooked a lock of hair behind his ear. Then, he returned to his work.

Phoenix glanced at the candle on the table near the window. Was it lower than it had been? She could have sworn she was looking at it only a moment ago. Her eyes ran over the ripples in the wax, counting layers.

"Stop doing that to me," she said. She crossed to the window and looked out on Hanuel. Kael made no reply; but of course, he didn't need to. Forcing her to stall was enough of a reminder of his power.

For the first few hours after they had exited the mindscape, all she had been able to think about was Damon. Now, reality set in. The bluish fires in the windows of the houses during 'nighttime' stared coldly back at her. She wondered if it was really nighttime above or if this was some arbitrary measure of time.

I have to get out of here. Phoenix knew the way, the only way. She turned back to face Kael.

"What are you doing?"

"Planning."

"These plans of yours involve me, I wager."

"You win your wager, for what it is worth." Kael smiled. She wanted to hit him. "You will execute my plans, my people will be liberated, and you will go to your Silan world to seek out Damon."

"So he *is* alive then!" She straightened.

"I said 'seek out.' I don't know his present state."

"But you could find out."

Kael looked at her but did not reply.

"Please!" She took a step but he held up his hand.

"What I have given you is enough for now. You will honour your bargain because you are a woman of honour."

Phoenix folded her arms. She tried to figure out if he was complimenting or insulting her or insulting her by complimenting her and then remembered that Ducal did not work that way. Once again, she could not decide if they played no games, or if their games were so far beyond her that she could not grasp them.

"Yes," she said eventually. What else was there to say? Kael's words returned to her.

You question the price because you do not grasp the magnitude of the thing you have asked for, nor what will follow.

Phoenix squared her shoulders and took a breath. She walked back to the bed and slung a leg over the frame, perching beside the shaman. "Show me these plans."

I will come for you, Damon. I swear it.

Damon found himself nodding in the saddle again. He'd switched from riding in the waggon to Silhouette for the last day of the journey. He was beginning to wonder if he'd made a mistake. *If I fall off, I'm going to be terribly embarrassed.* Casey rode his yak nearby, having refused to leave Damon's side even after the conflict had ended. Staruff, for his part, was still in a waggon with a few other wounded. He had spent most of the time asleep. It was hard to imagine something that could hurt the madman enough to make him stay down so long.

He sniffed the air. Something was amiss. No cooking fires. A weight settled in the pit of his stomach. *Did they get through? Were our defences enough?* He closed his eyes. *Please, I just want to go home and rest.*

There was a stirring at the front of the column as Lorne rode back toward them. He had gone on ahead to let the other Stonehearts know that they were returning. There were no horns calling between the steddings. A bad sign. Damon did not raise his eyes any higher than Lorne's horse's chestguard.

"There's no one there. Your house has been ransacked. I didn't ride any further than that. We'll have to spread out and check the other steddings."

"If we were attacked, they'd have the sense to go to the Hall," Erik replied, though his voice was darkened by anxiety. "We will go to my summer house first and see if there is anything salvageable. Assemble some search parties to assess the other steddings. We'll need all the supplies we can get for the winter."

He paid no mind to the parties peeling off from the main column. The faint jingles of armour and creaks of leather became fainter still. The wind seemed to pick up louder than before in the absence of sound.

Damon watched the snow pass under Silhouette's silver hooves, individual flakes catching the late afternoon light and scintillating like stars. He pulled his cowl up over his head, shielding his face from the light.

Did I choose wrong?

Boots hit the ground beside his horse and he realized that they had stopped. He lifted his head enough to see the front door of the summer house, caved in. Splinters of wood bristled as though it had been hewn with an axe. Erik ducked into the darkness of the broken doorway. Damon lowered his head again. For a moment, the snow was not there, but rather the damnable vision of armed raiders charging through the shallows of Lake Glasshammer. The mud churned up by their passage clouding the water like weeping wounds.

He put a hand over his face and swayed for a moment, keeping himself in saddle by virtue of leaning heavily on the pommel.

"Damon?" Lorne spoke close to his ear. He felt hands holding onto his shoulders. "Are you alright?" He sat up slowly, folding his hands over base of Silhouette's neck. Still, Lorne did not leave him. "Are you alright?" he repeated. Damon stared at the house. At the shards of leaded glass in the windows. The scraps of curtains waving weakly with every breath of wind. The broken wind chime hanging at an angle over the table. "Please, say something." His lips parted slightly.

What am I to say?

He shut his mouth again and resumed gazing at the snow.

A high-pitched wail of fear smashed through his thoughts. For an instant, he thought it was some lingering trace of the vision, but Lorne's hands jerked away. The lorekeeper jumped off of his horse and dashed toward the house.

Damon took his foot from the stirrup and let himself down. The impact of putting weight on his leg made him freeze for a moment. The muscles and tendons of his legs had not fully healed from the spikes driven through them and complained mightily if he tried to walk. Lorne usually chased him back to bed when he tried but his uncle was currently occupied with the commotion behind the house. He limped toward his kinsmen, using his sheathed sword as a cane.

"She's in the cellar!"

He blinked. The hay piled on top of the cellar doors to keep the snow from damaging the wood had hidden it from the raiders. As they pulled it away, throwing hunks of frozen fibers to either side, he saw that the lock was closed and untouched. The hinges too, were sound. Another scream came from below. The thin, strained voice of a young girl.

Rebecca.

They took a hatchet to the door. The house was in such disarray, Erik could not find the key and who knew how long she had been down there? Who had locked her inside? Damon's brain began to tabulate all the stores that had been put into the cellar before they had left for Emmesford. He tried to make it stop, but it would not.

Not enough. Oh Aervie, most of it was in the house...

Surely they had finished filling the cellar in their absence. Damon folded his legs under himself and sat. Almost immediately, the lances of pain in his ankles eased as the pressure let off. Sitting down, the snow was up over his hips. More was coming down.

Still, the hysterical screams continued.

At last the doors were wrenched open and two of his kinsmen jumped down into the dark. It took one more to haul Rebecca out, thrashing and struggling wildly. She was thin and smelled of sickness. The whites of her eyes showed around the dark brown irises rendering her face like a theatre mask.

Damon stared, uncomprehending, at her. Did she not recognize them? Lorne tried to calm her, to no avail. It was only when she saw her brother that she went still. The terror left her face and the blankness that replaced it was almost worse. They set her down on her feet. She seemed not to feel the cold, though she was only clad in a nightgown. She lifted her arm and pointed a blackened fingernail at Damon.

"You were supposed to save us."

Hollow, toneless words; they stopped the world, silenced the wind, held him pinned and stunned like one afflicted by elfshot. He had no answer. Not for her words or the empty expression in her eyes. Those eyes that had danced with light and life bored into him like a hole ripped in the sky where the sun should be.

Damon lowered his head. He did not hear what Lorne said and barely perceived others moving around him. A vague smell of smoke told him that someone had started a fire in the hearth. He had no use for warmth. The snow was soft under him and no dampness seeped into his clothing from it. It never did. He held a clump of feathery whiteness on his palm, knowing it would never melt in his hands, not on flesh that gave no heat.

Erik approached him cautiously, but Silhouette lowered his ears and warded him away, showing teeth. Repelled after a few more attempts, the chieftain went back inside. Damon could feel him watching disconsolately from the window. He did not look up. He leaned against his horse's legs and let the baleful chatter of his thoughts have the run of his mind. The tinkling of the broken wind chime pierced him with images of long white sleeves and he wanted to pull it down, silence it. He lifted his shaking hands and covered his ears.

"Damon?"

He blinked. Above him were the rafters of the barn and Casey's face. The giant waited for him to sit up before speaking again. He did not remember climbing up into the hayloft but he was there now. Silhouette whickered unhappily below.

"Yer sister's gone."

Damon stared at him.

"We can't find 'er anywhere. Didja see her? Her horse is gone too."

The black stallion was pawing the ground in agitation. He squinted. "No." He began climbing down the ladder, grimacing every time he grasped a rung.

"Sunev's been tryna find her trail but uh ..."

Casey did not need to finish. The stable doors stood open and the snow outside was falling so thick he could see barely a couple meter's distance. The passes would be closed. Surely, she could not have gone far? He began to saddle his horse.

"Wait ... Damon, yer in shit shape. I didn't come here te ask yeh for anything. You gotta rest."

"Have they found anyone?"

The mercenary stood silent for a moment. "No," he said quietly at last. "No bodies neither. But they gotta be around here someplace. They can't a just ... hey."

Damon swung up into the saddle and pulled up his cowl.

"Hey, stop. Really."

"She was right. I was supposed to save them."

Casey put up a hand to rest on the pommel. Silhouette turned to bite him but he rapped his knuckles against the horse's face.

"Oi! Stop bein' a cunt!"

Damon narrowed his eyes.

"I need ta get my gear on and saddle up Boob, yeah? C'mon, wait for me. Yer gonna need help." They stared at each other for a minute. "C'mon, I know I ain't a real Stonehart but I'm yer fuckin' friend. I'm coming with yeh."

Damon bowed his head in assent and rested his hands on his knees. He would wait. Then they would ride. He would not stop until he found her.

I don't know if there is still room for me in this prophecy, but there is no more room for failure.

Lyre sat on the floor before the cold hearth. The snow continued to blow outside, piling up around the small cottage. It was dark and this way-house had not been re-stocked in years. Perhaps no one hunted this far north anymore? Hunting with his father so long ago, the stone walls had not seemed so barren and unforgiving. How long had it been since he'd sat here as a child? After thousands of years, even the magic-infused stonework of old was beginning to wear.

He'd been born here. If he could not summon the power to light the wood, he would die here as well.

Life, what a cruel circle.

There had been enough energy to transport himself here. The Stonehart boy had given him the much needed burst when he had blundered into his mind and started hurling blood magic around. In desperation, he had cast the quickest and easiest shifting spell: it was a recall, putting him back at the site of his birth. An eternal waypoint open to all Stormforges with a drop of power in their veins. It really had been just a drop. He did not have the strength to cast another transport. Now, after days of waiting, surviving, and trying to think of a way out of this trap, the last vestiges of power had been used. The oil lamps stayed dark in their brackets and the aged kindling did not stir at his efforts.

There was no flint and tinder left in the supply chest. It had been emptied of anything useful. Even if there had been, his hands were too numb now to use such a thing. He looked down at his fingers, the tips yielding to frostbite. Without sufficient magic, he had no way to heal them. If the white hell outside would not offer him any means of starting a fire, he would probably lose them, possibly even his hands as well.

Survive. Such a vow ... in this hour, how shall I uphold it?

Torn shreds of silk from his robes lay scattered near his feet. They'd proven ineffective when twisted together in an attempt to light the wood bow-style. The sticks among the tinder were too brittle and the ornate comb from his hair was too small. The keening wind grated on his nerves, mocking him in one endless howl.

A shadow fell in the doorway and he felt a twinge in his chest. *Who, then, has come to end me?* He made himself rise and all of his joints screamed at him for it. *I shall meet you, my executioner. If you bring to me the long night, your gaze shall marry mine afore you give it me.*

A girl stood there. A small, shivering silhouette, blocking the light. She shuffled forward, keeping her arms locked around herself. Lyre looked down at her as she came near. Her thin face with its sunken cheeks was almost lost in the furs she was wrapped in. Large, dark eyes looked back at him. They were wide with shock, or perhaps terror, and he felt a knot of confusion settle in his brain.

Bear you no weapon? Why have you come?

Lyre lifted his hands and pushed the hood away from her face. He smoothed the dark, unruly locks and tried to read the words her mouth seemed unable to form. Her cheeks were warm against his palms. The first thing he'd felt in them all day.

Who are you?

He stared into those unblinking eyes and saw his reflection peering back, perplexed. His breath caught in his throat for a moment.

Then, he smiled. A golden glow suffused the tiny cottage as the hearth, and every lamp wick flared to life.

You.

About the Author

Ethan Kincaid is a Canadian author residing in Montreal, Québec. Blood of Midnight: Broken Prophecy is the first of three novels in his original fantasy series.